Rowan Blaize and the Hand of Djin Rummy

Published in the United States by Brightbourne Media
www.rowanblaize.com
Library of Congress Cataloguing in Publication Data applied for

ISBN: 0-6157-0875-7
ISBN-13: 9780615708751

Rowan Blaize and the Hand of Djin Rummy

Enchanted Heritage Chronicles: Book II

Jonathan Kieran

2012

Dedication

For K and D and everyone magical I have known

I

Of all the places I have decided to call "home" over the course of my particularly long and eventful existence on this planet (and in a variety of other universes of wildly varying qualities and characteristics), St. Augustine, Florida, should perhaps be regarded as one of my more unusual choices.

I have tended, due to a fairly observable trend of personality traits, to prefer living in magnificent cities that bustle and hum with relentless activity, metropolises redolent with what the mortal folk often call "exotic ambience." St. Augustine has its fair share of that, to be certain, but it is not a metropolis, not by any stretch of the imagination. When I first decided to hang around here for a while, I thought this might pose a problem.

For one thing, in the pell-mell madness of a grand city, it is easier for a magical being like me to blend-in and walk about unmolested without the inevitable strain of having to use deflective spells and other distractive techniques. In what mortals deem ancient times—but what to most of Us seems rather "last year" or "a couple of weeks ago"—places like Constantinople, Samarkand, Athens, Caesarea, Alexandria, Carthage, Rome, and Antioch were ideal spots in which to settle, at least for the urban-minded warlock. In such fretful, teeming hubs of the mortal world, someone of my persuasion could settle down with considerable comfort and observe the ever-unraveling secrets of Time at leisure. One could watch and interfere and indulge and perfect one's craft, all without much bother from the locals ... if one was powerful enough not only to conjure but to *maintain* the trimmings and trappings of a privileged lifestyle.

Yes, yes, I played the tourist quite a bit in the old days, gadding about in Peking and Osaka and a slew of other destinations remarkable and unremarkable, but I am a European magician, by birth, so when stationed in *this* world I have tended to patronize my own backyard, as it were, along with the various adjuncts, colonies, immediate neighbors, and dependencies of that ever-tempestuous playground. It pays to have a firm grip on one's travel arrangements. Contrary to what various legends about my kind purport to reveal, flying presents a rather complex, difficult, and sometimes dangerous magical endeavor. Great distances have always been far more wisely navigated by hitching rides on any number of those ingenious little conveyances so favored by mortals, like the caravan, the creaking but stately galleon, the camel, and, these days, of course, the automobile and the airplane. Beings like us have no problem whatsoever utilizing such methods, at least when it is not exactly convenient to snag and commandeer a six-winged Snow Seraph, a species that is practically extinct, anyhow, or saddle an obliging banshee and soar up, up and away toward imminent adventure.

Transforming one's self into some sort of bird may seem an ideal solution to covering lots of territory in economic fashion. Scads of well-intentioned and dreadfully uninformed mortal friends have indeed asked me about this over the years, but that method, while doable, is fraught with potential quagmires, not least of which is the likelihood that another larger, hungrier bird will attack and eat you as you travel. Just as troublesome, extended periods of time spent in Other-forms can be so intoxicating to the senses that many a warlock or sorceress has been known to lose all perspective and simply allow the Self to be absorbed by the spell—horrific cases of form overwhelming function. Two or three of my relatives have been lost to Transmogrification Syndrome, thank you very much. At least, we *think* that is what happened to them. Uncle Ashdod, unquestionably, flapped off into the beckoning twilight four centuries hither and is still hanging upside-down from a bat-cave ceiling in the Apennines, for all I know. Suffice it to say, this mode of journeying is approached with due sobriety and consideration, when it is approached at all.

But I must get back to the odd phenomenon of sleepy, satisfying little St. Augustine by rendering a full account of my contemporary travel history.

It is true that several in our European circle of friends and acquaintances had been intrigued or, at least, mildly aware, when rumor filtered through to magical enclaves that Spaniards had set off on yet another reckless and intrepid hunt across the boiling ocean in search of new shorelines to accost and colonize. My parents were still together in that century—more "together" than they were in the century before, at any rate—and I recall both of them speaking with some amusement about these various and endlessly competitive mortal explorers surging westward to please this queen or that emperor, hunting for fortune, titles, fame, future commissions, and, of course, any number of scurrilous-yet-storied treasure trails. Naturally, the New Religion (which was indeed still new in our far more expansive perspective) inspired and instigated a lot of this adventure, and the promise of new converts to mine from the vast reserves of indigenous "savages" was tantalizing. If I recall correctly, and I believe I do, for our existence is, in many respects, built upon the gleaming infrastructure and scaffolding of recollection, it was my father who first made mention of the Spanish landing in what is now the Floridian town of St. Augustine.

We were in Sardinia, spending a drowsy summer enjoying one of Pan's daughters' six-week extravaganzas in the alternating sparkle and secret shade of the Barbagian foothills.

"I spoke with Haziran and his wife the other day," said Father, lounging with a goblet of ambrosia by some dew-banked emerald pool. "Imagine this—they just returned on some Spanish commodore's galleon from the coast of the North Continent. It seems some stalwart named Pedro Menendez stabbed the soil with a cross and a sword and established yet another dreary colony in their beloved new territory. Named it after that loquacious Christian thinker, whatshisname."

"What *was* his name?" Mother had asked, her raven-shine hair being plaited at the time by a yawning little nymph and its coterie of distracted fey, each no larger than a hummingbird.

"Augustine. That's the one," replied Father after a thoughtful sip from the shimmering cup.

"Ah! The old fellow who used to bloviate in Numidia before the Vandals gave it a good sacking? Weren't his bits and bones housed here on the island for a time, near Cagliari or some such?"

"My pet! Who knew you were so well-versed in mortal ecclesiastical trivia?"

"Don't be patronizing, Enoch. Well, kudos to the Spanish mortals. That's what I say. They certainly are getting around these days. Why, that entire continent will soon be pockmarked with conquistador diggings and veritably clanging with the sound of church bells. I'm already getting a headache just thinking about it. Now tell me, dear. Why in the name of Cerberus did Haziran and Phoebe return on a Spanish vessel? I find that positively deranged."

Father had sighed, contemplating the glimmer of a nearby waterfall. "Phoebe's powers have always been a bit scratchy," he said. "She's never been able to fly much farther than a broody hen and, what with this last cycle of storms over the water, Haziran was more than a little tentative himself about expending the magic required to get them both back safely across the briny."

Mother had given a little shudder; she never liked to hear anyone speak of witches who possessed anything less than the most ripping magical talents. Deficiency offended her, for she was quite powerful. "If you ask me, the two of them have always spent far too much time flitting about the social circuit and not nearly enough at home, improving their skills."

"That's as may be, dear," Father had replied, "but they aren't the purest stock to begin with, are they? More than a touch of dryad in old Haziran's woodpile—no offense to you or to any of your relations," he had added to the nymph weaving wildflowers into Mother's tresses. "But a more sporting fellow simply cannot be found, and I should like to be most clear on that count. In any event, they were in the West, on the top half of the Clinging Continent, shopping for jewelry among the natives and looking at potential real estate. They found everything to be rather unacceptable. Swamps and Spaniards. One can get *that* sort of thing here. They had enough skill to transform their appearances to resemble deck-swabbers, or some similarly humiliating disguise, on that galleon. Then they simply mingled with the rest on the return trip to Valencia without having to do any actual work. They said the Augustine settlement had a bit of potential, though."

"More potential than Haziran and Phoebe, I daresay," huffed Mother. "Imagine Phoebe as a deckhand on a Spanish galleon! I don't care how crafty the glamor may have been, it's degrading. Moreover, they could easily have been lost in a storm or dashed upon rocks. Foolhardy to risk such a thing, unless one's skills are beyond reproach."

"Oh, they would have thought of something, had they wrecked, dear. Haziran may be a tad diffident when it comes to the ocean, but he is surprisingly calculating at need."

I had felt compelled to speak up, then. "Perhaps I'll fly over in a few months and see this new settlement for myself, Mother. The winter is going to be incredibly dull here and I understand that portion of the continent is a bit more tropical. It may prove a worthy diversion."

"Please yourself, Rowan. I would not soon worry about *your* abilities in the face of a storm, even at this time of the year. But in terms of discovering worthy diversions I would think you might wait a few centuries instead of a few months before making a visit. There's bound to be nothing to it. You've seen how these mortal settlements start off. Not worth haunting for even a week's curiosity. Wait three hundred years or so, darling. If it ever amounts to anything, it will still be around then and likely much more interesting. Do come with your father and me to Sumatra for the winter! Your Auntie Ariadne plans to throw some marvelous parties this season and you can collect your cobra-venom samples in the lovely heat. Everything is poisonous there—splendidly so."

I did not get on particularly well with either of my parents, at the time, and ended up visiting some friends in Marrakesh that winter. Even so, I did follow Mother's advice in regard to waiting a few centuries for a visit to St. Augustine. It is a bit strange, this "thing" about us warlocks and witches, even to ourselves, though we all have an ample amount of time to get used to our own quirks. For example, our kind tends, for the most part, to make our dwellings in the heart of a mortal city or somewhere along the margins of human civilization. There exists a sort of symbiotic relationship; mortals need us in certain respects and we find them occasionally quite useful. Perhaps it is all because we are essentially a different and far more complicated species sprung from a wayward branch of the same great tree, or at least from its root stock. Our kind, however, are exceedingly long-lived compared to humans and their mayfly existence. Then there are the magical powers, of course. Humans know these things about us, but what they do not know is that living for thousands of years (in some cases) is not always a phenomenon to be envied. Not by any means!

Indeed, even if we do not admit it to each other, we have all been known to envy the compact lifespans of mortal men and women from time to time. At least, we envy the ones who manage to pack an inordinate amount of adventure into their mortal coils. Yes, for them life can be, and generally is, far more tortuous than it is for us, but time and the perception of time—not to mention the way it plays-out in any sentient existence—is rather a relative thing. Our lives, for example can be intensely lonely, which is one of the reasons we are so restless and often walk the earth with insatiable wanderlust. To be certain, the more talented among us can spend an ample amount of time in other worlds, if it suits us to do so, and no matter what world we choose to inhabit, the vision before us is often the same. We witness kingdoms rise and fall, bright lives radiate and then vanish like gossamer drifting on a lofty breeze, and cherished haunts come and go. It can be a bit depressing, to tell the truth. The inherent conflict can often be made worse because the extent of our lives is not always commensurate with the scope of our magical powers. Some of our folk who live for six thousand years spend those six thousand years with only minimal innate magical abilities, while others in our number may live for only a few hundred years and yet possess the skill to conjure castles out of thin air! It is an odd business, in certain cases.

Spare a thought, I beg you, for the five thousand year-old warlock who has only the power or wherewithal to cast the odd fireball or perhaps confect a can't-fail love spell. That sort of magician is one who must perforce drag himself (or herself) through the merciless onslaught of weather-beaten centuries and eons, scrounging for a living as desperately as many mortals, only they must carry on the task for interminable ages. Think of the ingenuity required to survive that long with only a limited set of thaumaturgical skills. The existence of such types is even more intimately bound with that of mortals, who may pay them with food, shelter, clothing or funds for their potions, tinctures, and spells, but who may also turn upon them in the blink of an eye to disastrous effect.

Mortals, of course, are the most fair-weather and fickle of all thinking beings. One love spell that backfires, or one commissioned wax doll that sickens the wrong, unintended victim, and an otherwise reputable magus is in trouble. He or she could not only find themselves out of a local livelihood, but out of a life altogether! Matters can take a terrible turn if witches and warlocks mess up and subsequently lack the power to become invisible, shape-shift, repel small lynch mobs, or fly a respectable distance. It is true that the famous "witch hunts" of the so-called Dark Ages and beyond were responsible for exterminating thousands of innocent and decidedly non-magical human beings who were perhaps guilty only of possessing noticeable eccentricity, red hair, facility with herbs, strangely shaped birthmarks in the wrong places, or doddering old age. That being said, more than one hunting-craze has indeed been instigated by misadventures involving a genuine witch or warlock, and, on numerous occasions, a particularly vulnerable magician has been caught in the doom of some Inquisitor's net.

Suffice it to say that a glamorous life is not at all a guarantee for Our Kind, and what we consider "glamor" in the first place is far removed, quite often, from what mortals have concluded about us in that regard. Even so, our lives are bound-up with mortal lives and cultures to some degree or to another, and the majority of us are rarely found, for varying reasons, lingering too far from at least the outskirts of human civilization.

Much of this, of course, brings me back to St. Augustine, Florida, the charming and decidedly sultry Ancient City that I not long ago adopted as my home … however temporarily that may prove to be. The place is still considered by most history-enthused mortals to be the oldest permanent settlement on the North American continent. To this day, St. Augustine is a languid and, in some respects, beguilingly lonesome jewel-of-a-town, one that sweeps suddenly and swiftly alongside a tiny but picturesque bay-front and its adjacent *croisette*. On the whole, St. Augustine basks in a gentle resplendence against the friendly chop of the Matanzas Inlet, reclining and inviting as if to betoken some lazy but cheerful gateway towards an even more panoramic horizon of tantalizing possibility further on. The town entices without revealing much beyond a vision blossoming with a stately sort of grace. It boasts an allure that unfurls like the pennants fluttering along the clean, Spanish-inspired architecture of Avenida Menendez or Old St. George Street. As the Avenida sweeps southward in the midst of this fresh, palm tree-lined elegance, the redolent and almost dainty face of the little city seems to betray particularly heightened powers of intuition.

Beings of all persuasions have for decades admired the loneliness and almost lace-like ambience of mysticism that drapes St. Augustine. Whether staring from the grand walls of the town's sentinel fort, the Castillo de San Marcos, as jaunty swells slop relentlessly onto barnacle-pocked foundation walls of coquina, or tarrying beneath the moss-laden oaks that preside like belles dancing a cotillion waltz around the shadows of the old slave market, anyone with the most meager occult faculties can sense that St. Augustine is quite magical and decidedly ghostly. Perhaps the nexus of this peculiar attraction is to be found in the heady mix of piquant Spanish self-assurance and the blissful, somnambulant aura of Southern swamp. These features are duly gilded with a delicate-as-jasmine scent of stubborn old Confederate pride, lending the town an incongruous charm baked to perfection by breezy ocean-side summers and soothed by mild Mediterranean-style winters. Whatever the combination, it remains a place surrounded by secretive, forbidding tides, and has been something of a mecca for creatures of both real and imagined magical inclination.

St. Augustine *is* a witchy little hub, one populated by those unique mortals who, like thousands of their well-intentioned forebears across the world and down through the centuries, are convinced that they possess authentic magical aptitude, and who practice various forms of "witchcraft" in earnest. Dozens of psychics, voodoo priestesses, juju matrons, corner-calling Goth teens, and chemically depressed cat-owning women who waitress by day and dance—widdershins-nude—on moonlit beaches call the Ancient City home. Their "power," which is predominantly psychological (or psychotic, depending upon the intensity of any given delusion), nevertheless lends considerable spice to the rather savory melting pot of the community as a whole. But real witches, as old or much older than the city of St. Augustine itself, live here, too.

There are four genuine sorcerers in the Ancient City as I render this account, and believe me when I say that four are more than enough for a place of this particular size and temperament. Before anything else, it should be mentioned that True Magical Folk, as a general rule, are not known for getting along and forming close-knit communities or "covens" akin to those assembled in misguided imitation of us by our mortal neighbors. Oh, Persephone's Petticoats ... No! In fact, real witches, wizards, warlocks, and so forth tend to grow rather weary of each other, especially when close proximities are involved, and at the same time we are *aware* of each other—keenly so. As in the mortal sphere, a fair amount of competitive sizing-up occurs and territories are very clearly, if not officially, demarcated and understood.

Again, the notion of a coven is very much the product of overactive mortal imagination and of the fact that gathered groups of magicians have indeed been seen, spied upon, or encountered via perilous happenstance by inquisitive mortals from time to time throughout history. Otherwise, our folk prefer solitude and even our family ties are very loosely knotted, more often than not. In my opinion, a great deal of this springs from the volatile nature and flair for showing-off possessed by the everyday wonderworker, especially when stuck, for whatever reason, in the

midst of a group of peers. This phenomenon is the cause of a considerable amount of anxiety, especially in the less-skillful or marginally gifted
members of our diaphanous society. When in such circumstances, these
types often feign abilities they do not possess, or boast of strengths they
are not equipped to demonstrate when challenged. Challenges can come
fast and furious among our kind. The mortals have got that part right,
at any rate. Witches and warlocks enjoy a good duel, when it suits them,
and if someone ends up incinerated, transmogrified, or imprisoned in an
oak tree for seven hundred years … well, that's show-biz.

I do not, by any stretch of the imagination, wish to give the impression that all magical persons are incapable of getting along famously.
Far from it. When the slow and often grueling crawl of centuries begins
to take its toll upon any of us, we have indeed been known to forge lasting friendships. We can work together, as a unit, if you will, in certain
controlled environments, and those environments typically involve the
presence of a "leader" whose leadership qualities are so universally in-
disputable that duels and challenges are not ever matters of relevance,
except in cases of outright insurrection. Witches and warlocks can be exceedingly civil toward one another, we can enjoy one another's company
(with due caution), and even enjoy holidays and little outings together,
on occasion.

Sure, an entire city is apt to be burned to the ground and volcanoes have been known to belch a bit when particularly potent enchanters
make the mistake of going on an outright bender together, but these
days most everyone tends to maintain a low profile and opts for forced
conviviality. Mortals, after all, are more informed than ever they have
been in history, relatively speaking, and thus they are more apt and able
to stick their noses into our affairs—intentionally or not—which we do
not like. The more responsible and circumspect among our kind make it
a point to avoid meddling in mortal business … mostly.

At this juncture I feel it is crucial to reveal a bit about the other
three authentic magicians dwelling currently in St. Augustine. They are
all witches of the feminine variety, and all three were lodged here when
I decided to settle in the city after a series of most *unsettling* difficulties,

subsequent ramblings, and worldwide wanderings in an effort to ease my resultant distress. I was looking for a quiet, inconspicuous spot that was not too devoid of appeal after the horrific episode in London (more about that later) and wanted out of Europe for a few years altogether, at all events. St. Augustine seemed to be just far enough beneath the global metaphysical radar to afford a satisfying degree of enchanted incognito without leaving me isolated from an acceptably civilized dynamic. A certain amount of charm was non-negotiable, as was a certain amount of beach. I was in a beach phase when I decided to settle here. St. Augustine, sparkling upon what is known to proud mortals as Florida's First Coast, offered plenty of beach access.

I had once looked into New Orleans, but there was no beach to beguile me, the city's charm-factor was teetering on the brink of dereliction (I have seen this sort of decline all too many times in all too many different places over the centuries), and the place was positively rife with witch-drama. Warring warlocks, bickering sorceresses of dubious repute and questionable self-control, and entire magical families in various states of feud and fugue were the order of the day, there. I could have gotten that anywhere in Europe. Occult sensibilities were not required to discern that some sort of catastrophic event was on the horizon, so I took the advice of a bayou wraith I bumped into one evening while walking the banks of Lake Ponchartrain after enjoying a Zydeco festival and crab-feed. This had been a most talkative and helpful specter indeed. When I explained that New Orleans was not my proverbial cup of ambrosia, I was urged to explore the subtler, less frenetic ambience of St. Augustine and that was when I remembered my family's discussion centuries earlier.

"I have a sister who haunts the most cozy little drainage canal imaginable in St. Auggie," informed the wraith, whose name was Travinia. "Right next to a school for noisy mortal children with sticky faces, is this old canal. You would not believe the frights my sister is able to conjure in broad daylight when those brats walk home after their little lessons! That is noteworthy, for mortal children do not scare easily these days. In fact, they oftentimes scare *me*. Still, my sister, Destinata, can raise goose-bumps on any scrawny neck, I am proud to report. St. Augustine is a fine spot. You go see."

"How lovely for your sister," I had replied, though not terribly impressed by this initial recommendation. Wraiths are notorious for being easily amused and drainage canals certainly did not pique my interest. Travinia had more to tell, however, given the assertion that her child-spooking, ditch-dwelling relative allegedly travelled with frequency into the heart of the city via various drainpipes, sewer systems, and what-not.

"Destinata tells me that St. Augustine is sultry but lively," chattered Travinia. "Righteous and pleasing to the eye, yes, but very, very weird. The weirdest!"

That sparked a bit of curiosity on my part, and, best of all, there was the ocean. Though I had never bothered to visit the spot after familial discussion about the initial settlement, I had a firm idea of its location and was soon thanking the mournful and mist-addled wraith. The next day I made plans for an exploratory excursion with my current assistant, Miranda, and my loyal servant, familiar, and hulking English Mastiff, Bror. Upon arrival, I found myself enamored of the place for many of the qualities delineated heretofore.

"I can relax a bit in this odd little pearl-of-a-town," I murmured to the breeze. "I can also stay out of *Her* crosshairs, if indeed *She* has managed to extract Herself from the consequences of our little contretemps."

Within a month of my first visit, I purchased a newly remodeled and well-appointed five-story Victorian on a palm-and-magnolia-bordered acre of posh South St. George Street. Short escrows have never been a problem for me and, for this particular purchase, I opted to use the gold I had managed to recover from one of that awful Phillipe le Bel's tainted Lyons transactions back in the day. I christened the house in honor of Jacques de Molai, who had been a friend fated to suffer ruin as the result of one of Phillipe's schemes. This bit of real estate would be put to honorable use, if I had anything to say about it, and I did. Once we were all settled—me, Miranda, and Bror—I believed I was at least prepared to feel "at home" for the first time in several years.

It was not long before I met the others. It never *is* long, when a strange magician hits town. Any witch or warlock worth his or her pentagram chalk knows immediately when a strong new presence crashes the neighborhood, so to speak. I sensed their presence as soon as I had set foot in St. Augustine, as did Bror and, to a lesser extent, Miranda. Even so, I opted to let the others make their way to *my* door, if they were to make a way at all, and roll out whatever version of the occult welcome wagon they saw fit to roll out. There is no standard magical etiquette in this regard; one simply waits to see what transpires. Fortuna be thanked, we all hit-it-off well enough, though the initial attitude was one of guarded skepticism on all sides. This, however, is rather typical in such circumstances.

Allow me to introduce The Ladies.

First, there is the impressive duo of Leticia Beauregard and Gertrude Gokey. Leticia and Gertrude are best friends—witches who, to mortal eyes, would both appear to be roughly in their mid-seventies, but neither (at least thus far) has admitted to being a day over six hundred. I do not know all of the details concerning where they are from, or how, exactly, they hooked up in St. Augustine, given that they are presumably older than the settlement itself. I have managed to glean a slew of curious facts and tantalizing tidbits, but have refrained from forthright inquisition because it simply is not polite and they have not pried much into my background, though I can tell that they want nothing less than a complete run-down of my entire career and pedigree. Of course, the two of them have been scrying frantically in secret in an attempt to excavate information, but they have not been successful. I screen and block *those* kinds of "calls." Believe me. What I do know is that both ladies are equally impressive, each in her own manner, and yet they could not be more different, at least in terms of personality and disposition.

Leticia ("Letty") is arrow-thin and regal in a haughty Southern matriarch sort of fashion, though she has no offspring, to my knowledge, and is certainly not originally from the Old South. But witches can and do pick-up strange affectations when they linger in one place for a long time. Letty's iron-gray hair is braided in an impeccable, impenetrable helmet around her dignified, egret-like head, which protrudes in a perpetual angle of high-nosed disdain from the starched lace collar of her omnipresent robin's egg blue dress. She is all crossed arms, disapproving smirks, and warily raised brows atop her wrinkled-but-handsome face, and, if one did not know she had the power to summon at least six of the most dreaded Strangler Succubi, Letty could easily be mistaken for the stern, no-nonsense, eminently judgmental, and well-scrubbed wife of an aged Baptist minister. Indeed, Letty is a tough old baggage and she made certain I knew it from the first moment we met, though I could tell she was inwardly taken aback when she sensed that I was one of the Truly Old Ones. At that moment, she had been forced to get a grip on her own imperturbable demeanor for fear of revealing just how impressed she was.

The short and rotund Gertrude ("Gert"), on the other hand, is the most blissfully unconcerned vision of cotton-haired mischief that ever inhabited swaths of purple satin. There is ever a ribald gleam in Gert's glassy hazel eyes, which are set like almond-shaped stones in her luminous black face. From the start, her manner was as relaxed and as carefree as Letty's manner had been prim and uptight. Gert is all hearty chuckles, exotic turbans, heaving bosom, jangling bangles, and open-armed invitation. If one did not know she had the power to grab a lightning bolt out of the sky and twist it into a pretty bow before it even hit the ground, Gert could easily be mistaken for the affable, martini-swilling, devil-may-care hostess of the best soul-food joint in town.

The two of them turned up at my door a few weeks after I moved into the Victorian, gaily decorated jars of some strange preserve in their hands. We got to know each other over iced hemlock tea served by Miranda on the back porch, or, if we did not exactly "get to know each other" at that juncture, everyone was at least able to size things up. Letty and Gert own and operate a gift shop on busy, touristy St. George Street in the heart of downtown St. Augustine's sun-dazzled historic district. Their shop is called "Datil Be the Day" because it is an atelier devoted exclusively to the vending of products derived from or combined with the locally grown and unique datil pepper. This merchandise is offered in every homemade form the two women could think of, from datil pepper jellies and cheeses to spicy datil pepper chocolates and even love-tonic liqueurs (Gert's idea). The ladies run this wildly popular store with the help of no one, and they live together in a spacious Spanish-style adobe apartment with verdigris balcony railings and bright green shutters directly above their successful concern.

As longtime friends and business partners, their bickering is constant and almost symphonic, given Leticia's tart tongue and Gertrude's air of silky-smooth indifference to the general acidity of her companion's communications. Both have mastered the art of passive-aggression, which is not a magical skill at all, but which in witchy hands can become an exponentially terrifying phenomenon. In the magical department alone, I must aver that I was a little surprised to discover each lady to be remarkably gifted. It was plain to me from the beginning that each witch fancied herself to be more powerful than the other, but I also noticed with immediacy that their respective gifts were rather complementary. I guessed that this was the reason why they formed such a redoubtable team, and why only a potent spell-caster, like me, or someone who was *completely* daft would just wander arbitrarily into the territory these two seemed content to rule as a magical roost.

As I mentioned earlier, appearances can be most deceiving in our world. A sorcerer thousands of years old may veritably drip with power and yet appear to be a mere tender-horn, a fledgling. Others the same age may be wizened and hungry-eyed scrappers, dismal desperates who have scrounged across millennia with nary a worthy spell in their repertoire, while mages of much younger stock can appear just as decrepit but possess extraordinary gifts. Letty, Gert, and myself came to a swift and mutual respect over our cool beverages the day we made acquaintance, with me being the undeniably superior Power to enter "their" city. Even so, on that occasion the ladies were swift to inform me that, along with the potent spell-caster, there was indeed a place for the daft among the rustling palmetto bushes and shadowy groves thick with Spanish moss. This brings us to the third female magician in St. Augustine. Letty guffawed at the mention of her name and even the kindly Gert rolled her eyes and whistled through her teeth with dismissal. For my part, I met the city's "other" real witch exactly one week after Letty and Gert had paid their initial call.

Serenity Turnbull appeared on my doorstep bearing no jam, jelly, or Southern styled confection of any sort, but rather her recently published self-help book, *Bells & Smells: Unleashing the Sound of Your Life's Aroma*. She also brought a patchouli candle. Lovely Serenity was wearing worn, Roman-style sandals and a rumpled white sundress emblazoned with dully painted slices of honeydew melon. Atop her head was a knitted cap with the word "SUSTAINABLE" sewn in crude letters across a patch on the front and, from beneath this cap and its buzzword, fabulous tangles and tributaries and ringlets and rivulets of strawberry blonde hair emerged. To mortal eyes, she would have appeared about twenty-five— only a few years older than I have been said to appear, at least according to the contemporary Western gauge of human physical perception.

There was no doubt to me, however, that Serenity was considerably older than twenty-five, perhaps even older than the "Datil Be the Day" ladies, though I could not vouch for the state of her magical aptitude. Little could be surmised in that arena from sheer occult intuition, at least during our first encounter. It seemed she was hiding something, though this was hardly an insult or indication of rudeness; witches often hide all sorts of things, if they can, including the full extent of their powers. Otherwise, with a faint spray of freckles across fair cheeks and the bridge of her delicate nose, Miss Turnbull was a mild and cheerful spirit whose warm, cappuccino-colored eyes bid me sincere welcome to the Ancient City. She did not seem anywhere near as concerned with sizing-me-up as the other two, far more surreptitious, enchantresses. Standing on the flagstones of the veranda, Serenity assured me that she, too, had sensed my arrival in the usual manner (at least for witches) but did not have time to come inside for a visit. Moreover, she spoke not a word about Leticia and Gertrude, her fellow sisters in the local Craft. That was a bit more unconventional because witches and warlocks do traditionally take great pleasure in providing helpful, if unsolicited, information about each other, particularly in the presence of a newcomer, and even more particularly in the form of various "I-mean-this-in-the-best-possible-way" remarks.

Instead, Serenity (which I rather doubted to be her given name) handed me the bell-book and candle, begged my pardon, and explained that she simply had to run because she was teaching a class on biodynamic indoor herb-gardening to a group of students at the exclusive Flagler College downtown that very afternoon. She had hoped I was settling-in comfortably and that we might get together for *café au lait* and scones at a little bay-front patisserie as soon as possible. As she tacked off into the late morning sun in her bedraggled sandals, she encouraged me to send a message regarding my availability for coffee by telepathy, crystal ball, mirror vision, or tree-whispering but not, under any circumstances, via telephone, seeing as she had not owned a telephone since moving East from San Francisco ten years earlier.

"Oh, and don't send word via raven or any other bird or small animal-type messenger that you would actually want to get back, because my anaconda, Guadalupe, has free run of the house and she invariably captures, suffocates, and swallows any magical couriers from goat-size on down."

"How ... *sustainable* of Guadalupe," I managed to reply.

"Isn't it?" chirped Serenity as her sandal soles flapped on the radiating heat of the sidewalk. "She won't go near my familiar, Emory, of course. Even though he's just a little Shih-Tzu, he's quite intimidating. Can't wait for you to meet him."

"Nor can I."

Serenity had waved over her shoulder with a weak fluttering of thin white fingers, drifting in the honeydew sundress like a tired but determined butterfly toward her day's adventures. "Welcome to the Ancient City, Rowan Blaize. Do tree-whisper me when you can. At the very least we can lunch at my place. I live on Palmetto Street in Vilano. You'll have to drop by and enjoy some fresh-squeezed guava nectar in the crow's nest up on top of the house. The view is delectable. Enjoy the book, in the meantime. I'll be eager for your impressions. Absolutely lovely to meet you."

Then she was gone.

I had turned to Miranda and Bror, who had been watching from a window of the adjacent parlor with much skepticism.

"Don't stare, you two. Yes, I have met some odd ducks among my kind over the ages and have rarely batted an eye, but we are in a lazy little American beach town, now. This earthy little witch's story may prove mildly entertaining. One never knows. Have a look at this book she wrote. Here, Miranda. See what you make of it. Bror, your claws are going to ruin that window sill. Hop down and stop drooling, would you, please? She's gone. Thank you, old boy. You know, I'll bet our two pepper-purveying pillars of the occult community know a great deal more about Serenity's history than they let on during their first visit. Miranda, be a dear and ring them up at that Datil whatever-it-is shop. I know they, at least, have a telephone. It's only fitting that I repay their courtesy with a visit of my own. It would not hurt to get out a bit, now that we're settled. After all, we're on the … what do you call it?"

"The 'down low' is what we are on," replied my precious and icy green-eyed Miranda.

"That's the one. Right. We're on the down low in a magical Southern hotspot. Let's get to know the local gentry a bit better, shall we? Give the old biddies a call."

There had been no doubt about it; I was intent upon getting what our mortal confreres call "the scoop" and I was not going to need any magic in order to procure it. Southern charm—even though I had gleaned only a few weeks' worth of it at the time—was bound to do the trick.

That had been just a little over one year ago.

I did learn, eventually, following frequent visits to Letty and Gert's "Datil Be The Day" shop on bustling, sweaty, tourist-jammed St. George Street, that Serenity Turnbull had never been exactly *their* kind of witch. The ladies had reached this conclusion even after numerous (and alleged) attempts to grasp the value inherent in Serenity's "shockin' and deviant behavior"—this last according to Letty. Their witchy relationship with Serenity had always failed, even despite kindly Gert's attempts to be the diplomatic and broad-minded beacon of universal acceptance that she believed herself to be. Interestingly enough over the years, the two old witches could not seem to stop talking about this blight upon their otherwise immaculate social reputation in the Ancient City's supernatural circles.

"Letty, you have always been far too hard on that gal," said Gert as she performed a rather desultory dusting job at the pepper shop one balmy afternoon in late October.

"I'm not sayin' that Serenity Turnbull ain't never been welcome to bring a little bit of diversity to our town," replied Letty, counting the day's receipts as I leaned against shelves piled high with their namesake hot sauces. "But I'll thank you to keep your opinions about *my* opinions about the Turbull gal to yourself, Gertrude! What's your opinion on that, Rowan Blaize?"

"My opinion would only complicate matters between you two esteemed ladies, I fear."

"Ha! You hear that, Gert? Even Blaize agrees with me!"

"Now, I don't think I quite said as much as all that, Leticia Beauregard."

"Fine, fine, you can both forget I said anything at all," Gert muttered as she dusted idly. "Who cares about that blasted Serenity, anyhow? I wanna see this bit what's comin' up on the TV. Now hush!"

The display of datil pepper-infused olive oil bottles may have gotten short-shrift, but Gert's attention was indeed most firmly fixed upon the widescreen television above their granite-topped counter and its incongruously cumbersome World War II-era cash register. There had been a horrific shark attack off the coast of nearby Anastasia Island that morning and a swimmer had lost a limb. Gertrude Gokey, for all of her seemingly homespun qualities, possessed a ghoulish fascination for anything tragic or catastrophic that happened to mortals. Lost limbs were especially tantalizing to her curiosity. Letty, meanwhile, continued delineating her opinions about Serenity to me in more subdued tones.

"Anyone with any bit of sense knows that I am all for diversity and free expression, but our dear Ms. Turnbull has always been a pert little number, if you ask me," asserted Letty. "I think that *she* thinks she's better'n us, what with all her funny little organic and susta ... susta ... suss ..."

"Sustainable."

"Sustainable. Yes, thank you, Rowan Blaize. Anyhow, her sustainable ways may have been just dandy when she lived out there in California, but she's been in Florida now for over a decade and I think it's time she came down off her high horse. Besides, that gal sets her heart far too much on mortal trends ... to the detriment of her witchin' skills." Letty pounded a gnarled fist atop the granite. "I can't stand to see folks not usin' their gifts properly. I tell you I can't! It's a waste, is what it is, and nothin' brings about ill fortune like a witch that wastes her talents. Mortal trends. Ha! Those come and go with the breeze. That's why even the mortals are smart enough to call them trends! I seen plenty of that nonsense in my day, believe you me. But neglectful witchery? Why, that's an abomination. It's practically a ... a ... *cosmic disaster.* Don't you think?"

"I'm not convinced it's that ominous, Letty, but I do have the feeling that Serenity Turnbull may be a trifle scattered when it comes to the proper use of her gifts."

"You can say that again," said Letty, scowling absently at the lack of tourist traffic on the street between their shop and the town's famous Cathedral Basilica. The busy season was winding down like a forgotten clock and soon only the more transient "snowbirds" from ice-blasted northern states would be passing through on their way to Miami and Key West.

"In the ten years she's been here, I haven't seen Serenity ever use any magic worth writing home about," grumbled Letty, closing the cash register with a slam of disapproval.

"She flew her broomstick over to Ormond Beach when that sick old gray whale washed ashore," interjected Gert as she nibbled on a chocolate-covered pepper. "Managed to summon up enough of a swell at low tide to carry the poor beast right back out to sea when all them crybabies from the university were fit to be tied, pourin' their little cups of water over the thing and singin' songs to try and 'calm it down.' My stars! You can't get much calmer than an entire whale flat-out on the sand, unable to move. Heh! Serenity showed some good judgment—and power—in that case. Even you'd have to agree with that, Letty."

Letty glared at her cohort and adjusted the impeccable lace collar of her dress with fingers that were bright red due to centuries of ferociously scrubbing untidy surfaces. "The gal's got her head in the clouds, is all I was saying. And not the kind of clouds you can use a broomstick to get your head up into, either," she added. "Imitating mortals for purposes of sheer survival, or to blend in when the magic's on the blink, is one thing. Taking mortal ways so seriously that you want to *become* one is quite another. Why, it's patronizin' to mortal folk, I tell you what."

"Yet, you and Gert, here, run a retail store in the heart of the busiest section of a mortal resort town," I said with an intonation that was merely moderate in its baiting mockery.

"Ain't the same thing at all," snapped Leticia Beauregard, as if she had anticipated the comment and had been rehearsing an appropriate rebuttal all week. She stabbed a knobby index finger in the air for dramatic effect. "Great and respectable members of our kind have conducted commerce alongside mortals for centuries on end, Rowan Blaize, and you know it to be true. We've been in the marketplaces and bazaars and county fairs and nowadays even in them deplorable strip-malls, fulfilling a service to our neighbors and making our way in honorable professions. For centuries, I repeat! It's only the warped and fiendish magician who tries to conjure his money and his supper out of thin air, just for the ducks of it. I come from witchy stock that's never been ashamed to earn its keep in one way or another from the earth, all whilst using magic properly. Why, back in the Old Country, I had an Auntie who scraped and scrabbled and nearly broke her poor old back to run a successful candy shop, and everyone in the magical community said, 'Now there goes a *respectable* witch!' And they was right, too."

"As I recall, Letty, your Auntie Odina was also known for using her candy shop to lure-in some of the chubbier mortal kiddies. Kiddies who'd find themselves baked in her mincemeat pies, from time to time."

"That was when she got real old and a little 'baked' in the brain," hissed Leticia. "Besides, Gertrude Gokey, you know that happened only three or four times, and then the rest of the family got together and forced her to retire before the villagers had a chance to catch her in the act! Millions of mortal children have been the victims of far greater cruelty at the hands of their own kind, thank you very much. A hungry ole sorceress who's lost her faculties can't be held responsible, so long as matters are taken in hand. A few tots ending up in a bit of cobbler don't even put a *dent* in what humans do to their own. My point is that she was a sterling businesswoman in her heyday, and our kind has a long tradition of doing fair and square business with mortal folk. It's what happens *after* the shops close and the wagons are loaded that counts. Proper witchcraft is practiced behind closed doors and in the thick of the night, and I don't think Serenity Turnbull is a proper witch behind closed doors. I truly don't."

Gert waved a feather-duster weakly in Letty's direction and went over to lock the shop's front door for the day and flip the OPEN sign in the window to CLOSED status.

"Give it a rest, Letty," she sighed. "What Turnbull does within the confines of her own pentagram is her affair, not ours. It ain't everyone that can be exquisitely gifted and carry themselves with unwavering dignity, like us." Gert hitched a plump brown finger beneath a pinching shoulder-strap and adjusted the brassiere supporting her mammoth bosom with some measure of shuddering upheaval. "Plus, I know for a fact that Serenity *does* have some very witchy interests. If you ever gave the gal a chance, you might know the same."

"Like what?" I asked, figuring a bit of thaumaturgical gossip would do little harm. "What sorts of interests?"

"Well, for one thing, I gather that Serenity's been studying to become a certified amateur archaeologist, or some such," said Gert, scratching at a bit of stubble on her chin.

"She never!" gasped Letty.

"It could be true enough, and don't act so surprised." Gert placed the feather-duster atop a crate of Datil Pepper Sassy-Salsa and rested a bit from her dubious labors. "You know she's got herself that warlock boyfriend over to the university there in Gainesville. The boyfriend who goes looking for trinkets and what-not from a buncha digs in Macedonia or wherever. Can't think of the feller's name, but sometimes he sends her stuff and she uses her computer to do research. She googlies things for her boyfriend, you see."

"She WHAT?" gasped Letty, a hand flying in prudish horror to the cameo of Artemis at her collar.

"She *Googles* things," I said with a reassuring hand on the old witch's shoulder. "I believe that is what Gert is attempting to tell us."

"Whull!" said Letty with an obsidian glint of suspicion in her gimlet eyes. "I ain't never heard of a spell like that."

"Googlin' ain't no spell, Letty," said Gert, whose patience was well-practiced. "It's one of them searches you can do on the computers and phones and stuff these days. Ain't that right, Rowan Blaize? Find anything in the world with the Googly, you can."

"Hmmpf!" sniffed Letty. "Mortal magic. It'll never catch on and it won't last, neither. I'd put an earthenware pot full of good clean scryin' water up against their Googler any blessed day of the week."

"The Googles is actually quicker," informed Gert, warming to her sudden role as technological informant. "Though it won't amount to a thing if all the electric and all them satellites whirling around up in space go to pot."

Letty flourished a hand in triumph. "My point exactly. Mortal trickery can't be counted upon for posterity, and before we go any further with Serenity and this boyfriend of hers, just how did you come to know so much about these wicked computer contraptions, anyhow, Gert? It was bad enough that we were forced to abide the abomination of television and radios and cash registers and credit card machines, although them last two things are real useful, I'll have to admit."

Gert shrugged and swung her stubby legs childishly from side to side as she sat atop a straining and groaning crate of "Datil Be The Day" salsa product. "I am a woman and a witch of the Twenty-First Century," she said, beaming a display of magnificent teeth that might cause the world's whitest pearl to discolor with envy. "I keep up with the times, because—magical or mortal—the times'll be quick to sneak up on all of *us,* if we don't."

"That's as may be," admitted Letty, "but I still can't picture what sort of nonsense that Serenity has apparently gotten herself into now. Archaeology, my eye. Why, last year she was hell-bent on making a go of it with that awful turquoise jewelry-stand down at the once-a-week market on the Plaza. All proceeds to benefit endangered sea-turtles or some such, if I recall correctly."

"Nothin' wrong with makin' ugly jewelry and sellin' it, Letty. We make all these datil pepper delectables and folks come from miles around to give us money for the stuff we brew-up in the kitchen back there. Best part of all is folks keep comin' back for more, in spite of themselves, even if they can't stand the taste of datil peppers! Hee hee!"

Letty sneered.

"Never said there was anything wrong with jewelry, Gert. But there's a difference. We put little charms and a smidge of enchantment into our merchandise so people can experience a bit of unobtrusive uplift in their daily lives, a touch of contentment. Not enough to mess with their outlooks or anything, but enough to take the edge off."

"Like wormwood martinis," I offered.

"Exactly, Rowan Blaize. That's what altruistic witchcraft is all about, when a witch engages with mortals in a bit of friendly commerce. We give them a little extra in return for what we take from them in or-der to live alongside. Last summer I went down to that dilapidated craft fair and I said to Serenity, I says, 'Serenity Turnbull, this is a mighty fine jewelry booth what you have set up here in the miserable heat like a com-mon gypsy, and your turquoise bangles aren't too bad to look at, neither.' I was trying to encourage the girl, see. Then I said to her, I says, 'But tell me, Serenity, what kind of spells do you put on your goods to give poor mortals a touch of comfort for the hard-earned money they are throwin' away on this foolishness?' Do you know what she said to me?"

"Yes, Letty! You told me a dozen times last year!" squawked Gert.

"What did she say?" I asked, for I had not been thus privileged.

Letty whirled around behind the checkout counter, thrilled to have a more marginally interested audience for her oncoming rant. "Serenity Turnbull said to me, 'Oh, Mizz Beauregard, I do not place any sort of magical influences upon my creations. That would compromise the authenticity of my art.' Can you *believe* the nerve?"

"Yes, I can believe it. But how did she come to the conclusion that placing a charm upon a bangle would compromise artistic integrity?"

"That's just it!" said Letty, nearly breathless by now in her enthusiasm for discussing Serenity Turnbull's occult deficiencies. "Witchcraft *is* the proper 'art' for a witch. It's the only authentic art a witch can possess. Oh, I tell you, Rowan Blaize, that gal's blithe disregard for her heritage was like a slap in the face to hard-working sorceresses everywhere. Mark my words ... when a witch gets too caught up in harebrained mortal philosophies and trends, she is travelling down a reckless and wanton path, indeed."

Letty was undeniably passionate about her assessment of Serenity Turnbull. Her aquiline nose was held higher than ever and twitching a bit; the flesh of her spectacular cheekbones was so flushed one could barely see the wrinkles. Witches and warlocks are excitable beings in the calmest of times, so I thought it best to proceed with caution.

"I admit that some of Serenity's views are rather unorthodox for an enchantress ..."

Letty snorted in recognition of what, to her, was a maddening understatement.

"...but one ought to give her some credit for maintaining such a broad spectrum of hobbies and enthusiasms. Since I've been in St. Augustine she's gone from publishing self-help booklets to environmental activism, beekeeping, the craftsmanship of terrifically gaudy jewelry, and now, according to our dear Gertrude, she is enraptured with an unnamed warlock from Gainesville and sharing his fondness for ancient artifacts. I call that positively adventuresome."

"Aha!" said Gert, as if emerging suddenly from a deep trance among the salsa crates. "I've just remembered his name. It's Percival something-or-other. Serenity started to keep him company not long after you came to town, Rowan Blaize. Why am I becoming so forgetful in my old age? Such a sorry pass. I used to have everything right on the tip of my tongue."

"Seems to me you still got an awful lot positioned there," informed Letty.

Gert stuck out the tongue in question for a moment and then continued. "Yes, they've got eyes for each other, Serenity and that wormy little warlock, Percival. Met him only once, down near the Bridge of Lions when they was taking a stroll and I was on my way to the Cobalt Lounge for a whiff of happy hour. They're a mousy little couple, and no mistake about that. I suspect it's just another passing fancy on Serenity's part, but fancies are helped along considerably when someone sends you ancient coins and baubles dug up in them old, exotic stomping grounds. I think Serenity likes the attention, to tell you the truth, and I think she likes it even better that he's out of the country all year earning that doctor hat or whatever it is he's trying to earn over there by Gainesville."

"They strike me as two peas in a pod," noted Letty. "This Percival character probably has about as much practical use for his magic as she's got for hers. He's probably stricken with mortal fever, too!"

"I see no harm in Serenity hanging on to a long-distance romance and a few dusty knick-knacks sent by her beau, ladies. In fact, with her interest in archaeology and archaeologically minded warlocks, she may even have an entertaining story or two to share with the rest of us. I plan to invite her to my All Hallow's Eve party this Sunday. Hopefully she will accept the invitation this year. It behooves all of the city's primary enchanters to be gathered in one spot on such an auspicious occasion. I would hate to think that Serenity might continue to discard *all* the trappings of her immortal heritage for the mere sake of being contrary and affected."

"She'll be a no-show at your fine party this year, same as she was last year," declared Letty. "The girl has no respect for her elders and would rather be seen hawking trinkets, or protesting the mistreatment of them buggy-draggin' horses down by the bay with all those sanctimonious college students, instead of sipping nightshade juleps with the swamp goblins, like a proud witch ought to do on a major holiday."

Gert shoved her round self off the crates and sauntered awkwardly over to the counter, her elaborate purple turban slightly askew. "Turnbull is going to make her own choices and learn her own lessons and no amount of huffing and puffing from you or from me is gonna make a whit of difference, Letty. Give it a rest. The important thing is that our dear friend Rowan will have St. Augustine's two most *prestigious* witches in attendance at the All Hallow's Eve party, and that's us."

"True enough," agreed Letty, albeit with a begrudging frown. "We wouldn't miss the party for the world—seen or unseen."

"There now," said Gert. "See how nice things go when we mind our own affairs? Say, Rowan dear, would you mind reaching up and pushing that little volume button on the TV, the little button on the lower left over the stack of Datil Dumpling mix? I lost the remote last week and haven't had a chance to scry for its whereabouts, yet. Yeah, that's the button. That shark attack piece was gripping and all, but I been waiting since Monday to see these two characters up there on the screen right now! I heard they was gonna be interviewed on tonight's six o'clock news."

Gert had become visibly excited, balling her stubby fingers into fists and burying them deep in her gargantuan bosom.

"Don't turn that chatterbox up and humor her," begged Letty. "Please, Rowan Blaize. Gertrude Gokey watches far too much television for her own good. Why, back in the Old Country we were quite content to conjure-up entertaining scenery on the surface of pond water, when things got boring. We could get a real nice look at what the elves and the nixies and all sorts of little buggers were up to, if we wanted. Remember, Gert?"

"Hush, Letty! I want to hear this."

"Magical eavesdropping, eh, Miss Beauregard?" said I, increasing the set's volume for the starry-eyed and utterly fascinated Gert. Foot traffic outside the shop was non-existent now in the thickening shadows of sunset that began to spread across St. George Street and the walls of the nearby cathedral.

"I would hardly call our efforts in the old days 'eavesdropping,' Rowan Blaize. Witches in them times had to stay on top of things for our own self-preservation. There was a practical part to all of that. This mortal TV stuff is what's eavesdropping, if you ask me, and the worst kind, too. Dolled-up housewives pulling the hairs right out of each other's heads. Mortals swapping their spouses just to see how insane everyone'll get after the switch. Greedy, illiterate people in them trailer-houses calling each other all sorts of vile things and throwing sharp objects around. Swarthy Armenian trollops. That's entertainment? It's shameful, is what it is."

"No one wants your opinion on this subject right now, Letty," said the mesmerized Gert. "Besides, this TV is half mine. I like all them shows. Gives you a good look at a side of humanity we never got to see gazing into a patch of old pond scum."

"Ha! They *are* the pond scum, now!" bleated Letty, but Gert was not to be thwarted.

"Say what you will, my friends, but those two mortals up there on that TV screen this minute are what I call the *upstanding* sort of mortals."

Letty stared up at the television in spite of her misgivings about modern entertainment and clucked her tongue loudly in disapproval.

"What in the world is that oily man with the gold tooth doing next to that child in the tiara and all the frightening make-up? Is that a ball-gown she's got on? The girl can't be more than six years old."

"Quiet, Letty! That there is St. Augustine City Councilman Chesterfield Rummy and his darling little daughter, BonSashay. She's been entering all sorts of talent and beauty contests across the state and now she's fixing to go all the way at the upcoming Pint-Sized Princess Pageant being held right here in town in a few days. It's the statewide championship. Don't you know anything? Dear little BonSashay has been practicing so hard her whole life to win this thing. Don't you even read the entertainment section of the paper?"

"No, I do not," replied Letty, folding her arms and glowering at the scene on the screen in mounting distaste.

"Then pipe down for a minute," urged Gert. "I can't hear what they're saying."

The older man on the screen, dressed in a three-piece suit and a frightening hairpiece that resembled portions of various animals often seen smeared alongside Florida roadways, was sweating profusely from every pore on his rotisserie chicken-tanned face. He and his six year-old daughter, who appeared to be gearing up to trick-or-treat in attire befitting a courtesan, were being interviewed by Channel 6's own Bobbi Jo Mickler.

"So just how long have you and BonSashay been working toward the ultimate goal of taking the Pint-Sized Princess title on November first, Councilman Rummy?" asked Bobbi Jo.

"Thank you for taking the time to welcome us, Bobbi Jo," drawled the man in tones as slick as boar grease on an outdoor Floridian doorknob in August. This was a man who seemed quite comfortable around microphones and eminently at home in the glare of any spotlight. "The real credit for all this hard work and success, though, goes to my beautiful daughter, BonSashay Rummy. This is her dream, you see. Her mother and me have just been along for this exceptional child's fabulous ride. Isn't that right, honey?"

"Are we going to Dairy Queen or Cheeseburger in Paradise tonight, Daddy?" said the porcelain-faced child. Her Joan Crawford eyebrows arched outward from an astonishing explosion of golden ringlets and Shirley Temple-worthy curls, all topped with a gigantic polka dot bow. "You said we could go to Dairy Queen or Cheeseburger in Paradise if I nailed that pole-dancing routine in practice today and I *did,* so when can we go?"

Chesterfield Rummy laughed as if his child had just told a rather harmless knock-knock joke, but the chuckle was laced with anger the way clouds are sometimes laced with heat-lightning before a storm.

"Heh heh. That's so sweet, darling baby girl. Isn't she just the sweetest thing you ever saw, Bobbi Jo Mickler? Why, you'll get yourself a cheeseburger soon enough, honey. First we have to spend a few minutes talking with this nice TV lady who's agreed to interview us before the biggest opportunity of our—of *your*—life. You precious thing. Heh heh."

Bobbi Jo Mickler shoved the microphone closer to Chesterfield Rummy's fiendish grin and to the set of large outer teeth that were almost as yellow as the shining gold one in their midst. "Now, Councilman Rummy, as I am sure you are aware, there is some degree of controversy about the whole pageant culture, about the idea of parents pushing their very young daughters into competitive events that many people feel are more suited to seasoned adult women."

"Ha! More suited to seasoned adult women of ill-repute, too!" hissed Letty at the widescreen.

"Silence!" commanded Gert. Against the grand backdrop of the Castillo de San Marcos, where the sunset interview was being held, Chesterfield Rummy waved a well-manicured hand as if brushing away an insignificant bit of cobweb that had dared to somehow attach itself to his soul.

"Oh, we have heard all the naysayers and the haters, Bobbi Jo, but what most folks fail to understand is that these kinds of competitions are great for little girls like BonSashay. See, they build a fortress of character that provides a lasting foundation for the rest of their lives." He gestured toward the Castillo as he uttered the words "fortress of character" in his honeyed, meaningful tones. It was a convenient and convincing prop, at least in the eyes of Gert, who clapped her hands in giddy approval. "Besides," continued Rummy, "I couldn't stop this little dynamo from pursuing her dreams if I wanted to! Isn't that right, honey?"

"I have wanted to be an actress and a dancer ever since I was a little girl," said BonSashay, staring directly into the camera on robotic cue.

"But you still *are* a little girl," said the visibly uncomfortable Bobbi Jo Mickler.

"I mean since I was a littler little girl," said the little girl, enunciating every word to perfection. "I have reached new levels of awareness in my life since the very young days. I did not have a clear vision of what I wanted at three, but now that I am six, I can see an entire world of opportunity opening up before me like a tan pajama."

"Uh ... that's, er, *panorama*," Chesterfield Rummy informed everyone in TV-land. "She meant to say panorama. Is there any way we can shoot this bit over again?"

"No, I'm afraid it's live, Councilman Rummy," reminded Bobbi Jo Mickler, bending lower with her microphone to the pint-sized hopeful. "So what you're saying to us, honey, is that you have been wanting to do this ever since you can remember. Is that right?"

"Yeah, yeah. Just like that," replied BonSashay with a little shrug.

"My, she certainly is precious, isn't she?" said the unconvinced Bobbi Jo.

"You took the words right out of my mouth," said Chesterfield Rummy as BonSashay unleashed a cavernous yawn for the camera. "We're hoping that the esteemed Pint-Sized Princess panel of judges sees the exact same qualities that you see, Bobbi Jo. Namely, we want them to see all that preciousness backed up by second-to-none vocal styling and cutting-edge dance moves that no other contestant will be able to touch in terms of ability and execution. BonSashay brings a veteran's work ethic and a wealth of hardcore experience to the mix, and her mother and I believe this will give her the winning edge on Monday night."

"What song are you planning to sing for the pageant judges?" asked Bobbi Jo.

"Are you kidding?" blurted the weary BonSashay, whose mascara was beginning to run at the corners and was soon smeared across one cheek as she ran the back of a white-gloved hand across her face. "We don't reveal our secret weapons until the day of the pageant. I can just see that nasty Brenda Bob Parson stealing my whole act if I was dumb enough to tell you about it on national TV, lady!"

"Oh, my," said Bobbi Jo Mickler of Channel 6. "Well ... um ... this is only a local news program after all, sugar."

"Yeah?" squeaked BonSashay. "Well, Brenda Bob Parson lives just a few miles away over in Spuds, so I'm sure she and that turkey-necked mama of hers are watching this program right now so they can try to come up with any little clue they can use to bring me down on pageant night."

"Now, BonSashay, doll, we must remember to be respectful to our fellow Pint-Sized Princess competitors," interrupted the now wild-eyed Mr. Rummy, seizing his own little princess somewhat roughly by one of her puffed satin sleeves. "She's tired," he mouthed to the fascinated reporter.

"Daddy, if you rip this gown, I swear I'm gonna pee the bed for a whole week!" threatened BonSashay.

"Can we at least edit some of this? Time-delay or something?" begged Chesterfield Rummy in a desperate whisper.

"Sorry, Councilman," replied Bobbi Jo Mickler, gesturing outward to the thousands of North Floridians she hoped were watching the scene unfold. "We're live but we're not *Saturday Night Live*."

"Now, these young professionals do tend to get a bit excited as pageant time draws near," stammered the elder Rummy, wracking his brain for some new track upon which he might dash off to rescue the listing interview. "In fact, all of this pressure and hoopla can really bring out their sharp competitive drive and that's a good thing, Miss Bobbi Jo, because these girls thrive on pressure, and no one enjoys the challenge of the spotlight more than my little BonSashay!"

"Daddy, you are *choking* me with my *own* rhinestone rainbow necklace," gagged BonSashay. "Cut it out!"

"Sorry, precious."

"Mr. Rummy, the Pint-Sized Princess Pageant is one of the biggest events St. Augustine has hosted in, probably, weeks," continued Bobbi Jo Mickler, "and I understand that one of the greatest obstacles to national success in the little girl beauty pageant racket—er—*industry*, excuse me, is funding. Am I correct in understanding that you have been actively seeking sponsors and even going door-to-door soliciting tax-deductible donations to offset the cost of your daughter's tour on this grueling and competitive kiddie circuit?"

"Absolutely," said Chesterfield Rummy, loosening his grip on the rhinestone rainbow necklace and also his child's extravagant mane of hair and hair extensions. BonSashay had been getting a little too pale, even in the relentless blaze of the camera crew's lights. "Talent and personal integrity are two of the most important things that carry a sweet young prodigy like BonSashay toward her All American goals, but I'd be a liar if I told you that hair and outfits weren't crucial, too. And those things are expensive. Hoo wee. So are the hotels, entrance fees, vocal lessons, dance instructions, personal trainers, make-up artists, massage therapists, and psychological consultants. All of these things can play a vital role in snatching that big brass ring. We are a family that takes a very holistic approach to the nurture and promotion of a talent as earth-shattering as BonSashay's. For that reason, we have gladly mortgaged the house, again, and we will be stepping-up efforts to seek out and welcome new sponsors in the next few days, folks who may wish to hop aboard this little angel's runaway train to stardom. Getting in on the ground floor of BonSashay's journey is not just an investment in what'll become a mind-boggling multi-media empire—one that will pay the visionary contributor jaw-dropping dividends!—but it's an investment in something much bigger, Bobbi Jo."

"What's that?"

Chesterfield Rummy turned to face the camera with all the pathos and pontifical self-assurance of the most persuasive of Pentecostal preachers.

"That bigger something, my friends, is an investment in the God-fearing values of wholesome family togetherness, values this great nation was founded on. This is an investment in raising-up young Christian girls into women who will Biblically exemplify the best of what American ladies have to offer. Winners like BonSashay will lead by example, and this is a chance to guarantee a future generation of wives in this country who know how to attire themselves and style their hair properly for the appreciation and admiration of their husbands. Together we can make sure that America is filled with mothers who will not rush their children to the corner bus-stop dressed in slovenly curlers and bathrobes. No! We want mothers the way they used to be, able to practically spring right out of bed in impeccable make-up and fashionable frocks that'll allow kids to greet the day with pride and say to their little friends on the school-bus,

'*That* is my beautiful mother. She was once a Pint-Sized Princess pageant contestant and winner. My mother ... is an *American* mother.' "

Letty snorted in disgust and flicked off the set with the remote control just as Chesterfield Rummy looked on the verge of shedding a few manly tears and little BonSashay was perhaps about to warble a few bars of the *Star Spangled Banner*.

"Hey! What'd you do that for?" screeched Gert. "And where did you get that remote control?"

"I could not stand to watch another second of that charlatan, and I been hiding the remote control on you for a week because I knew you'd be getting caught up in drivel like this if I didn't," said Letty, stuffing the remote into the datil pepper-embossed apron at her waist as if tucking away the keys to some notorious killer's jail cell.

"Whull, you know I never really needed the remote. I can go right ahead and turn that set back on with a spell!" growled Gert. The glorious ostrich feather sticking out of her turban quivered with indignation.

"You do that and I'll blow the thing to smithereens with a spell of my own," retorted Letty. "You can go pollute your mind with that mortal claptrap on your own bedroom set upstairs, but I'll not have the hallowed confines of this store besmirched with any more of that filth! Really, Gertrude, even a grizzled, slightly vulgar old witch like you ought to exhibit some amount of umbrage at the circus act we all just saw with our own eyes. I've seen some mortals bent in the head in my day, but that Chesterfield Rummy is the most warped one in a while. The kid can't be blamed, but just wait until she grows up. There'll be no end to the twistedness. I can't abide seeing that garbage, I tell you. I just can't! Can you truck with that brand of depravity, Rowan Blaize?"

"I have to admit, I am on your side in this regard, Letty. The father and daughter act is rather akin to something we might have encountered in Caligula's time, for example. Oh, the attire has changed and so have the flimsy ideological trappings attempting to justify matters, but the *modus operandi* appears to be quite the same. Unfortunately, this sort of behavior among mortals has never gone out of vogue. One can detect it in every era, in one form or another. Repellent."

"There, you see?" crowed Letty, a victorious finger jabbing once more toward the ceiling.

"Now hold on just a minute, you two," said Gert, clearly offended that her interest in the Rummy Family Adventures was being so categorically dismissed. "What if that man simply wants his little girl to have her moment in the sun, huh? How can we judge them? If anyone in this world—or any other world, for that matter—knows how important it is to have one's moment in the sun, it's a witch or a warlock."

"Moment in the sun?" said Letty slowly, grimacing as if she had just been force-fed a handful of toads. "I've seen dried-up old carcasses on the roadside that've looked more respectable after their 'moment in the sun.' Can't you see clearly, Gert? That man is using his little girl to satisfy some sick fantasy of his own. Rowan's right. It ain't as if we haven't seen this sort of behavior from humans before, over the centuries. I figured we all learned ages ago, however, to look away in disgust instead of being entertained by it. American family values indeed! Hecate only knows what the mother in that sad unit is like, or what she's doing as we speak. The husband's prolly got her locked up in some basement, sewing more of them hideous ball gowns for that spoiled little brat."

"But Letty, what if a life in show business is what this girl wants and her Poppa is only trying to help her along?" pleaded Gert.

"What she *wants,* Gertrude Gokey, is one of them cheeseburgers she was talkin' about at the start of that insane interview. She wants a cheeseburger. Got it? You heard her with your own ears, presumably, unless you was too hypnotized by her ridiculous outfit. I say, you have always been one to go straight over the moon whenever you get a gander at mortal children in outlandish costumes. Remember how you used to ooh and ah back in the Old Country when maypole time came around and human parents used to deck their kiddies out in all them bells and ribbons and what have you? You couldn't get enough of it. I have to tell myself that you're just obsessed with silly outfits and that's what's blinded you to the dark underbelly of it all. Mortals have been using their offspring like chattel and mucking up the world without need since they first came around. It all seems like it's been getting worse, too, these past hundred years or so, when they've got less excuse for mucking things up than ever before. When they've got more knowledge and information telling them they ought to *know better* than ever before! At the very least, we are certainly hearing a lot more about it than ever before. That's your beloved television for you, Gert. And them computers and phones and what not. I've had enough of it, certainly for today. I'm heading upstairs to make a cup of … um, *tea,* and I suggest you come along. Rowan Blaize, you are welcome, as always, to join us."

"No, thank you, Letty. I need to get back to the house. Miranda and Bror have been left to hash out the rest of the plans for the All Hallow's Eve Party and they are probably at wits' end by now. There's still a few things to be arranged. Besides, I have a feeling that you two are going to continue debating the merits, or lack thereof, of Councilman Rummy and his prize winning progeny. It is not my desire to get in the middle of a dispute that is not likely to abate anytime soon."

"Oh, it's abated, alright," assured Letty, her jaw set in a most determined square, her shoulders straightened in a display of triumph. Gert looked rather crestfallen.

"You needn't run off without a cup of tea on my account," she murmured. "I'll allow Letty to have her little say about this … for now." She snuck a swift dagger glance at her friend beneath her brow. "I'll mention one thing more and that'll be the end of it. If that nice fellow and his tiny gal should come to the shop looking for a donation so she can wear that Pint-Sized Princess crown on Monday night, then *I'll* not turn them away."

"Good," said Letty over her shoulder as she gathered her apron and skirts and headed up the stairwell to their private apartments. "If they show up at the store when you're alone, you can give them all the cash they crave, but if they show up when *I'm* behind the counter, I'll turn them both into titmice. Good Evening to you, Rowan Blaize. Best wishes on the party preparations." The willowy witch vanished up the stairs with a terse nod.

"Good Evening to you as well, Leticia Beauregard." Rowan turned to make his own way to the shop's front door, Gert in tow to lock up again behind him.

"I hope you two come to terms with mortal eccentricities soon, so there'll be no squabbling at my party," he said playfully as the portly old witch saw him out. Gert paused to glance up and down St. George Street, reveling drowsily in the charm of the famous cobbled avenue. Other shops were closing and only a handful of tourists straggled here and there, finishing ice cream cones and nibbling at pretzels in the unseasonably sultry embrace of the October twilight and its burgeoning shadows.

"You know Letty and me well enough by now," said Gert with a mischievous wink of a shiny, black olive eye. "We'll be quibbling about something entirely different by the time we get to the party. I'm sure the argument will be much more interesting by then."

"No doubt it will," said Rowan, strolling off toward the town square and thereafter the leisurely walk up the brick-paved residential stretch of St. George Street. "All the same, do keep me posted on the Pint-Sized Princess pageant drama. It might be amusing, after all, to see how those two creatures end up in the scheme of things. Just don't tell Letty," he added conspiratorially. "Also, if you happen see Serenity Turnbull in the next day or two, try to persuade her to come to the All Hallows Eve Party. I sent a last-minute invitation to her yesterday. Hopefully she's not preoccupied with pining for her archaeologist friend, or researching one of those corroded old coins or whatever it is he sends her. It would do her some good to hobnob a bit with our set, at least for one night."

"Oh, I think I could convince Serenity to make it this year," said Gert with a final wave and a toothy smile from the doorstep of the datil pepper shop. "I daresay that nothing her wormy ole Percival sends her will *ever* be as exciting as one of Rowan Blaize's equinox parties!"

അ∽

II

Serenity Turnbull sat at the table in her pomegranate-colored and biodynamically wallpapered kitchen and stared at the enormous ruby ring. What in the world had Percival sent her this time? She was, in fact, getting tired of cruddy old coins, potsherds, and ampullae piling up around the house but, if she wanted new jewelry ... well, then she was more than capable of making her own, thank you very much. An entire bureau drawer of unsold turquoise bracelets, bangles, and squash blossom necklaces could attest to that, along with a stone polishing kit collecting dust next to the spider-infested pottery kiln in the garage.

She tossed her floppy hemp hat onto a chair next to her loaded dry goods pantry and blew an errant strand of sun-bleached hair toward the ceiling. It had been a long day. Now there was one of Percival's love letters to contend with. She thought about dropping the letter and the ring back into the postal package she had opened automatically upon returning home. The whole distraction could wait until tomorrow and a cup of ginger passion-fruit tea would be ideal, along with a leisurely sit on the porch, playing with Guadalupe, her anaconda, or perhaps in the backyard hammock with Emory, her Shih Tzu familiar, listening to the last cicadas of the lingering season. It would be glorious to kick back and enjoy the cooler currents of autumn air as they mingled with summer's ever more elusive tropical remnants. She could smell the intoxicating mustiness of the nearby ocean, even inside the house.

The suddenly kinetic, almost spritely, verve of Percival's otherwise stolid handwriting, however, intrigued her just enough to delay the evening's relaxation ritual. She wanted to see what he had to say this time, from wherever on the planet he currently happened to be digging. She could tell from the florid, messy penmanship of this missive that her suitor had been writing quickly. He was giddy with excitement about something. This had happened a few times before in letters, usually involving an obscure discovery of stultifying magnitude. Serenity yawned. Surely, she thought, his present eagerness could not have anything to do with the warped golden band and its garish, poorly cut, and cloudy jewel. Percy had not even bothered to polish the enormous ruby, which was a style she favored in turquoise but never in other gemstones. Fastidiousness counted for something, after all. This was just a dull, dusty, and depressing red rock clutched by golden tines that looked like talons reaching out in desperation from the clumsy band.

Oh, Percival.

Serenity opened the letter and sighed, hoping to Hestia that she was not about to feast her dreamy caramel eyes upon a marriage proposal. Percy had been hinting about that matter for almost a year, beating around the bush in his signature diffident fashion. He *is* a bit of a wormy warlock, she mused. The old Gokey battle-axe at the pepper shop was right about that much. Still, even Percival would not have sent an actual marriage proposal—and an accompanying, hideous engagement ring—halfway around the globe for her consideration. Surely he wouldn't do *that*. Certainly he had enough moxie and class to tender such an important invitation in person.

Then again, it's Percival, she reminded herself. Not much would surprise her.

She wrinkled her nose a bit and peered over her cat's-eye spectacles at the correspondence.

My Indescribably Magnificent Serenity, it began.

"Oh, good grief," said the reader.

You would scarcely believe the bounty we have uncovered at this new dig site in Turkey, but I can tell you that it is the most promising that anyone has come upon in decades! Practically Constantinian in terms of date, we suppose. This spot appears to have been the burial chamber of some old Byzantine senator's Chief Eunuch, as the loot is especially worthy—you may already know that the eunuchs got all of the

best trimmings and trappings, for a variety of reasons which I shall not now delineate.

Of course, I sent you a little "something" as a token of my unflagging esteem. No museum is likely to miss it. Ha! This time, I am pleased to say, it is much, much more than the odd coin or cracked lead ampulla. It is a ring! I am certain you have discovered this by now, since I intend to wrap it up with the letter itself and you are going to see it the moment you open the box!"

"Great Gaia, how did I ever put up with this ninny?" muttered Serenity, but she read on, fearing the worst and unable to quell her morbid curiosity.

The ring was, of course, a risky item to send you by way of the postal service. After all, I am not in charge of this dig, unfortunately. But, if there is one thing I do know, it is that high and mighty Professor Bleecker cannot put spells on various packages and parcels in order to get them safely past those insatiable, inquisitive and sticky-fingered customs officials! Ha! I may not have the razzle-dazzle and pedigree of a sorcerer like that arrogant Rowan Blaize—Is he still traipsing around your beloved little St. Augustine? I hope not. I should not _ever_ like to meet him—but I do have a trick or two up my sleeve. I made certain to put the most potent combination of protective spells and camouflage charms (at least, those with which I am familiar) on this box so it would wend its way to you unmolested.

In case you were wondering, this letter is indeed the one you have been especially waiting for! You know, of course, that I am a bit shy when it comes to discussing matters of the heart, but given the intimate manner of our pleasant and steady acquaintance, and the openness with which you have accepted so many of my admittedly frustrating ways, I was supreme in my confidence that you would read (and accept) this letter of marriage proposal with the same ecstasy I enjoyed while writing it! Accept as well, my dear Serenity, the rather grand ruby ring (aforementioned and included) as a token of my devotion, as the visible contract encapsulating the pledge of my troth. It is, as you can see, a trifle large for your delicate-yet-environmentally stalwart and ever-sustainable fingers, but I thought you could have it resized at the little jeweler's shop on King Street, the one we used to admire as we strolled of an evening? The proprietor has several pet ferrets, if I remember correctly. Perhaps you even know a spell that might shrink it down to size for the dainty digit in question. Wear it about your neck with a string of hemp-rope, if you wish, like you did with that fetching bit of old sea-turtle shell you once dangled about your décolletage as a symbol of protest against night-time driving on the beaches.

Just wear it!

I know you will love the ring itself—far be it from me to forget your fondness for large, rather rough-hewn, and uncomplicated gemstones. I found it in the tomb I mentioned earlier and thought this stone was right up your earthy alley, my dearest. No one will miss it, here, because no one knows I found it. Do you think Prof. Bleecker doesn't keep special tidbits for himself? Think again! But I digress. Though doubtless you are now overcome with *elan* and maybe even a tad tearful as you read these words, I urge you to keep in mind that I still have another year left in my commitment to this ongoing series of excavations—one final pass across the lonely calendar before I can return to Gainesville and complete my doctorate. Then, perhaps, I can find some suitable teaching position at Flagler College and we can settle down in St. Augustine together. I know how fond you are of that place. Either way, in one year I will be able to take you at last in my arms as Beloved Wife and Cherished Mate henceforth. Your happy acceptance of my proposal is, of course, already anticipated, but please render me the grace of a formal reply the next time you send one of your own endlessly fascinating missives. No doubt you will be eager to start composing that letter forthwith, so it is with deep satisfaction and excitement that I bid you much affection and bring this letter of mine to a close.

Yours Forever in Blessed Betrothal,

Percival

PS: There is the small matter of that unusual inscription along the outer edge of the ring itself. It appears to be some sort of obscure variant of ancient Babylonian, but I'll be an uncle's monkey if I know what it means. Never seen the like of it before in all my travels, or in any of the many reference books we have about the encampment. For obvious reasons, I could not show it to Prof. Bleecker. Please picture me rolling my eyes as I wrote THAT sentence! In any event, we can have the inscription removed and the band re-inscribed with something germane to our upcoming union. If you are curious regarding the meaning of the inscription and have nothing better to do (as if!), perhaps you could engage in some research or attempt a translation spell. Mine, alas, were ineffective. Better yet, rummage around for that old ciphering talisman you said your grandmother left you before she retired and turned herself into an oak tree wart. Kisses—P.

Serenity placed the letter on the table and weighed the awful ring thoughtfully in her palm. Her freckled cheeks were flushed with the splotched hues of deep-seated annoyance as she turned the ring over to peruse the inscription.

"Probably says 'Always drink upstream from the herd' in ancient Babylonian," she muttered. Her cheeks grew redder.

Around the kitchen, inanimate objects suddenly became quite animated. The NO MORE MOON LANDINGS! lunar clock shuddered and its hands began to race madly around the surface of the Sea of Tranquility. The Portuguese rooster-shaped teapot began to whistle atop the stove, even though there wasn't any water in it, and the stove was not on. A wooden bowl full of bright green organic apples rattled noisily and then the apples turned dark brown and withered into shrunken lumps, as if ready to be sewn onto stuffed bits of gingham and serve as wrinkled heads for an army of Appalachian granny dolls. Two bottles of Cabernet Sauvignon and one bottle of Malbec flew out of the wine rack and smashed like missiles into the wall above the sink. Guadalupe the anaconda came floating through the room, tied into a knot, and flicking her tongue in snake-perplexity. Emory the Shih Tzu pranced into the kitchen and took one look at his mistress, and at the way every hair on her head was standing up and outward, like the curious child who places her hand upon an electrode during a science museum daytrip. He whined and turned tail, running for the darkest recesses of the upstairs bedroom closet. Serenity sat, expressionless, amid the outer storm, and, in a moment or two, it subsided. She looked around and made a little irritated face and then rose from the table to make herself a comforting bit of tea in the now silent rooster-kettle.

So Percival had proved to be a complete loser after all, proposing to her from a distance and making sure to do so in his unmistakably offensive manner. Well, it was not as if she hadn't been expecting something that ridiculous to emanate from him at some point. Still, she was not quite prepared for the degree of umbrage and insult she felt as the recipient of his clumsy foray. Was it a character weakness to feel insulted by idiocy even when you were fully prepared to be the victim of an idiot? She had to wonder about that. Even so, she could not figure that part out, at the moment, and this angered her slightly more because she had always believed that a woman—and especially a woman witch—ought to know better. Presently she took a saucer and steaming teacup into the living room and sat, forlorn, at the bottom of the stairwell.

When she truly lost her temper about something, like the injustices wrought upon innocent sea turtles, for example, clocks continued to keep proper time in her presence and wine bottles stayed in their racks. It was only when she repressed her misery that things got messy, and she despised this about herself for a number of reasons, not least because a mortal psychologist and an aromatherapist (who knew far less than she did about both subjects) had been counseling her against the repression of her angry emotions for years. Another reason was because she had purposefully taken the name "Serenity" while hanging around Berkeley in the 1960s in order to underscore her determination to live a new life. This name was supposed to herald an existence emancipated from the free-floating anxiety that had always gotten a girl named "Eudoxia" in trouble due to untimely telekinetic manifestations of ire.

Name-changes, causes, and the adoption of heart-hemorrhaging ideals only went so far, however, when it came to becoming someone other than the person you really were, and Serenity did not like to be reminded of this fact. The shattered glass and pooling California vintages on her kitchen floor were the damnable proof, but only the latest bits of proof in a rather long line of evidentiary materials. It was bad enough to be a witch with an anxiety disorder, yet worse to be a woman who was not only anxious but completely misunderstood in both the natural and supernatural spheres! Kitchen floors can be cleaned up the next day, anacondas can be unknotted, and fluffy, frightened familiars can be soothed with a little pat on the head and perhaps a belly rub, but there was no cure—mortal or magical—for being terrifically misunderstood.

Serenity grimaced and sipped at the rim of her cup. She wasn't a crying witch (a "problem"—according to her aromatherapist), but if she were, she figured she deserved to indulge in a thorough cleansing of the spirit right about now. Then an even more unpalatable thought struck at her core: what sorts of awful things might occur if she *really* let loose with a spate of boo-hoos? Entire flocks of birds and swarms of bees would possibly fall dead out of the skies, like they did during the crying jags of other emotional and nerve-shredded witches Serenity had known in the past. That would never do; Serenity could not truck with dead flocks of birds, even if they were annoying pigeons, or with dead swarms of bees, even if they were those "killer" ones of African strain. She remained in a funk as the last glimmer of day faded in the somewhat salty haze of a saffron sunset, visible through the atrium window overhead. Guadalupe the anaconda slithered out from behind the sofa and headed for the laundry room, giving her mistress a wide berth.

Serenity drained her teacup. After everything she had worked so hard to give herself in terms of spiritual self-protection, after all of the numerous psychological walls she had erected—some more sincerely founded and maintained than others, it was true, but all of them useful—she had allowed a sniveling little skink like Percival to get under her skin. This was all the more galling because, truth told, Serenity had never liked Percival all that much in the first place. Oh, he had been *likeable* in that he had never judged her as an inferior—which was not saying a lot about him or her, she realized—and he had also warmed to many of her causes and little preoccupations, the ones helping her cope with whatever new, evolved personality she was becoming.

Percival, with his nebbish mania for mortal archaeological history, had at least understood the value of evolving things and knew the importance of personal evolution in the existence of a long-lived witch. She had to give him credit for that as a fellow magician, even if he was hopelessly misguided on so many other counts, and even if she would not marry him were he the last mage on earth ... probably. The most annoying part was that she had never fished-about for any sort of long-term union during their time together. Well, that wasn't exactly true, now, was it? In some roundabout, obtuse fashion she had managed to lead him on a merry little chase, of sorts, and worse, was *aware* of doing it in some loathe-to-admit-it degree or another. It was just that she had wanted the idea, the possibility, of a proposal, rather than the reality of one, especially from Percival. Percival was welcome to proffer possibilities so long as he never delivered, and now that he had delivered in the most insulting way imaginable, all walls were down and everything was muddled.

There were nuances to her conundrum, she had to admit that. One nuance was that she had wanted a "potential only" proposal to come specifically from a warlock, even such a warlock as Percival, or from some other suitably magical being. She had made the mistake of marrying mortal men twice already in her life, despite the sage advice of her mother and grandmother. Neither marriage had gone particularly well. It was not that Serenity had not loved her previous husbands. She had, in fact, adored them. The disastrous aspect came in that she had naturally—or, rather, supernaturally—outlived them both in rather glaring and obvious fashion. It is one thing to marry a man when you and he appear to the rest of the world to be all of twenty-one years old, but it is quite another thing when your man turns seventy-two and you have not visibly aged a day since the wedding. That is when your husband's relatives, in particular, begin to whisper with unsettling enthusiasm.

When your husband gets old and needs a cane to walk, needs help getting out of bed, and has lost every tooth in his head while you do not possess a wrinkle, can dash swift as deer across a meadow, and still enjoy the noisiest bite out of the orchard's crunchiest apple ... that is a problem. By that time, your husband's family members (the surviving ones, anyhow) have long since bypassed the tried and true methods of bated mutterings and fireside gossip. Indeed, by that time, your husband's relatives are sending for priests, and not to perform last rites on your dying spouse, either. Serenity shuddered a bit in the stairwell at the memory.

Her first mortal husband had been a knight—a dashing, hairy, hungry, lovable beast, but he had had one whopper of an extended family and he had insisted upon remaining in their veritable bosom. Serenity knew and possessed a respectable repertoire of spells, and excelled at several of them, but she had never been one of the great enchantresses by any shake of the stick. Though she could certainly craft a convincing glamor, an illusion to appear as old as her husband at any given moment during the progression of his years, she did not have the power to maintain that glamor for extended periods of time. Some sorceresses could manage that sort of thing for a century or more, but she could swing it for a week, at best. As a result, a great many of her husband's closest relatives and fellow townspeople would have had to die early, at all kinds of odd and staggered junctures, in order for her to have gotten away with any glamor. Serenity had not been the sort of witch inclined to separate her spouse from his dear kinfolk, much less kill the kinfolk off just for the sake of keeping-up household appearances. Neither was she about to come out and announce, "Hey, everyone, no worries! I'm a witch. That's why I haven't aged while the rest of you are withering away like prunes in the sun. Sorry I forgot to bring that up during the courting process!"

Such a revelation was not a wise choice for any witch who lived exclusively among mortals in those times, powerful or not powerful, even with all the hoopla of the Crusades as a bit of a distraction.

Human beings came to have grave suspicions as time marched on and the humans waned as you kept waxing, but blind eyes could be turned, too. Being especially kind, adept with medicine, and always around to welcome *another* outstanding local harvest—when other villages were in the throes of famine—were rather helpful things. These things could buy a suspected "witch in the family" a certain grace period. Even when matters became obvious to the point of being ludicrous, and nagging suspicions morphed into personal convictions, a reasonable amount of leeway could be enjoyed. Eventually, however, someone (or several someones) always became hysterical and pointed the grave Finger of Accusation. Usually, it was a more distant relative with an unimpeachable record of church attendance, but it could just as easily have been someone closer, someone who felt slighted, for whatever reason, and who chose to seek the ultimate form of vengeance.

Serenity had never quite managed to fully understand that tendency in the mortal world. Oh, she had always been able to relate very well to notions of anxiety and worry and painfully repressed emotion; this was, perhaps, what made her especially comfortable around mortals. The inclination of humans to secretly or not-so-secretly hunger for the destruction and death of other people over the most seemingly insignificant trifles … *that* part she had never been able to fathom. When her first husband had died, the proverbial jig was up for her, and a faction of his relations and neighbors that had been waiting for years to raise a ruckus about the "perpetual maid of Morgarten" finally played the unsavory hand. Serenity, for her part, had seen that coming, too, just as she had seen Percival's asinine proposal coming and, since she had never been, by any means, a witch of pithy talent, she had been able to remove herself quite easily from the incipient fracas.

In the case of the first marriage, her removal had been, by necessity, permanent. The situation was all the more difficult because she had been forced to leave behind her two children, who had, by that time, just begun to "out-age" her in appearance, for they had been born predominantly mortal, as the offspring of such unions sometimes are. Serenity had been able to essentially run home to mother (who wagged considerable and consecutive fingers of I-told-you-so) but she could not bring herself to spirit-away two grown mortal sons about to seek their own wives and ways in the world and cart them into the mysterious depths of her native enchanted realm.

Achingly, she had returned often to her husband's estate, but only on the outskirts, in the concealing shadows of magic, to make sure the crop remained bountiful, and to ensure that her sons were unharmed due to their association with a sorceress-mother who had compounded her "evil" by abdicating her position in the family. She had observed things beneath the cover of ethereal mists and through tear-splattered mirrors over the years until, eventually, all those she had loved, along with those who had betrayed her, were wiped out by the Black Plague. She possessed admirable gifts, but averting that particular menace on behalf of mortals had not been among them. Thus it was that she had moved on, and had moved extensively, through worlds and times, as all of her kind must do. Much later, she had even married another mortal, on a bit of a lark, in New York City in the Roaring Twenties, but she had not made the error of bearing children with this one. After a few years of flash and festivity, that husband had ended-up "roaring" from the window of a skyscraper to the pavement following the crash of 1929. A witch sees a lot of things in her day.

My, how things had changed! Things had changed in all kinds of worlds and ways, and Serenity knew that she was now the product of all her experiences and decisions, like any other witch ... or mortal, for that matter. The 1960s in the United States had been a revelation, even to her, who had seen so much and had lived so long, just as it had seemed a revelation to her young mortal friends. She had always worn names lightly when cavorting primarily among humans, but their wealth of innovative ideals seemed to kindle a strange new fire in her that had never had a chance to sputter into existence before. Still, a witch's life is a series of fires kindled and rekindled. It had been a flowery and rather whimsical path that had led her footsteps to old St. Augustine, and it was probably the whimsy of her particular waltz into town years ago that had put her on the outsider's list with the two old bats she called the "Pepper Sisters."

To be certain, Serenity never had anything against Leticia Beauregard and Gertrude Gokey, and she was fairly certain that neither of them harbored any deep-seated resentment toward her, beyond perhaps a token disapproval of her perceived "flakiness," which was what Gert called it, and her "mortal fever," which was what Letty called it. Even so, she had never been interested in much interaction with them to begin with, and she was certainly not obliged to kowtow to them, so she remained relatively content to enjoy the roots she had put down in the Ancient City thus far. She had also been able to enjoy the qualities that had drawn her to the spot in the first place. Serenity had always been an ambient witch. In her estimation, St. Augustine's amalgamation of lazy Mediterranean coastal charm and Southern Gothic drama had played with considerable allure against the backdrop of big, New Money bravado exemplified by the grandiose architectural contributions of Henry Flagler. The ornate ambition and scale of Flagler's direct and associated foundations—the college, the museum, the now-restored Bridge of Lions—had reminded her, fondly, of those heady years spent with well-heeled mortals in flush, electric 1920s Gotham.

Ambitions had changed, but Serenity had sensed at once that St. Augustine remained a magical hub that basked in its own languid resplendence, a town that coaxed its occupants to drift here and glide there within its confines, enrapt in the balm of some delicate luxury fueled by one coquettish sea breeze after another. The Ancient City was mystical. It was friendly. It was intimate, with a wealth of secluded side-streets, cobbled alleyways and moss-drenched groves. The town was winsomely vain without realizing it and, best of all, cast a sleepy-eyed gaze of indifference toward those who were, indeed, quite different, to those who were misunderstood, be they mortal or immortal, man or myth. An aura of gentle acceptance seemed to drench the air, winding aimlessly like a lost tourist through the exotic but uncomplicated avenues. St. Augustine was one of the most natural mortal communities Serenity had ever known in her extensive travels and "natural" was her latest *cause celebre*. She felt she could be the witch she was currently attempting to be in St. Augustine and, even though she had lived in other places far longer and had enjoyed them just as much, and even though she knew her life would meander elsewhere at some uncertain point in the future, she was where she needed to be now.

Though most of Serenity's acquaintances were mortal students she taught at Flagler College, and even though her best friends comprised a loose horde of over-energetic, under-informed environmental feminist types, she had never shied away from the city's plentiful array of magical denizens. She unleashed a smug little laugh as she rose from the stair, her empty teacup clattering in its saucer. The old Pepper Witches looked down their noses at her in part, she knew, because they believed she did not associate as frequently as she ought with the occult inhabitants of St. Augustine.

"Goes to show what those magpies know," she muttered to herself with some satisfaction, traipsing back into the kitchen and stepping gingerly over the broken glass bottles to contemplate the scope of the mess.

Aside from Percival who, of course, did not live in town and who was one of the most magically underwhelming warlocks she had ever encountered, Serenity possessed other confidantes, and the "Datil Be The Day" doyennes did not know (or apparently care to know) about her associations with them. For example, St. Augustine was a town positively infested with ghosts, wraiths, imps, incubi, succubi, phantoms, bridge trolls, dryads, nixies, pixies, naiads, poltergeists, gremlins, ghouls, ghastlies, and all sorts of the more peripheral fey beings that tended to congregate in witchy towns, or in towns that exuded inordinate amounts of occult energy. For a number of metaphysical reasons, St. Augustine was one of those particularly energetic locations. Some places simply had it, while others did not. Serenity herself had always been a little surprised that there were not more real witches and warlocks in the neighborhood, but then again it was a relatively small community with a rather concentrated locus of power. Plus, the overbearing presence of Leticia and Gertrude had likely been enough to discourage most enchanters from pondering a bit of real estate in the seaside idyll. Like all witches, Serenity knew that magicians get along tenuously, at best, even in vast metropolitan locales. Under the wrong conditions, having five or six witches lodged in a town the size of Auggie could be akin to staging a gladiatorial circus in an arena roughly the size of a postage stamp. Being a pleasantly odd town, even for mortals, St. Augustine attracted sufficiently weird sorcerers, along with the typical rag-tag, flotsam, and jetsam in their wake.

Ghosts, in particular, found the Ancient City to be a most nurturing environment and Serenity was on a first-name basis with dozens of the Dead. The joke among the spectral community was that St. Augustine's mortal inhabitants, while being keenly aware of the presence of ghosts among them and eager to make a profit via promotion of various Ghost Walks and other haunted tours, had fixated and singled-out all the places that were *not* occupied or frequented by ghosts. As usual, mortals had a "dead-on" insight regarding the reality of supernatural forces around them, and then fudged the details completely. St. Augustine's most renowned ghosts were supposedly named "Elizabeth" and "Lily," but even kind-hearted Serenity had to laugh at the fact that the *actual* ghosts in town had never heard of either of them.

Serenity's best friends in the spirited category included a shrimp fisherman from a prominent local family who had died when his boat capsized during a particularly virulent Northeaster in the late Nineteenth Century. He had been unfaithful to his wife on the very evening before his fateful cast-off and the guilt had kept his lively soul glued to the town with no desire to secure a chance at the requisite "rest." Mortals could be so stubborn, especially where immense guilt is involved, and then all that is left of them, literally, is a conscience wrapped in a bit of ectoplasm. The fisherman's wronged wife was of course now long-gone to her own reward, whatever it was, but he had grown rather accustomed to hanging about the bay-front and watching the tourists, as well as "overseeing" the shrimp-trawling industry that remained, such as it was. Serenity encountered him often while taking her weekly constitutional along the bay's panoramic esplanade and across the Bridge of Lions.

Dominic was always eager to give her the latest ghost-gossip and tourist news, though he did have the rather unseemly habit of recounting the more tawdry happenings. These constituted tales about activities in which locals and tourists engaged once downtown bars and hotspots closed for the night and patrons staggered out into the darkness where all sorts of troubles—and trysts—could occur. Dominic had once even come over to her house on Vilano Beach, waking her at three in the morning to inform her that a particularly inebriated young woman— "She reminds me so much of my own poor Angelina, Miss Turnbull!"— had bumped and banged a path all the way from Belle Watling's bar down to the bay, where she promptly toppled over the barrier chains headfirst into the swells at high tide. On that occasion, Serenity had promptly donned her back velvet cloak, grabbed her oaken flying staff, which was ever at-the-ready in the crow's nest atop her house, and had taken off toward the scene of the accident, Dominic surging alongside in the sticky night air. The woman, unfortunately, had drowned by the time they arrived, which made old Dominic both distressed and slightly hopeful. Since the drunken woman had reminded him so much of his beloved earthly wife, to whom he owed a debt, he wondered whether the poor, waterlogged and splayed corpse bobbing along the seawall might spawn a lingering essence of its own to keep him company. But the woman had left no ghostly presence to speak of.

"I was so sure her spirit might stay behind," Dominic had lamented.

"I'm afraid one spirit or another proved to be her undoing," Serenity had countered, scowling at the floater in the dark. "Are you sure you didn't spook that poor creature over the wall with one of your little manifestations?"

Dominic had sworn his innocence on that count and Serenity believed him. He was a goodly ghost, for the most part, and no more inquisitive, at least in the dangerous sense, than others in town. Serenity had called the local police department from a payphone, at that time, which caused its own stir in the papers and among the chattering towns-folk, who wondered if the poor besotted woman had been pushed to her watery demise by the "mysterious caller." There was always an excessive amount of drama attached to the phantasm community, so even witches tended to keep their distance to avoid exasperation.

Another loiterer Serenity knew particularly well was the shade of a woman named Rowena, who had tried to kill her abusive husband with a double-barreled shotgun, missed his head, but had hit a cast-iron skillet, from whence a shell had ricocheted back to take off the top of her own skull. Rowena had formed a support-group in town for spirits trapped between worlds due to domestic violence. Her circle would put on quite a clinking, clanking, clunking display of group catharsis when they met on Saturday nights in an abandoned trailer-park lot near the airport on US 1 North, but no local "ghost tour" ever had the sense to organize visits to that particular paranormal jackpot. In other immortal categories, Serenity allowed two down-on-their-luck nixies to occasionally inhabit the little koi pond she had installed behind her studiously ramshackle beach-house. These ladies were at times a trifle off-putting and oversensitive—it is tough to be a freshwater faery in a saltwater nixie's world—but their prickliness came in handy when Serenity's beloved fish needed protection from the prying paws of raccoons or marauding gulls, pelicans, and egrets.

Without question, Leticia Beauregard and Gertrude Gokey had long ruled the roost when it came to being well-connected with and firmly in control of St. Augustine's magical minions, but Serenity was proud to have kept her oar in, as it were, and she refused to let the nit-picking and chronic condescension of her fellow witches make her feel unduly excluded, as if she were not really part of the occult landscape. She knew she was different, but as much as any of them, she had a right to belong and share her gifts and opinions. Gamely, she had tried her best to win the confidence and respect of the datil pepper witches when she first moved to town, but it had been a losing battle. Just when one of them seemed to be softening up, the other would tighten the screws, and then both would descend upon Serenity in some nightmarish tag-team scenario of sarcasm. The whole thing had left her disillusioned and reluctant to participate in any communal acts of sorcery or celebratory gatherings whatsoever. Little wonder that she had been practically forced to content herself with the meager and long-distance "company" of the feckless Percival.

Now, Percival had proposed, and the two old crones would certainly get wind of it, sooner or later. They always got wind of everything, mainly because the two of them had the wind in their gainful employment in these parts. My, how they would cackle at her expense! Worse, Serenity knew she was doomed in regard to Percival, at least as far as Letty and Gert were bound to view the proceedings. If she revealed the truth that she had absolutely no intention of marrying Percival, they would both cluck like disgruntled hens that she was putting on airs and was so enamored of mortal ways that she was in danger of losing all her occult credibility. It did not matter that neither of the Pepper Witches thought Serenity's occult credibility was very credible to begin with. If she married Percival, they would squawk to the heavens at how poorly she had "settled" when it came to choosing a proper mate, for they were bound to consider Percival ten times the magical joke that she was supposed to be. She had seen the skeptical look in the short, tubby one's eyes the solitary time all three had met by the Bridge of Lions.

Faint, combined light from the banished sun and a rising oval of moon began to brush the kitchen in milky hues as Serenity placed her cup and saucer in the sink. "Emory," she called to the upstairs bedroom. "You can come back down, now. I think the worst is over for the evening."

Fragments of glass amid the great puddles of wine made it seem like a shimmering pool of blood had been spilled in the creeping darkness on her floor, as if some terrible crime had been committed in her cheery breakfast nook and the victim had somehow managed to just get up and walk away from it all. At this thought she cracked a wan smile. After the deadening weight of Percival's daft proposal and thoughts of the bossy witches downtown, Serenity *did* feel a bit victimized on this particular night. Oh, how she wished she were clever enough—or even powerful enough—to put those two nags in their places just once! That, however, was an impossible aspiration. Though Letty and Gert were as cantankerous with each other as they were with those unlucky enough to dwell in their magical orbit, the two were still as thick as thieves and ready to defend (or at least fill-in for) each other … if one or the other happened to be lacking in the usual gifts of passive-aggression on any given day. For the time being, and ostensibly for as long as she dwelled in their territory, Serenity knew she would have to continue to content herself with the wobbling pillar of her own self-respect; there would be none forthcoming from her peers.

Well, except for Percival, who respected her in *some* sense. But Percival did not really count in a million years. That much was now apparent.

In the fading light Serenity stepped on tip-toes over the mess scattered and splattered across the tiles. She sighed with dismay at the results of her own tempestuousness. Wanton magical emanations were such an annoying reminder that she lacked self-control at crucial emotional junctures, and that realization always hastened the onset of anxiety. Looking at the scene of destruction for even another minute was not acceptable, not in her current state of mind. Perhaps a Reconstitution Spell was in order. It was always draining to waste magic on household duties that could be handled with elbow grease and some spare time, but Serenity had harbored a niggling phobia toward mops and buckets since the Middle Ages. She had been bitten by a Blue-Backed Gremlin Tick while crossing the Carpathians one summer and, aside from debilitating chronic fatigue, the resulting loss of her powers had forced her to take work as a Baroness's chamber-maid in Budapest for almost a year. She had not been very good at it. In fact, the episode had been a nightmare and, as practical as she now fancied herself to be, Serenity remained scarred by the thought of swabbing a floor—even if it happened to be her own.

Cabernet and malbec pooled and streaked everywhere, along with splintered glass. Any effort to sop it all up would only succeed in spreading the disaster in a wider radius. The witch tapped thoughtfully at her chin with a fingernail and considered a few options. There was a useful incantation she had once known in old Brythonic; Serenity enjoyed translating archaic verse into English, when possible. It was her current tongue, after all. She narrowed her eyes at the detritus and extended a hand to channel her effort.

"Spawn of Puck and Azriel, concerned with lesser tasks ..." she began, a bit uncertainly, "... hearken to this witch's call and do thou as she asks. Sons that ride the Western wind, O daughters on the breeze ... imps that stir the minor storms, ye gather as I please. Behold the mess on yonder floor, with which I am annoyed. By gentle cyclone gather and ... um ... deposit *in the Void?"*

She took a few quick steps back, hoping the entire floor would not be uprooted in a howling tempest, but she was fairly confident the translation had been impeccable. It was mainly about the power wielded, of course, but one never knew—some spirits were curmudgeons and absolutely resented translations. She stared and listened and, soon enough, a faint whistling and whirring sound grew to a sharp whine as the air shimmered above the floor, like a mirage hovering across some desert horizon. Glass shards clattered and fermented California varietals were together sucked up in the vortex of a mini-tornado that spun furiously for a few seconds and then vanished with an exclamatory hiss. The floor was spotless.

Serenity cracked a smile, pleased with herself. Some ecologically oversensitive witches argued that use of the Void as a magical dumping ground was irresponsible, but she had never gone down that particular ideological track. "It's a *void,* for Hecate's sake!" she had once told an earnest finger-wagger. "What good is a void if you can't banish the occasional nuisance into it?" There were, to be certain, other important aspects of the Void, but few witches ever liked to discuss *those* at length.

If only the Pepper Witches could have seen how efficiently she was able to manipulate her skills. It was only a little spell, true, but nicely rendered and executed, she thought. Ha! The newcomer warlock, Rowan Blaize, might have some appreciation for her talents, even if Beauregard and Gokey did not. Serenity allowed herself the luxury of a little chuckle. When push came to shove, the Pepper Witches placed a great deal of value upon the kind of hearty cackle that would melt the marrow in a mortal's bones, but Serenity had always been a chuckler, not a cackler. This was yet another reason she was suspected of sub-par sorcery. Still, there might be some glimmer of hope for her local fortunes, after all. Though Letty and Gert would never likely admit it, there had been a subtle but decidedly tectonic shift in the enchanted equilibrium of St. Augustine ever since Rowan Blaize had moved to town.

The shop-keeping crones carried on as if nothing in the world of worlds had changed, but Serenity knew that, in their hearts, both women were daunted by the presence of Blaize. Like her, they could sense the enormity of his power, even if he didn't show it. Like her, they could practically smell the considerable antiquity of this relatively recent arrival, who looked to be no more than a mortal youth of perhaps nineteen or twenty years. Serenity also knew that Letty and Gert hobnobbed with Blaize, a bit, while never having managed to extract much concrete information about him, and the extraction of information was one of their tag-team specialties. She rather doubted that either witch had done any scrying on-the-sly in order to delve into his background. This meant that both witches were afraid that he would "know" if they attempted to know, by use of magical means, more about him than he was prepared to share. Witches only tried that sort of rude intrusion on other witches they deemed inferior or incapable of retaliation. She was certain they had attempted to gaze into *her* business, but Serenity had put a metaphysical "freeze" on her history as soon as she had met the two busybodies years earlier, and she hoped it was still holding up.

As far as Rowan Blaize was concerned, however, there were a number of rumors floating about—whispers shared among magical underlings in the city—that he was a rather infamous magician from centuries of the deep past, in places worldly and otherworldly, far removed from cozy little St. Augustine. Serenity found it remarkable that none of the dryads, nixies, pixies, faeries, ghosts, goblins, gremlins, imps, succubi, incubi, or other entities had ever been able to offer more than vague speculations and enigmatic mutterings. How remarkable that Letty and Gert were content to observe him without the invasive prying that was one of their favorite pastimes. For her part, Serenity was more than a little afraid of Rowan Blaize, though he had never offered anything except the most cordial words to her when they happened to meet, which was admittedly infrequent. Perhaps there was a new dynamic that could be made to work in her favor as far as attaining some measure of status in town, something she had hitherto failed to explore.

She glanced at the pile of things on the kitchen table: Percival's tedious letter of proposal; the gaudy ruby ring; and, amid a few bills and other bits of mail, the unmistakable invitation to Rowan Blaize's All Hallow's Eve Party on Sunday night. She knew it had been sent last-minute, but was hardly offended. After all, she had refused to attend the event he had hosted the year before and tongues had wagged in town … at least among members of the supernatural set that actually possessed tongues. No one seemed to care that she had declined out of sheer intimidation. She knew the Pepper Witches attended the party, which had been more than enough to keep her away, along with scads of St. Auggie's other enchanted folk. Indeed, the reports she had received about last year's event had been exceedingly spectacular. Perhaps it was now time to leave aside the Happily Independent Witch persona, at least for an evening.

At any rate, attending the feast would afford her one less evening in which to think about the glowering look that would occupy Percival's face when she tendered her rejection of the proposal. She planned to do that in a couple of days, and her correspondence would certainly *not* be sent by way of the postal service. Dear Percival would feel the full weight of her displeasure at being so misunderstood, and it would reach him via magical response—one he would not soon forget, out there upon the desert sands, amid the relentless sounds of shovels and pick-axes. He could take a shovel, alright, go dig a hole, and bury himself for a few hundred years for all she cared. Thus, it would be a "Yes" for Rowan Blaize (Festivity and Camaraderie) and a "No" for Percival (Misguided Marital Imprisonment) and all his particular invitation might stand for. Somewhere between those opposing forces she might also find a way to reassert—or assert for the first time, actually—her identity as a worthy witch of the Ancient City. Any datil pepper product-vending snobs had better be prepared to applaud … or kindly get out of her way.

Emory, her familiar, had at last emerged from hiding to come downstairs. He peeked around a corner and rolled his bulging Shih Tzu eyeballs toward the former zone of destruction. Serenity crouched to coax him over.

"It's alright, love. A snappy little spell cleaned everything up. No more projectiles tonight, I promise. Speaking of things that ought not to be flying about, I have to go and find Guadalupe. Hopefully she's not in knots somewhere behind the washing machine, like last time. We'll never get her out."

The dog panted and wagged his tiny curl of a tail. Serenity picked up Rowan's ornate invitation, Percival's disastrous letter, and the ridiculous ruby ring, glancing once again at the arcane inscription on the band before turning off the light and making her way upstairs for the night. "At the very least," she said to Emory, "I might be able to amuse myself tomorrow by fishing-out Grandmother's old cipher-stone and discovering what this inscription says. It would be marvelous if I could tell Percival it reads: 'Not intended to be worn by those already bored to tears with wimpy warlocks or considering marriage.' Hmpf! I have half a mind to tell him that's *exactly* what it says, no matter what."

Serenity chuckled again, softly, grimaced at the absurd weight of the ruby ring in her palm, and wondered if the dreary Percival, pottering about the musty dark of some ancient eunuch's tomb, would even grasp the sarcasm of such a response.

෨ᴥᴥᦕ

III

St. Augustine City Councilman Chesterfield Rummy was unsatisfied with his job, his wife, his home, his car, the media, the world, and his existence in general. Over the years, he had honed the talent of publicly masking a pervasive dissatisfaction with Everything to the level of an art form. Appropriately enough, he was not even satisfied with his ability to do this. The one person with whom he was never, ever too terribly unsatisfied was his six year-old daughter, BonSashay.

Little BonSashay was Chesterfield's sparkling pride. Though she was, in fact, a bit more tarnished when it came to being his constant *joy,* the child would one day—and one day very soon—pay-off like a winning lottery ticket. Of this, her father was certain. Indeed, that sunbeam of a dream-child was going to make him Rich and Famous, both of which Chesterfield Rummy had always believed he was destined, even entitled, to enjoy, like new twin identities taking the place of 'St. Augustine City Councilman' and 'Entrepreneur.' These designations loitered beneath the name on his business card, a name which, due to either the ineptitude or uncanny intuitiveness of the printer (or both), currently read in large block letters:

C RUMMY

The telltale glory of this blunder aside, Chesterfield believed he possessed special gifts and the kinds of world-mesmerizing charisms reserved exclusively for the Rich and Famous. He had furthermore believed himself to be on a direct collision course with Rich and Famous from the time he had been BonSashay's age, though his opportunities for the unfettered pursuit of stardust and its accoutrements, down to the remotest collateral perks, had been few. The glittering chances that managed to present themselves to Chesterfield Rummy over the years had all been shot down like so many clay pigeons at a skeet-shoot by his unimaginative father, a talent-blind array of cynical elementary and high school teachers, the bitter barbiturate-receptacle who had been his mother, and, alas, by his incessantly intoxicated wife, Fancy Rummy, *nee* Fancy Badcock-Chapel (of the Jacksonville Badcock-Chapels).

Fancy had stopped believing in him as a matter of doctrine right after the failure of his ostrich farm in DeLand, and she had offered mere token support as a holy helpmate when he had attempted to transform his defunct ostrich-barn into the Community Church of God's Glorious Gospel Prosperity. Chesterfield Rummy had had no formal or even self-taught experience as a scriptural scholar and man of the cloth (or, in his case, a man of the $700 three-piece-suit), but these things were hardly prerequisites to founding a church in the South. Chesterfield held a firm conviction that all reasonably well-bred Southern males possessed the genetic wherewithal to spontaneously form new and enticing religious denominations of the fundamentalist Christian variety. So, he took a stab at the ministry.

It did not pan out. Potential converts were reluctant to attend services in the stifling humidity and summer heat of a three thousand square-foot, hastily converted, aluminum former ostrich-barn with no air conditioning. The promise of soul-stirring hymnody in said sanctuary proved to be another bust. Chesterfield's brother, Lloyd, who had been hired to hard-wire a "state of the art" sound system in the barn-church, abandoned the project after getting arrested for shoplifting a sixty-pound bag of dry dog food and a key lime pie from the local Winn Dixie. Worse, Chesterfield discovered that he was not particularly gifted as a prophet, and even less so as a preacher. Being unable to properly pronounce simple names like Hazarmaveth (Genesis 10.26) and Sephar-vaim (Isaiah 36.19) had indeed contributed to his undoing in the eyes and ears of the initial dozen-or-so Old Testament-obsessed occupants of the pews, but the infancy of his darling BonSashay had contributed, too.

Chesterfield felt certain that the ultimate failure of his religious endeavor was directly linked to the fact that his offspring, still crawl-ing around in dirty diapers at nine months, had been unable to bolster the Gospel Prosperity Church's success by virtue of her (at the time) still-hidden star power. Had BonSashay been old enough to belt out a number like "When the Roll is Called up Yonder" while wearing one of her puffiest gowns, Chesterfield believed he would have packed the worshippers in like so many sardines. Therefore, the entire evangelical flop and subsequent bankruptcy filing were primarily the result of regrettable timing.

Things had changed when the Rummys moved to St. Augustine and Chesterfield made two amazing discoveries. First, he learned that he was something of a dab-hand at small town politicking. Second, his golden-haired daughter possessed a knack for charming her way to child beauty-pageant crowns and runner-up ribbons throughout a tri-state area ... once she was able to stand on two legs, grab hold of a microphone, and caterwaul a few verses of *God Bless America.* Ever since, all resources upon which Chesterfield could lay his hairy and somewhat sausage-fingered hands had been channeled toward BonSashay's attainment of immortality. The Rummys would settle for nothing less than the kind of immortality that guaranteed multi-media entertainment deals, new cars, ostentatious homes, the chance to kiss-off local sewage treatment disputes and zoning intrigues, and good riddance to the flyblown oyster shack on San Marco Avenue that was barely keeping their dreams aimed at the stratosphere even now.

As Chesterfield pulled his wheezing Cadillac Seville into the garage of their home off South Street, he glanced down at the Ticket-to-Opulence sleeping on the seat next to him and sighed the sigh of a man on the razor's rustiest edge. BonSashay had been way off her game during the TV interview with that obviously child-hating Bobbi Jo Mickler from Channel 6. They could afford no further missteps, not with the Pint-Sized Princess Pageant only days away. BonSashay was not only the hometown hopeful, she was the odds-on favorite to take the coveted crown, a crown that would come with the precious lining of a $50,000 check and immediate "wild card" entry into the hallowed 'Lucky Little Lady Las Vegas' World Championship next March. In the meager light of the garage, Chesterfield was horrified to see that BonSashay had smeared

Dairy Queen cheeseburger grease and ketchup all over the front of her white satin Empress gown. He found his mind once again having to force itself to resist one of the strange and disturbingly oft-recurring new urges it had been experiencing—the urge to wrap his bejeweled sausage fingers around her precious little neck.

He took a few deep breaths, turned the engine off, closed his eyes, wiped beads of sweat from his forehead, popped a couple of aspirin that had been disintegrating in his breast pocket, and chewed them with some measure of ferocity. He reminded himself that she would not be able to reuse that particular gown, anyway. They had already risked enough allowing her to wear it during two separate competitions *and* to the TV interview with that despicable woman reporter. Chesterfield Rummy knew better than anyone that child beauty-pageant judges were everywhere—veritable will-o-the-wisps—staking out the favorites for upcoming competitions and taking copious notes while they staked. There would be a new gown for BonSashay's crown-clinching showstopper at the imminent pageant. They had already commissioned its design with a Jacksonville *cotourier.* Now, all Chesterfield had to do was pay for the miserable thing so Fancy could sew-on the last set of BonSashay's trademark bugle beads. That would be tomorrow's work. They still had one crucial day in which to raise funds and root-out hitherto untapped sponsors hiding among the local populace like woodlice in a pile of kindling. Still, Chesterfield could not do it alone.

He needed BonSashay and he needed her to be on her very best, most wheedling, most harp-pluckingly angelic behavior when they went door-to-door in some of the nicer neighborhoods of Vilano Beach in the morning. He was determined that his daughter, his font of endless pride, would stay out on the streets and work her adoring public until it hurt, and a rather dark little edge of his soul hoped that, somehow, some way, it might indeed end up hurting. A lot. If she had to come home with nothing but bloody stumps in place of her dainty feet, she would get the rest of the money they needed to seal the deal. Chesterfield had not come this far to lose the Pint-Sized Princess Crown. No, Siree.

"That little monster is gonna *perform* tomorrow," he whispered, pounding the steering wheel.

In the worn, brown leather seat beside him, like some garishly overdressed and rouged ventriloquist's dummy that had come to life upon pronouncement of the magic word "Perform," little BonSashay awakened from her engorged burger and fries induced coma. She stretched from toes to fingertips and emitted a little whimper.

"Daddy? We home already?" she croaked while rubbing the sleep from her eyes with tiny white-gloved fists.

"Yes we are, precious superstar," cooed Chesterfield, and then his tanned cheeks grew red hot in the stuffy interior of the Seville. He reached over and smacked his daughter's hands away from her face.

"Hey! Whatcha doin'?" bleated BonSashay. She bared her whitened teeth, which gleamed like menacing little peg-shaped pearls in the dinge. She was ready to take a bite out of the canned hams that masqueraded as her father's hands—several pearly little rat-bites, if necessary. It would not have been the first time.

"How many times have I told you to keep your hands out of your eyes, girl? Especially when you got the white lace gloves on and you're still in full make-up. Now see what you did? You smeared the mascara all around your eyeballs. You look like a raccoon in a wig. And them gloves is probably ruined."

BonSashay considered the delicate lace gloves, smudged with dark streaks and even one set of false eyelashes that had come off in the rubbing process and which now clung to a bit of lace like a dead, curled-up spider.

"Oh, gimme a break, old man," said BonSashay as she reached to open the passenger door. "I need a new set of stupid gloves for the pageant, anyhow. You said so yourself the other day."

Chesterfield took his daughter roughly by one of her puffed sleeves. "You listen here, Miss Lady Locket. I said we was gonna get you a new gown. Them gloves have got to be worn again! The judges won't dock you any points for wearin' the same set of gloves in two consecutive Class A competitions, but what they gonna say if you mince out on that stage looking like you just changed the oil in this lousy sedan with your own two hands? What is it that I have told you time and time again about show business, girl?"

His child rolled her raccoon eyes and sighed. "Yeah, yeah. I heard it all before. 'The scrutiny of the spotlight is unforgiving' and all that other crap you bark at me until I wanna tear the dadburned hairs right outta my own head! Can't I go in and get some more sleep? It's been a long day."

"Oh, you gonna get some sleep alright, little girl. You got yourself one mighty big day of fundraising tomorrow, in case you forgot." Chesterfield was beginning to feel the weird strangling urge wash over him like a mighty wave again. He had to grab hold of his necktie and squeeze for dear life. "And tomorrow had best not be a day like today was, you hear? You laid an egg at that Channel 6 interview, child. A big, bratty, cracked-up, stinkin' egg. What in thunder do you think we spent all that cash on etiquette lessons for, huh? Playacting in front of the mirror at home in your bedroom? No! I needed you to perform on target during that interview tonight, exuding the kind of ladylike graciousness and decorum befitting a Southern Belle. Instead you went completely off-script and blew it."

"But I was so tired from dance classes all day, and that news lady had the worst breath I ever smelt in my whole life. It was like she'd been suckin' on a onion all afternoon or something, Daddy. Then she gets right in my face with it. I thought I was gonna pass out, standing up there next to that dumb old fort. You'd get cranky, too."

Chesterfield Rummy considered this.

"She did have some godawful gnarly fumes coming out her pie-hole, I'll grant you that," he said, scrunching his face up at the memory. "But real stars don't blink an eye when the media comes at them like fire breathing dragons! You stay poised and you charm them until they are all putty in your hands, girl. That's what separates the great ones from the also-rans."

"Is that filthy little Brenda Bob Parson an 'also-ran,' Daddy?"

"Honey, listen to me. Little Brenda Bob Parson is nothin' but a bottom feedin' parasite, a boil on the backside of humanity, a disgrace to pint-size beauty competitors everywhere. But she *does* have excellent stylists and a mama with enough wolverine fangs in her head to make sure her daughter is *on* when she *needs* to be on, and no messin' around! I just hope your little brain freeze with the Channel 6 folks hasn't cost you the pageant before it's even started."

BonSashay's face became a twitching mask of horror. "Oh, Daddy, do you really think any pageant judges out in TV land saw me mess up tonight? I'll just crawl under my day-bed and die if I've ruined my chances and that snotty little Brenda Bob wins the tiara!"

"I daresay certain judges were watching that flub of an interview you gave, BonSashay Rummy. You know how I've told you that pageant judges can be lurking around any ole corner at all, watching you get into your jammies from a dark curbside with binoculars in their hands, even going through your garbage, girl—going through your garbage to see whether your garbage is the kind of garbage a *real* lady would take out to the garbage!"

"Oh no!" squeaked BonSashay, tears coming from her eyes as if there were a miniscule but leaky backyard sprinkler whirling around inside her skull.

"Now don't get yourself in a nervous tizzy over all this. That's the last thing we need. There's still plenty of time for damage control, darling. Don't you fret."

"You really think so?" sniffed the girl with rhinestone dreams.

"I do. We have all day tomorrow to hit the streets and knock on doors and shove your irresistible little face into people's homes so you can sing, dance a little, and beg them for everything they can spare to help you achieve the dreams they would sell their own souls to achieve, only they can't, on account of they're all too old and used up. Look, BonSashay, you gotta make all them empty, aimless souls believe they can live vicariously through you, honey. I mean, we have done this sort of thing often enough. You know the routine. Push the fat old ladies with two or more cats the hardest. Give them a glimpse of limelight and razzle-dazzle and they'll open up their pocketbooks right quick."

BonSashay tweaked her enormous satin puffed sleeves and straightened her shoulders, as if preparing for battle. Chin up in the dank old Seville, she managed her finest "Show Must Go On" smile.

"I promise you, Daddy. I'll knock them dead when we go door to door tomorrow. I will prove to you how successful I can be."

Chesterfield Rummy patted the remnants of his daughter's elaborate but wilting bouffant and grinned. "That's more like my best girl. You really *do* want that Pint-Sized Princess tiara and the Little Lady Las Vegas wild card, don't you, honey?"

"I sure do, Daddy, more than anything I have ever wanted in my whole, entire life. And you are gonna be there to see me take it *all* in just a couple of days. But fundraising is the most important thing right now. I'll be ready in the morning."

"Good to know, honey, good to know. Now, what say you and me go on inside and let your mother out from underneath the stairs. I locked her in from the outside again so she could finish stuffing them press kits for the Hollywood people, and I'll bet you a dollar to a doughnut she's been scratching at the inside of that door like a mad dog. Thank heaven I had the sense to put that leather padding around the frame. Come on, girl, or else the Beauty Sleep Fairy is gonna leave you high and dry tonight and then we'll *all* be out on the streets soon enough."

᠅᠅

IV

Rowan Blaize drew a woolen sweater tightly around his chest and even felt compelled to lift the hood portion of the garment up over his head, hiding his haystack shock of raven hair. He stood and observed the night from the third floor widow's walk of his merrily lit Victorian. A cool rush of sour, briny air rustled through the palms along the edges of the well-manicured property, making the treetops shiver and whisper while fronds scraped and rattled against each other, as if annoyed by the unfamiliar chill. More air blew in. More oak leaves and palm fronds chattered their displeasure. Sun-baked husks that had been bright, mischievous comrades through the summer were certain to be snatched away from the ranks and lost in the rhythmic gusts. Rowan nodded once to acknowledge the feisty display.

On a warlock's property, every living thing is entitled to its feelings and opinions at any given time. Quite often, those opinions are actually sentient.

Autumn is settling down upon us at last, thought Rowan, and his attitude was one of welcome, sparked by the same fiery stir of delight he had felt for centuries of seasons, in hundreds of places. Gone for at least the next five months were the sultry breezes that drifted and whirled and insinuated a decadent path across the city, enveloping everything in a sleepy, tropical cocoon. Gone, too, were the almost daily electrical storms and torrential downpours that still managed to give Rowan a slight sensation of alarm, an almost imperceptible shadow of apprehension that hovered like a cloud above his thoughts. It was abhorrent to him, the way one horrific encounter with a tempest had scarred him, how one instance twenty years prior, in which his great power had been humbled in the face of earth's elemental forces, had managed to make such a lasting impact.

He had indeed been flung from the pummeling blows of a fateful storm on that Cursed Day, but still bristled at the repercussions. Of course, he was careful to remember that it had been far more than thunder and lightning and wind that had wreaked such havoc upon his being. *Far* more. Thanks to unexpected assistance, that seemingly inescapable episode had been eluded and conquered, at least for a time, and the memory of ultimate victory provided its own soothing antidote, a host of edifying reassurances to counter the memory of humiliations that preceded his triumph. But Rowan could not bring himself to look up at the cloudless sky and scan the stars tonight, particularly those stars sequestered in a dense quadrant along the western border of the Great Square of Pegasus. He did not wish to bother himself with the most unsettling reminder of all—not tonight or on any other night, if possible.

Instead, he breathed deeply of the fresh evening air and luxuriated in the safety of his surroundings. St. Augustine would not be his home forever, not by any means, but it had thus far proved to be a worthy retreat after so much restless meandering, and after the uncertainty that had entered his existence following the Grim and Terrible Encounter. A wayward strand of hair started whipping as madly as the palm treetops in the latest rise of wind, so he tucked it up beneath the hood of his sweater and glanced back within the house at the crammed but comfortable library and Spell Chamber. There, Miranda sat at a cluttered roll-top desk examining RSVPs for the All Hallows Eve party. Thus far, everything had been stacked in the "I Accept" pile, at least in terms of invitations that had been sent and returned in material form. Enthusiastic ethereal responses had been arriving over the past few days, as well.

There was really no need to keep track of the guest-list, except for purposes of catering. One could not feed a distinguished family of hobgoblins the same *amuse bouche* prepared for the palette of a succubus, after all. This year's event, like the one that had come before, was shaping up to be a marvelous success and Rowan had Miranda—his faithful companion and stalwart muse—to thank for that. Watching her bent over the desktop, inscribing meticulous party notes and details in a leather-bound journal (which would later be transcribed to her iPhone, of course), Rowan took great comfort in knowing that she was a talisman in her own right, living proof of the extraordinary escape from doom and the mastery of malignant powers that he had managed to achieve not long after first meeting her.

What a pitiful waif she had been, but what a cherished friend she had become!

Now, her deadpan personality and watchful, contemplative presence reminded him each day of what victory had gained for him, and what it had cost him, too. It never ceased to impress Rowan how fluidly a mortal like Miranda had adapted to the strange and itinerant lifestyle of a warlock in his position, always without complaint or quibble. Years ago, he had been rather concerned about her ability to keep up with his constant relocations and the vagabond phase that had spurred his feet to stay on the move like they were clad in a pair of red-hot iron shoes, after the horror of his Great Unsettling. She had proved more than up to the task of being personal assistant and friend, and now … she was getting older. Miranda had been fourteen when he met her. Today she was a lovely, sometimes dangerously no-nonsense woman of thirty-four years who nevertheless looked almost old enough to be his mother, to the outside world. On several occasions he had respectfully offered to "arrest" the aging process on her behalf—he had the power to do that, under certain conditions—but she had declined, just as politely, every time.

Rowan was not surprised by Miranda's durability. A "childhood" like hers could not easily be shaken and she never had wished—or, at least, she did not *yet* wish—to abandon certain familiarities associated with her upbringing. Rowan had thought her chances for happiness to be grim when, not long after her emancipation twenty years earlier, they had discovered that both of her parents were dead, one from cancer and the other from a possible broken heart. Nevertheless, fourteen years as a Changeling in the court of a bitter faery king had given Miranda a steely resolve, and now she only spoke of her own mortality in order to compare it to that of her parents, whom she had never known.

"Mum and Dad died the way humans die," she had said to him once during a conversation about her parents. They had happened to be sitting atop Notre Dame at midnight, sharing baguettes and *foie gras* with famished gargoyles and admiring the elegant sprawl of the City of Light. "I may not be fit to live in the mortal world after all that's happened to me, but I know I can die in the mortal world, now, just as they did, and whenever and wherever and however that might happen, I want to share that one thing in common with them—just that one thing, at least."

She had been as unshakeable in that conviction as the stones upon which they were seated, at the time, and Rowan had never failed to admire her candor.

He left the autumn nightfall and went back into the library. Shadows from two dozen flickering candles (Miranda adored tapers) danced upon his hooded visage as he denied entry to inquisitive winds behind the door. Bror, the Mastiff, was curled up near the hearth on his favorite surface in the world—a Persian rug they had brought from his former mistress's house in Holland Park. The great dog, Rowan's adopted familiar and occasional servant, twitched and snorted and whimpered in-between mammoth snores. His gigantic paws paddled a bit; he was dreaming again, possibly about a cattle bone, possibly of a cozy, crackling fire. His huge black eye-patch was slightly askew, as usual. Rowan glanced at the empty fireplace and considered arranging a cheery conflagration in the blink of his own eye, but it was not yet nearly cool enough for that, and the candlelight provided more than enough ambiance.

"That cold front tells me we've seen the last of the big heat, at least for this year," said Miranda absently, not bothering to look up from the pile of RSVPs. She swung a colorfully tinted, braided ponytail over her shoulder and adjusted her cat's eye glasses. "Most all the names are crossed off the list." She indicated the parchment scroll on the desk. "Everyone's coming, of course. The wraiths that patrol the old mission grounds sent an ectoplasmic response just a few minutes ago, while you were out on the balcony. A couple of the cranky Old Moultrie Road faeries sent word, too," she added, pointing with a pen to the baroque mirror above the fireplace. "The ecto-replies are in here, if you want to listen."

She tapped a pale green alabaster jar with the pen. "That stuff gets everywhere if I don't bottle it up. Sticks to the walls something awful. Look at this reply from the troupe of werewolves who run that dinner theater down by Cordova. They're *so* obsequious!"

Rowan said nothing. Miranda finally looked up at him, pushing her glasses up the bridge of her nose with the handy pen. "You okay, Blaize?"

"Quite," answered Rowan, after another moment's silence. He folded his arms and moved inward to scan a few titles on his bookshelves. "You're correct about the weather, by the way. Autumn is finally in full blast. I rather enjoy this time of year, even in St. Augustine, where there's no grand show of foliage to mark the changing of seasons. Our party will have to be the 'grand show' once again, don't you agree?"

"The party will be the usual tonic for an autumn like this one," said Miranda. "What's the matter? Are you really pining for the sight of drifting colored leaves that spiral to the ground? A sheet of dew glimmering on the grass until it shivers itself into a blanket of frost? Runny red-noses and people bundling themselves up against bone-chilling breezes that whip and whistle?"

"I pine for none of those things, and don't be so smart," said Rowan, peering more closely at the bookshelves. It was, a bit unfortunately, a rather abbreviated collection culled from his permanent (but currently abandoned) home-base at the castle in Tarascon, but he had been wise enough to bring along some exceptional volumes for this stint, all the same. *Winged Creatures of Am-Duat.* Now *that* was always good bedtime reading, and the illustrations were choice—done *pleine aire* by a wizard named Isidorus in the fourteenth century. Isidorus had been a friend of Rowan's, until one of his more irascible artistic models ate him, sadly, in 1374. Ah, the pitfalls of artistic wizardry, thought Rowan. *Some Little-Known Doorways to the Sixth Archipelago of TanTanTua* was also promising, though Rowan had read it two hundred years ago, had gone to TanTanTua himself, and had found its "little-known doorways" to be less than accommodating, to say nothing of its perilous archipelago. No, this would not be a night for perusing dusty old travel-guides.

"Pumpkins," said Miranda over the snores of Bror.

"What?"

"Pumpkins," repeated Miranda. "I can tell you're brooding about something. You need to hear about cheerful, seasonal things when you're in such a mood, so I'm choosing pumpkins. You'll be happy to know that there are pumpkins galore, all over town," she said, stretching her arms wide over the walnut desk. "All the little kiddies, and, frankly, just as many adults, are jamming the supermarket aisles in order to select the ideal jack-o-lanterns for their doorsteps. I noticed the hullaballoo yesterday when getting groceries at Winn Dixie. Halloween is definitely upon us!"

"Or what's left of All Hallows Eve," said Rowan. "At least among mortal types." He selected the *Winged Creatures of Am-Duat* book and slipped into a red velvet-upholstered chair. "As usual, ninety percent of those purchased pumpkins will not be properly carved out and candled to frighten imps away from the aforementioned doorsteps, so people are going to be complaining about all sorts of little accidents and anomalies the day after All Hallows Eve. Only they won't realize the cause of any of this trouble because they don't *believe* anymore, or because the adults have spent the festival utterly confusing it with an occasion to repeat the debauchery of Mardi Gras. On All Hallows Eve, such people will return to their dwellings far too drunk, weighed-down with plastic beads, and disillusioned to notice that magic is still afoot, and that enchantment is very much all around them. Thus, for yet another year, I shall focus exclusively upon *my* private party and not pity any mortal victim of faery mischief, be that mischief minor or major."

"Nor will I pity them," concurred Miranda, deflating not a bit. She had never been adept at stirring Rowan out of a mood, and she knew it. No one had ever been good at it. "I daresay you have a point, too. It's come to something when humans so blithely neglect or twist the real meaning of the whole affair that the magical community is left with no choice but to actually intensify its own celebrations, just to compensate!" Miranda risked a little laugh, one that caused her still delicate, still pixie-like facial features to contort with the faint evidence of sarcasm.

Rowan peered at her with steel-pale eyes over the top of his book. "Oh, I have seen mortals confuse, blend, syncretize, rename, reconfigure, and ultimately *regret* what they have done to mangle and mash all sorts of holidays and festivals over the centuries, my dear. As we have discussed before, this little American trend of turning the autumnal equinox into a big endorsement for cheap tequila drinks served at smelly dance-clubs to people garbed in mass-produced carcinogenic costumes from China … *this* does not surprise me. One could see that coming a century ago. If I'm a bit disappointed in the subject of All Hallows Eve, it's because the Europeans are now starting to follow the same trend, and I had always hoped the European mortals would know a bit better."

"It's the fact that *kids* really don't appreciate Halloween anymore that gets me a little miffed," confessed Miranda. "Not that I like to bring him up, but crusty, rotten old King Narzell truly knew how to scare the daylights out of the Sutton kiddies every year, along with his minions. Even I was allowed to get in on the fun, once or twice. Nowadays, children don't even wear frightening costumes anymore. It used to be that if a kid went out dressed as a witch, for example, it was with a stereotypical hag-mask and pointy hat, which, as we know, is actually a true stereotype, at least insofar as your garden variety crones and hedge-witches are considered. But they don't even do much of that, lately. It's 'sexy witches' in lingerie, which, of course, is also not terribly far from reality because great enchantresses have been known to slip into something slinky when the fancy strikes them, but the whole nonsense is so affected when mortals do it."

Rowan rolled his silver eyes. "Of course it's affected, my foundling. That's the point of wearing a costume. Total affectation. Yet I, too, wish for their own sakes that they displayed better taste and some respect for the Deeper Meaning and all that. Even so, it's their current version of the holiday. If they are prepared to suffer the consequences of what happens when mortal and magical worlds collide for a night, then that's their lookout. Not ours. We have authentic revels to mark the occasion."

From the floor, Bror let out a gargantuan yawn and stretched on his back across the length of the Persian rug, this time to resume snoring in a completely upside-down position.

"As I mentioned, looks like all the usual suspects will be showing up for the party," noted Miranda, yawning herself, contagiously, after the dog's display of comfort. "I take it you stopped to pay a call upon Misses Beauregard and Gokey?"

"I most certainly did pay a call, but you'll have to excuse me because I forgot the box of Datil Dumpling Mix or whatever it is you asked me to pick up. I wasn't in the store five minutes and everything was sidetracked by one of their chronic squabbles. You know how they are."

Miranda raised a brow and whistled through her teeth. "Oh yeah."

"Both Leticia and Gertrude are excited about the party. They'll be there with bells on, and by that, you know I mean that each will try to outdo the other with a showy entrance, much like last year."

"Who could forget last year?" cried Miranda. "Letty Beauregard arriving in a sandstorm on the beach, of all places—*a sandstorm!*—while tubby old Gokey shows up riding that luminescent swell of sea foam in a monstrous clam shell, half naked. Oh, most disgusting! A total 'Birth of Venus' rip-off, and then the wave she rode in on dashed Beauregard's sandstorm and covered the whole lot of us in mud! It would have ruined the entire event, had it not gotten such a round of laughs. I would think they'd both be too embarrassed to even think of trying anything outrageous again. Why do old witches do that sort of thing, anyway?"

"For the same reasons mortals do. Competitiveness and drama," said Rowan. "Making the 'grand entrance' at a sorcerer's council or enclave is a tradition that goes back thousands of years, love. You would not believe the lesser lights and lurkers that have been snuffed-out forever—disintegrated!—due to some glorious personage's need to make an unforgettable first impression. Rather foolish, I realize, but that's why witches and warlocks tend not to congregate in tight clusters, at least at the beginnings of important get-togethers. One simply never knows when someone else will choose to come hurtling down out of the sky in the form of a meteor. I've seen everything but pink elephants raining-down, in my day, and even that would not surprise me. Still, we mustn't be too hard on Letty and Gert. Neither of them has had occasion to get out much and let their hair down at supernatural soirees, certainly not since they settled in St. Augustine so long ago. I imagine that the temptation to relive a bit of their youthfulness with a touch of dazzle at my All Hallows party can be overlooked. We will have to warn the Swamp Goblins ahead of time this year, however. The one that got sucked out to sea on Gert's undertow last year was never accounted for."

"Mmm. The goblins are still upset about that, too," informed Miranda, who had had occasion to chat with a brood of the victim's relatives off of Highway 16 only a week earlier. "All the same, everyone I have spoken with seems pleased that the party is not going to be held at the beach this Halloween. I say, it was a splendid idea for you to decide on holding it inside the Castillo. The fort seems such a fitting place, though I imagine security will be a bit of a challenge, seeing as it's right downtown. All the mortal revelers will want to get in, too!"

"Trust me, they won't get in," said Rowan. "I have already arranged everything with the Historical Preservation Board, and by 'arranged' I mean I put one wallop-of-a-spell on them all during their meeting last Wednesday. The Castillo is the very emblem of the town's antiquity. That panel would never have allowed us to borrow it for a night if I hadn't exerted some measure of influence. As for security … well, let us just say that it shall be rather tight for this most private and exclusive event."

Miranda was not surprised. Hollywood film crews wishing to use the fort for their productions were routinely turned down by the stringent and unshakable supervisory council of the Historical Preservation Advisory Committee. The "magic" of Hollywood, however, was not on a par with the magic employed by Rowan Blaize. Miranda had watched as her emancipator and friend accomplished some extraordinary feats in their twenty years together, and she had seen things that would frazzle the average mortal brain even before meeting Rowan. After all that, the logistics of his exploits never failed to fascinate her.

"Then I gather you have also 'exerted some measure of influence' on the local police department, the town, the National Guard, and any observational satellites that might be drifting overhead in view of the pyrotechnics that are bound to be a feature of the evening's festivities?" she said with a knowing grin.

"Not yet, but I'll see to all of that the night of the party," answered Rowan. "No one from any earthly authority will intrude upon the gathering. Those invited to the feast will see things for what they are, of course, but for anyone uninvited, whatever is seen taking place in, on, around, or above the Castillo de San Marcos shall pass through the mind as a thing of no consequence, to be ignored or forgotten the instant it is encountered. No mortal recording device of any sort will be able to capture the proceedings."

"Huge magic!" gasped Miranda.

"Significant," agreed Rowan, turning a page to explore more winged terrors of the Land of Am-Duat. "But not as taxing as you imagine. I only have to put a certain kind of cloaking spell upon our company and the location in question, not upon everyone and everything else in the neighborhood, much less in the stratosphere. All should be quite tidy."

"Leave it to you," said Miranda, leaning back in her desk chair and noticing one important name that had not yet been crossed off her guest-list. "What about the odd little witch, Serenity Turnbull? Have you or the St. George Street sorceresses heard whether or not she is going to be making an appearance this year? I sent her an invitation again, as you instructed, but once again, *s'il vous plait,* she has decided not to *responder.* Such a weird duck, that one, even for a witch. She very much goes in for all the mortal trimmings and trappings, doesn't she? I don't blame her, in certain respects. I know that I certainly longed for a normal mortal life when I was in the hands of Narzell and his cheerless court. Then again, I was a human girl just wanting to be human, which is not quite Serenity's position. My empathy may be a trifle misplaced. Funny, isn't it, how things turn out in this world? I wanted one sort of life, the one I had been born for, and when I was finally rescued from my magical captivity, my reward was … a magical existence!"

Rowan closed the ancient book and placed it on his lap.

"Do you regret it, Miranda? If so, you know that I have always assured you that you are free to strike out on your own at any time, and that I would more than provide for an excellent start in a thoroughly non-magical lifestyle. I could do that and even erase your memories of all magical trials and tribulations in a way that would not harm you or compromise your identity. You could certainly manage a 'normal' mortal life, as you describe it. Of that I have no doubt. You've grown into a capable woman who has seen more than any mortal's fair share of the world's mysteries splayed-out for full inspection, and you have learned well from your experiences. Study has been your constant companion, every bit as much as Bror, there, lazy and large, or me, for that matter. No university in the world could teach you the nature of the peculiarities you have beheld and the oddities you have fathomed, though perhaps a well-rounded, non-magical setting with college and friends and your own troubles and triumphs experienced exclusively among your own kind would benefit you. You have only to say the word and I will help you and leave you to it. Moreover, I would understand completely."

Miranda smiled a little and shook her head, but it did not require a magician's immortal instinct to discern a certain sliver of wistfulness, a thread of taciturn regret in her response. It was there, and both of them knew it, but it was blessedly faint.

"Rowan Blaize, that's not what I was angling for, if I was angling for anything at all with my silly comments." She placed a stack of return invitations neatly in one of the desk drawers and tried to distract herself from the flush of embarrassment she felt rising upon her cheeks, which was a thing that happened from time to time, when Blaize truly confronted her in his probative but compassionate way. "I appreciate the reiteration of your promise, Rowan, and your encouragement. It means as much to me now as it always has. But if there is one thing I know, it's that a genuinely 'normal' mortal life is not possible for me, and I suspect you know that, too. Given the circumstances in which I was raised for the first fourteen years of my life, I don't think it's fair for me to even *imagine* a normal life as being possible. I have always given the facts a very careful examination. I don't shirk from them. Magic ruined my childhood, yes, and it ruined the lives of my dear departed parents, whoever they were, and yet the kindness of magic has balanced the chaos and cruelty, in my case. This is a thing that must always be accepted and appreciated. There's a reason for that balance. I've been around you long enough, and have learned enough about the world of magic, to know that balances are not to be disturbed. Besides, I'm a woman in my thirties in a beachside resort town and loving it. I'm happy where I am. You need not question me."

She smiled broadly, more affectionately from the deepest wellspring of her complex spirit and moved with grace to one of the hearthside chairs, a lithe and fair-skinned woman in faded jeans and a pullover emblazoned with the University of Florida's colors and reptilian mascot. Her feet were bare and she put them on top of Bror for warmth, rubbing his considerable belly at the same time. The Mastiff slobbered a bit in the midst of his dream, wriggling beneath the touch of her toes, but he did not wake up.

"What's the matter, Rowan? Were you hoping I might drift off? Are you looking for a younger secretary?" she said playfully.

"Don't be ridiculous, Miranda. You're no secretary. You are a friend. I do not want you to drift off unless that is what *you* would like to do."

"I know. But no matter what I want, one day I will … drift off. For I grow older and you do not."

"We all get older, each in our own manner," said Rowan, reopening the enormous book and turning its gold-leafed pages. "No being—no created being, I should say—can avoid getting older, even though Time itself seems, to some, a mere plaything, a brief reflection glimpsed in a mirror that is swiftly passed and then forgotten. Every magical entity knows this to be true, even, as you put it, a 'weird duck' like our dear Serenity Turnbull. And now that the subject gets back to her, I must confess that I believe a great more is going on with that particular duck than meets the eye. There is much about Serenity that she is not willing to reveal, but it is hardly unusual for a witch to keep overly inquisitive minds at a comfortable, or in her case *uncomfortable,* distance. She certainly keeps Letty and Gert in a healthy state of speculation."

"Little wonder, then, that old Gert and Letty find her so confounding," remarked Miranda. "If Serenity is putting up some sort of magical smokescreen to keep them from getting to know her too well, then surely they perceive it and disapprove of her all the more. Of course, you put up the same—or shall I say a far more impenetrable—wall to keep those two old biddies from grasping the vast scope of your identity and past. Still, the dotty dears think you walk on water, which you can do, of course, but that's beside the point. They don't feel the same way about Serenity, and never will."

Rowan laughed. "Well, they know enough to know that I am no Serenity Turnbull," he said. "They know enough to know that I am to be handled with much greater care and prudence than is typically reserved for objects of their interest and in-depth analysis. But, champion bickerers and complainers that they are, Leticia and Gertrude are a pair of fine old witches and they, too, have more in the way of secrets than any of us will ever imagine. I guarantee it, because that is the case with us all. Respected privacies notwithstanding, I admit I have grown weary of their condescension toward Serenity, at least as far as my All Hallows party is concerned. If their attitude is what has kept her from joining us on a night sacred to all magical folk, then I plan to rectify that. Tomorrow afternoon I am going to pay a call to Miss Turnbull and underscore our firm desire that she grace our Equinox Bash with her welcome presence. She may quail and find an unexpected house-call from the likes of me somewhat gauche, but I'll risk it. Serenity is someone I think the two of us would appreciate knowing. Secrets don't have to be traded like wampum in order to achieve that, either."

A dark cloud seemed to pass across Rowan's brow; Miranda thought it was a momentary trick of the candlelight, but it was not.

"I shall remain quite careful about things, Miranda. Quite watchful until I am absolutely certain, to the tips of my phantasmagoric nerve-endings, that She Whom I Banished twenty years ago is no longer a threat to me, or to anyone I care about."

"Then you *do* intend to lay low in this languid little city for the foreseeable future?"

"Perhaps for what you can see of the future, my dear," said Rowan. "Not for as much as I can see of it. For the present, however, I do think it best."

Bror came suddenly to a thumping, bumping, rolling, rocking, drool-spluttering wakefulness, knocking Miranda, who burst into laughter, out of her chair and onto the floor. The grand canine stood, immense paws splayed across the hearth rug and head lolling in bewilderment. Who knew what inner vision haunted dreamscapes with enough potency to startle such an imposing magical beast?

Rowan had some ideas.

He patted his companion and scratched behind the great, drooping gray ears as he rose to head for bed and further delving into *Winged Creatures of Am-Duat*. Miranda was still giggling on the floor in amusement at the Mastiff's clumsy display.

"Not to worry, dear Bror," said Rowan as he departed the room. "Waking nightmares fade as swiftly as they appear, unlike some others. Count yourself fortunate. I'll see you both in the morning."

–§

V

Leticia Beauregard and Gertrude Gokey were at it again, though to anyone remotely familiar with the pair across the centuries, use of the word "again" would seem downright superfluous. It is best, perhaps, to say that Letty and Gert *are at it,* as if no past or future exists. Consider them locked in a perpetual "now," at least in terms of their mutual and relentless fidget.

Luckily for St. Augustine and various other parts of the world, theirs was a low-grade magical antagonism of viral proportions, and no one was ever injured in the fallout. Well, that is not exactly the truth. Only rarely did injuries occur, and then not necessarily on purpose. Most were victims of collateral damage due to dangerous, hurtling objects caught in perfectly understandable magical vortices, shockwaves, and minor explosions. In short, neither witch ever intended to injure anything or anyone hapless enough to be located within a reasonably distant radius of one of their arguments. They did not consider themselves responsible, however, for those unfortunate enough to be located within *unreasonable* radiuses.

Leticia's lanky frame was draped like a crumpled, worn garment that had been casually tossed across the length of a recliner and its footrest. She was an almost horizontal figure, from her slipper-clad feet to her dignified but eagle-beaked hook of a nose. A cool compress of cucumber water, chamomile, and deadly nightshade was placed over her eyes, both of which were weary from having to stare for hours at straggling tourists on St. George Street and then at tourists poking, prodding, and (if they knew what was good for them) *purchasing* distinctive products in the pepper shop itself. Letty Beauregard was not a witch to suffer looky-loos lightly, except perhaps at the very end of the shift, when so much commerce and interaction with mortals took its toll upon her, along with the constant drain of bickering all the livelong day with Gert. This last, however, could sometimes be an invigorating and ever-renewable source of energy, too; it all depended upon the subject under "discussion."

Unwittingly, and without any overt magical influence whatso-ever, Letty and Gert seemed to have invented a Perpetual Motion Machine of Squabble. Others, of varying degrees of skill, had attempted and perhaps come close to such exquisite craftsmanship, but these examples were so many mere stabs in the proverbial dark, compared to what the witches had accomplished. Had mortal scientists ever managed to observe and experiment, they might have found a means of channeling the energy of Letty's and Gert's Incessant Wrangle, duplicating its dynamics in order to build the elusive device that would garner every prize and plaudit imaginable, to say nothing of the alteration of history's very course through the cosmic continuum.

For now, however, the world of scientific achievement would have to settle for a distant second place.

Letty's long, sinewy arms half-rested upon and half-dangled over the plush arms of the recliner, her knuckles barely grazing the tiled floor below. Gert, for her part, was fifteen feet away, perched on a sofa at the other end of the living room, watching her beloved television set and listening via the headphones Letty had insisted upon gifting her for her birthday in lieu of "gifting" her a television set that would be teleported directly out the window, through the muggy Florida air with lightning speed, and plunged with considerable explosiveness and satisfaction into the deepest part of the bay. Both witches were in their evening house-coats, sipping their preferred after-work liquid refreshments, which they described to anyone who ever asked as "iced tea" in summertime and "hot tea" in winter, but which was in fact datil pepper-infused vodka (with a splash of wormwood) all year round ... and Bloody Marys with the same stuff on Sundays, when the shop was closed. Fondness for the datil pepper and for any alcoholic beverage that could be derived, concocted, or distilled from said pepper constituted particularly sacred ground—*rare* ground—upon which both witches were always united in unflappable agreement.

Like most witches, Letty and Gert had stomachs of steel and livers to match. A week earlier, Gert had even informed Letty that she once "Knew an old sorceress who actually had herself a zip-out liver! Why, this old gal could drink a jug of white lightning every morning for breakfast, burn down an entire forest with her breath by lunchtime, take her liver out before bedtime, give it a good wring into a bucket, put it back inside her belly, zip herself up, and pick up right where she left off the next day!"

Letty, of course, had told Gert to stop being such an idiot and go soak her own head in a bucket of moonshine, but for all she knew, the story could have been true. Gertrude Gokey always had some rather unusual and mystifyingly weird acquaintances, even for a witch.

Their tidy, spacious apartment above the store was cheerful and redolent with near-textbook grandmotherliness: lace doilies atop parlor tables; elaborate cuckoo clocks; framed embroidery upon the walls; large, blossoming glass bowls piled with cookies and nuts; potted ficus trees and window-sill planters lush with herbs and dainty flowers; knitting baskets crammed with yarn; little rolled-up tubes of Ben-Gay jammed between the sofa cushions or forgotten on knick-knack shelves. The casual onlooker would never believe that the two occupants of such a quaint space were frequently guilty of summoning-up any number of denizens in the Hierarchy of Hellspawn to exact little measures of domestic revenge or mischief upon each other in return for someone forgetting to wash out the teacups or empty the lint-filter in the dryer.

This particular evening in the House of Beauregard and Gokey was, so far, a relatively mild one in terms of attritional wars. Early on, both women had been in exceptionally pleasant moods, at least for them. Traffic in the store had been much better than usual, considering the busy season was over, and Rowan Blaize's swanky All Hallows Eve party was very much in their thoughts. Gert had her ideas about what kind of grand entrance Letty was planning to make, and Letty had her own inkling about what Gert might try to do, but neither woman would dream of revealing to the other so much as a glimmer of open curiosity in that regard. Their minds were, in fact, spinning like windmills in a gale. Despite outward appearances of evening relaxation, each had been preoccupied with plans to outdo the other in grandeur this year, in ways that did not include stinging mud-baths and the drowning of Swamp Goblins.

Next to the satyr-headed coatrack by the "garage" (broom closet), a mammoth grandfather-clock was close to striking ten and Letty, as if aware something had been too long awry in their universe, finally found a reason to harangue Gert.

"Hey! Turn that blasted TV program down, Gertrude Gokey. I can hear fools jabbering right through those headphones, you inconsiderate old baggage!"

To Letty's surprise, and to the disappointment of her habitually cultivated sense of antagonism, Gert grabbed the remote and complied without one of her usual, dagger-like retorts. Turning down the set, she leaned back on the sofa and took a luxurious sip from her martini glass, which was nearly the size of a small fishbowl and, like Letty's, always magically chilled to a tantalizing, frosty temperature. Letty lifted the comforting compress from her eyes and yelled across the room.

"You figure Rowan Blaize remembered to invite Mr. Wagswrath, that old troll what lives up under the Bridge of Lions, to the party this year? He forgot to invite him last year and look what happened. Nice little family from Japan gets eaten up in a fit o' pique and a whole country goes off-the-boil wondering what happened to them. Tokyo blaming the scandal of our American crime rate. Ha! The secrets we have to hold onto as witches! Take off them headphones, Gert, and listen to me. You think he remembered the invitation this year?"

"Wagswrath got invited. I remember Rowan telling me himself the other day!" shouted Gert in reply, never looking away from the TV set. The miniscule images of contestants waltzing on some dance competition program could be seen reflected in the twin shimmering black pools of her fixated eyeballs. "The troll's lucky Blaize didn't annihilate him for what he did to them poor Yakimotos. But Rowan knows as well as the next warlock—trolls'll be trolls. Wagswrath has been invited this year, right enough."

Then she took another swig from her martini glass and belched. There was not even a perfunctory "Why in the name of Nineveh are you asking *me* such questions?" from the lips of La Gokey.

Letty was not best pleased. She removed her compress and flung it onto a nearby end-table with indignation. She struggled for a moment and then gritted her teeth; a swiftly muttered spell brought her LaZboy into the full upright position.

"And what about Iggy the incubus, the drunk?" squawked Letty. "You think he got invited again? I only ask because the nasty little varmint got good and tossed at last year's party and tried to put the moves on that Miranda, Rowan's foundling or assistant or whatever she is. You think *he'll* be allowed back?"

Gert shrugged her plump shoulders. "Who knows and who cares?" she yelled. "Everyone gets a bit tipsy at that party and even if he does show up, Miranda knows how to look after herself. At least, well enough for a mortal. I don't expect Rowan *or* Miranda will hold too much against the lecherous Iggy. He'll be there. Count on it."

Gert's eyes continued to devour the action on *Dancing with the Stars*. Letty's eyes, riveted with umbrage, continued to devour Gert. After a moment, her stern, paper-cut of a mouth twisted as if chewing upon the world's tartest lemon and she rose, imperious, from her recliner, marched across the floor and ripped the headphones off her housemate's cornrowed skull.

"What's the big idea?" squealed Gert, slopping a precious bit of Datil Vodka onto her lavender bathrobe. "They're just about to give Misty and Puffy their scores for the Paso Dobre!"

Letty's eyes darted with serpentine speed and cunning toward the television set. The screen went dead with a swift static sound and the remote in Gert's hand evaporated, completely, in an acrid puff of black smoke.

"Well, I NEVER!" gasped Gert. "What do you think you're doing, woman? I suppose I'm to be thankful my TV set didn't blow-up just now into a million pieces of confetti, like last time?

"Don't doubt that the thought crossed my mind," said Letty, arms akimbo.

"What manner of bewildered bee has burrowed into your brazen bonnet *this* time, Beauregard? I thought we was having a real nice, re-laxin' evening, savoring our voddies and generally staying out of each other's way, for a change. I can enchant that set back on just as well as you can shut it off. No remote needed. So kindly tell me what's on your mind or let me get back to my show!"

"Something very ominous is on my mind, Gert Gokey, and I don't mind telling you it's giving me a slight chill down the spine and frankly down the backside, too."

Letty glowered down at Gert like a towering pinnacle of doom, her slightly bloodshot but emerald green eyes ablaze with portent. This was certainly worth the interruption of a dance program. Gert took a bracing sip of her martini and considered her friend's gloomy counte-nance. The grandfather-clock began to strike its mournful hour.

"By the jingles, what's got you so spooked, Letty? I ain't seen this kinda look on your face since that time we were back in the Old Country and that miserable Mephisto beat you at cards, and, on account of you being the loser, he gave you the choice of getting turned into a skinny black swan for a hundred years or else going upstairs to his room and ..."

"Shut up about that, you sour old gossip!" snapped Letty. "This is something completely different." She sat down with a thud on their blue velvet settee, staring at the hem of her housecoat and then at her slip-pers, as if the solution to her sudden panic might be found amid the worn tufts and tattered edges of terry cloth. "Something big is comin' into this town, Gertrude. I can feel it in my marrow."

"Whaddaya mean by 'something big,' Letty?" Gert reached for a datil pepper gumdrop in the crystal candy-dish near the sofa. She was entranced. Forget about the dance show. Letty's forebodings were al-ways top-notch entertainment. "What do you see? A storm brewin' out over the ocean? A bad Northeaster, maybe? It's a little early, yet, but you always did get a crick in your back when a nasty wind was about to blow. Remember when the old pier got taken out back in 1984 and you warned everybody who'd listen that—"

Letty waved her crabbed hands as if swatting away some invisible, buzzing cloud of gnats. "Nothing like a storm," she said. "A storm is occasion for concern, sure, but not for outright foreboding."

"Then what, exactly, are you feeling, girl?"

"I wish I knew, *exactly.*" Letty nibbled with vexation on a bony knuckle. "I've been feeling some sort of weird vibe coming on ever since we closed up the shop this afternoon, but at first I thought it was just my eyes getting tired, or that we weren't clucking at each other like old hens, as we normally do. Now it's gotten bad. Real bad. There's this huge sense of trouble, Gertrude, just at the very outskirts of my intuition. But it's massive. I been trying to focus and get some kind of hold on it, but it's eluding me. I even tried the nightshade compress, but nothing clear is coming through."

"Could be those cabbage rolls you ate last night," ventured Gert. "They fairly gave you the head-sweats, you put so much Boomslang Curry on them."

Letty shook her braid-reinforced head and placed her hands around her ears, wincing in terrible pain. Gert began to actually worry about her friend for the first time in ages.

"Hey. You ain't kidding when you say there's something off-kilter somewhere, are you?"

"No," croaked Letty, lowering a hand and motioning to Gert. "Give me a sip of your drink. I'm too dizzy to get up and fetch my own. Ain't even going to try and levitate it over to me."

Gert carefully handed Letty the sloshing, ice-cold martini and watched with fascination as her companion took a long, burning draught.

"Here. That seems to have hit the spot for now. Thank you, Gertrude. Oh, I say. Yes. That hit the spot and then some." Her eyes widened as Gert took back the empty glass. "Say, do you remember that feeling both of us got just around the time Rowan Blaize first came to St. Augustine? Only it wasn't necessarily an *uncomfortable* feeling?"

"Yeah, I remember," said Gert. "It was just a sense that something, well … BIG … was on the scene and we didn't know what it was. But we could feel the weight of it, couldn't we? We could feel the power. That's how we knew Rowan was one of the real Old Ones, one of the Mighty Ones, once we met him in person. Only we never give him the satisfaction of telling him that we knew—and that we know—how powerful he really is. You said we didn't want him putting on airs, no matter who he was, and you were right about that, Letty. But sure enough, that was the feeling we felt when he came. Something big. And you're saying this premonition or whatever it is you're having right now is like that, too?"

"In a way, yes. In a way, no. This is big trouble. Danger, even."

"To the city?" asked Gert. "You positive it ain't no hurricane the mortal weather people might've missed on their Doppler? Surely you can't be feeling anything that's a danger to the two of us. What have *we* got to be afraid of?"

"I tell you I don't know, yet!" snapped Letty. "But I know enough to know that we would be well advised to feel afraid, Gertrude Gokey. Possibly *very* afraid, from the feel of things."

"Blast it all!" said Gert, chewing her gumdrop and gathering the folds of her housecoat and nightdress. She, too, could intuit momentous things and events, being a witch of considerable skill and experience, but she did not have a knack for getting a preview of coming catastrophes the same way Letty did. Her inner spirit was too optimistic—or, at least, more optimistic than Letty's—to be an Oracle of Impending Cataclysm. Leticia Beauregard, on the other hand, had been predicting plagues, wars, earthquakes, eruptions, and everything from mob uprisings to mudslides since they had been girls back in the Old Country. If Letty hung her head in her hands and told you that trouble with a capital T was on the way, you would be wise to sit up and take note, because it was on the horizon.

"Something outrageous *would* have to crop up now, just as we're ready to get some nice rest after a busy summer," griped Gert. "Just as all my programs are getting really good and even that Pint-Sized Princess pageant is coming to town!"

At this, Letty's hands flew again to her temples and she was wracked with pain.

"What'd I say?" gasped Gert, now thoroughly perplexed. "Can't be the pageant coming to town that's got your feathers ruffled. I know you don't approve of all that mortal fuss and vanity, but it's just a two-bit kiddie show meant to tickle softhearted old gals like me. Ain't nothing *evil* about it."

"Don't you think I know that, Gokey?" Letty's voice was now husky and subdued. "Fact is, I've been getting odd little jolts all day, now that I think about it. Ever since you started watching that ridiculous business on the TV down in the shop, when Rowan came in for a visit. I'm sure you mentioning it again is just some reminder that set me off automatically, some awful reflex, but it doesn't change the fact that I'm getting one doozy of a dark message, loud and clear, but without any actual shape or shine to it. You wouldn't believe the pain caused by being unable to get a grip on the exact form of it, whatever *it* is. I feel like my head has either been split wide open with an axe, or else I'm gonna be begging you to split it open, before all is said and done!"

Gert set her slightly mole-addled and somewhat stubbly jaw with determination and leaned forward on the sofa. "I may not understand the frustration, Letty my girl, but sure as Saturn's Seventh Sister I believe it's real, and that means we have something well worth a proper investigation!"

She rose with buxom enthusiasm and stalked into the kitchen of their spacious quarters. In a moment, Letty heard the sounds of pots, pans, and various other items of a culinary character banging and clanging against each other and the cheerfully painted pastel cupboards. A dish crashed onto the rust-red tile and shattered.

"Drat," grumbled Gert.

"What in the world are you doing in there?" called Letty. "The headache's bad enough as it is. When I said I might need my skull split with an axe I didn't mean for you to go rummaging around for one. Get back in here and help me talk this thing through! Ain't no time for you to prepare one of your evening snacks, not at such a troublesome hour."

"Not looking for no axe or snacks, Letty, though a slice of that key lime pie in the fridge would be just the thing right now, what with my nerves. And it is way past time to 'talk things through.' I do believe you have said enough."

Gert emerged a moment later from the kitchen, triumphant. Her bosom swelled with take-charge confidence in the doorway. "You think we need to talk, Letty, when what we really need to do is ... *wok!*"

Letty rolled her eyes and flung herself backward in a show of despair upon the settee, lanky legs sprawled out across the faces of the jolly monkeys sewn into the pattern of their tropical-motif area rug. "Why, by the treacherous trade winds of Tartarus, did you go and fish *that* ridiculous thing out at a time like this?" she asked, forlorn.

"Because we need it at a time like this," said Gert, brandishing the most powerful and magically utilized member of her vast collection of kitchen utensils, gadgets, gewgaws, knick-knacks, and novelties. It was a large, dented, heavily tarnished, and not at all well-scrubbed wok. Her nephew had sent it to her all the way from some crowded, dingy street market in Peking nearly a century ago, and though she had since used it only half a dozen times in her desultory experiments with Chinese cooking (a cuisine Gert never cared for in the first place, but how was poor Horatio, her least-attentive nephew, to know a private thing like *that?*), she had nevertheless found the clumsy, shelf-hogging object to be a most unexpected and indispensable talisman.

While the dusty spell-corner in Gert's otherwise spotless bedroom was stocked to the ceiling with crystal balls, obsidian shards, silver-lined jade bowls, and ampullae full of exotic inks meant specifically for purposes of diehard divination, ethereal eavesdropping, and surefire second sightings, the wok was *not* to be trumped. Never, in all of her years as an enterprising and methodologically inquisitive witch, had Gert managed to conjure up more accurate and informative visions than she had in her wok. It wasn't much to look at, and not the least bit esoteric compared to her other, more overtly enchanted and mysterious implements, but she would not trade the wok for all the Magic Mirrors in the entire panoramic history of Wicked Queendom.

"Oh, for crying out loud, Gert," bleated Letty from the settee. "Don't tell me you're gonna start playing around with that beat up oriental cooker!"

"I am," asserted Gert, clearing off the coffee table and arranging her warped wok upon the thick glass surface between them. "We'll both feel a heck of a lot better for a little stir-scrying, tonight, don't you think? Why, the way this thing's worked for me in the past, we might even get to the bottom of your migraine premonition toot sweet! You could irritate the tar right out of them pits in LaBrea, but you are my best friend, after all. I can't rightly stand to see you so bent out of shape. Besides, if there's something nasty on the way that can put a couple of old pros like us to serious inconvenience, then I'd prefer to get me a good solid look at what it is, ahead of time, so we can figure out a way to calculate an ounce of prevention, if necessary, or ponder, if at all possible, our pound of cure."

Letty groaned as she pulled herself into an upright position and hobbled over to the recliner to retrieve the nightshade compress, which was still visibly steaming due to the intensity of her oracular fever. She placed it back atop her sweat-soaked braids, anyway.

"You really think you can tune that dumb thing well enough to get a decent read on what's eating away at my brain?" she asked, sitting down stiffly next to Gert on the sofa. "If I recall correctly, the last time you fetched that cooker out of the cupboard to have a gander at something unforeseen, you claimed a great brush fire was gonna sweep through Marsh Creek all the way to Crescent City when, in fact, you was really looking at a burnt-up old piece of broccoli you never bothered to scrub outta that fry-bowl. The Broccoli Incident was more than a bit embarrassing, if you want to know the truth, especially since you got me all worked up about it and we ended up calling the entire fire department down on the south side of the city. When the fire chief asked you exactly *where* you'd first seen this ragin' brush fire, you were so overexcited you forgot yourself and told him you saw it in the Chinese cooking pan! Gah.

We had to employ actual Memory Dissipation spells on the poor fellow, or else we'd never have been able to live that one down!"

Gert pursed her lips and pretended not to be bothered too much by Letty's dour skepticism, or by remembrance of the admittedly unfortunate screw-up with the broccoli floret that was supposed to have incinerated half of North Florida. Witches who are brave enough to pioneer hitherto unexplored expeditions into the paranormal possibilities of common cookware are bound to make mistakes once in a while, Gert figured. That was the price one paid for being a maverick. Besides, the wok had worked wonders for her on past occasions when she had peered into its smudgy depths to perceive any number of pertinent secrets unjustifiably withheld from her deserving curiosity.

Why, there had been the time only last year when one of the sweet old sisters of St. Joseph had wandered away from her room at the majestic convent just down the street on St. George and no one could find her. The entire town had been beside itself, seeing as Sister Mary Eusebius had a slight touch of dementia and was a frail thing no sturdier than a water lily. The wind might have blown the dear old soul most anywhere, but Gert had yanked the wok out from under the sink the moment she heard the news and muttered a particularly incisive spell in which the word "nun" was craftily paired with "on the run" and, not a few moments later, there was Sister Mary Eusebius, plain as plain, wedged between a chipped, life-sized statue of St. Anthony, with her habit snagged on a spoke of St. Catherine's wheel, way up in some discarded statue room of the convent attic.

No one had ever entertained the notion that eighty eight year-old Mary Eusebius could make it up all those stairs into the most forgotten junk nook of the convent, but she had done so. Gert had promptly called the authorities to inform them that they could call off the citywide search, because Sister had somehow wafted upward on breezes unknown to be with the saints ... the dusty wooden and plaster ones, anyhow. At the time, the whole city considered Sister Mary Eusebius's rescue one of the feel good stories of the month, if not quite a miracle (little did they know), and even Letty had paid Gert a compliment, saying that it had been "a very ecumenical thing" for her to do, "what with helping out the Catholics and all."

Gert now reminded her friend of *that* stir-scrying success and a couple of other select examples from past spellcraft involving the fryer. "I think this could solve your conundrum lickety split," she said while pouring a stream of crystal clear water from Tarpon Springs out of a vial she had also brought from the kitchen. The liquid made a happy little splattering sound against the cast iron surface of the pan. Gert licked her lips with anticipation. Riddle solving was great fun, especially when she was the one using power to do the solving. Given the pain Letty was in, however, and the volatility of her moods even in the most tranquil circumstances, Gert was careful to explain that this was going to be a joint magical venture.

"Letty, you got the gift of Catastrophic Foresight," she burbled pleasantly. "Anything disgusting, vile, and hideous ends up in your head when it comes to that."

"Gee, thanks," sneered Letty, adjusting her compress and peering doubtfully down her nose into the quivering little pool inside the wok.

"I don't mean no offense, of course," explained Gert. "But here's where the two of us can use our powers in tandem to accomplish something crucial. Your head gets saddled with all manner of evil and filth, whereas my vision is occupied with things of beauty and day-in day-out practicality. If we combine our magic, I can pierce through the veils, as it were. I can work my side of things with what you've got to give me."

Letty blinked, wearily. "What sort of spell are you fixing to cast in this particular instance?"

There were literally dozens, as both witches were aware—a slew of spells that could potentially be employed to achieve the desired effect.

"More to the point," added Letty, "what sort of spell am *I* supposed to give you, so that our magic can work in tandem, as you say?"

Letty knew a few spells that fell under that description and was a little vague on the particulars; proactive divination had never been one of her enthusiasms, not when harrowing visions and forebodings tended to descend upon her out of the blue, with no extra effort required what-soever.

Gert bent low over the table and blew gently upon the surface of the spring water. "Oh, you ain't gonna need to use no spell, Letty."

"But I thought you said we were going to work magic together to get to the heart of this."

"We is. Or we are. I'm going to do the spell. Don't worry. It's a good one my Aunt Odina learned from old Baba Yaga when she was ap-prenticing as Baba's housemaid back in the day. You just have to give me some of your magic to gaze through."

"And how do you want me to do that without a spell of my own?" pressed Letty.

"Easy," replied Gert with a colossal and sparklingly white grin. "You just have to spit."

"What?"

"Hold your head back, clear your throat once or twice, and work yourself up the biggest loogie you can. Then give the thing a good ole hawk right into the water, see? But not too forceful that it splashes any liquid out of the vessel. That might damage the framework of the charm. It has to be the right amount of phlegm. Best if you let it just kinda plop gently into the wok, and then I'll cast the enchantment and have myself a good look."

Letty looked at her friend as if not quite certain which one of her ears she intended to smack first.

"Have you lost your mind entirely, woman? What kind of half baked, two-bit hedgewitch nonsense are you trying to put over on me? I've a good mind to send you out on an evening stroll down St. George wearing that wok for a bonnet, and nothing else but your knickers. Do you not realize how serious this predicament could be?"

"I absolutely do," countered Gert, who was more than a little of-fended, given that she was trying to help out of genuine concern for her stricken sidekick. "I wouldn't be going to all this trouble when my most favorite programs are on, one after another, tonight. Not if I thought this was some sort of joke. Really, Letty, you have always been a regular snob when it comes to using the really good, backwoods nitty-gritty my folks taught me when I was just an up and coming practitioner of the Unspeakable Arts.

"That's right. You've always fancied yourself too good for the meat and potato, down and dirty aspects of the Craft, just because you happened to grow up in a big city amongst the type who sipped their nectar from pretty little cups and kept their pinky fingers stuck out straight in the air like they was ready to poke some poor slob's eye out, if that slob was fool enough to get close to y'all, get right nearby as you sat around and talked about how much better you was than the rest of us. As you well know, Leticia Beauregard, I grew up in the woods, where we had to scrape and scrounge for every little bit of magical advantage we could get! We didn't have them fancy spellbooks bound in unicorn leather and decorated with gold leaf made from the dust of dead faery wings. No, ma'am, we did not.

"When I was a tender-horn, we had to learn our hexes the hard way, just so we could keep ourselves from getting chewed up by certain kinds of faeries, swarming thick as mosquitos in them days, as I recall. We had to make our magic work with sticks and stones and scattered bones, while your folk were off fine-tuning your diction, and messing about with the most poetic ways possible to cast your spells. We didn't have the luxury of poetry in the shadow of those big old broody mountains. We couldn't waste our breath crafting epic chants when it behooved us to conjure up just enough wind to get our broomsticks off the ground while being chased by werewolf packs! Our ways were rough around the edges in the big woods, and they weren't very pretty, but you knew you were a sorceress right down to the marrow when you could take a strand of some measly old spider's web and stretch it out long and fast enough to wrap-up an entire gaggle of Wood Wart Ogres that had you cornered, and was about to club your brains out and scramble them up for lunch."

"Oh, why was I born at all?" lamented Letty, but Gert was not to be thwarted.

"You make fun of my methods and cluck your tongue at the very notion of using a little sweat, blood, elbow grease, or spit to activate a spell, but let me tell you one thing: Old Baba Yaga didn't think twice about stuff like that. She would stand up to an Ice Daemon as big as a hillside and you know what she'd do? She'd cackle that awful cackle of hers, hawk a spit-wad right in its eye from two hundred feet, and melt the no good thing down until it was flooding like a river around her boots! Ha! Let me tell you, honey, when ole Baba got to cackling in them deep woods and them beastly black mountains, the troublemakers would make tracks and dare not show their sorry faces again, if they knew what was good for them. Baba lived in a little cabin made of gnarly logs and had but one kettle for cooking, tea, and doing her laundry, and she never so much as stuck out a pinky when she swigged from her jug of liquor. That's right. Baba never wore much but a tattered rag on her head, either, with burlap sacks for skirts, and she wouldn't pluck the bristles from her facial moles for all the gold in a dragon's trove, but she was mightier than mighty!

"You know what else? She stunk—stunk bad enough to clear a forest of every sensitive nosed creature for a two mile radius, but she never fussed with fancy spells. She'd just narrow her one eye, stomp that peg-leg of hers, and cackle. The job got done. My strain of witches didn't have access to elite forms of magic, but what we did have were the no-nonsense wiles passed down to us through the tender mercies of Baba. She was probably the least fancy witch on earth, but the name of Baba Yaga struck fear into the hearts of rotten old kings who wouldn't think twice about carving up their own children for supper! When it came down to hex for hex, fireball for fireball, shamble for shamble, and cackle for cackle, there ain't many witches that live now, lived before, or shall come to live—in this world or any other—that could go toe-to-toe with Baba Yaga, my friend. You're a skillful witch, Letty, and you've come a long way towards getting down from that high horse your folks raised you on, but sometimes I fear you'll never lose that arrogant streak that runs through you like a vein, pumping hoity-toity impulses from that aching head of yours all the way down to your crooked toes. You're a grand witch, Letty, but you ain't no better than me, and you *certainly* ain't no Baba Yaga. If the occasional spit ball or loogie was good enough for her, well, then, it's sure as heck good enough for the likes of you."

Gert set her jaw like stone and regarded the gobsmacked Leticia with an even stonier, yet somehow girlish and mischievously encouraging, gaze.

"So what do you want me to do, Gokey? I can't listen to another word of this jabber."

"Just spit in the wok like I told you, Letty," said Gert, nodding up at her friend's braids. "Because judging from those little drops of blood starting to trickle down your forehead, we may not have a whole lot of time."

VI

The pale, bristling light of a late October dawn cheered the horizon and streaked its way over the Atlantic to dab at the shadows and corners of Serenity Turnbull's kitchen. Near the oceanfront window over the sink, the coffeemaker was wheezing and grunting out the last streams of freshly ground Ethiopian roast while Serenity yawned to greet the waking day. Along the pristine stretch of Vilano Beach, the tide was ebbing and sandpipers darted in manic zigzags, dodging the last, weak surges of foam. A few early risers were getting an industrious start to the day with groggy morning jogs atop the firmest part of the shoreline near the receding surf. A line of pelicans tipped and wheeled seaward to scout the murky chop for signs of breakfast.

"Getting a bit colder, today, Emory," Serenity commented to the Shih Tzu imp, which was gobbling up a bowl of Sustainable Suzie's Biodynamic K-9 Kibble. "The runners have got their sweatpants on for the first time I've seen this Fall, and the pipers look like bright little ice cubes sliding all over the sand."

Emory was unimpressed. *It's warm enough in here,* he noted as his mistress shrugged in agreement. Then the dog abruptly turned off his telepathic signal to gripe to himself about the quality of food still being noisily consumed. It was the worst brand of pet fodder she had come home with to date—like noshing on the cedar wood-chips she had strewn decoratively around a statue of Cerridwen in the backyard. Serenity had been a fair and even-tempered mistress, except for those intermittent fits of panic and pique, and Emory knew full well that there were plenty of poor familiars in Timbuktu who hardly *ever* got a thing to eat, but he did wish she would snap out of the "organic" and "authentically sourced" phase she had been cultivating for the decade he had been at her side. He had served other witches and warlocks in various animal forms down through the centuries, but the Shih Tzu incarnation Serenity had imposed upon him after summoning him up for the job had been the most annoying manifestation he had worked under in ages.

It was worse, even, than the asinine canary one half-deaf old enchantress had made him squeeze into from 1842-1848 in a grungy little Paris flat overlooking the Tuilleries. Had he ever been glad when the bird-body keeled over in its cage while the witch who owned him was down at the market puzzling over baguettes and beignets! That witch used to rap her cane against the cage to keep him tweeting for hours on end, which was an exercise in futility, especially when one was forced to sing for the satisfaction of a crone who could barely hear a thing in the first place. Pure torture. Still, the canary-form had croaked while she was out and that meant he could take a well-deserved breather in the Void ... until the next mage in need of a companion/consultant/spy/pet rang the old incantation bell and, if you were not an especially potent spirit, like Emory, up drifted your shade from relative peace and quiet to begin your next tour of duty.

Luckily, Emory figured the Shih Tzu had only two or three years to go before succumbing to the torment of organ failure or perhaps sheer gastronomic boredom, what with the unconvincing grub. As a familiar spirit, he had always found small lapdogs to be good only for the amusement of neurotic, socially stunted masters who had trouble relating to their own kind. They were also good for irritating the life out of virtually every other creature on the planet. Thus, Emory was currently deep in a self-loathing complex, especially when he chanced to pass a floor-length mirror and behold his scraggly, smashed-in looking face, invariably bug eyed expression, and trademark under-bite. That was the pitfall of being a Third Class Spirit.

You simply weren't strong enough to turn down job offers from lesser witches with bad taste in dog breeds.

Emory let out a snorting sigh of relief as he finished the last of the "Nutritionally Cohesive and SUPER YUMMY!" crap in his dog bowl. Things could have been much worse; Serenity might have displayed a thing for Yorkies, after all. Hopefully, there was an inattentive possum or perhaps a swamp rat loitering about the yard, something he could thrash and mangle when she let him out to do his "pooties" before bedtime. That sort of activity was his only form of pleasure, these days, and even that had to be done with discretion, since M'Lady was such a softie.

Serenity filled her coffee mug with a steaming flourish and trudged upstairs to her bedroom. There were things to accomplish today, before getting ready to teach the afternoon "Best Friend Within" class at Flagler College. First, there was the matter of sending an RSVP for Rowan Blaize's All Hallow's Eve party. The more she had thought of it in the wake of the previous night's episode, the more galvanized she was to attend the bash and find some way of showing the Pepper Witches that they were no longer going to force *her* into some permanent "category" in town by the sheer weight of their condescension, no matter how helpful they mistook themselves for being. Attendance would also afford an opportunity to pay a little more attention to Rowan Blaize himself, and he was due some attention, as she sensed he liked her to some degree that was quite distinct from the way he liked the Datil Duo. Besides, had she not a bit of a duty to make an appearance at such a gathering, being one of the four genuine sorcerers to inhabit the unassuming Ancient City? Perhaps for this reason alone, she thought, she ought to have bucked-up and attended the previous year.

Better late than never, she opined. There was still time to take control of her image as a witch in the community and mold it according to her own designs. Though she did not like to lord her powers over the slew of other magical beings in St. Augustine (like Letty and Gert did all the time—Did Rowan do the same?), she contemplated the possibility that her reputation as a spell-caster might be in question, and that gossip amongst the eerie hordes might have painted her as a timid or weak witch. Even Serenity knew that this sort of publicity was never, ever good. Next you knew, the imps were raiding your pantry in the middle of the night and a witch might as well clear out of town if word like *that* ever made the rounds. There was a slight responsibility when it came to keeping up appearances, for a witch—even such an unconventional witch as Serenity. The timing of her decision to finally accept Rowan's invitation might be ideal.

Of course, there was the matter of proper attire. Serenity did not think that Rowan Blaize adhered to any sort of strict supernatural dress code. Everyone had seen him, or his mortal Girl Friday, Miranda, outfitted like any other respectably fashionable Ancient City-dweller—smart khaki shorts, linen short-sleeves, leather sandals and sunglasses in summer, jeans, dress-shirts, blouses and tailored jackets in winter. That being the case, Serenity was also aware that every true magician owned work clothes appropriate to their occult status and reserved these much more elaborate and ceremonial trappings for special convocations and other occasions. She herself had two or three flying gowns that were nothing to sneeze at. One, spun from *argiope* silk, had been handed-down by her mother, who had always been self-consciously witchy, and another ensemble Serenity herself had commissioned a little caravan of wandering Shadwocks to run-up for her around the middle of the Seventeenth Century. The poor things had skulked through her village on the Normandy Coast one evening, next to starving for lack of reputable work, and she had taken pity upon them. The resulting garment was splendid—a flowing but form-fitting number fashioned from reconstituted pixie tresses and dyed with indigo from Alexandria.

Serenity sat down with her coffee at the little vanity table by her bed and resolved to wear the Shadwock dress to the party. Perhaps, if they were still on hand, she would get one of the nixies in the koi pond to do her hair up into something a little—or a lot—more regal than the hemp-like folksinger's braid she often sported about town. She looked in the mirror, turning her face this way and that. Yes, with one of her grandmother's Chimaera pendants and a pair of dangly, platinum Hypnalis earrings, it would be possible to make a significant impression at the feast, one that would leave no doubt about her position as one of the quartet of thaumaturgical pillars in town.

But there were other things to accomplish today, as well, including another very important RSVP, of sorts. Percival's proposal was going to get the speedy response it merited, enhanced by a hefty dose of her magical disapproval at his presumptuousness and all-around lack of romantic finesse. A brief but remonstrative strangling-spell would be just the thing, if she were a much meaner witch. She would at all events make it clear to him that, while she was very much a non-traditionalist and encouraged such traits in other supernatural creatures, she was not, by any means, *that* offbeat or outré. Basic manners still meant something, even to a religiously liberal witch like her.

The absurd ring, of course, would have to be sent back along with her refusal.

She slurped a little more coffee and stared at the humongous ruby on her dressing table. It seemed to shimmer in the reflection of the large mirror, which was bedecked along the framework with a collection of environmental activist stickers and individualistic, life-affirming slogans. She grimaced. It was a truly ugly ring in every respect; Percival knew that she disliked rubies and worshipped turquoise, and she thought him most lackadaisical to have sent her a gem with a band sized for an ogre's thumb. Who cares if it came from some royal eunuch's tomb from the depths of the past? Serenity also came from the depths of the past, though certainly not that deep. Oh, well, a rather healthy sprite would have to be conjured to make the return delivery, and the power required for such a summons would likely leave her exhausted and moody for the rest of the week. Still, she was determined to deal with it. Not another day would she allow to go by with Percival thinking she was across continents and oceans pining away for him, simply swooning with satisfaction at the prospect of being his bride. Back to the archaeological dig in Damascus (or wherever he was) would go the offensive gift along with a piece of her mind written carefully down on thrice-recycled papyrus.

She fished around in her bureau drawer for a pen and some of her favorite stationery. Emory came grumbling and puffing to the top of the stairs to see what she was up to. A laser-like panel of the rising sun's light pierced her bedroom curtains and danced upon the mirror before cascading down in a radiant waterfall upon the clumsy ring. The long, etched inscription on the golden band was illuminated until the lettering had an almost fiery sheen. The glow caught Serenity's eye and she paused to consider a slight adjustment in her strategy. Placing the fresh envelope and paper upon her tabletop, she wondered whether Percival's folly might offer the benefit of some minor amusement before she fired off the fateful note to her suitor. Translating the ring's inscription would also provide an opportunity to utilize her Grandmother's most treasured heirloom. Where had she put that old cipher-stone, anyhow? Her highly disorganized closet was the likeliest spot, so she went to hunt for the talisman, now mildly intrigued.

"It would be a fine thing if that wretched inscription turns out to preserve some archaic words of wisdom or another timeless adage that might show silly Percival the error of his ways and offer insights to help him improve his worldview in the future, when it comes to seeking a proper mate to share in his dry-as-old-toast existence!" she grumbled with an emphatic nod toward Emory. The familiar sat on its haunches and watched his mistress rummage with the kind of disconnected interest that only the bulging, crazy eyes of a Shih Tzu could convey.

"Aha!" said Serenity after a moment foraging through the heap of old boxes, faded protest signs, Greenpeace bumper stickers, stacks of old Mother Jones magazines, bins full of slightly smelly seashells, and other bits of paraphernalia that had made the transition with her from Berkeley to the coquina-rich shores of St. Augustine. Beneath a coffee table-sized cookbook devoted exclusively to eggplant and lentil recipes, Serenity found the Charm Trove, which was really more of a box than a trove, but the most ornate and exquisitely crafted thing she possessed, and with good reason. Roughly the size and shape of a small, oblong sewing basket, the darkly polished and stained alder-wood container was carved with intricate scenes detailing the life and times of Cerridwen, who had long been rumored to be a distant relation by some of the older and more socially self-conscious branches of Serenity's sprawling and labyrinthine family tree. No one in her surviving family, of course, had ever actually had Cerridwen over for dinner and drinks, at least as far as anybody knew, but witches liked to advance the dignity of a muddy pedigree whenever possible, and a goddess-in-the-woodpile was always a solid reference, even if the lineage was a tad difficult to trace back for the most intrepid occult historians and genealogists.

No matter the authenticity or lack thereof when it came to this particular connection, Serenity's Charm Trove was a work of crafts-manship befitting, if not a deity, then certainly one of the deities' most favored handmaids. Embossed at the outer edges with jewel encrusted dragon-bone, elaborate gold hinges at the back, and a front latch fastened from the clicking front fangs of a Northumberland Were-Goat, the pre-cious container had been the greatest inheritance in Serenity's magical journey. It had belonged to her grandmother, Thecla, who had herself in-herited the thing and had sworn to the veracity of its divine provenance. Trends and fads and men and travels and familiars and adventures all passed by in a blur across the centuries of Serenity's life, but this gift had been the one piece of luggage she had brought through the muck and mist of the ages, along with her very self. She had never misplaced the Trove, and no one had ever managed to steal it—not for very long, anyhow—thanks to the complexity of spells her grandmother had placed upon the thing before bequeathing it to her.

Though brigands and thieves of various skill-sets had been vouch-safed a glimpse of the beguiling box over the years due to Serenity's pro-clivity for wanderlust in diverse global environments, no one, mortal or magical, who had ever attempted to meddle with the thing had walked away unscathed in return for their machinations or mere curiosity. A sort of ethereal homing-device had likewise been woven into the spell surrounding the protective features of the box. On one occasion nearly two hundred-fifty years earlier, Serenity had been obliged to retrieve her Trove on the fast-fleeing pirate ship of a particularly enterprising Ja-maican rumrunner. The ordeal had been a considerable bother. To begin with, the captain's hands had been turned to stone the moment he had tried to break open the fanged Were-Goat latch, and the hardscrabble hearts of his jaunty, pillaging crew may as well have been turned to mush when Serenity had come swooping down out of the boiling clouds on her flying staff, honing-in on the box's signal.

All of that kerfuffle had come to pass because Serenity and the entire crew of the *Redheaded Doxie* had spent the previous evening kicking up a bit of a row at one of the inns in old Kingston and, though all had come to respect Serenity for her ability to drink the most seasoned seadogs under the table, none of them had been prepared for the sight of the same maiden flying, vengeful and distraught, down upon their heads the next day after sleeping off her share of the grog. They had stolen her Trove and, in return, Serenity had landed on the ship's deck and made her stern-faced, accusing way without incident or impediment past the quaking, rather sudden and outwardly religious crew to the captain's quarters, where the fearless leader was blubbering like a baby and attempting to drag his hands—now made of diorite—up from the floor planks.

"That'll learn you to mess with a witch's belongings," Serenity had said, wagging a lily white finger of admonishment. "And to think you boys robbed me after such a pleasant evening of cocktails, too!"

Then she had lifted daintily the hem of her skirts and flown off into the Caribbean sunset with her most cherished possession, while the boson, first mate, and a few toothless swabbers jumped overboard wailing prayers and holy names they had not used since the innocence of childhood, if they had ever a shred of innocence—or childhood—at all.

Though she might have tried, Serenity had done nothing about Captain Gallanty's heavy hands. She had not been quite as compassionate and forgiving a witch back then as she was now, at least when it came to the outright theft of her rather limited belongings, and even less when she was on holiday. In subsequent years, she had often wondered whatever became of the man. She imagined that his career on the high seas must have been effectively halted. There was not much point in trying to make a living, even an illicit one, atop the vast surface of a substance you would never, ever be able to move successfully around in, except for straight down. His had probably ended up being a difficult life, if he had even managed to go on living much longer at all.

Spells like that could take the starch out of even the hardiest mortals. Certainly, no legends of the "Stonefingered Captain of the Doxie" or the "Ruin of Rockfisted Gallanty" had filtered down to her through the years since the theft. It might be interesting, she thought, to spend a day at the library, or waste one plumbing the depths of Google, to see if there was any trace of relevant folklore. Almost to the last, witches loved folklore, and the folklore they loved best was the folklore in which they, personally, played starring roles, or instigated some adventure or other. Serenity Turnbull, bleeding heart that she was, was not immune to her own apocryphal allure.

For now, however, as she lugged the little box out from amid the clutter of the closet, the encounter with the pirates was just one more happy memory related to the container, and to its somewhat colorful history as a marker of the not inconsiderable travels she had undertaken in search of Herself. Genuine magic boxes were undeniably handy for such journeys; they not only managed to repel the majority of thieves, but, by their very nature, deflected dirt and dust-bunnies, too. It was all due to the inherent metaphysical energy fields. That was a superlative bonus in the eyes of a witch with allergies, and Serenity worried about sneezing. If Serenity sneezed, things had a tendency to shatter or crack. Like fine china, if any happened to be nearby. When she happened to be dining with royalty. That, however, is another tale.

She sighed with nostalgic satisfaction and cleared a space for the box on her dressing table. It would open only at her touch, and even then only with the recitation of the proper spell, which she had never forgotten since it had been drummed into her head by her grandmother, who had been on her very death-grove at the time. She passed her delicate hands over the box and whispered the incantation now:

"O Trove that holds my heart's delight,
unlock thyself so that I might
behold the treasures safe inside,
where's love's bright splendor
doth abide."

Serenity rolled her eyes. It was admittedly a rather twee "old lady incantation" and her grandmother had never bothered to change it into something more appropriate to a granddaughter's personality or unique set of interests when she passed it on. It worked, and that was the important thing. The Were-Goat fangs unlatched with a sharp click, the cover of the sacred box sprang open a few inches, and Serenity smiled to think of her Gran. Even a somewhat jaded witch's heart could be a deep and secret wellspring of romance and she was suddenly quite glad the old girl had never altered the Opening Spell. The only things her grandmother had ever kept in the Trove had been a handful of small amulets, assorted talismans, and every love letter she had ever received from her six century-long affair with a dashing faery lord named Branthus. All but one of the love letters had been burned, but one remained in the box and Serenity touched it with the tip of her finger. *Where love's bright splendor doth abide, indeed,* she thought. All the sad sea turtle injustices in the world could not trump sappy sorceress-sentiment in the rich, nougaty center of Serenity's pulsating and earnest spirit.

She opened the lid wide and gazed at the small collection of personal treasures she had accumulated and stored in the box since it had been given to her so long ago. There were blue velvet-tied locks of hair from both of her mortal husbands and some from her half-mortal sons—all she had left of their physical presence outside of memory, and it was only the magic of the box that kept these things from becoming dust. She touched each lock gently and moved on with the ingrained acceptance of mortal ephemerality that characterized most all magical creatures, even if they had enjoyed intimacy with mortals and, in Serenity's case, had passed on a bloodline that was never guaranteed to lift a hybrid offspring from the specter of eventual death—the Fate that Countenances No Refusal for the human Sons and Daughters of Earth.

A tiny, moldering book of all-purpose enchantments was next to the cuttings of hair. No larger than the plate covering the light-switch near her vanity table mirror, the volume contained much of what she knew and had needed to utilize for quick reference as a girl. Its translucent pages were lined with endless rows of miniscule script in Latin and other tongues, some lost and some still hanging on in various forms, along with intricate illustrations and sigil arrangements. That book had been a gift from her mother, written and crafted by a rickety old warlock who had been posing, peacefully, as a Greek Orthodox hermit on Mount Athos for years.

Serenity picked up the book and smelled of its musty, powerful aroma. She still knew most of the contents by heart, her retentive powers on par with those of other respectable witches who made it a point to never forget the basics when it came to spell-casting. Certainly, she had browsed through more complicated magical tomes in her time, and had written down a number of trickier, more convoluted rituals, but for the most part she had gotten along quite nicely with the generic material, helped more than a little by the fact that she did hail from inherently powerful stock with a robust occult metabolism. This suitably potent natural ability always made even the most pedestrian charms more effective and imposing. That was the nature of individual witchcraft and its wide-ranging spectrum of practitioners. As a result, the marginally gifted had to work very hard, the truly talented had to expend only a modicum of effort, and the geniuses seemed only to have to will things into being, even though Serenity knew full well that the best specimens of her kind were wise enough to keep their flame burning brightly due to constant practice and study.

For a moment, she pondered the enchanted hierarchy of drowsy, intoxicating St. Augustine within such a framework. She was not a vain witch, or a delusional one, and would put herself squarely in the "respectably gifted" category, while the Datil Pepper witches had undeniable talent, and Rowan Blaize ... well, Rowan Blaize was one of the Old Ones, and unquestionably a genius. If not more than that. The most shiftless witch in the world could smell the superiority emanating from him. Nevertheless, in the presence of Letty, Gert, Rowan, and certainly any of the lesser supernatural folk about town, she was like most of her race and would not be caught dead intimating that she, too, was anything less than a prodigy. It simply was not done. Witches and warlocks knew that it was always advisable to keep everyone guessing on that count— especially each other, if possible. A sliver of doubt could mean the difference between parting company with a terse bow and a muttered "Good day to you!" or engaging in a duel wherein someone ended-up as a column of ash, or worse.

Even the most earth-shatteringly potent magicians, however, appreciated the value of a rare tool, a mighty talisman. Indeed, the greatest sorcerers were the ones who usually invented such things (or managed to wheedle them away or even steal them from the Archons, the Ruling Powers), and Serenity was quite proud of the fact that she possessed such a coveted object for her very own. At least, it would be coveted if any of her peers over the years had known she actually had it. There it was, bequeathed to her along with the Cerridwen Box that contained it—a smooth round disc of amber no larger than a teacup saucer, with a hole the size of a quarter through the center. Dangling on a chain or a bit of hemp twine, the thing would appear no more interesting than one of the hippy pendants Serenity used to make with her stone-polishing machine and sell every summer from her booth in the shady oak plaza across from the Cathedral Basilica downtown. But the Cipher Stone was much, much more.

She picked it up and savored its cool surface before clutching it almost protectively against the front of her pastel green nightgown. Wouldn't old Beauregard and Gokey steam like a couple of boiling kettles if they knew she owned such an item! Doubtless they would tell her she was much too "airheaded" and "misdirected" to be entrusted with the proper care of such a dainty.

"Imagine!" gasped Serenity to Emory, who was still squatting near the top of the stairs, tongue lolling and eyes popping. "Those two bats would quibble with me over my own property. What dark chasms of insecurity must exist to prompt an envious heart down the lonesome path of its own destructive foray!"

She wasn't really conversing with her familiar so much as she was conversing with herself. Serenity was an expressive creature and believed a decent rhetorical flourish ought never to be wasted, especially if there was only one in the audience and you were both the audience and the flourishing rhetorician.

"Those two in their high and mighty brass brassieres would dare to believe that they know better than my own grandmother knew about the handing-on of her legacies. Letty and Gert would have the audacity to believe that, in a perfect universe, this sort of trinket would somehow find its way into their clutches, not mine. Then, of course," added Serenity, waving the cipher stone back and forth in front of Emory, as if to drive home a point, "they would end up squabbling over it between themselves, if one or the other had it!"

Emory tilted his head and pondered his mistress and her penchant for self-amusement. *Witches are so imaginative,* he reasoned. *They really do have to create little hypothetical scenarios and potential intrigues, complete with extensive dialogue, just to entertain themselves. Just to keep those brains and synapses on rapid-fire ... or whatever it is that makes them tick.*

Of course, he had witnessed this sort of display from Serenity before, and did not deem her latest self-production to be as relevant as his need to wander over to the drapes at the far end of the bedroom and pee on them with lifted leg when she wasn't looking.

Serenity, for her part, studied the cipher stone.

"Why, I imagine that Rowan Blaize, whoever he is and wherever he comes from and from whatever marvelous history he emanates, would fancy having a look at this little bauble owned by daffy little Serenity Turnbull. But we musn't ever let him have a look at it! Heavens, no. I'll go to the great All Hallow's Eve party, but they can all mind their own affairs when it comes to poking their noses into my personal life and my interests. Not one of them has ever bothered to try and fully understand my intentions, and no one can admire what they don't at least attempt to understand. Not Rowan. Not Letty. Not Gert. And certainly not that diffident little egret, Percival!"

She picked up the ruby ring by its hulking jewel. Next, she brought the cipher stone into the light of her vanity table bulbs and the rays of sunshine that swelled through the window, positioning its see-through hole over the golden band. The cipher stone had been created by some Extraordinary Power, supposedly, in the very snaking mists at the dawn of time, and even her grandmother, great as she was, never had a firm idea about its exact origins, or even how such a magnificent thing had passed into their family, which was not a particularly noble or infamous brood among the citizens of the magical realm. There were a few, shimmering edges of myth, however. Vague tales, like flecks of gold managing to shine up from the silt of muddy streams, collided with whispers among the Very Knowledgeable and with writings in various tomes, about a series of faded yellow discs that had once been stolen from the rubble of the long-destroyed Tower of Babel. No one had ever been able to authenticate or prove such a thing, one way or another. There were, in fact, many ciphering stones and similar devices littered about the witchy world. All Serenity knew for sure was that this artifact had somehow come into her family's possession, where it had been ferociously guarded and kept quite secret.

Its power was clear and direct—one did not need an incantation to activate it. The cipher stone could render an exact translation of any written inscription in any language that had ever existed in magical and non-magical worlds, or worlds not yet even in existence, supposedly. By looking through the stone as one passed it over a bit of unknown writing or inscription, the exact nature of the words would be revealed in whatever language was desired or willed by the wielder of the stone. Chewing with curiosity on her lower lip, Serenity passed the amber stone over the faint etching on the ring's rugged golden band. As she did so, she read aloud what she saw, for she was also the sort of creature which often read things aloud without actually thinking or realizing that she did so, which, in her capacity as a sorceress, must be considered a professional flaw, since all witches are advised to be quite conscious of the possible repercussions of speaking words of uncertain provenance aloud, no matter when spoken. Words were power, and magicians tended not to take them lightly, or if they did, they were fairly certain they had a firm grip on their surroundings before taking them lightly.

Serenity read, one eye closed, staring through the hole in the stone, speaking in the slow, mechanical monotone of an archaeologist— perhaps even an archaeologist like Percival—struggling to accurately transliterate a line of faded temple hieroglyphics in an inconveniently dim light.

"Whoever … has the … grave misfortune … of speaking … aloud … the words … of this secret … inscription … that I, Marutha … inscribed … hereupon … will break … the infernal … seal … and … find …themselves … at the mercy … of mighty … Dedwen."

"Dedwen? Who's *Dedwen?*" muttered Serenity, standing straight and cocking her head toward that spot in the universe where Foolish Questions are indeed sometimes rewarded with the Forthright Answers they so richly deserve.

The ring began to wobble a bit in her hand and, at first, Serenity thought that this was due to the fact that the gemstone was so outlandishly large and unwieldy that she had merely lost a proper grip on the band. Then she realized, in a flash of achingly black and perhaps infinitely abysmal despair, that, yes, she *was* a bit of a careless, scattered, and sometimes flat-out airheaded witch, after all.

The ruby ring flew out of her hand and bounced off the vanity mirror, which smashed into a black widow's web-work of crazed glass. Clattering amid her hodgepodge of sustainable and thoroughly mineral-based cosmetics, the enormous ruby began to pulsate with a most discouraging and disturbing light that flashed blood-red bursts throughout the room and across Serenity's increasingly horrified expression. She backed away toward the closet, clutching the cipher stone and nearly tripping over Emory, who was dancing in bug-eyed, frenzied circles around her retreating feet, Shih Tzu shrieks at full volume. It was then that a gently boiling, almost metallic blue smoke, like a glint of the Nile in full flood at its southernmost source, began to grow in a billowing cloud from the surface of the vibrating gem, extending in mere seconds outward and across the bedroom, then upward from the floor to obscure even the ceiling fan that hung from the arched roof. Madly, reflexively, Serenity reached over and switched on the ceiling fan to its third and most high-powered rotational speed, as if this act of technological convenience would dissipate the roiling blue and ominous supernatural presence that was taking over her boudoir.

This plan did not work.

Serenity's eyes widened in grave concern, bulging almost as crazily as those of the bedraggled dog-familiar, which had ceased shrieking and was now hiding behind the hem of its mistress's Japanese silk kimono bathrobe.

"Ohhhh …." squeaked Serenity, faintly, as tiny but jagged bursts of lightning were manifested here and there throughout the blue-green wall of cloud, sizzling and snapping as if the angriest coattail of some churning electric storm had happened to spin off from its host and somehow get trapped inside her house. But this was no storm, and Serenity had the unnervingly distinct sense that she was the only thing "trapped" in this place.

Aye yi yi! Surely Leticia Beauregard would describe this feeling as one very similar to her famous forebodings, Serenity thought with the random, ineffectual displacement activity of someone who shall soon end-up the victim of a potentially traumatic and incapacitating shock. Meanwhile, the manic veins of lightning flashed with even greater frequency, an apparent crescendo of fury coming from the midst of the dire cloud, now accompanied by a low peal of thunder that sounded as if it had made its laborious way across many millions—perhaps even billions—of years to impress her alone with its stark solemnity.

"Ohhhh …" squeaked Serenity again. Her eyes darted about the room. There was the ring, still on the dressing table next to her smashed mirror, but it was no longer connected to the horrible veil of acrid blue smoke it had produced. Perhaps she ought to go and grab it? Perhaps there was an inscription on the inside of the band that might reverse the monstrous display that had been burgeoning before her eyes. But she did not move, for she did not believe there was really another inscription on the inside of the golden band. There never was, in such cases. She had a dreadful certainty about that. In fact, it was likely not a very good idea to even handle the ring again at all.

Just then, a terrible new ruckus occurred, something that looked and sounded like a searing, cyclonic sandstorm began to whistle and whir and roar within the surface of the blue bank of smoke and doom. Serenity gulped and Emory began to whimper. The string of hemp tying her strawberry blonde ponytail at the end snapped and whizzed across the room and her hairs, to the last, began to creep up and stand on end. Various objects all around began to rise from their surfaces and fly from nooks and crannies, spinning wildly as projectile manifestations of her near-hysterical concern. Guadalupe, the anaconda, who had been lurking beneath the bed, whizzed by in knots and promptly flew out a bedroom gable window that was now banging open and shut of its own accord.

"Ohhhh ..." Serenity whined. She had to pull herself together, for things were not apt to end with the fireworks and other atmospherics that had been set in motion by Percival's wretched engagement ring. Then, as swiftly as she realized this, her mind also produced a bitter confession: *It wasn't the ring that set whatever-this-is in motion ... it was YOU, you fool, by having the nonchalance to read an unknown ancient inscription aloud, and not even having the good sense to STOP reading when it literally warned you of woe halfway through! IDIOT!*

Still, there was no time for self-recrimination now. Her thoughts bounced frantically, one off of the other. Some sort of protective or defensive spell was in order, given her hunch that she would discover the source of this supernatural tempest presently. What else could she do? Her flying staff was downstairs—drat!—and there'd be no time to get to it, anyhow, because the stairwell was blocked by the noxious and pervasive cloud. A spell, a spell! She yammered a bit and then opted for the most powerful Sheltering Chant she knew. But she had to concentrate to impart the full extent of her power, and it was very difficult at this moment to focus. Still, she did her best:

> *Ye hidden hosts that haunt the day,*
> *now heed my spell and wend this way.*
> *Around my form protection place*
> *to spurn the gaze of Evil's face.*
> *Come Maids of Isis, Leto's Lads!*
> *Come one, come all, in droves, in scads.*
> *A potent shield do now erect ...*
> *... Withstand the doom that I suspect!*

Serenity spread her arms wide and felt the shimmering inrush of mystical air as the unseen forces she had summoned began to coagulate in an ethereal chain, building the classic witch's sheltering enclosure around her person. Whatever strange force or phantasm had found its way out of the awful ring, it would have a fearsome challenge ahead if it were to penetrate the intricate tapestry of spiritual entities she had conjured to her assistance. In seconds she felt the fulsome security of her spell take effect as she squinted through the slightly quivering air of her magical force-field at the hissing, explosive cloud, trying to gain some sense of what it might possibly be, what manner of unclean thing had been unleashed. If successful, she could perhaps fathom a means to control and manage the intrusive presence, or flee, if necessary. She had never seen anything quite like this, that much was certain.

Alas, she was to accomplish neither management nor flight, for no sooner had her sheltering spell achieved the full force of its sanctuary effect, when the entire enchantment she had cast was smashed—smashed as if by a trillion grains of stinging sand and dispelled into nothingness by a downburst of superheated air. Serenity and little Emory were hurled head over feet across the bed and against the wall with a sickening thud that sent their crumpled bodies slamming, at last, onto the floor. The witch landed on her hands and knees, severely injured, her hair blown forward to cover her face like a mask of straw. Emory howled in pain and tried to drag himself on front paws beneath the cover of the nearby desk, both of his hind legs shattered by the brutal impact.

A different kind of smoke could now be sensed in the room. Serenity wiped a bit of blood from her lower lip with the palm of her hand and, panting in terror and shock, parted the hair in front of her face and looked up. There, standing with fiendish supremacy amid the remnants of the unholy blue cloud, was a daemon the likes of which she had never encountered in all her centuries of adventure and inquisition, a hulking beast of such fetid and muscular malevolence as she had only ever heard about in stories and tales told to frighten even the children of witches and haunt their already enchanted midnight dreams.

Covered with pockmarked skin as thick and rugged as rhinoceros hide, the gargantuan legs and arms of the monstrosity exuded a grotesque mist the same color as the cloud from which it had materialized. Each appendage was covered in warped, oblong scales that resembled the plated armor of some long extinct reptile of the archaic world, and venom-dripping spines jutted out between these scales at almost every edge, especially around the behemoth's audibly creaking joints. Three shiny black digits clicked and rasped and grasped with nervous, threatening movements at the ends of the thing's feet and hands. A small, sinewy waist ballooned into a massive torso covered with writhing tendrils of seaweed-like skin growths, patches of brown and matted fur. Exposed sections of red-raw pectoral muscle were pierced by dozens of jangling silver ringlets, like the chain mail of some hell-spawned knight. Most terrifying of all was the head that rested, or rather seemed to protrude, from a leathery collar of flared and upturned horns around the neck and over the impossibly broad shoulders that were nearly half the width of the room.

Serenity could do nothing but stare at that awful head. Its maw of central fangs dripped pus and viscous pink saliva onto the floor as great mandibles on either side of the orifice clacked and clattered to slurp up the oozing stream. Three eyes, each as large as a dinner plate, were dominated by irises the color of volcanic fire and pupils that were hazy green and feline. These orbs stared down and around, at the room, at its own body, as if disoriented, weary, or bewildered. Serenity tried not to gasp, even as her body was wracked with a spasm of searing pain. The eyes—yes the three eyes positioned above insidious black holes that served as nostrils!—gave the nature of this intruder away and the fallen witch was mortified. This was, without question, one of the djinn, and *not* a member of the minor hierarchy.

This was one of the Exceeding Ones—Serenity would have bet the very breath in her lungs upon it ... if she thought she would continue to *possess* breath to use as collateral for such a wager! Desperate, she tried to steady herself, but was seized by another jolt of pain. Her ankle was broken, she could sense it. Probably a couple of ribs, as well. Never had she suffered such injury in all of her long life. Her gaze darted toward Emory, who was now peeking out from behind the antique desk amid the pungent blue mist and remaining billows of smoke that floated and swirled.

Think, Serenity, think!

She had never been innately powerful enough to employ dematerialization spells, or even to risk casting one so that she might vanish in a puff of her own vapor and reappear somewhere else—anywhere else!—for the sake of a moment's safety. Only the greatest sorcerers could use such magic without fear of ending-up trapped between the suffocating walls of adjoining worlds, or of drifting endless and alone amid the forgotten currents of another dimension. Serenity knew a rather strong relocation spell, one that ought to at least get her outside the house and perhaps able to hide beneath one of the oleander bushes in the backyard like a chastened, scurrying rat, only there was still the risk of making an error in her weakened condition and vanishing forever without hope of rescue. Trapped!

She was on the verge of panic. She thought foolishly of an invisibility chant, but that would only be a waste of power: a djin of *this* caliber would easily be able to see through any cloaking charm she might finagle. Why, its mere emergence had blown her strongest Sheltering spell to bits! What fireballs she could expel from her fingers—and Serenity was actually adept with fireballs—would have about as much affect upon such a monster as tossing balls of cotton at it. Even if she had had her flying staff handy, the thing would have been able to catch her in a heartbeat, if it so desired. Everyone knew that the djinn could fly rings around the world, down to the most meager members of their race. Still, Serenity wished the staff were in the room so that she could at least blast through the now-shattered bedroom window and give a swift getaway one good try. Perhaps the colossus was not interested, or would not be interested, in pursuing her. It did not matter; there was no flying staff at hand and all she had now at her disposal were her wits.

Djinn were fearsomely powerful and built for trouble. Even mortals, however, had been known to outsmart them or outmaneuver them using only their wiles and, sometimes, a bit of witty repartee. A solitary djin—mighty or meager—was not a being that necessarily thought in linear ways akin to other supernatural beings. Twists in logic and puzzles and riddles could sometimes fool them, even as they employed such methods to the ruin of others. Serenity gritted her teeth. If a common mortal pickpocket like Aladdin had been able to manipulate such incomparably harrowing spirits, then certainly a witch who had the experience of centuries under her belt stood a chance at some successful bit of parley. But the Aladdin brat's case had been quite different, she knew. *His* djin had been unwittingly released but was bound by magic to remain at the service of its liberator. Serenity had set free this nightmare unwittingly, too, but the translated words of the ring's inscription blazed across her mind, taunting her even now. The emancipator of this djin was not destined to be served, but was instead at the mercy of the escapee, and djinn—at least ones that looked and smelled like this specimen— were not noted for their mercy. Throughout the many years of her vagabond existence, Serenity had gleaned that much about the natures of such beings, though she had never personally encountered them. Until now.

What to do? *What to do?*

The hideous thing was now looking straight down into her eyes, as if from the top of some storm-shrouded mountain. Little bolts of lightning snapped from the collar of horns to the top of the gruesome head amid dank clouds of steam roiling off the summit. Serenity was paralyzed by its tripartite gaze. Moving its bulk forward one step, the sheer weight of the great devil caused the floor to groan and start caving in. The repulsive head crashed into the ceiling fan, which snapped like a toothpick, as did one of the rafter beams extending from one side of the arched roof to the other. This bottom-to-top display of structural instability distracted the slime-drooling djin, which puffed an exhalation of sulfurous fire from the triad of nostrils. It looked askance and lifted a great arm to tear down the rest of the dangling beam it had dislodged. The floor lowed like a cow with a broken back beneath its gargantuan feet and Serenity sensed her chance. The forceful punch of a well-aimed disintegration spell would weaken the strained surface beneath the creature and ensure its collapse, allowing her to use the djin's own weight as a weapon and send it crashing through to the floor downstairs. This would be no great injury to the mammoth malignance fifteen feet away, but it might just buy her the time she needed to confuse it or at least drag herself to the balcony and perhaps levitate down into the shadowy cover of the nearby oak grove and hide, if she had any strength left at all. The beast grunted in annoyance and, with clutching black talons, plunged the splintered beam and ceiling fan through the dry-wall above the staircase as if shoving a birthday candle through the frosting on top of a cake.

Serenity clenched her teeth, drew back her bruised and battered arm, and struck for all she was worth.

"Crumbling surface, failing hold—Mind my spell and do as told.
All that keeps thy form intact, I sunder with this potent act!"

The force of the incantation was hurled from Serenity's lips and fingers as if she were pitching a scorcher of a fireball, and the magic leapt from her being, drawing upon the occult forces she had maneuvered into one concentrated burst. With a shuddering impact it struck hard at the floor beneath the djin and rocked the entire house. A circle of Berber carpet caved in with a deafening crunch and it appeared that the startled invader was about to plow through to the bottom, taking most of the upstairs down with it. Alas, with a malevolent narrowing of its feline pupils the djin lifted its arms and gashed great holes through the rooftop on either side to gain immediate purchase and restore its compromised footing. It stretched one enormous leg against the corner of the stairwell and wedged the other upon a portion of the bedroom flooring that had not fallen victim to its oppressive bulk.

Stretched wide and awkwardly, but stabilized, the djin glared in anger at the cowering witch and snarled. Muttering deep and devilish words Serenity could not understand, the djin undertook a spell of its own and before her despairing eyes it morphed, rippling and bubbling almost as if it had become a liquid entity. It did not, however, assume some other form, as the djinn are so often fond of doing. Rather, it merely reduced its enormity by half—rendering it ever as loathsome and intimidating in appearance, but now quite agile enough to sidestep the upstairs sinkhole and stride menacingly toward the quivering, exhausted form of Serenity Turnbull. She was still in a semi-kneeling position, huddled near the wall against which she had first been flung.

She did not scream as the enemy approached. Witches, above all, know that screams are usually pointless in a world full of screams that are routinely ignored by the indifferent, and she did not take her own eyes away from the accursed trio of orbs now fixed upon her. If this was to be her last moment of existence in *this* existence, she was determined to carry the moment with as much dignity as she could muster. That is another thing witches are known to manage, if they can: obstinately haughty demises.

Emory the Shih Tzu shook like a leaf in a gale as his mistress was lifted up by a talon placed carefully (and thus far bloodlessly) beneath her chin. Up, up, up she was hoisted, wincing as she felt a bone in her leg grind where it had been fractured in the initial blast of the djin's emergence. Pain was a relatively foreign sensation to most respectable magicians, but Serenity managed the intensity of hers with a deepening calm. She did not blink an eye, though her head was covered in drywall dust and blood trickled from her nose. She tightened her talon-suspended jaw as much as she dared. The djin tilted its abominable head this way and that as it studied her tiny skull.

"XXrbxx Nyyrrt vrrkkkwlln Zjjvvrb, Marutha?" said the creature in a voice like the low but resonant sound of a great booming drum echoing upward from incomprehensible depths, from a dark abyss that would shame the very Void Itself.

Serenity could tell that she was being asked a question in some dialect of djinn-speak, but she had traveled seldom in the portions of the world known to be especially frequented by such spirits, knew not a bit of their language, and was not about to regret it now. The djin narrowed its bulbous eyes and allowed the vile talon to just barely break the skin under her jawbone as it held her high above the floor. Oh, it knew exactly what it was doing, for it had done this sort of thing to female creatures before. The venom from its multitude of quill-like spines began to spurt and hiss, raising swift little smoke-columns in burnt spots across the carpet. The horror clacked its mandibles and opened the rancid central maw to speak again, but Serenity beat it to the task.

"You might as well keep that disgusting mouth of yours shut because I ... do ... not ... speak ... your tongue, Foul One!"

The utterance had required nearly all of her strength without impaling her chin on the razor sharp talon, but Serenity thought she had enough energy left for a final, perhaps flaming, spitball into one of its dreadful eyes. The djin, for its part, had listened to her words with an intense interest that caused the tattered, shark fin-shaped ears to curl forward. It continued to study her face intently for another moment. Then it growled and suddenly dropped her on the nearly ruined bed as if she were a rag doll casually discarded by a petulant child.

"I do not recognize this place, Woman," it bellowed. "Where is Marutha?"

Serenity's jaw, aching and lacerated though it was, dropped in astonishment. She rubbed her neck and throat protectively as the djin began to pace around her bedroom, flooding it with stench, seemingly impatient to find something that had been lost.

"Y-you speak English, I see," she said, her own voice hoarse and injured from the fray.

"Is that what this tongue is called?" croaked the demon, lifting its head again in deep thought. "Ah. I see that it is."

It turned back and approached her once more; Serenity cringed against the headboard of the bed as Emory tried, in vain, to drag himself deeper behind the desk.

"I do not 'speak' this language," said the djin. "At least, I did not speak it until this moment, until I looked inside your own words and discerned the manner in which this language ought to be spoken."

"You're a very swift learner," whispered Serenity with growing alarm. If the thing had somehow been able to see within her mind, then there was certainly no way, in any world, or by virtue of any wise word or wonderwork, that she might escape its incredible power.

"I ask you again—*where* is Marutha?"

The demon hissed and its outer mandibles sprayed noxious flecks of venom upon the walls of her room, singeing holes in the sandstone-colored paint.

"I don't know anyone ... or anything ... called 'Marutha,' O unwelcome guest," answered the witch, somehow determined to make as impressive a show of bravery as she could muster. Though her mind raced, she recalled reading (or hearing) somewhere in the annals of the distant past, in some far-away fire circle, or by virtue of some spell book, that djin daemons respected bravery above all things.

"Ha! I do not suppose you would know Marutha, after all," rasped the creature. "He was not inclined to consort with witches, unless they served his devious purposes. Though I must say, Marutha's *friends* would have little trouble burning a witch, if they were to catch one."

"So you know that as well, do you?" said Serenity. "That I am a witch?"

The djin shrugged a spiny shoulder. "It was easy enough to sense your feeble spells ... the protective one around you when I broke free from the Strangling Shadow, and also the one you used to try to cast me into whatever dungeon lies beneath this floor." The djin cast a baleful glance at the concave wreckage of the bedroom's latest and most unbecoming renovation.

"There is no dungeon down below. Just my living room," offered Serenity.

"So be it. Your spells are not powerful enough to trouble the likes of me."

The thing appeared to be grinning, if a grin was even possible on a putrid maw like the one that protruded between the ever-twitching, clacking mandibles. The hundreds of metal rings and piercings on its torso and in its ears tinkled in eerie passes as it moved, pinging like the sharp patter of rain bombarding a tin rooftop.

"What is this?" snarled the djin, gazing out the bedroom window that had been smashed by the shock wave of its appearance. "Are we near the Great Sea? I know what manner of trees I behold," it added, focusing upon the rows of palms swaying toward the nearby beach, "but what are those?" The moss-draped live oaks seemed to stymie the brute.

"That's the Atlantic," choked Serenity, recoiling at the billowing odors that seemed to emanate from her visitor in currents of invisible, twisting layers. "The ocean. You are in the United States of America."

The djin stared back at her in consternation. "I know these words, for they are words that *you* know, but I do not yet know their significance."

This was true because, even though the djin had the power to assume the language of another mind, it could only apply that language to thoughts and concepts with which it was already familiar to some degree.

"It is clear to me," continued the great daemon, oozing contempt for its new surroundings, "that I am far from the scene of my downfall. Exactly how far, in regard to time and space, is something I intend to discover in due course, and you shall assist me, witch."

Serenity stole a glance at the half-ruined vanity table. Its mirror was now thoroughly in pieces due to the thunderous meanderings of the djin, but she could still see the light gleam of the ruby ring and its golden band amid the shards and debris.

"Were you imprisoned, by chance, in that ring, yonder?"

The djin's eyes followed her gaze to the little table and it stalked its thudding way over, snatching up the ring and inspecting it as it dangled and rolled on the very scimitar tip of one devil-talon.

"This was indeed the jewel the vile old he-goat used to trap me! I remember well how he brandished it before me in triumph. What I do not know is how I have come to be released from this prison and *where* I have come to be released. Suppose you enlighten me, witch, and none of your tricks. I guarantee you that further spells will be of no avail in the presence of one so great as I!"

Serenity gulped, remembering the name she had read from the ring's inscription through the cipher stone. "Dedwen is your name, is it?" and for her query she was rewarded by a pelting of spit that she was able to dodge only by a fraction of an instant. The sticky stuff was burning a foul and corrosive hole in the headboard behind her when she dared to look up again.

"I am the one who utters names in this place, if they are to be uttered at all," cautioned the djin. "But let us say that you are correct. If so, tell me how it is that you have come to guess my name? Famous and feared though that name has been across the shifting sands of Punt and throughout the jungles of Kush, few are those who know the face that belongs to the name ... few alive, that is. What, pray, is your name, witch?"

"Serenity," said Serenity, lifting a trembling finger to point at Dedwen's murderously curved talon.

"There was an inscription on the outer band of that ring," she confessed. "It has the word 'Dedwen' on it. That's how I knew your name."

Dedwen spun the thing around with a calloused thumb and held the jewel close to its middle eye, which narrowed at the side-lids even as its hideous convex pupil swelled like a living thing apart from the rest of the organ. The djin peered at the miniscule etching across the circlet of gold and, upon reading, threw back its head and howled with a vibrating chortle that rattled the pane of the remaining bedroom window overlooking the sea of oaks, palms, and ocean beyond. Emory yelped in spite of himself and covered ears and eyes with his forepaws. Serenity heard a car alarm go off somewhere outside, down the tropical little beachside street. The djin was too busy bringing its amusement under control to notice, apparently. It pointed a hand the size of a small boulder in mockery at the witch.

"Can it be that you were so foolish as to read the words of this inscription and set me free?" Dedwen bent forward with a cruel, sweeping bow as Serenity's cheeks burned with embarrassment. "I must thank you for being so careless, witch," added the djin with chuckles that sounded like rocks being tumbled over and over in some great rolling barrel. "I daresay, however, that Marutha would gnash his rotting old teeth and pluck out great tufts of his louse-ridden beard when he finds out that his enemy was turned loose by a sorceress! Oh, but I would give a dozen wishes to the mangiest mortal of Meroe just to see the look on Marutha's wrinkled raisin of a face when he *does* find out."

"Then why don't you use that great power of yours, Dedwen, and summon up this Marutha person, so that you can reckon with him properly, now that you're free and all?" Serenity was up for a little mockery herself; in her estimation, there was not a whole lot left to lose. "Or perhaps you are too frightened of your friend Marutha. After all, he was presumably the one who put you inside that lovely ring. Tell me, djin, or whatever you are—how was life inside the ruby?"

More venom spewed from the vile mouth to sizzle against and then through the walls, the carpet, and even the rafters above, but Dedwen did not make another threatening approach. Instead, the djin appeared solemn and hesitant for the first time.

"There was no life in the stone," growled the daemon. "Nothing, save for a constant drowning, a ruin, a torment that did not cease. Dare not, witch, to call Marutha my 'friend,' even in jest. I would contend with him, if I knew where he might be. Yes, in good time I will contend with him, but for that encounter I must plan with greater care. I recognize nothing that surrounds me, save for the ring, and now you, a fool of a being—and even you do not look like a proper enchantress." It gestured toward the wreck of a ceiling, and touched the mangled edge of a steel reinforced beam, along with the now shredded live wire that was once connected to the ceiling fan. It snapped and crackled upon his talons to no effect.

He glanced, then, at the rooftop drywall, which had been painted in a soft purple hue. "This manner of structure I have never before seen, nor have I seen furnishings quite like unto these. These decorations, those trees with beards outside, your strange garment, that repellent breed of dog—if dog it be—whining in the corner, seeking to hide from me. I assume that is your familiar spirit? Rest assured, it is one upon which I shall enjoy feasting! Oh yes, I shall. Even the air smells. It is the smell of a salted sea, no doubt, but there is oil and metal and filth and a thousand other stinks I do not recognize. These are smells that do not belong in the air of the world—this world or any other world."

"Just how long were you trapped in the stone?" ventured Serenity.

"Are you deaf as well as foolish?" hissed Dedwen with a snapping click of his mandibles. "I told you that there is no time to be passed, knowingly, in the ring. Marutha saw to that."

"And just who is this Marutha, by the swine of Circe?" moaned the witch, who was beginning to reel from a new pain throbbing upward from her crushed thigh.

Dedwen snorted, a terrifying sound replete with a triple-projectile emission of demonic snot. "You mean to say that you are a true witch and yet you do not know Marutha of Maipherkat?"

Serenity blinked. Maipherkat? *Maipherkat?* That place she knew, at least by reputation and legend, but, as far as she knew, the location that once possessed that name had not possessed that name for a considerable age. She looked up at the djin through sweat-drenched strands of hair splayed across her brow.

"Maipherkat was a city in Persia, centuries ago," she related in tones of smug wonder to her adversary. "The place—the ancient city, at least—has been ruined for ages. All that remains of it is mostly beneath the earth, forgotten by everyone except for a few nosy diggers," she added, thinking bitterly of Percival. "If you encountered this Marutha in a place called Maipherkat, and if it is the Maipherkat I am thinking of, then this means that you have been imprisoned for a rather long stretch, O djin. Perhaps a thousand years or more. Was Marutha a Muslim caliph or imam who subdued and banished you to exile in the ring?"

"What is a 'Muslim,' little witch?" queried Dedwen. "Or an 'imam'—what is that? Marutha of Maipherkat is a bishop in the fold of those who follow the One from Nazareth. Marutha is bishop of that fell city, and a more irascible, devious, contemptible bishop among the horde of his fellows cannot be found! Not even that chatterbox they called 'Chrysostom' could equal Marutha in guile!"

"Oh my," said Serenity, a rueful smile curling at the corners of her mouth. "You were brought low even *before* the coming of the Muslims, those people who, to this day, preserve a deep belief in your treacherous species ... and in those of your number who are indifferent or even beneficent to the race of mortals."

Dedwen's claws clenched and unclenched as he reached for Serenity, meaning to clutch at her anew.

"You speak in riddles, my broken enchantress. I know nothing of this people that you claim 'preserves a belief' in Us! You speak of preservation, as though a world exists in which it is possible *not* to believe in me!"

"Oh, but it is, my lost and long-relegated devil. You now stand in such a world! Your kind has existed since the beginning of the world in some form or other, and you have seen mortal lords, kings and holy men rise and fall. In your case, you were trapped and tossed out of Time, even before the rise of one such holy man, one whose legions did indeed keep strong their belief in you and your companions, who they knew to exist long before them. But things have changed, O djin, most certainly in the Western reaches of the earth. You would not recognize a thing, now, not even in your old haunts, and your bishop Marutha, if true mortal bishop he was, is not even so much as a bit of dust lingering in the dark corner of a tomb, anymore."

"It was the year four hundred-nine, as the followers of the One from Nazareth reckon time, when Marutha fought against me and I was undone by his curse," informed Dedwen.

Serenity laughed low, shaking with pain but also with the exhilaration of knowing more about the nature and circumstances of her opponent's predicament. Knowledge, however slight, could be the only effective power at her command, now.

"This is beyond the two thousandth year of that era," she drawled triumphantly, "as the followers of the Nazarene *still* reckon time, at least in this portion of the world, and it is in this very different portion of the world that you now find yourself, Dedwen! You have been lifted from the smothering sands that were layered upon you by storm and by century, by sunset and by sunrise, by tedium and by the time that has forgotten you. You have come and gone and come again, even as the race of mortals has risen up with the magic of their own machines and has, for the most part, long ceased to see you as anything more than a harmless child's tale! Even the old wives and wise women of their kind speak of your people, and indeed of mine, with naught but the ringing of laughter, the attitude of jest, and the quaint dismissal of nostalgia. All of this has reduced you to nothing more than a mere exotic tale for purposes of entertainment, and a rarely engaged entertainment at that. While you, O djin, have agonized in the limbo of the gemstone, centuries have plodded by and you, along with your confreres, have been pushed to the margins like so many others."

"You lie!" roared the djin, trembling with anger.

"Oh, your kind still haunts the desert crossroads of a night, one suspects, and I daresay they haunt the bazaars and kitchens of the stubborn East, wreaking mischief in little ways, here and there, but few these days find themselves enthralled by the likes of you. You are no longer the great dread of the midnight traveler, Dedwen, for now the mortals speed across the world! Most assuredly, they fly above it faster than we can, and they have no time to be concerned with you these days. They have no time to notice you, or to give countenance even to your memory. These days, you are fortunate if you are the cause of the most meager goose-bump raised on the arm of some wanderer in unfamiliar territory, the momentary rise of a few hairs on the back of someone's neck when they enter an empty room, or a long abandoned dwelling, and can't put a finger upon the reason for such a brief chill.

"Oh yes, Dedwen. Things have changed, and you may even come to discern that you would be much better off had you remained in the perpetual annihilation of Marutha's ring. You have been lost for centuries and, through all that time, the centuries were gradually losing *you*."

The djin drew itself up, making a show of confidence even though Serenity could sense its rattled uncertainty. Over one thousand five hundred years trapped in stone, along with the revelation that mortals had conquered even the magical word and banished it to the outskirts, could not be matters of negligible interest when it came to Dedwen's sense of stability. The behemoth, great as he was, could not quite conceal the flicker of shock now pervading its spirit. Confusion was Serenity's greatest chance, and chaos her ally at this ruinous juncture.

But Dedwen was also moved to anger by what he considered to be the ravings of this witch, ravings he was inclined to believe were deceptions and obfuscations. In his thousands of years of existence he had never encountered a magician of any caliber who did not revel in the need to disarm, equivocate, betray, destroy, control, and subsequently manipulate all things material and magical, stationary and spiritual. Duplicity and intrigue were in the blood of sorcerers, he knew, and though the djin could veritably smell that certain things in the world had changed, perhaps on an enormous scale, his previous centuries of observation told him that there were a great many things that time and tedium, shifting sands and searing storms, could *never* change. These were the enduring things worth counting upon when forced to master whatever new age he had come to inhabit.

"Let me assist you, great Dedwen, to fathom the intricacies of this altered and unfamiliar landscape." Serenity breathed the words with a steady enthusiasm tinged, just barely, with a hint of persuasive magic that she hoped would charm the djin amid its uncertainty. "This world is one you *could* possibly dominate once again, but much will seem to you as upheaval, and much will rob you of the advantage of time, when it comes to reestablishing your rightful place in this existence. I have lived through the ages from which you were so harshly and unfairly excluded, and I have seen much. My help will be crucial to your successful reemergence and the reclamation of your vaunted status. Allow me to serve you as guide. Accept my help, O djin, for I offer it freely, and it is of considerable value!"

Dedwen did not possess—at least in his innate and current manifestation—the ability to smile, but if he could have smiled he would have done so at that moment. He had been expecting a plea for life from the tiny yellow-haired witch, one disguised as an offer of assistance. That was an offer, however, that he fully intended to reject, at least according to the vague guidelines that had been delineated for his supposed benefit. He would have been genuinely shocked by grave changes in the fabric of the world if the whiny spell-caster had not proffered *some* sly attempt to save her skin. She was still apt to concentrate all of her efforts upon escaping him, or trying to gain some surreptitious measure of power over him. Oh yes, these magicians had their ways. But this little squab would not have her way, not entirely.

The djin drooled onto the hissing carpet and thought of how easy it would be to destroy her. How satisfying it would feel to annihilate something after so many years of inactivity and exile! Her magic was impressive, he had to admit that much if only to himself, but it was not strong enough to withstand even one solid thrust of his own power. Moreover, the witch was already weakened and injured from the encounter, which was a considerable bonus. The familiar, the ratty dog-thing, was obviously ineffective and of no consequence as a guardian for its mistress, even if it came to stealing away and seeking help. Dedwen wanted very much to kill Serenity, then and there. Brute that he was, however, the djin was not foolish enough to believe she could be of no use to him whatsoever, particularly under conditions wherein he maintained absolute—and, if necessary, absolutely *painful*—control over her.

That was it!

He could have his way very easily. He could use her until she was drained of all the life that remained in her, or until his need for her became superfluous and he killed her: whatever came first. It was time to explore this new age against which he had been so severely cautioned. He cleared his rancid throat. Another flying blob of venomous phlegm dissolved a yawning hole through the wall above Serenity's headboard.

"It is true that I have reason to proceed with due caution in any unfamiliar clime, little witch. Never has Dedwen the Great required assistance from *any* being, but as you emphasized, times seem to have changed and my own situation has hardly been conventional for a djin of my elite breeding. Unusual circumstances do call for unusual alterations of behavior in order to restore balance and regain what may, regrettably, have been lost."

On the floor, Serenity licked her dry lips and raised herself with as much earnest appreciation as she could summon, given the extent of her injuries.

"You are wise and resplendent with sound judgment, O Dedwen the Great," she uttered with a brief bow of her head. "With me at your side to reveal the nature of all the nuisances in this strange land, all the gadflies that might hinder your smooth journey back to a place of power, no one shall match you! Why, there is even a chance for vengeance, perhaps, against the descendants of your enemy, Marutha, for it is within our power to discern the whereabouts of any such whelps, should they exist. The djinn love cursing entire family trees, do they not? Many witches do as well, I must confess. Heh heh. In any case, with me on hand to facilitate and brush aside all needless obstacles, the pathway to your reclaimed glory shall well and truly be paved!"

Dedwen snorted in derision. "Oh, my way to glory shall well and truly be paved and you will most certainly help do the paving," he thundered. "But you will not be doing so at my side."

He aimed the talon still holding the ancient ruby ring and wagged it fiendishly in a widening swivel before Serenity's eyes. Then he began to speak in hurried, guttural tones. Translated in the English he had so easily acquired by magical osmosis, Dedwen's incantation was forthright:

"Where once I was ensconced in stone
now *thou* art sent by blood and bone.
Within the red and fateful jewel,
I banish thee to limbo, fool!"

This time, Serenity did manage a very un-witchlike scream of fear, for there is nothing a witch (or any super-sentient being) might fear more than the suffocating agony of confinement in a state of limbo. Poor Serenity began to gabble the words of a Dematerialization Spell that likely would have smashed her essence into a fragmentary, floating existence in the Void, which would have been preferable. But she had little time and even less power to confect a means of her own preventative destruction, whatever its chances for success or ultimate failure. Dedwen's power was beyond resistance for her, and in the form of a roiling, boiling, swirling cloud of smoke—hers being colored a pleasant strawberry blonde, like her hair—Serenity was sucked swiftly into the ruby-stone ring, as if spinning into a vortex.

Emory, still on the verge of a seizure behind the desk, could only peek in helpless terror. He knew more than a little about djinn daemons—in fact a fair bit more than Serenity herself had ever known. Through his own long tenure as a doleful, minor servant-spirit, he had, during periods of unemployment in the Void, stayed well away from any phantasm with even a taint of djin ancestry. No species of devil was speedier when it came to eating and relishing the taste of lesser spirits than were the djinn. With this in mind, poor Emory had already resigned himself to a gruesome doom. He could not depart the body of the Shih Tzu until Serenity herself allowed it, or until she was dead, or until the dog-body itself was dead, which was what Emory wished had happened earlier. Yet, even if Serenity had somehow managed to release him after the djin's initial attack, he was now much too weak to withdraw properly, anyway.

I'm a Shih Tzu-kabob for a djin! he yowled in the despair of his quavering spirit.

His bloodied eyes rolled upward. At least this djin's maw was so huge and its mandibles so razor-sharp that it would all be over swiftly. The monster was bound to be famished, after centuries inhabiting a stupid gemstone.

For his part, Dedwen bounced the ruby and its new occupant up and down in his palm, satisfied with his decision. When and if he encountered any particularly puzzling inconvenience while blazing a noteworthy trail through wherever-the-Hades-he-was, he could always summon the wormy little wench out of the ring as his personal roadmap and tour guide. It would be ideal, but Dedwen, most vain and confident of all the djin, did not envision too many inconveniences that would last long enough to qualify as inconveniences.

He reached down and lifted the yelping, dying Emory up from under the desk by the scruff of the neck.

"Oh, stop wriggling," muttered the slavering daemon. "Surely you knew this was coming. You're a runty, desperately ugly specimen of a dog, and I have never been partial to dogs, even in the days when jackals could be plucked up and gobbled like dates from a palm tree. But, after well over a thousand years of malnourishment, you will do as a snack, for the moment."

Dedwen spread his mandibles wide and exposed the cavern of his fanged, slimy maw. Just as he was about to bite Emory clean in half, however, the front doorbell rang downstairs, seemingly a world away. Galaxies away. Dedwen, of course, had never heard such a peculiar sound before. Serenity's doorbell had been installed to chime the first few notes of "Dixie"—she disapproved of the song's politics, naturally, but had taken pity on a desperate door-to-door doorbell-salesman, once upon a time.

So, there were to be some particularly puzzling inconveniences already! What a pain. Still, Dedwen did not feel like extracting Serenity from the ring to explain, not so soon, not when she was likely just getting "comfortable" in her state of agonizing suffocation. Instead, he drew Emory closer to the dripping, clicking mandibles.

"What, pray, is that noise? Speak, runt, or I'll eat you rather slowly instead of in two quick bites, starting with your scraggly little toenails."

Telepathically, Emory responded.

It's the doorbell, downstairs. Someone is ringing it and wants in.

"Someone at the bell, eh?" growled the djin. "Another sorceress, perhaps?"

Not likely, answered Emory. *The witches in these parts tend not to call on my witch. Probably a mortal neighbor wanting a cup of sugar or a bit of gossip. It might be the man from the electric company. A Jehovah's Witness. Who can say? Mortals are always bothering each other for nonsensical reasons in this neighborhood.*

"Mortals, eh?" Dedwen dropped Emory to the floor in a writhing, yelping heap. "Don't stray too far, my upcoming meal. I believe an investigation of this accursed new era into which I have been loosed is due to begin at once. But look at what a mess has been made already! It may behoove us to proceed with a caution to match our burgeoning interest. I assume that appearances still mean as much in the stupid world of mortals as ever they did?"

Dedwen reached upward with his mighty, spine-whiskered forearms, and with the talons of both hands, proceeded to peel away the moldering skin atop his bald head. Instead of exposing the abominable sight of a great and bloody skull, however, the lethal claws ripped away the entirety of the leathery hide as if stripping off a mere suit of clothing. Underneath it all was a perfect replication of Serenity Turnbull, right down to her green nightgown and silk kimono, not a single strawberry-blonde hair out of place. She belched a bubble of sizzling green acid and put a dainty, alabaster hand to her pink lips.

"Oops. Musn't do that."

Smiling and satisfied, the new Serenity pried the rest of the gelatinous, rank layers of djin-skin off her arms as if removing nightmarish opera gloves, wriggling out of the bits around her ankles like a snake from its husk of skin. Into one of the undamaged corners of the bedroom the mess was thrown, where it instantaneously burst into a bright blue ball of flame and vanished in a toxic updraft of smoke that whisked through the smashed window nearest the bed.

"That was easy enough. Now let us go and see who nags incessantly upon this bell I hear. With any luck it will be someone far more worth eating than a dismal little rat-snack like you. A djin of my status requires sustenance before embarking upon an ambitious expedition of the sort I have in mind. Try not to die while I am down below, will you? I much prefer to crunch the bones of something that still has a bit of spirit left in it."

The bell rang for a third, and rather prolonged, time.

"On my way!" cried Dedwen in Serenity Turnbull's buoyant chirp-of-a-voice. The imposter placed the ruby ring next to the cipher stone on the wrecked vanity table and, lifting the hems of the kimono and nightgown, minced down the flight of stairs to answer the front door.

"Neighbors come to call," it said, licking the pale lips. "The first in over one thousand five hundred years, too! How very exciting."

❧❦

VII

The fire was a five-alarm affair, requiring two extra trucks summoned all the way from Anastasia Island, just in case matters got particularly out of control. The disaster seemed to be contained, more or less, by the time two additional units arrived from Ponte Vedra, but the entirety of the Datil Be The Day shop—right down to its daintiest jar of datil pepper dipping sauce—had been consumed in a conflagration of apocalyptic proportions. Early morning mass attendees still flocked in tongue-clucking wonder on the side lawn of the Cathedral Basilica across from the smoldering framework of ruins, and a few dozen firefighters continued to scurry about, directing the last jets of hose-water onto four or five whipping columns of flame that refused to surrender.

News crews from the St. Augustine Record and from television stations as far away as Jacksonville had been on hand for most of the morning, and virtually every other shop owner on otherwise evacuated St. George Street had gathered to behold the shocking inferno. Present, too, were the paltry ranks of particularly intrepid offseason tourists, who had been milling about in hopes of entering shops and boutiques at the very instant doors were unlocked for the day. Everyone was kept at a safe distance by officials, of course, but there was still plenty of room to gawp, take hundreds of pointless photographs, and procure battery-frazzling amounts of digital footage on smartphones.

This fire had been a resoundingly successful attraction for the smattering of bargain-basement shoppers and drowsy weekend getaway types, all of whom would have a brush with catastrophe worth bragging about when they returned to the bosoms of their own safe and unscorched homes and worksites. A few budding cinematographers in garish tees and comfy sneakers were already itching to get back to hotel rooms and upload their documentaries of disaster onto YouTube. These were the citizen journalists who had been fortunate enough to capture images of the pepper shop blaze at full, towering inferno intensity: twisting flames and great plumes of black smoke burgeoning into the sky like a volcanic cloud of doom.

Far more extraordinary than all of that, however, was the look of incomprehension (bordering on madness) that crossed the sweaty face of the chief of the St. Augustine Fire Department, who dropped his axe and his bullhorn, when the two old women emerged. They were somewhat singed and sooty around the hands and ears, and rather crispy about the hemlines of their dresses and lace collars, but they just sauntered, all of the sudden, as if strolling blithely out of hell, into the otherwise gentle morning sunlight and waiting hullaballoo. They stepped gingerly, these women, a bit bewildered themselves but nevertheless upright and accounted-for, traipsing out from within the still-licking patches of flame and churning spirals of dark smoke, brushing ash from their shoulders.

The fire had earlier been roaring like a glimpse of some imminent micro-apocalypse for half an hour, but the twosome—the tall, turkey-necked one with the bobby-pinned gray braids, and the chunky little black one with regal bearing and a scorched purple turban—emerged from it nevertheless. In addition to the chief's axe and bullhorn, several cameras and smartphones dropped to the pavement, too. These old ladies were as relatively unscathed as were the adjacent shops and buildings on either side of what had formerly been Datil Be The Day, shops and buildings that ought to have been incinerated by the sheer intensity of the central blaze, just as the old ladies themselves ought to have been incinerated. Such were the sorts of things on the minds of the onlookers, in any case.

Under normal circumstances, potentially viral YouTube viewership and national talk show guest-spots would have become exponentially more likely due to the series of theatrical maneuvers undertaken by the "miracle women" (observers from tourists to TV news crews were indeed already forming such monikers in stunned brains) as they tacked through the debris toward the slightly awry, extended arms of the gobsmacked fire-crew nearby. The lanky, bird-like old girl had started muttering and stamping her feet in a show of consternation as members of the rescue team tried to take hold of her.

"Get your hands off, boys. I'm alright. Stop that. I thought I *told* you I was alright! Now, if anyone here can see where I dropped a bobby pin? I swear it's impossible to find anything small that falls on these blasted shell-stone sidewalks."

She had even slapped the hand of the Fire Chief himself when he approached, beckoning to a foursome with a gurney behind him.

"Do I look like a woman who can't walk out of her own burning home?" she had squawked. "Out of my way this instant! It's been a rough enough morning as it is, and I won't put up with any poking or prodding."

Yes, it had all been caught on cameras and smartphone-videos, complete with sound, and it was, for the most part, fabulous coverage.

"It's come to something when a perfectly capable woman gets treated like a doddering old bag as she's standing in her own former doorway. Get that oxygen mask away from me, son, I can breathe just as good as you can. Get yourselves off the street and stop acting like a mob of headless chickens, if you want to be of some service. Gertrude Gokey, are you COMING?"

Of course, dozens of cameras and phones had also fixated upon The Other One, who was much less agitated and far more eager to allow burly firefighters to assist her, it seemed. *That* old lady paused amid the fray to adjust her smoking but still positively sparkling bejeweled turban.

"Did my ostrich feather burn off?" she asked several flabbergasted rescuers. "I can't tell in all this smoke and what-not, but it doesn't feel like it's there. My hand's a bit numb, if you want to know the truth. Can you fellas see my ostrich feather? I've had that feather since ... well, for an awful long time, put it that way. You wouldn't believe me if I told you where I got it."

"Gert Gokey, stop fussing with your fancy do-rag and get yourself out from amongst those men this very minute! They've got to put out what's left of the rest of the shop, not to mention the apartment, and as you well know we have got *work* to do."

"I am on my way, Letty. Can't you give a girl a minute to make herself remotely presentable? There are news cameras over yonder. Hey there, y'all! Have a look and see for yourself. I spied 'em through that backdraft right before we came out. Letty never did have a lick of patience," she informed the ring of stunned firefighters to her left in conversational tones.

Just then, the remnants of the upstairs balcony collapsed in a crunching, thunderous cascade of fiery ruin behind them.

"Mind your heads, now. Y'all don't want to go getting your necks broke, or a headache. A headache was what caused this snafu, sure enough. A headache of Letty's."

"That's what caused it, Gert Gokey? You're blaming me? Why, I'll send you back to the Dark Ages without so much as an Evil Eye to bestow upon your worst enemy!"

Both women balled fists and seemed, for an instant, prepared to brawl amid the screaming chaos of men and fire and smoke and shocked churchgoers and EMTs and tourists and police, until one onlooker bellowed for his wife to get a "better close-up" as they were standing at the guarded parameter behind the Cathedral lawn walls.

"Zoom in on the fat one, Mabel!" the man yelled and jabbed a finger on her spandex top. "If that chubby one cold-cocks the tall skinny old bat it'll be money in the bank!"

"Hey, Letty," said the "fat one" with an elbow's nudge against her partner. "There's folks filming us with them intelligent phones. Filming us like we're some sorta joke."

"Whuh?" said the tall one, whipping around and zeroing in as personnel dashed everywhere, suddenly seeming to lose all awareness of the two women who had walked straight out of Doomsday.

"Yeah, them two," said Gert pointing, and, with a jab of one stubby finger, the cinematographic careers of Mabel and her hectoring husband came to an abrupt end. Their little rectangular phone melted, suddenly, warm as tar. Its remnants dribbled like black licorice that had liquefied, right through the woman's fingers, falling in streaky splotches onto the cement barrier wall of the Cathedral-Basilica lawn.

"It ain't nice to take photographs and movies of people during an emergency!" yelped Letty, as if lecturing a class of woefully uniformed schoolchildren. It ain't proper manners. Not at all. Ain't that right, Gert?"

"Most correct, Letty, most correct."

Then, with the store still dangerously pulsating flame and charred devastation, with the emergency crews suddenly, strangely walking around the ladies as if they were no longer present, returning to the business of extinguishing the magnificent mess ... very slowly the two women, standing indignant and proud in their dishevelment, did indeed begin to disappear.

They disappeared from the coquina-paved streets of St. George.

They disappeared from the maddened, mystified crowd.

They also vanished from every camera, phone and recording device that had taken footage of their incomparable debut.

Most significantly, perhaps, the two disappeared from every memory of every person that had seen them that morning. The last thing anyone possessed as even an elusive, fiery feather of remembrance, was the slow and ghostly fade-out—both women smiling triumphantly, but the tall one as if she had never smiled a day in her life. They were gone, and the store, the *Datil Be the Day Pepper Emporium,* had continued to smolder, exhausting the men and women who battled the little explosions and bursting spark-storms amid its bleak and ruined remains.

VIII

"No one's home, Daddy," whined BonSashay Rummy, elbows outward and little white-gloved fists resting on the hips of her most surefire
donation-soliciting outfit.

Across Florida and into more than a handful of Georgia counties,
the white satin hoop-skirt, knee-high stretch-stockings, and gleaming
patent-leather black tap shoes had never failed to secure the oohing, aahing, cooing, bosom-clasping approval—not to mention pocketbook-
snapping financial contributions—of bored old women and unfulfilled
housewives. It had never failed to dazzle those who coveted shiny tiaras
while sporting curler-crowned heads as impenetrable as armadillo skin.
This was the Little Princess "look" that won hearts and dollars; other
dress and hair arrangements had been tried and found wanting when
it came to securing all-hallowed ink on the signature line of a check.
That morning, Chesterfield Rummy had nearly clubbed his daughter repeatedly with a bedroom slipper after she spilled chocolate milk on the
faux fox-fur hem of her hoop skirt, but he had stopped himself in the
nick of time. Luckily, the lethargic Mrs. Rummy had proved as adept at
chocolate milk stain-removal as ever … once she had been temporarily
released from her "special room" in the mad dash to get everyone ready
and out the door for the day.

"Daddy, did you hear me? Are you even listening to a word I say?
No one is home and we have rung this stupid doorbell three times. Ugh!
The sun shines right onto this porch, too." BonSashay cupped a hand over
her brow and gazed toward the East. "See, Daddy. Soon it'll be roasting
and my foundation is gonna get all tacky. Let's go on to the next place!"

"Now just listen here and hold your horses, BonSashay," said
Chesterfield. He already boasted a glistening forehead, the hairline of

his flat-top buzz-cut toupee exuding rivulets of sweat that seemed to be competing with each other to see which would be the first to drizzle down and soak his reddish, Hair Color for Men eyebrows. "This here is one of the nicest neighborhoods on Vilano Beach, baby girl, and I looked up the info to learn that the very kind of person who is most likely to help you skyrocket to Pint-Sized Princess glory lives right here, in this very house."

BonSashay stamped a tap shoe, but she was not about to perform her trademark Dance of Desperation, not just yet.

"Don't tell me it's another stinky old woman," she complained. "I hate stinky old women. They all smell like used-up teabags. Mother once told me that's because old women don't like to use pumice stones to exfoliate themselves, and that if *she* had anything to say about it, she'd take a pumice stone to old stinky people and scrub the dead skin cells right off their bodies until they bleed and scream for mercy, just like she used to do to me, before she started spending most of her time in the Special Room."

"Yeah, well, your mama says a lot of things, Sugar, but she's not the one taking you around and building the everlasting launch pad of your future superstardom, now, is she?"

"No. You won't let Mama take me around or even come to the shows anymore since she started getting those ... what did you call them, again, Daddy?"

"Uncontrollable urges to bite the other pageant mothers on the breasts and get us sued," replied Chesterfield promptly.

"Yeah, since she started getting *those* urges," continued BonSashay. "I guess she wasn't all that good at helping me raise funds, anyhow. Not as good as you."

"You got *that* right, darling," muttered her father in a husky drawl, prying with a sausage finger at the horrible starched collar that made his throat look like an ambitious, eggy soufflé, slowly rising from his gray pinstriped and suited shoulders. "You just go on and ring that bell one more time like I asked you, and you put on your pageant-face, child. We can't leave any stone unturned today, of all days. A boffo dress needs to be paid for and this is our last opportunity before the competition."

BonSashay reached up and jammed a gloved finger into the bell with all her nine year-old consternation, angst, regret, and a feral stretch of lips brightened by Cherry Bomb Delight gloss. Her perfect, white, peg-like teeth were clenched. She was tired of the fundraising process and was not going to pretend otherwise. In fact, if Daddy wasn't careful, if he did not find a way to ease up and start spoiling her with an extravagance to match the discipline he was meting out, then she *might* just have to sabotage one of these little exploits. She had done it before, when her father's stress-level had gotten on her last Little Lady Nerve and he began to get "The Look" on his face—the one that creeped-out even the primordially self-centered child-brain of BonSashay. It was a look that even her marksman-like senses could not exactly interpret, but one in which she experienced disturbing flashes. These were visions wherein it would not be terribly difficult to imagine Daddy—her hero, her champion—choking the life right out of her and tossing her, gown, tiara, and all, into some nasty place that probably served as the habitat for an inordinate amount of alligators. She knew she could "work him," but it was a tight-rope walk at best and there was always a need for caution.

Still, BonSashay had not taken that grueling nine-day Ballerina & Circus-Trapeze seminar in Pompano Beach for naught. If any Pint-Sized Princess heels could grind a staccato Watusi all over Daddy's disposition and bring him into proper submission, it was hers.

BonSashay pushed the doorbell until her teeth were grinding audibly.

"That's enough, girl," bleated her father. "You don't want to break the dang thing!"

The door opened, slowly, but without the usual kind of trembling, peekaboo timidity they observed in most rich old lady domiciles, on other rich old lady porches. In fact, this was no rich old lady at all. The portal opened to reveal a pretty strawberry-blonde in her mid-twenties, at most, with gentle eyes, a slightly freckled milk-white face, and buoyant crab apple cheekbones. She was dressed in some sort of shimmering, pale green exotic housecoat, and white terry cloth bedroom slippers.

BonSashay frowned. This did not look promising at all. If she had to dance for the dollars, even *she* knew the right kind of audience for it. Housecoats and bedroom slippers were okay—sometimes even preferred—but only insofar as the women wearing them were fat, visibly about to collapse from chronic ennui, and stricken to their blowsy souls with pangs of regret for the bright Baby-Doll Days of their own, long-lost youths. Whether those salad days had been dressed with sassy raspberry-mango vinaigrette or plain old vinegar, BonSashay knew her particular suckers on sight. To BonSashay, this hausfrau did not look as if she pined with barely repressed angst for giddy girlhood. This one was pretty without needing so much as one slathering of foundation make-up, much less the standard four slatherings to which BonSashay herself had become accustomed. A rubbing of rouge would add not a thing to this woman's naturally healthy complexion.

BonSashay hated this specimen in the doorway with immediate and irrevocable passion. Like her father, she could detect the telltale scents of liberalism like a Best-in-Show bloodhound. Pretty hippie-type ladies *never* doled out the dollars. They only doled out lectures and sometimes strange granola cookies that tasted of bellybutton lint. They never gave you money for purposes of pageant primacy. Worse, they muttered cryptic things that addled BonSashay's carefully constructed worldview, odd rejoinders about the complete immorality of zircon tiaras, high heels, and Xtra-padded training bras. They spoke blasphemies against Nair and other depilatories. They rarely if ever seemed to possess checkbooks. The only paper item that sort of woman ever offered, in BonSashay's experience, was a leaflet invitation to some group discussion centered upon the mysterious and confounding Hell-word "sustainability"—a word that frightened BonSashay to the core of her cheeseburger-craving soul, a word that haunted her cotton candy-draped dreams. She clasped her father's plump, sweaty hand with a most ostentatious flourish of her ivory glove.

"Come on, Daddy. We must've got the wrong address," she intoned while staring upward with icy contempt at the Liberal Lady of the Beach-House.

"Please. Do not feel the need to rush off so soon after I have answered this rather persistent ringing of my bell," said the hippie lady in the calmest, most pleasant and persuasive tones of command that BonSashay and her father had ever heard amid their seemingly countless porch-front sorties and pageant barnstormings. "What a privilege it is to receive a visit on such an exquisite morning. Tell me—was I expecting you?"

"Excuse me, Ma'am?" croaked Chesterfield, losing his focus more than a bit, mesmerized by the stare of a cobra in a cheery kimono.

"I mean, of *course* I was expecting you," said their hostess in the portal, making a slight, robotic motion with her head, as if realigning some errant inner circuit. "Surely you must both be parched after journeying. Why do you not tie your camels to the palm tree, yonder, and come within for a cup of something … refreshing?"

"Er … camels, Miss?" said Chesterfield Rummy.

"You couldn't have been expecting us, lady," piped BonSashay with a sneer. "We ain't never hit you up for money before. Trust me, I'd remember. And what's with the camel stuff? Daddy, let's go! She's nuts, just like that monkey what tears its own hair out and pees on people at the Gator Farm. Just like Mommy. Let's try the next houses. Please? I think I saw an old grammaw in a Mercedes drive into her garage a few blocks away. That's more our style."

She yanked her father's hand like it was a bell-pull summoning the most harried, yet intractable, of household servants.

"Money? Is it money you seek, my friends?" said the lady with an arch of one pure, corn-silk brow. "There is plenty of that on hand. You ought to come within and visit, most assuredly."

She moved slightly out of the way and opened the door wide, gesturing and blinking with kind, languid eyes for them to enter. BonSashay tugged her father's hand harder than ever.

"Daddy, I said 'Let's GO!' This place gives me the heebie jeebies."

Indeed, the pageant hopeful, the voracious little seeker of uncon-ditional love, adoration, envy and vicariously misplaced dreams, had long been adept at reading the odd ticklings of true thought that moved about in secrecy behind the otherwise controlled gazes of adults who beheld her. BonSashay had become skilled—sometimes uncomfortably so—at discerning various hints and catching brief glimpses of things adults actually expected, or wanted, from her, as opposed to what they *pretended* to desire. Never had her aspiring showstopper's heart, howev-er, felt more unsettled than under the watch of this particular stranger. Those eyes were, she knew in a sudden, precocious epiphany, the same eyes she had when her father kept her waltzing, waving, singing, smiling, dancing, posing, and baton-twirling all day on the Treadmill of Fame ... without so much as a break or a slice of bread, and she would chance to spy the golden arches of a favored burger joint. BonSashay knew what her own eyes looked like in those desperate, lip-licking moments at the end of a wrenching day at Beauty Boot-Camp. She had seen them all too often in the side-view mirror of the sedan.

This woman in the lovely beach house—pelicans gliding over-head, palm fronds rustling in the morning gusts, one bedroom slipper tap-tap-tapping in a barely suppressed mix of expectation, exaltation—had the exact same gaze.

"Daddy, for the last time, I—"

"BonSashay, honey, why don't you be a good little girl and shut your bossy piehole for once in your life? This nice lady has just offered us the grace of her hospitality and you seem awfully ready to spurn such a rare and refreshing invitation. Why, anyone'd think you forgot how im-portant it is for an authentic Southern Belle—and future chart-topping Billboard recording artist with a multi-film deal—to reward gentility with a heaping helping of her own. Heaven knows gentility is a rare thing to behold in these times of inconsideration and apathy. Pleased to make your acquaintance, Miss. My name is Chestferfield Rummy."

A blotchy, hairy-knuckled hand was extended and a business card was brandished in its palm. The name on the card read:

C RUMMY

"I am a member of the St. Augustine City Council and proud father of the next Pint-Sized Princess pageant champion," he continued. "This here is my lovely daughter, BonSashay Rummy, who is fixin' to become the aforementioned champion."

His oafish fingers were gently clasped by the thin, white, chilly, and inexplicably goosebump-inducing digits of their hostess.

"And you, my dear lady, are, uh … Miss Serenity Turnbull, if I am not mistaken?" added Rummy in his finest mélange of King James Bible-preaching, snake oil-selling, Lady-charming tones. "You may wonder how I know your name, but I urge you not to be alarmed. We are not salespeople, nor are we Jehovah's Witnesses, as you may have rightfully suspected, seeing that a perfect stranger has brought a child to your doorstep and has lingered a bit on your bell. No, this is very much a neighborly call, a friendly communication from one good citizen of this upstanding community to another, all for the purpose of expanding the horizons of our world's most treasured resource—its youth—beyond the scope of their hopes, beyond the narrow confines and suffocating limitations placed by the dream-dashers and the star-smashers of this cynical globe upon the least among us, the littlest talents, the first-fruits of a better future as human beings. And thus … er … uh … Did I hear you say that you had money with which you would be willing to part, dear lady?"

A sly wink and a frantic "your secret is my secret" series of nods provided Rummy with his reply.

"Well, in that case, let's get right down to the nitty-gritty," chortled Chesterfield. "Miss Turnbull, I understand that you are a single female who teaches down at Flagler College? Now, don't be concerned. I researched your name, address, and occupation via public records and various online investigative sites at absolutely anyone's disposal because we target—I mean, we are very eager to *include*—only select members of the local community to act as contributors to my stunningly world-class talented little girl's campaign to win the Pint-Sized Princess Beauty and Talent Competition, which, as you most undoubtedly already know, is about to be held at Sandpiper Auditorium, right here in our own, beloved city of St. Augustine. As you may also know, a competition of this kind provides a virtual powerhouse of giftedness, like BonSashay, with an opportunity to build unimpeachable character, and a set of unshakeable God-centered American values that will surround her like a golden shield as she hopscotches her way across the entire panorama of life experiences, and film sets, that await her as a career-oriented female of the Twenty-First Century. BonSashay, honey, introduce yourself to the nice lady."

"Hello," said BonSashay, warily gathering the hem of her faux fox fur-trimmed hoop skirt, rendering a little curtsey and trying, simultaneously, to hide behind her father.

"Greetings, young lady. I am Serenity Turnbull. *Indeed* I am. This is your lucky day, for I have found artistic children to be very much to my taste for a long, long time. It would be such a treat for a lonely, unmarried spinster teacher, like me, to welcome into her home ... a future queen."

"Well, it's just 'princess' at this stage," corrected Papa Rummy with a nervous chuckle. "We don't start to tackle queenship until we get to nationals." His shirt was now nearly transparent with sweat beneath the pinstriped suit jacket.

"Not to worry. Slightly lesser royalty is also welcome, I assure you. Why do you not both come in and keep me company for a spell? Your delectable little girl can show me all the amazing feats of which she is capable, and then we can see what it is that I may do for the two of you!"

Chesterfield Rummy slapped a somewhat greasy pinstriped knee with giddy enthusiasm and proceeded to yank the now-whimpering BonSashay by one of her opera gloves.

"You got yourself a deal, Miss Turnbull! What a pleasure to discover a citizen so immediately open to the personal advancement of her community's brightest young geniuses! Besides, I swear it's getting hot as the Devil, standing out here on this porch, even for the end of October. Come on, BonSashay. Get your little diddycan together, girl!"

They went inside.

෯෴

IX

"Rowan, you're never going to believe who's downstairs in the drawing room," said Miranda, poking her head around the library door.

Rowan Blaize cocked a skeptical eye in her direction, but did not put down his copy of *Little Known Uses for Lapis Lazuli in Spells Concerning the Weather.*

Miranda shrugged as Bror stretched and belched at his master's feet among the book stacks.

"Well, the word 'never' *is* sort of stupid," admitted Miranda. "A person, especially one like you, must always be prepared to believe most anything. But you'll be very surprised, I think, to learn what condition they're in, to say nothing about what has happened to their shop. In fact, I guarantee you'll be surprised."

Now, Rowan did put down the book atop the elaborately carved alder-wood table at his side, the table that had been a birthday gift from Phaethon's granddaughter, centuries ago, when they had spent summers playing hide-and-seek with the naiads in the watery Chasms of Grovalda.

"Leticia Beauregard and Gertrude Gokey are downstairs? In my drawing room? Both of them?"

"Umm hmm."

This *was* a surprise.

"How long have they been here?"

Miranda tossed her head and flicked an adventurous strand of multi-colored hair back among its companions across her scalp. "Not five minutes," she said as Rowan pursed his pale lips.

"How unusual that I did not hear them knock. I guess I was more engrossed in the storm-summoning attributes of lapis lazuli than I realized. It'll never do to have me so distracted when witches are on the very doorstep."

A dark shadow, like one of the mammoth storms about which he had been reading in the book, seemed to cross his countenance, only to pass swiftly and vanish somewhere in the region of his heart, where everything seemed to end-up these days.

"Don't be too shocked that you failed to see them coming," counseled Miranda. "They weren't exactly on the doorstep. As a matter of fact, the two of them just sort of 'appeared' in the kitchen while I was taking a bowl of minestrone soup out of the microwave for my lunch. Nearly made me jump out of my skin, if you want to know the truth. Lucky I didn't scald myself."

"They actually materialized in the kitchen?" gasped Rowan, rising from the chair and stepping carefully over the mountain of dog that was Bror. "This tale of yours grows more intriguing by the minute, Miranda. Those two never use that kind of magic for traveling, and they never ever simply turn up in one's kitchen, announced or unannounced, invited or uninvited. Something is wrong. I smell it."

"Oh, you'll smell it, alright," said Miranda, moving out of the way as Rowan strode from the library toward the stairwell. "It's like a smokehouse down there, but nothing they said made much sense to me. You know how those two bicker and talk over each other incessantly. It was impossible to get a grasp of what might be really going on."

"Ha!" said Rowan. "Easier to grasp one of the wriggling eels in Amphitrite's swimming pool!"

"Well, I *can* tell you that their feathers are good and ruffled, but you'll have to figure out the reason why. I put them in the drawing-room, despite their condition. There's no way I was going to hang around when witches are that far off the boil. Hot soup all over myself would have been the least of my worries, given the state those two old bats are in. You'd better have a look."

"I shall," said Rowan, and down the graceful stair he descended to the spacious and sun-washed living room. His aquiline nose wrinkled from the acrid smell of smoke even before he turned through the hallway to enter the normally peaceful salon. Things were anything but normal and certainly not peaceful when he got his first look at the unexpected arrivals.

Letty Beauregard sat bolt upright on the very bitter edge of a cushioned tapestry armchair near the empty fireplace, scowling like some dowager empress who had discovered the bulk of her throne to be studded with pins. She was balancing more than she was sitting, and Rowan half guessed that, were the chair to be suddenly whisked from its spot, pure cantankerous sorcery would keep Letty suspended in her rigid position. She was also muttering like a Fury trapped in a crystal jar, shaking a finger at Gert Gokey, who sat, lumpish and a bit slovenly, muttering back. Gert was shaking her head slowly back and forth, her eyes closed in almost placid counterattack to her companion's chastisement and frantic finger-wagging.

Both women had soot on their faces and considerable portions of their dresses were slightly scorched. Neither of them bothered to notice Rowan's presence, in his own house, as they carried on what he had no doubt was only the latest installment in a contretemps that had been going on—at least in low-grade fashion—for centuries. This, however, did not interest him, this chronic feud, in and of itself. He was rather curious about the condition of his callers and surmised that there was indeed more than a marginally interesting story lurking behind the scent of burnt lace, singed velvet turbans, and ash-saturated sorceress-hair. It behooved him to get to the bottom of it, particularly since tendrils of smoke still appeared to be rising in faint curlicues from the spot where Gert's famous ostrich feather used to be, and from where the blackened remnant of Letty's prim collar now straggled across her shoulders like the twisted legs of a Caltressian Swamp Spider.

"Ahem," he said. It was as good an opening as any he could think of.

The witches continued their *sotto voce* swashbuckling.

Rowan coughed.

The witches began to squabble more feverishly than before.

"Ladies!" shouted Rowan, with a block-quaking stomp of his Cat Colorado boot. The house vibrated for a few seconds. The chandelier above the tea table rattled and swayed and tinkled. Birds throughout that part of St. George Street abandoned even the most comfortable of perches and hit the skies.

The witches paused and looked curiously about as the temblor dissipated and then they glared at Rowan Blaize as if he had thwarted a debate that might have led, at any moment, to the solution of certain Great Mysteries that even the grandest and most philosophically inclined supernatural beings had never managed to fathom.

"Whull!" huffed Letty Beauregard.

"Hmphh!" snorted Gert Gokey. "You didn't have to risk bringing the whole house down to get our attention. Had about enough of houses coming down for one day, in fact. Ain't that right, Letty?"

"I should say so," agreed her friend with an offended nod. "Why didn't you just say 'Boo!' at us, Master Blaize? We was only having a discussion."

"Discussion? More like the most potentially volcanic *tete a tete* I've seen in many a year from witches who ought to know better. What an undercurrent of antagonism! Besides, it was beginning to seem like I had been in the room for hours as you two kept at it. Now, enough of this foolishness, if foolishness it be. I demand to know what in the name of Persephone's Powder-Room has precipitated a visit like this? What, pray tell, has happened to the two of you? You look and smell like Rome after a particularly productive visit from Atilla."

At this, both ladies let out little gasps of indignant air and tried to gather themselves, patting a bit of soot off a cheek here, brushing an elbow-crease lined with ash there, tucking in braids and bosoms and generally settling into more respectable poses. All the while they clucked like award-winning hens who realized they had just been denied their annual blue ribbons for incomparable pedigree and the laying of dependably premium eggs. Rowan, for his part, could scarcely wait to hear what had happened, if he could manage to keep himself from laughing. He called up to Miranda and asked her to bring everyone some iced ambrosia with mint. Then he sat down next to the softly smoldering Gert on the divan.

"Well? Out with it. You first. What has brought the two of you hence in such a state? Miranda tells me you just faded into the kitchen out of thin air."

"Mighty thick and smoky air is more like it," interjected Letty, a bit gruffly. She was still insulted, even if she knew that their intrusion was beyond the pale even for them … *especially* for them.

"We didn't mean to scare your little foundling-girl," said Gert, laying a plump hand upon Rowan's knee. "But we haven't had to maneuver like that in quite a while, at least not together, and it was a little bit cramped in the atmospheric continuum. Had to kind of feel our way through. We knew we were heading here, but we initially aimed for the front porch, like proper visitors, not for the kitchen. Sorry about that."

"Yes, we're very sorry," added Letty in earnest, her umbrage forgotten. "We ain't never been the kind of witches who don't have enough sense to knock on a friend's front door, if we can help it. You ain't mad at us, are you?"

Rowan put a few fingers to his forehead. "No. I am not angry. Just forget, for the moment, how you came in and tell me *why* you came in!"

"It was all *her* fault!" said both witches in perfect synchronicity, pointing at each other, then lowering the digits of accusation and opting to burn the air between them anew with frightful scowls.

"One at a time, if you please."

Letty sighed and sagged, as if all the backbone that kept her at such rigid right angles with the world had turned to rubber. She collapsed into the armchair, her gnarled hands dangling weakly off the griffin-clawed armrests. She looked for the first time eternally exhausted.

"The whole pepper shop is gone," she sputtered. "Burnt to a crisp, every last bit of it."

"What?"

Gert nodded pitifully. "Yep. The apartment up above is lost, too," she added. "Never saw such a bonfire o' the vanity."

"But we shoulda saw *that* one coming," croaked Letty. "I knew when you started playing little divination games with that dreadful China cooker that we were in for trouble!"

"But I only did it so's we could get to the bottom of your blasted premonition," countered Gert. "If you'd only have let me channel the pain of your headache into the scrying water instead of pulling back at the last minute and letting all the power ricochet off the mirror and blast the bathroom sink!"

"Wait," interrupted Rowan. "There was an explosion in your bathroom?"

"It was a bonfire of the vanity. Didn't you hear me the first time?" replied Gert. "And seeing as the power behind it was fueled by the worst foreboding migraine that Letty, here, has ever endured ... well, neither of us could get a handle on it and, before we knew it, angry fireballs was flying all over the house."

"We had to get out of the way," explained Letty from her crumpled state in the chair. "My head was spinning too fast from the spell to try and conjure-up a quick fix and Gert was down on all fours behind the couch, her wok knocked all over the upholstery, which only made things worse because she insisted upon adding the most flammable scrying oil to the spring-water mix, oil made by the most fly-by-night GnostiKimps imaginable!"

"I defy anyone to stand in the way of one of *your* headaches that's been suddenly let loose upon the world to run amok!" retorted Gert. "A gal has got to protect herself. Oh, but the Bear Cubs of Baba Yaga couldn't have done more mischief. We've gone and lost everything we own!"

"Don't you start to cry, Gertrude Gokey," said Letty, only a blip more discernibly comforting on the Richter Scale of Consolation. "It's hardly the first time this has happened. Remember when I left the door to the Grab-Goblin's cage unlocked—accidentally, of course—and then we woke up the next morning to find that the little bugger had cleaned us out?"

"Please!" begged Gert, holding up a chubby, ringed hand to bar the onslaught of memory. "You know I don't like to talk about our days back in old Boston, what with all the nonsense that befell poor Cousin Tituba and that fractious Deliverance Hobbs. Lucky they got out of that jam, but what a stir!"

"I am just trying to illustrate the point that these sorts of tragedies have occurred before and we have always managed to find our way through them with our wits intact," said Letty through clenched teeth. "Besides, it's a terrible thing for witches to get too attached to material things and possessions and what-not. Our lives are much too long and our associations much too transient for that. I've always said it, and you know I'm right, Gert. Ain't I right, Rowan Blaize?"

Letty stared Rowan down like a weathered schoolmarm not quite certain of her ability to handle the day's curriculum, much less the student body. Her hands were beginning to shake, a little, and she buried them in the folds of the ruined dress atop her lap, embarrassed.

"I am still rather out to sea regarding the events which precipitated whatever catastrophe you two are attempting to describe," said Rowan. "You claim the store has been burned down along with your flat above and everything you own?"

"Yes," said Gert. "I'm surprised the whole city wasn't down at the end of St. George Street to get an eyeful. The entire firing squad was there!"

"Firefighters!" snapped Letty. "They come to put the darn thing out, not line us up and shoot us."

"Miserable Mephistopheles!" growled Rowan. "Was that the cause of all the commotion we heard a couple of hours ago, with sirens blaring straight down to Hades?"

"That'd be us," said Letty with a woeful crack in her voice.

"Miranda, Bror, and I all heard it, but I was settling in the library to do some research or else I might have ventured out to see what was going on. Now I regret that I didn't take the fuss more seriously—I might have been able to help!"

"Don't you go worrying about that," said the kindly Gert in a drawl as rich and unhurried as molasses being poured from a jug. "I'm glad you stayed to do your research. You're a warlock what likes to keep his incantations up to speed. Heh! We oughtta be poring over spellbooks as often as you do. And it was a lot of mortal hullaballo, anyhow. You know how they love to hear themselves blow horns and make all manner of exasperating noises just to amuse the world, even when there ain't no actual emergency to speak of."

"But your store is apparently destroyed!" said Rowan.

"Right you are, but look, we eventually got hold of things from the inside, once our scattered wits were collected. We had to really hop-to-it, though. Woo hoo. It was a furnace and then some, I'll tell you. Letty chanted one of Mother Gorthwog's old spells to at least prevent neighboring structures from catching fire, and I managed to put the two of us in a FireBane Bubble so we didn't go up in smoke like the rest of our stuff. Wasn't easy, neither. I had to draw upon every ounce of power I had to contend with a burn *that* ferocious. Even then it zapped the Veldarnian ostrich-feather right off my nightcap and you can see what's been done to Letty's hair. Lucky she's got anything left at all to braid around her aching head."

"You did good with the Mother Gorthwog spell," noted Letty. "And a little teamwork at the very end kept things from becoming a lot worse, I suppose. We managed to find our way out of them smoke clouds and flames, eventually, but we were not best pleased to be greeted by such a nosy lot once we got outside. Fire trucks and camera crews and bored tourists all amped-up taking movies on their phones and such. And then there was us, hardly looking our best to top everything off! Insult to injury, was what it was. But we put the fix on all the shutterbugs, at least as far as the two of us were concerned."

"We sure did!" crowed Gert. "None of them will remember even seeing us and no film of any sort could capture us. We both cast the net of that particular spell pretty wide, and then we figured it was best to just dematerialize and try to find our way here. Oh, thank you, Miranda, sweetie. I sure could use a nice glass of ambrosia right now. That last push to get us into your kitchen took the starch right out of me."

"Me, too," said Letty, accepting a cool glass of supernatural refreshment from Miranda, who hurried out with her serving tray as quickly as she had hurried in. These nerved-up witches were still volatile and her own wealth of experience told her that the far end of the house—if not the back garden—was still the safest place to be.

"I'm a bit surprised that y'all didn't see any coverage of the fire on the TV," mused Gert, sipping the salvific beverage. "We didn't block out anyone's ability to film the *overall* disaster … just us two disasters."

"I wouldn't have seen anything because I don't keep a television in the house," explained Rowan. Gert, denuded of her precious ostrich feather though she was, found herself most pleasantly fascinated by this tidbit of information.

"You mean you don't even have one for poor dear Miranda to watch?" she queried.

"No. Miranda, if you'll recall, was not raised among mortals, so she has no particular attachment to the things and, for my part, I can't abide them."

"And that's a fitting approach, too," encouraged Letty. "Some people in this room would not be inclined to agree, however, seeing as how they would rather drop undead than miss a little girl beauty pageant being shown on one of them chatterboxes."

"Oh, stow it, Beauregard," rasped Gert.

"Serves you right, in that sense," countered Letty. "You won't be watching no pint-sized princesses strutting around like little peacocks, now."

"Please, ladies! Before you set my own house afire, I would ask that you clarify these matters just a little bit more to satisfy my own curiosity, seeing as you're here. You say that this tragedy began with a headache and a piece of cookware? Given those oddities alone, I simply must know the details."

Gert placed her now empty glass on the marble tabletop at her knees and licked her lips with a sigh, eager to tell the story of their dramatic morning. In her estimation, this was certainly not the first time in history that some great domestic catastrophe had been the direct result of things like headaches and cookware, in natural or supernatural worlds.

"It all began last night, after we closed up shop, or not terribly long after. I was busy counting the till, but right around then, Letty started to whine a little bit about one of her premonitional headaches, or what have you. It started to get real bad, too. Believe me, as long as we've been housemates I have never known Letty to get one of these migraines and not have something really serious come to pass as a result. Back in the old days, she used to be able to get a pretty clear read on her premonitions. Remember, Letty? Her mother was the same way. People in them days either paid attention when she smelled trouble and did something to look after themselves, or else the cow patties hit the fan and you were liable to get caught right in the middle of the spatter. Some folks back then—mortal and not-so-mortal—didn't pay her mother enough heed, and look what happened to them!"

"Her mother?" said Rowan.

"Yeah, Letty's mother once worked a stint as the Hag of Vesuvius. Ain't that a thing? But I digress. Nowadays, when Letty gets these attacks of hers, sometimes the big deal about to happen ain't always a *bad* deal, if you catch my drift. Sure, Volkswagen-sized meteorites might explode over remote portions of wintry Russian woodland, leveling every tree within a hundred mile radius, but one of her headaches might also mean that some old rock and roll band is about to make an announcement that they are set to reunite for a 'limited time only' world tour. You never know. One of her headaches might mean that some elf queen in the Amazon is gonna have a royal child, or that there might be a brief outbreak of zombies in Jakarta. Again, you frankly never can tell with one of Letty's thumpers, and even though she's usually pretty good at working her way to the heart of the oracle and giving folks fair warning or timely prediction so's they can send out announcement cards or take shelter, she was not getting anywhere with last night's case.

"Once that became apparent, I knew dramatic measures would have to be taken or her head was gonna explode off her shoulders, along with half the shopping district on St. George Street. So I figured I could get hold of the occult energy hammering at the inside of her thick skull by using a Phlegmatic Transcendental Override, you know, like anybody *sensible* would do, and then redirect the fallout from the spell into my scrying pan. That wok was the best vessel I have ever encountered in my travels, when it comes to things that work well as transmission material for divination magic. Hands down! Now, Letty likes to draw undue attention to one or two little mistakes I've made with my wok in the past …"

"Ha! One or two?" blurted Letty.

"But I'd put its accuracy up against any sibyl from Delphi to old Siwah, if push came to shove," continued Gert.

"Fact is, Blaize, the old goat really was trying to help me with her banged-up vegetable cooker," interjected Letty, squirming with agitation on the edge of her chair. "But I don't think neither of us was prepared for the magnitude of the hidden vision that was tormenting me."

"But what was it?" said Rowan, exasperated. "What in the world and worlds-within did you end up seeing?"

At this, both women glowered helplessly and tried to avoid their broadsided host's inquisitive gaze.

"Trouble is," continued Letty, clearing her throat and sitting up straight in an effort to regain some semblance of her usual, cantankerous dignity, "we lost the vision just when Gert was yanking it out of my head and into the waters of her wok."

"That's a fact," nodded Gert, sad eyed and curling at the lip. "I never felt such a stinging, furious, fiery ball of magical mental weight in all my days. 'Hold on,' I screamed at Letty while I was chanting the spell to maneuver the pain into the pan, but she was half in and half out of consciousness because it hurt so bad. Then, just as I got my first glimpse in the scrying waters, Letty pulled away and broke the Harmonic Bridge of Enchantment. The pent-up power of her unrealized vision boomeranged and whiplashed outward, hitting the mirror in the bathroom, which was bad enough, as I said before. That's when the whole place turned into a conflagration. It's a terrible thing, you know, when a witch gets a mighty vision that she can't elucidate. The power just builds and builds like a boiler about to blow and then——"

"Yes, yes, I am familiar with the scenario," interrupted Rowan. "Such circumstances are not to be taken lightly, by any means."

"Nor handled lightly," offered Letty in tones decorated at the edges with the frosting of accusation.

"Hey, my spell was working just fine and you were about to be headache-free, if you weren't such a belligerent old bandicoot, even when you're half-comatose!"

"Bandicoot, eh?" spat Letty. "I may be more than a little spent after the morning we just endured, but I think I have enough strength to turn you into an *actual* bandicoot, Miss Fumble Fingers!"

"I did not drop or fumble-finger your psychic ball of brain-freeze, Leticia Beauregard! If you hadn't been raised to be so contrary——"

"Enough!" said Rowan, tempted to give his boot another stomp, but wary of attracting unwanted attention from seismologists in the relatively earthquake-free zone of North Florida. "Don't you two think the more important issue right now is what shall become of your home and shop? If you say it's been destroyed, then the mortal authorities are certain to be searching for two elderly and charred-beyond-recognition bodies. It's not as if the two of you are unknown in this town as business owners."

"Especially Gert, after that margarita debacle at last year's Chamber of Commerce gala!" clucked Letty in triumph.

"Whull, at least I wasn't batty enough to take off into the midday air after too much hemlock sangria at a dryad baby-shower and crash, drunk as a skunk, right into the cathedral bell tower. Tell Rowan how you explained being found ninety-five feet up in a belfry one morning by a sacristan, with nothing but a bad case of hiccups and a broomstick! That was in 1967, mind. Folks around here weren't quite as open minded as they are now."

"Can we dispense with this eternal needling, ladies? In fact, I insist upon it, because I am about to develop an explosive headache of my own. You're both rather sad cases at the moment, in my regard, but I do consider you dear friends and, until you make other arrangements, the two of you are certainly welcome to camp here. It's times like this that I wish I had not allowed Miranda to convince me to build that guesthouse in the back garden, but you'll be most comfortable there."

Both witches bristled appropriately. "We certainly do not wish to put you to any inconvenience, Master Blaize," enunciated Letty, setting her iced ambrosia down as if it were suddenly a glass of poison.

"That's rather correct," added Gert, directing her words just as primly. "No one has ever been able to say that we have been forced to rely upon the charity of others. At least no one who remains in their original form, I should mention. Ahem. We journeyed this way because it seemed as if it were the most palatable option before us, at the time."

"Moreover," said Letty, with the measured trajectory of a world champion dart-thrower, "we always did consider you to be a worthy acquaintance, despite your status as a newcomer to our charming community."

Rowan rolled his icy gray eyes and held up a calming hand. "Look, you're both welcome to stay with me as long as you like, or need. There's plenty of room, whether in the guesthouse out back or in the main house, and, as you may or may not know, I *am* quite fond of you two."

"Now, isn't that just the sweetest thing to say?" gushed Gert, transforming from offended interloper into mushy, cherished guest in an instant, though she did not reach over and pinch Rowan's cheek as her impulse was dictating. "What a darling thing to say. Isn't that a darling thing to say, Leticia?"

"It's friendly enough," agreed her companion with a weary and reluctant grin.

"There does remain the issue of how you'll deal with what's taken place within the framework of the mortal community," reminded Rowan. "I realize better than anyone that our kind plays fast and loose with their rules, but explanations of some sort will be required."

Gert propped her lavender-slippered feet on the marble coffee table and made herself exceedingly at home, seeing that they had officially been invited to move in.

"Now, don't you worry your handsome head over that, Rowan Blaize. We can always tell people that we were off visiting relatives when the awful fire occurred. And we have excellent insurance."

"Not to mention a fair amount of money in the bank," added Letty, a bit more proudly than she intended. "It'll be a snap for us to rebuild the shop, if that's what we want to do. *Is* that what we want to do, Gert?"

"I daresay we owe it to our legions of loyal customers, Letty," came the response, and then the two started clucking at each other over the virtues of faithful clientele in such erstwhile touristy climes.

"That's all well and good," said Rowan, mustering his coolest, black iron expression, "but what about the headache?"

"What are you talking about, honey?" cooed Gert, genuinely perplexed.

"Miss Beauregard's oracular headache. Her vision. Her premonition. You said her headaches are always harbingers of considerable magnitude. Through all of this drama did either of you manage to ascertain anything remotely useful before the aborted attempt to unravel the tangle in Letty's second sight?"

The witches stared at each other for a moment and then Gert shrugged. "Before everything caught fire and our place went up like Mrs. O'Leary's cow had kicked my wok off the table, before I lost my grip on Letty's head-trip, I did manage to see ... er ... a *little* something in the scrying water."

"And?"

"That's the thing," continued Gert, scratching her scalp up underneath the disheveled purple turban. A puzzled look flashed across her brow. "It wasn't anything terrible or untoward, in the sense of a tragedy or some other ominous happening or event. In fact, I can't even be sure I saw exactly what it is that I saw. All the excitement afterward may have skewed my memory a bit."

"Humor us all the same," insisted Rowan.

Gert straightened her plump shoulders and her enormous bosom heaved with a mixture of exhaustion and relief.

"It was Serenity Turnbull. Serenity Turnbull and something dark hovering all around her. That's it. I coulda swore I saw her, just standing there in the wok water, plain as plain. Nothing else unusual about it, unless we take into account that Serenity Turnbull is just plain unusual in the first place. That's all I glimpsed. Oh. I think she was in her jammies. There was that, too. Her in her jammies and that awful shadow. Then she was gone. So much for visions and premonitions, eh? I was expecting maybe a tidal wave based on the intensity of Letty's discomfort and all I get is little ditzy dormouse Serenity Turnbull." Gert shook her head and laughed, hoarse from smoke inhalation. "My vision must've jammed-up when I lost—I mean, when Letty inadvertently *yanked away*—her part of the charm. Serenity may be an awful lot of things, but she ain't no catastrophe and she ain't no ominous event."

"Took the words right out of my mouth," agreed Letty, who was now on her feet and inspecting the surface of Rowan's mantelpiece for signs of dust, since she might be settling in these parts for a while. Rowan was bothered, but not by Letty's brazen investigation. Rather, elusive shadows of his own were beginning to crowd his thoughts.

"Yes," he murmured after a moment. "It was probably just a strange side-effect of a reckless bit of spell-casting gone terribly awry." The witches both glared daggers at him. "But it pays to be safe, rather than sorry. I had been planning to pay Serenity a visit later today and convince her to come to the All Hallow's Eve party, and I think I'll head over as soon as possible, just to make sure everything is in order."

"Oh, that is such a gentlemanly thing to do," said Gert admiringly. "And look at me! I had almost forgot about the big party. I guess now we can go together, us three, seeing as we're temporarily in residence with the host himself!"

"We can even help with the planning," suggested Letty, eyes wide and determined. She looked comically frightful even to Rowan, standing bolt upright near the hearth with her now-black and crispy lace collar upturned toward her chin. "I knew your All Hallow's Eve parties would become the highlight of the occult calendar in St. Augustine, but there's always room for little improvements here and there, ain't that right? For example, at last year's party I noticed that—"

"Thank you, Letty," said Rowan, "but things are well in hand between the work of Miranda and my own efforts to pull this event together. Your recommendations alone have proved more than enough contribution in the past. Besides, all of the arrangements are finalized, and I mean for it to be the most spectacular gathering yet. I *predict* it will be ... without even having the benefit of a psychic headache."

Letty's mouth screwed up as if she had just bitten into a lemon.

"I do appreciate your offer of help, but after you two have rested a bit and made yourselves ... er ... *presentable*, Miranda will show you to the guest house or to the guest bedrooms upstairs, depending upon your preference. I think you'll both have your hands full attending to the disaster downtown and to the local authorities, whom I guarantee will wish to see you both alive and well, and in the flesh."

"Oh, we can handle that!" assured Gert, as if the infernal eradication of her home had always been a routine part of her long and colorful existence. "Now how about asking that precious little Miranda to rustle us up some wormwood martinis, eh? This ambrosia was positively restorative, but now my nerves need something a bit more steadying, before I have to go and look at my poor ole ruined store, not to mention my home, and then act all surprised and distressed for the mortals."

Rowan nodded. "I'll send Miranda to attend you in a moment. Otherwise, make yourselves ... well, *more* at home than you already appear to be, I guess. I'm glad that you're both safe and sound. Bror needs to be fed and the library tidied up, and then I shall pay my quick visit to Serenity after sunset. The four of us can have our dinner here at eight. Would that suit you?"

"Sounds grand," replied Gert. "You bring the wormwood martinis and we'll bring ourselves. Oh, and be sure to give our regards to Miss Turnbull and tell her we are very much looking forward to seeing her at the party, so long as she doesn't wear her jammies to it."

☙❧

X

Chesterfield Rummy was on his knees, trembling like a man stricken with some virulent and exotic fever, but indeed his problem—or, rather, one ought to aver that his PROBLEM—was in actuality far more virulent and far more exotic than any fever.

BonSashay was kicking and trying to squeal through the kitchen towel that had been shoved into her mouth, hanging from the hem of her fur-trimmed hoop skirt on the blade of a stainless steel ceiling fan in the middle of Serenity Turnbull's living room.

The djin, Dedwen the Mighty and Heinous, was no longer cloaked in the illusory form of the ruby ring-imprisoned Serenity, but had reverted to his true and pestilential, petrifying self. It was a showy act of transformation that Councilman Rummy and his fame-hungry offspring had not quite been expecting to witness when they first followed the blonde maiden-in-a-fancy-housecoat through the front door.

Madness, of course, had toyed briefly with Chesterfield's already tenuous mental faculties and, had he been a man of science, or machinery, or learning, or an atheist, he most assuredly would have succumbed to the white-hot fingers of insanity clawing at his cerebrum because of what he had seen with his own, bulging eyes. Even so, Mr. Rummy, in addition to being a charlatan of considerable criminal imagination, was, like most of the people in the South who don neckties and suits for whatever reason, a soul rooted in and raised with an almost innate respect for the teachings of the Holy Bible—King James Version.

Devils *exist*.

Here, in this otherwise decoratively pedestrian beach house, in this twee living room, was one of those very beings, one of those devils, idly spinning his frantic daughter round and round on the ceiling fan with a talon as large and as sharp as the samurai sword that hung on the wall above the bar in Chesterfield's favorite Japanese restaurant in Jacksonville. Therefore, the elder Rummy did not go mad. Instead, he believed. He believed and he fell upon his knees and he trembled with the sheer agony of his overweening belief, with the shock of it. Yes, he thought, for an instant, of diving headfirst out the nearby sliding glass door onto the back yard. But he figured that would hurt too much and, quite frankly, a being like the one hulking before him seemed capable of catching a person, if that person tried to make a run for it. Yet, more than anything else in his heart—an organ somewhat swollen with arterial plaque and existential bitterness—Rummy felt the flickering hope of a potential deal that could be wheeled, a shady bargain that might be struck.

Devils exist.

Devils strike deals.

Chesterfield had read that or heard that; it was something that anyone with an ounce of mischief knew, or ought to have known. Thus, he had Hope of the most shameful and deliriously dirty variety.

Sweat poured from his glands like thick oil. His eyes continued to bug out of his phony flat-topped head. His piggy knuckles were white and held up in clenched position before him, as if in prayer. He had already bitten a small chunk out of his tongue due to the trembling, and the devil, the enormous festering devil, had watched all of this with mild interest, at best.

"It is quite obvious to me that I am far removed from my accustomed climate," growled the djin in a voice like the settling of great rocks in undersea caves after an earthquake. "Even the weakest mortal men of my native habitat, and time, would have conducted themselves with more dignity than you have done."

Dedwen nodded his repulsive head, mandibles dribbling venom, toward the large puddle on the Saltillo tile, the puddle currently pooling outward beneath the crotch of Chesterfield Rummy's drenched trousers.

"But you may be of some amusement to me, despite such distasteful cowardice," continued the djin. "For one, you have not gone mad at the sight of me, which indicates that my kind still has some measure of odd influence in this age and place, whence and wherever it is. You are a believer. Is that not so?"

"Yrrghhhh … ghurghgggg … ynggghug," said Rummy.

"Just nod, my good man," rasped Dedwen with a resulting yawn that withered the fourteen-foot ficus tree in the corner to a rancid, drooping twig and seared every curling hair in both of Chesterfield Rummy's flaring nostrils. "Nodding is a most acceptable way for your kind to answer my kind when asked a question."

Rummy nodded, or tried to do so. He was now shivering with such violence that his head went sideways as much as it went up and down, and his yellowed teeth clacked and chattered like dice being shaken in a cup.

"That leads us to the next point," continued Dedwen, spinning the feisty, muzzled girl in shiny tap shoes around once again. There was an almost poignant delicacy to the flick of its gleaming talon-tip. "You may be a believer, but you are not, decidedly, a *good* man, as I first termed you. In fact, you are anything but good, like most men."

"Yrgghhghh … flnghhnch," said Mr. Rummy.

"No, no. No need to comment," instructed Dedwen, wagging a terrible finger before he spun the tiring BonSashay anew. "I can see straight through to your greedy, grimy, little fluttering moth-of-a-soul. Indeed. You, Sir, would like to strike a bargain. It is plain to see. Again, you prove marginally amusing, if predictable in the extreme. Despite my prior confinement—which we shall not now or ever discuss in detail— I had existed quite long enough beforehand to learn that, even though mortal men, women, and their tragic kingdoms evolve, their whining wickedness never seems to benefit from periodic advancements. As a result, their souls remain ever-prone to the tawdry and to the gluttonous. It is amazing to have watched a species so mired in its own vulgarity that it cannot ever learn enough from the errors of its past to secure its future. It has been one long and tedious affair watching you fools lift yourselves, literally, out of the primordial mud, build castles and fortresses out of the same dirt, essentially, tear them all down or watch as they are destroyed due to your own avarice, then POOF! You pick yourselves up from the filth with astonishing determination, only so you can repeat the entire ridiculous process all over again."

"Mnmnphhgccck!"

"Pray do not interrupt me, little man. It is most unwise. Now, where was I? Oh yes. We djinn are beings that have certain advantages, it is true, but we are not bound to your dismal fate, by any means. At least ... not yet," added Dedwen with a lurid glance ahead into centuries and veiled eons of time that even he could not dare to fathom. "Until the Resolution of All Things, if All Things are indeed ever to be Resolved, we have sought to entertain ourselves as best we can and thus all the world is our amphitheater, so long as you unfortunate buffoons are moving about in it. Bargains, I must confess, have always proven rather irresistible to us, and even we do not know why such a thing should be so!

"To be certain, there are a few Powers greater than Us, flitting about, dwelling in this world or shifting in and out between the very many worlds that do indeed exist. Perhaps They know why even the worm-fodder of humanity can so easily beguile our vastly superior imaginations with the dangling carrot of a bargain, of a game. Alas, They do not reveal much as to the reason, if any reason exists at all, and I would very much like to hear *your* proposal, little man. For your sake, it had better be an interesting proposal. Now speak, you miniscule bag of angst-ridden cognate primeval ooze."

Dedwen lowered his three pulsating, soul-scorching eyes to Chesterfield Rummy and waited.

"I ... I ... I w-w-want to l-l-l-live!" jabbered the quaking councilman.

The great djin's eyes closed in contempt and its slavering mandibles clicked in what could perhaps best be described as the hellspawn's version of "Tsk, tsk, tsk."

"Surely you can do better than that?" grumbled Dedwen. "I took you for a snake of much more complex colors and coil formations than first-glance would indicate. Every idiotic mortal 'wants to live.' That is the only thing, in fact, that your kind all seems to agree upon, universally, as a species, in fact. But where is the art, little man? Where is the offering? A bargain involves a delicate exchange of goods or interests. Come, come! You want to entice me with something and I wish to be enticed. Whatever could be the matter, when matters are thus so clearly understood and set before us? Rally yourself, toad! I don't have all day and neither shall you, in a completely different sense, if you fail to rise to the occasion. Still, let Us be merciful and give you a moment to collect what paltry wits you possess. A diversion is required. Let us discuss your name, for instance."

"Any … any … th … th …thing you want, Your Greatness," answered Rummy in a terrific spray of spit, sweat and snot.

Dedwen blinked and scratched lazily behind a membranous earlobe. Drooping from the ceiling fan, BonSashay had finally passed out.

"Yes. Crummy, I believe it was, according to the card you brandished at the portal. I have little doubt that your name is a most common and reprobate title amid a sea of garish and repugnant mortal monikers," noted the djin, "but you did well to include an honorific when addressing me just now. Things *appear* to be looking up. And this squeaking little tidbit is your offspring, I gather?"

Dedwen gave the fan another push with a talon and a dazed red face lifted momentarily to peek out from a tumbling mass of blonde curls. Round and round she spun again, her father's head making open-mouthed little spirals as he watched.

"Y-yes, Your Greatness. Your Excellence. Th-that there is my little girl, BonSashay. Hi there, honey. Daddy's right here. Now don't you fret about a thing. I'm just gonna have a nice talk with … uh … with Mister … um …with this gentleman, with this demonic gentleman, here, and everything is gonna be okay."

BonSashay squirmed and tried in vain to wriggle her way off the fan, but her frilly fundraising fur-trimmed frock was irrevocably impaled on the blade. She did, however, summon enough moxie to attempt a kick at Dedwen's glimmering talon as she spun by.

"Now don't struggle, darling. It'll only make things worse, I suspect."

"Not really," said Dedwen with some sincerity, narrowing one blue bloodshot eye at the girl. "She is very young. Too young even to give away in marriage, unless things have truly changed on the planet since I was away. Tell me, Crummy: why is she dressed like one of Caligula's harlots?"

"Excuse me, Sir? I mean, Your Hellaciousness?"

"The child," replied the djin. "Why is she garbed in the adornments of an imperial circus monkey? Can it be that some traditions have survived the long dark of the ages? And I have never seen such exceedingly golden hair on a child. Is it real?"

"Y-yeah. It's real. It's my daughter's hair. She's a blonde … or, mostly a blonde. Sort of. My wife gives it a little help, what with the bottle treatments. My wife's real good at that sort of thing. Or she used to be. But I don't know what you mean about the other, the harlots and circus monkeys and all. My precious little baby girl is a beauty pageant contestant, not a hook … uh … not a working gal."

"What do you mean by 'pageant' little man?" Dedwen leaned against the marble-topped counter of Serenity's kitchen. The countertop immediately cracked down the middle to accommodate his enormous elbow. "I have witnessed mortal pageantry in my day. Great processions in honor of the gods. Festive altars and costumes and such. Is your daughter some sort of priestess?"

"Priestess? Gosh, no, not at all, your devilry. We started out as Baptists, then we got involved in the tongues movement for a while, but still Christian. In fact … Oh, Lord! I oughtta be calling upon my Savior right this very minute, seeing as we're trapped here in the clutches of—"

"Don't bother," breathed Dedwen with a lazy but dismissive wave of his claws. "Doesn't work that way, at least not in your particular situation. Now tell me what the two of you were doing here? I seem to have forgotten. Why is it that you came to the witch's dwelling?"

"The WHAT?"

Dedwen blinked in hideous triplicate. "Are you telling me that you did not know a witch lives—*lived*—here?"

Chesterfield gulped and sweated some more. "Golly, no. We sure didn't know that. But a witch living here would sure enough explain a devil hanging about the place, begging your pardon, of course."

"Hmm. It might explain that, yes. But believe me when I say that the witch was about as void of a clue as are you. And do stop referring to me as a devil. I sense that this is a rather generic term in your abrasive and most unpleasant tongue, a tongue to which I have adapted for purposes of sheer convenience. I am more properly termed an *ifrit*. I belong to the race of the djinn, little man, which is a race quite apart from that of your common devil. Most assuredly. I say! I am becoming rather adept at your disgusting language, which is a fine magical accomplishment, considering that I have heard more intelligible syllables emitted by zebras writhing in the jaws of Nile crocodiles. Still, far be it from me to dismiss local custom, particularly when the striking of a bargain is imminent. So let us come to it. Tell me why I should not smite you down where you kneel, mortal! I grow weary of your ugliness and there is an intriguing old world in new adornment that I am most eager to explore."

Chesterfield Rummy quailed and cowered. He knew what the word "smite" meant, having heard it so often during his youth in the church pews and having used it threateningly himself on numerous occasions during his failed attempt at a ministry, and also upon his wife when she committed any number of her usual infractions.

"Please don't smite me, Mighty Afright!"

"That's *ifrit,* you idiot."

"I … I meant to say afreet. I mean, I'm not exactly sure where you come from or what you're doing here, or even if I'm awake right now."

"But you are, Crummy. You are."

Chesterfield licked his lips and tasted the dried blood that had dripped out from his bitten tongue. Yes, he was wide awake, and likewise was his maniacal instinct for survival, the black flickering finger of wickedness, or whatever the djin had called it. If his skin was on the line and this thing from the pits of Hell demanded some sort of deal to smooth things over and save that skin, then Rummy knew that he, a man who had parted starving old women from their paltry life savings for the most deviously fabricated reasons under the sun, was a man who just might be shifty enough to make a deal with the devil ... or, rather, with the *ifrit*.

Suddenly, there on the knee-splitting floor tiles, Chesterfield Rummy's heart, such as it was, formed a powerful and almost sentimental bond of solidarity with the endless array of connivers, cheats, tricksters, con men, grifters, sharps, and hustlers who had come before him in the Bloodline of Sordidness. In that dire and surreal moment, he embraced the nattering ghosts of Deceivers Past and let the dank, slightly greasy aura of their collective metaphysical dishonor wash over him in a fortifying wave of psychic ill-repute. Suddenly, Chesterfield Rummy felt more religious than he had truly felt in forty-three years and, in full communion with the unseen spirits of his despicable ancestry, beneath a cloud of witnesses swollen with the acid rain of moral erosion, he regained the hyena gleam in his eye and veritably reveled in the walls of his wheelhouse.

He rose a bit from his crouch. "Let's you and me strike up some kind of mutually beneficial deal, Mister ... uh ..."

"You may, for the moment, call me Lord Dedwen."

"Alright, Mister Lord Dedwen. Let's talk about this. Now, I can see, plain as plain, that you are a being of some ambition and flair. Why, I can tell by them hundreds of piercings and them wonderfully drawn tattoos that you are someone who likes to assert your unique identity."

"Is that so?" said Lord Dedwen.

"Abso-freakin'-lutely it's so! I recognize gigantic talent when I see it. Heck, I am in the very business of recognizing talent, Mister Lord Dedwen, and let me be the first, or probably just the latest in a long line of admirers to say that you are just exploding with talent. Explosive. Heh. That's right. You are also someone who has probably been very misunderstood by the world, am I right?"

The djin shrugged, with only one shoulder. It was all the same to him.

"I knew it!" said Rummy, now rising cautiously from his knees, hands gesturing with all the carnival ringmaster authority inherent to the dusty interior of his fly-by-night Big Top soul. He wasn't about to fall down in terror any longer. Here was the opportunity he had *really* been waiting for all his unfulfilled-but-not-for-lack-of-trying-all-the-wrong-things life.

"What do human beings know about the plights and personalities of glorious creatures like yourself? Why, devils and demons and genies and such—they all get the short end of the stick in this shallow culture. Portraying y'all as good for nothing else except spitting pea soup and whirling heads around, and maybe living in filthy oil lamps to be summoned at will by greedy, good for nothing whippersnappers!"

"I know nothing about this soup you mention, but I see that you have heard at least some of the more popular stories concerning my race," noted the djin.

"That's just it, see," continued Rummy. "They's all nothing but legends and stories. Big distortions of the truth that have been blown way outta proportion for purposes of cheap human entertainment, and human entertainment is in a sad state of affairs, Mister Lord Dedwen, take it from me."

"Hmph!" snorted the djin.

"But a presence like yours could change all of that in the biggest, most profound way ever achieved in all of earthly history."

"How, pray tell, could that be accomplished, little man?"

"Through the power of television!" said Rummy with the brightest twinkle he had ever summoned to his molasses-colored eyes and a panoramic sweep of his pudgy hand, as if caressing an invisible rainbow.

"What, exactly, is television?"

"Why, it's only the greatest feat of human magic and ingenuity ever conceived," exuded Chesterfield. "Television is a means by which important images are transmitted to millions and millions of other human beings simultaneously, in their homes, all at one time! It's a means of grabbing countless legions of folks right by their craws and shaking them down right to their very toenails! Now, I have little doubt that you are a fiend of practically immeasurable power, but I also have a hunch that even you could not beam yourself out to be seen by literally millions of people all at the same time."

Dedwen bristled, but gave the matter some consideration. "You are correct. I can do a great many things, but I cannot do that. Nor do I believe that mortals have the power to do such a thing, either. You lie, Crummy!"

Three swift plumes of fire sizzled outward from the djin's nostrils and he loomed over the wildly grinning Chesterfield Rummy, bending forward with menace.

"Now, now, hold on, hold on. I can show you, Lord Master Dedwen."

He sidled over to the television set in Serenity's half-destroyed living room. It was covered with dust and a bit of debris from the wrecked bedroom ceiling above, but the remote was still atop the widescreen. He was about pray that the thing worked, that the witch—or whoever had lived here—had full cable, and then he thought that, under the circumstances, prayer might not be such a good idea. He had to play to one Side only, now, and he had chosen that Side. It wouldn't do to turn back just as the game was getting good. He fumbled with the control and flicked on the set, treating the behemoth djin to another flourish of his fat fingers and an episode of *Jersey Shore* already in progress.

"What manner of sorcery is this?" fumed the ifrit. "More, even uglier, pig-like harlots bouncing around in a magic box? This is a witch's trick!"

"No, no, no, no!" said Rummy with the calming gestures of a Cadillac dealer about to blow the most important sale of his life. "Not true. I mean, the part about the pig-like harlots is right on the money, but this ain't no witchcraft. I know you said the little lady that lived here was a witch, but if so, then she had herself a TV just like everybody else in America. Nothing magical about it. It's all science, you see. Technology is what they call it."

"I grasp the meaning of that word, and I knew of mortal scientists in my own time" said Dedwen, staring at the set, gargantuan arms akimbo. "And you say that all mortals possess one of these contraptions?"

"Aw, heck yes! Sometimes even two, three, four of them in one house. Even the little brown pygmy people over in Africa got themselves little pygmy TV sets, I hear tell."

"They have this power in Africa?" rumbled the djin, fascinated.

"Darn right they do. They may not have toilets or running water or anything to eat, but they got TV sets and cellphones, believe you me. I got a brother-in-law who made a small fortune setting up signal towers for this kinda stuff all over Morocco or Tanzanibia or some godawful place like that."

"Let us suppose that you are not deceiving me," said Dedwen, poking a talon through Chesterfield's sweat-soaked shirt and just barely piercing the flabby shoulder beneath. "How is this mortal magic or technology of any benefit to the likes of me? How is it of benefit in the bargain you seek to strike?"

Chesterfield Rummy leaned forward as much as he dared to share a conspiratorial whisper. "Between you and me, one of the most prestigious events in the whole nation is about to take place, day after tomorrow, right here in this town."

"What event?"

"The Pint-Sized Princess Beauty and Talent Pageant," answered Rummy, breathless from the pain of the talon still sinking into his shoulder. "Little BonSashay up there on the fan is slated to compete. The whole country is gonna be watching them pretty little dolls prance out on that stage to vie for the tiara, the title, and the timelessness. The winner gets a shot at going on to compete for world champion in Las Vegas. I swear, Master Lord Dedwen—this Pint-Sized Pageant coming to town is gonna be carried on the History Channel and everything, right after that hot new show they do about folks in trailer parks who make candles outta their own earwax."

"What sort of competition involves little human girls?" spat Dedwen, still staring at the horrors of mortal degradation languishing on the widescreen.

"Well, the usual little girl stuff," replied Rummy. "Bikinis. Hair and make-up. Lip-synching. Dancing. Poise challenges. Some of the girls even perform a few magic tricks."

"Magic tricks?" Dedwen raised one cactus-spined brow.

"Course, not the kind of magic tricks you're used to. I'm talking about stuff with cards and hankies and rabbits and hats and such."

"And you say that millions of mortals will be watching these painted little squabs perform their tricks, all at once, on a device like the one I see before me?"

"Yes. Millions who tune in. They'll all be expecting to see it!"

"I sense a proposal," roared Dedwen. He roared until the pane-glass window over the tidy backyard began to shudder.

"I propose that we give these millions some tricks that they *ain't* expecting to see!" said Rummy with a wink and a deal-sealing slam of one fist into his open palm.

"Ah! I surmise that you do indeed possess reserves of potentially useful but derelict wisdom, Crummy."

"You bet I do, Mister Lord Dedwen! But that's my bargain, see? My life for your debut on national television so you can scare the living daylights out of humanity, so you can show them what a real whatever-it-is-you-said-you-are is all about. I am especially equipped to help you achieve this once in a lifetime opportunity, due to my vast experience in this very genre of entertainment. You see, I have been BonSashay's agent for quite a while, but I always thought I could do even better with a more explosive, controversial act. Truth be told, my little girl ain't got much talent. But she's got big hair, and outfits. Big hair and outfits is really all it takes in the little girl beauty pageant game. Oh, I can't imagine the looks of horror when a handsome brute like you walks out on that stage, bold as beans! And I'm the one who knows how to get you in to set up the money shot! But it's gotta be planned just right, so I can't emphasize enough how much you need *me* to help."

"Fool," snarled the djin. "Do you think a Power of my pedigree lacks a sense of proper showmanship? I have seen mortals perform everywhere, from Athens, to Caesarea Maritime, to Samarkand. I know the value of a dramatic turn! We go in with subtlety and then launch the 'money shot,' as you call it, at the proper instant. Tricks? These millions of unsuspecting humans will see such tricks that their pattering little hearts will leap right out of their throats! There is nothing an *ifrit* loves more than working a crowd, and this television, this mortal vessel of passable ingenuity, will allow me to make a most auspicious debut in this new and foreign age. I will set my seal upon this era, and all the other djinn will be howling and tearing their tails out with envy. But first, we would require a proper disguise."

Dedwen reached over with an arm that easily crossed the span of the living room and plucked BonSashay from her dangle on the ceiling fan. He lifted her swiftly into the air above his reprehensible head, tilted his neck backward and, spreading his mandibles, allowed his rancid maw to unlatch, like that of a boa constrictor. The djin-mouth opened with a terrible bone-crunching sound until it became a throbbing and slimy pink canyon, ringed with fangs into which the kicking, squealing child would soon be dropped, curls, hoop-skirt, and all.

"Sweet mother of mercy!" yelled Rummy. "What you gonna do to my darling little girl?"

Dedwen paused and turned to look at him, annoyed.

"I am going to feast upon her. What does it look like?"

BonSashay tried to kick the djin in the forehead, but Dedwen held her away like a spider holds back a particularly irritating and energetic insect trapped in its web before getting down to the act of envenomation and mastication.

"B-b-b-but ... is that really necessary, O Great and Powerful Lord Dedwen?" bleated Chesterfield Rummy. "I mean, I thought we had a bargain, you and me."

"We do. The bargain is that you offer your unfailing services as 'agent' to me in exchange for your life. Unless you would like to change the terms of your bargain, in which case I would be happy to feast upon *you* and secure your daughter's services instead. I imagine she knows a thing or two about televisions and procedures at these bizarre competitions. In fact, she could prove most helpful. Probably more helpful than you."

"Then you're telling me it's necessary for you to eat one of us?" wailed Rummy.

"It is. Not only am I famished, but it is crucial for the spell I have in mind, as you—or one of you—shall see presently. Now decide according to the terms of our original bargain, Crummy. Hold to them, or withdraw. Keep in mind, however, that a significant amount of worldly fortune is very likely to be added to the benefit of the one who assists me in my endeavor. There is also an outside chance for inordinately long life."

Chesterfield Rummy froze, and the world, the universe, and the universes within universes, seemed to freeze with him.

"Did I hear you say 'fortune' and 'long life,' Mister Lord Dedwen?"

"You did."

"Would that fortune, by any chance, have something to do with, say, actual pieces of genuine gold?"

"Unquestionably."

"Eat her."

ৡৡ

XI

Rowan was relieved to depart the house and the nervous, fussing witches and soar upward into the gentle cool of the evening sky. It was not routine for him to fly as a means of travel in and around St. Augustine—the magic was exceedingly draining, it had always been draining, in its way. More to the point, it was not a very discreet mode of transportation, particularly where the terrain was flat and one could not coarse alongside the camouflaging curl of a mountain range, or skirt seemingly endless woodland treetop expanses. Everything was ocean, earth, and vast horizon in Florida. A body speeding across that horizon, whether one hundred feet or one thousand feet in the air, was conspicuous and invited attention that was in no way desirable, for many reasons.

This evening, however, Rowan was hurried, worried, and eager to enjoy the whistling caress of the wind upon his face while borne aloft. After sunset, he donned a black woolen cloak and went up the circular stair to the little widow's walk fronting the top of the stately Victorian's façade. Pausing to glance around the quiet neighborhood of upper St. George Street, he saw that there were no troublesome onlookers. The palm tree-clustered block was winding down for the evening and, around his house, the additional encircling army of Spanish Oaks drenched with moss provided superb cover. In the cobbled street beyond the walkway, a few youngsters rode bicycles in the thickening shadows around a lone streetlight, and to Rowan's ears came the noise of families settling down for dinner, or returning from a long afternoon of work, shutting car doors and opening windows to catch a draft of refreshing October air. All of this was like background music to which Rowan, the exile, had become not unpleasantly accustomed during his residence in the Ancient City, thus far.

As he stood, a hazy pillar of shadow on the widow's walk, the smile on his lips was an ironic one. So many of his kind were stricken with wanderlust but also with the ability to linger enjoyably in whatever region they deigned to inhabit, for however long they desired to pause, two years or two hundred. The Blaize family tree of sorcerers, however, always seemed to harbor some nagging form of discontent or antagonism when it came to their more impermanent surroundings. Rowan's mother, for example, was notorious for lurching unplanned into new territories, building elaborate accommodations, staffing them with phalanxes of servants, as if determined to irrevocably root herself in the world, and then, just as swiftly … she would change her mind in a fit of anxiety or melancholy restlessness, and abandon everything, lock, stock, and barrel. This had happened quite often to the amazement, and the enrichment, of looting local mortal populations. Indeed, his mother was the source of numerous and colorful legends around the world, and all of them seem to have an indelible motif. A beautiful, mysterious Lady moves to town, or the edges of town, establishes an estate replete with every indication of opulence, hosts parties of incomparable splendor, and then vanishes like a thief in the night, with all of her entourage, never to be seen again. Riches and valuable possessions left behind were of no consequence to this Lady, and it usually took less than a year for curious locals and outright thieves to clear out one of this Lady's foundations.

Of course, a great many of these brought home far more than they had ever intended to "salvage" since his mother's immense magic tended to spill over and dawdle about her discarded things, like a trail of gossamer lace in one of the gowns she favored, brushing gently over the surfaces of objects and imbuing them with little remnants of her fancies, her mischiefs, and, occasionally, her maledictions. A sticky-fingered forager in one of Mother's lonesome decampments might bring home a gilded mirror and revel in the exquisiteness of the craftsmanship and the unusually radiant clarity of its reflective powers, all the while unaware that, deep in the dead of night, beings from any number of magical worlds might slip out through the glass and snoop around, play tricks both hilarious and disturbing, and often steal things back into their own domains ... even as their gateway to another prowl-about world had it-self been stolen.

Whether one knew it or not, one simply had to be careful when it came to Mother—mortal or mage, person or pixie. She was eccentric, even for a sorceress.

Standing in the light breeze near the night-shrouded rooftop, Rowan thought about her. He had not seen his mother in two hundred fifty-nine years, not since they had last met for *qahwah* in a café near the Hagia Sofia in Constantinople. She had been shopping, then, combing the bazaars, murmuring nervously, her ivory fingers fluttering over all that was elegant and intricate, speaking of decorating another house, this time to stay put "for a good long while." They had spoken, too, of the slightly more strange changes occurring in the wider world, wondering whether or not it would behoove them to pass through one of the various Veils and dwell for a time, times, and perhaps half-times in some other dimension. They possessed enough power and talent to do so, though such excursions were never for the faint of heart and dangerous even for the most gifted. Rowan himself had already done it on a number of occasions, with some measure of enjoyment. In the shadow of the brood-ing, long-usurped sanctuary, he had spoken to Mother of the glorious solitude he had experienced in the Land of Kelnia, where hundreds of years in *that* world were but a fraction of a day in the present one. She had expressed a brief interest in visiting the place herself, and had wagged a perfunctory and distracted maternal finger at him, warning in rote terms of how unsafe it was to crisscross worlds.

"Look at your father," she had cautioned, sipping at her tiny steam-ing cup. "He approached the Shimmering Gates of Punojem, by the Wa-terfalls of Bibb, and has never been seen or heard from since."

Rowan had been hearing that line for years, indifferently deliv-ered as it was, but the tale was true, of course. Even though the most powerful families were always prepared to lose a mother, daughter, son, father, or spouse to the perils of magical curiosity, unable to find them in another plane of reality, having slipped betwixt and between layers in the fabric of Existence, Rowan knew that his mother had taken his father's prolonged disappearance rather personally. Then, amid the noise and beguiling turbulence of the Constantinopolitan streets, he had made the mistake of assuring her that "Father could well reappear any day and soon have us all enthralled with tales of misadventure."

She had not appreciated his attempt to mollify. By that time, Father had already been missing for over six hundred years and, in the blink of an eye, he would soon be unaccounted-for for the span of a millennium, which was highly unusual for Earth-originating witches and warlocks still alive, wherever they might be. But that was part of being such creatures as they were. Rowan's mother had left that day and, to his knowledge, had never built a house along the Golden Horn, as she had intimated. He was not certain what had become of her, though several reliable sources maintained that she had taken up residence in the Mountains of the Zerhoun, of all places, and was haunting that particularly grim corner of the world most infamously. Then there was the rumor that she had been spotted in Portugal, opening a vineyard that produced Madeiras of exceptional vintage, and another rumor that she had been seen on the arm of a mortal billionaire in Hong Kong. Still another tale purported to insist that she was touring Canada with a circus troupe of goblins disguised as tumbling clowns.

One or all of these scenarios were possible, he knew, but Mother had not been in touch for nearly three centuries and Rowan suspected that the truth was likely to be found in the typical string of ornate but inexplicably abandoned houses here and there across the globe. Rowan himself had lived long enough to know better than to attempt to track her down and honor her with a surprise visit, much less try to spy upon her through magical means. One had to be invited by Mother and, even though it was well-understood that "young" Rowan was the prodigy, the most talented and powerful member of their clan, down to its remotest collaterals, even *he* was not inclined to risk a row with his mother under any circumstances. She was powerful, too.

So he had left her alone, and she did not ever see fit to contact him, and that was the way of their world. The state of affairs had not bothered him quite as much when he still had the pleasure of his endlessly fascinating Aunt Ariadne's company, but now she was gone, as well, in the worst possible way, and the memory of *that* departure sent a cascade of chills from his heart to the tips of his toes as he paused upon the widow's walk, troubled in his thought and preparing to fly to the house of Serenity Turnbull.

It was little wonder that he dwelt upon it, even now, for all of the various matters could well be intertwined in the weave-work of impending doom he had been sensing at the edge of his intrusive but carefully managed anxieties for the past two decades. Due to this ever-encroaching fear he was separated from his friends, as well. They had always served as a welcome replacement for the camaraderie of family, but after what had taken place it was still too dangerous to risk associating with them, for their good as well as for his. All of them would cringe at the very thought of Rowan Blaize hiding-out in a place like St. Augustine. He could veritably hear the disbelieving hiss of a longtime companion like Sorana, the Grimmer-Witch of Athlone: *Whatever possessed you to inhabit a place like that?*

Rowan sighed and then he frowned, and finally he pulled the woolen cloak tight about his shoulders as he watched an osprey speed across the emerging blanket of starlight above.

This current and itinerant tour of exile would have to do, for now, and he had been determined to make worthy friends whenever possible, even with the likes of the exasperating Misses Leticia Beauregard and Gertrude Gokey. At least there was the clamor and social excitement of the upcoming All Hallow's Eve party to look forward to, along with its magnetic draw upon the wildly diverse specimens of the Ancient City's magical landscape. There was also Serenity Turnbull—that recalcitrant witch who had been more than a trifle enigmatic, though perhaps with good reason, given the overbearing presence of Letty and Gert.

It was amazing to imagine that the latter two were now guests in his home. What a muddle! The catastrophic fire itself had not stunned Rowan so much; fires and accidents far worse than fires can occur whenever a witch or warlock fails to be careful with their powers and peculiarities. What surprised him the most was that such an abject disaster had befallen *those two*. Despite their folksy veneers and obvious proclivities for absorbing the trimmings and trappings of Southern mortal culture, and despite their titanic bickering, Rowan knew that both witches were considerably more complex and experienced than either would ever let on. They were powerful, as well—idiosyncratic spell stylistics notwithstanding. Scrying pans, indeed! Witches were chameleons. They had to be. Artifice was often such an ally that it became first-nature, instead of second, at least in terms of externals.

Still, Letty and Gert had *not* succeeded in frying themselves up like the datil pepper fritters they used to serve tourists in their now-annihilated shop. That alone testified to the scope of the skills they both seemingly wished to downplay or deemphasize. Letty and Gert were "tough old birds" as Miranda had correctly deduced when they first arrived on the St. Augustine scene. Miranda, too, knew her hags from her hedge-witches, possibly with as much discernment as any full-blooded mortal had ever possessed.

If a witch like Gert had even the slightest inkling that something of considerable magnitude was about to befall the airy and elusive Serenity Turnbull, and Gert had gotten that inkling from the atomic migraine experience of a witch of Letty's caliber, then the matter was more than worth checking into. It behooved Rowan to meddle in the affairs of local witches at this juncture. He was not going to risk ignoring the resurgence of a foe he was now uncertain he had defeated, not when he was already taking the tiresome precautions of his present exiled lifestyle, not when he had estranged himself from his usual circle.

Poised against the balcony railing, Rowan braced himself for the spell, gray-blue eyes reflecting the liquid sparkle of a bright and nearly full moon that sailed out from the spectral, finger-like claws of cloud streaking the sky. Sensing the air, the thickness of it, the humidity, the undulating current, he directed his mind toward the upper reaches where he intended to cruise. He had not flown in six months, which was far too long to go without the enjoyment of a gift that very few, even of his own kind, possessed with such innate capability.

Indeed, many were the sorcerers who, by quirk of magic, or due to a crinkle in the thaumaturgical warp and weft, could enchant various "props' and endow them with enough magic to carry their bodies over great distances in flight. Animals, crooked tree limbs, broomsticks, carpets—these could all become favored talismans. Rare, however, were those who could connect with the heavens in a direct physical sense and not only repel the gravitational forces that ruled (at least in mortal estimation) so much of reality on the great globe of boiling rock that hurtled through space and time. Rowan was one of those beings who commanded the power and skill to manipulate these "laws" to his own design and make himself essentially one with the zephyrs. He was one of those who could mesmerize the very air and trick it into accepting his form as part of its own substance. In his existence through the lonely, slow surge of the centuries, he had mastered this ability and never had he known another of his race who, possessing similar skill, failed to savor its advantages. The experience of flight without need of talisman or crutch was simply thrilling.

The frail, clutching clouds soon coagulated and closed around the moon that shone on like a probing searchlight through the velvety cover. The darkness grew more complete, more attainable. Rowan lifted his arms and summoned, with words and syllables too primordial to even be ancient, a panel of wind from the East, as was required of those who sought to tame the very atmosphere and its gusts. The swirl of air came as commanded, very slight and able only to rustle his mane of black hair and whip ripples on the surface of his cloak. He did not require a great draft or a mighty funnel, just a mere whisper, a weary exhalation of the night, and presently he felt the always exhilarating power activate and flow through his being, conquering the very space around him and vanquishing its grip. Slowly and with difficulty at first, as if he were tugging himself gently from the space around him by force of will—and this was indeed the point in the spell when inner power combined with willfulness and entered the battle, the symphonic fugue of magic and desire— he felt the instant release and the grip of Earth had no claim upon him. It let him loose without argument.

He soared and rode upon the air, moving with a rush of speed into the seeming emptiness, away from the muted light of the moon and northward over the gently cracking tops of the oak trees and sandpaper rustling of the palms. He flew and seized great command of his pathway, untroubled by the sight of land below, firmament above, or sky all around. Rowan set sail on the wind with ease and with grace, and once again, as had been so for centuries, the sensation was that of an exquisite, unstoppable escape. Claiming immediate authority over the night he smiled at the rush of power, undaunted by his speed, but wary and watchful as is the need of all who dare thwart the hungry reach of the earth. His black cloak snapped and undulated like swelling ribbons of water on an angry sea.

Rowan spread his fingers to feel the resistance of the oncoming air. It was so good not to be earthbound, even if only for the few moments it would take to race over town and bay to the northern stretch of Vilano Beach where Serenity Turnbull lived. He chastised himself a little for not venturing skyward more often, but flying witches and warlocks, however they achieve it, are apt to attract more than mortal attention and jaw-dropping double-takes as they pierce the heavens. Magical beings of all kinds sense the thrill of another's flight, acutely so. Rowan swallowed hard at remembrance of a journey that had ended in disaster for him twenty years earlier, when his trajectory just beneath the caress of the clouds had attracted a great deal of magical attention indeed—the wrong kind of attention.

What a day it had been! Everything, or most everything, had been settled as far as Letty's and Gert's cataclysm. Once their nerves had been soothed and they were assured of the authenticity of their friendly lodgings, the two proceeded to make excellent use of Miranda as secretary. Cleaned up and composed, they had been driven in the foundling's battered old Jeep, first to the police department to report that, "Thank Heavens!" they had both been out of town during the horrific event and all would be well and good. Letty, with a shockingly facile gift for crying on cue, had said: "We aim to rebuild and vend the beloved local pepper and its associated products with more gusto than ever before." Furthermore, their "loyal and worldwide following" would not be let down and shelves would one day be restocked with their signature "Datil Learn Ya' Super Spicy Cha-Cha Salsa" ... among other delicacies.

Of course, they had made the requisite tour of the charred ruins, gasping and boo-hooing a bit for the news cameras and reporters who were still quite enamored of the "human pathos" side of the story. Gert, in particular, offered a few dramatic sound-bites to satisfy interviewers, and the rest of the day was spent wrangling with their insurance company, only the wrangling part did not last long and segued swiftly into a "Yes, Ma'am, Certainly, Ma'am" display of world-class customer service and hop-to-it results on the full-coverage front. Letty wasted little time putting The Influence upon any agent, associate, or underwriter throughout the company who entertained the slightest hint of a quibble, and that, of course, included them all. It was resolved that everyone would meet the following week to discuss how much bigger and better both shop and apartment were going to be rebuilt, to say nothing about the replacement and compensation due for the loss of precious possessions and inventory.

That had been the extent of it. Letty and Gert had caused their own disaster, rued it briefly, and got on with the business of setting things in order as survivor-type witches are wont to do. Afterward the two set up court in Rowan's drawing room and apparently planned to rule from there, even kicking old Bror out of his favored spot on the downstairs hearth rug so Gert could find a better position for her footstool and the knitting-basket she had purchased that afternoon to further placate her rattled psyche. Rowan wondered what manner of weird afghans, mittens, or socks she would concoct in such a context; the magical infusion was bound to be off the charts. He also wondered how poor dear Miranda would cope, even though she had escaped to the library and locked herself in. He would have to have a reassuring talk with her—and with Bror—when he got home. Presumably they would all make it through supper in one piece.

For a moment, however, it was liberating to let darkness afford him a chance to detach himself from the hullaballoo. Banking slightly westward, he risked a low swoop over the Castillo de San Marcos, where the All Hallow's Eve festivities would be held tomorrow, beginning an hour before midnight. The fort itself was shrouded in the misty glimmer of moonlight that washed over the sprawling and ungainly four-pointed structure. It was a grizzled mountain of mortar and coquina stone that rose, gray and lumpish, like a monstrous starfish that had crawled up from the murky bay onto the green knoll, died, and fossilized—only to be hollowed out and used for war games, and later the amusement of curious visitors and earnest period reenactment aficionados.

Skirting the fort, Rowan propelled himself like an arrow toward Vilano Bridge, stopping for just an instant to stand upon the tip top of the town's famous stainless steel cross, which rose two hundred-eight feet above the marshes of the Matanzas Inlet that filled the bay. The monument was situated in the heart of the shrine to the Nursing Virgin, *Nuestra Senora de la Leche*. There, silhouetted for a daring moment against the drowsy, emerging lunar disc, he stooped to retie one of his boots, for even the magician cannot bear to travel with laces undone. Slow-moving curls of cloud approached in the next few seconds and the moon hid its face again, as if embarrassed to flash such grandeur. Rowan leapt from the steel cross and roared downward with a dive that nearly took his breath away and left him skimming, for a bit, just above the chop of the bay. A few scattered flocks of nighttime waterfowl kept well away in the pungent, salty air; beasts, above all, know when a sorcerer is out and about, roaming in their territory.

Soon the roof of Serenity Turnbull's house peeked up from the thick grove of oak trees a block from the beach and he descended gently to the quaint crow's nest situated at the very peak of the house, his black cloak billowing in a play of dark wool upon moonstruck shadows. He began to walk down the steps that wound from the crow's nest all the way to the front door of the house in a masterful maze of decking and then he stopped, on guard and solemn, upon spying the smashed window of the master bedroom. No lights were on. His warlock eyes narrowed to peer within and he saw that the entire room had been ruined, with a portion of the floor caving-in, as if slammed by a wrecking ball that had bounced out and moved on. A sudden wall of wind rushed up behind him from the hissing oaks and he whirled about, startled.

It was only the wind; that much he knew, for all of his senses were on maximum alert. He felt he could even hear the mole crickets, digging, digging, digging deep in the dirt beneath the front lawn. The sliding glass door to the upstairs bedroom had been partially smashed as well; shards of glass were sprayed across the outer deck. He unlocked the latch with a swift spell muttered under his breath and one pass of his cupped palm, then stepped inside, boots crunching on more broken glass upon the carpet. There was no time to search for the light switch. Making a fist, Rowan blew softly into it and, as he gradually opened his palm, a small sphere of pulsating orange light was manifest, its surface turning and swirling and crackling as if it were a miniature version of the sun, plucked from the abyss of space. He bounced the sphere delicately, once or twice atop his palm, until it floated with a languid rise to the ceiling and there expanded to three times its original size, casting a warm and revealing radiance over the entire scene.

He pressed his lips in dismay.

Something extraordinary—and terrible—had clearly taken place. Roof beams, bed, curtains, floor, burnt holes in the walls … all of these things amid the general wreckage spelled trouble of the worst kind. Rowan enshrouded himself immediately with the most powerful Sheltering Incantation he knew before calling out.

"Serenity Turnbull! Show yourself at once, if you are present. It's Rowan Blaize. Come to pay you a little call."

There was no reply, but that did not surprise him. He had not been able to sense the witch's presence anywhere near. There was, perhaps, another very slight presence. A tingling at the edge of his perception indicated that someone else was lurking about the room. The remnants of something alive still clung to the ruined scene.

"If there be any fell spirit or untoward power in this place, let it come forth at once and show itself!" commanded Rowan in the soft glow of the light he had shed upon this new disaster. Yet no force or malignant entity responded to his summons, which was well and good, because even though he was fully prepared to confront any potential danger, to the very last fiber of his being, there was one force he feared above all else as a possible source of this upheaval before him. It was the same source he had been worrying about for almost twenty years without cessation. It was the one source he did *not* feel prepared to confront—not now, not again, not at any cost, if at all *in*humanly possible.

The room remained silent, save for the slight creaking of the damaged structures, the wind singing and whistling against the jagged glass of the ruined window, which looked like the wide open maw of a lunging, glass-toothed shark. Listening for a moment longer, Rowan felt certain that he was, in fact, alone, and was prepared to let down his guard and investigate matters more thoroughly when, from one corner of the space, he heard a whimper that set his shoulders rigid once again. Gathering his cloak around himself like a shield, he crept, a tall sliver of midnight, to the nearby desk and knelt down. There, half crushed beneath a splintered set of drawers, with blood trickling from his nose, was Emory, who Rowan recognized as Serenity's ever-bedraggled familiar.

This was the presence he had sensed. The spirit, cloaked as usual in Shih Tzu form, was still "alive" and breathing in a belabored fashion that indicated its living status was not likely to persist much longer. Tenderly, Rowan lifted the offending burdens of wood and detritus away from the little dog and he passed two hands in graceful crisscross fashion over its broken form. There was indeed very little life left in the thing's body—too little even for Rowan to attempt a healing spell. To have done so would have risked overwhelming the constitution of such a small and injured body, and if that happened all would have ended in a swift and rather messy explosion. There did not need to be another of those, not in this particular space, not tonight.

Presently the Shih Tzu rolled its bulging, now glassy eyes up at the warlock, who was gripped with a keen but dignified pity.

"Do you have the strength to communicate, Emory?" probed Rowan. "I believe you do."

The familiar shuddered as if on the verge of a rather agonizing and final seizure.

You must allow me—or better yet help me—to depart this mangled body, came the telepathic reply, faint as the very last thread of sunset against the darkening horizon.

"I will most certainly allow it," responded Rowan, "but I will not assist just yet. First you must tell me what has transpired here and where, pray tell, is your mistress?"

The dog grimaced, exposing even more prominently its underbite of jutting lower canines, and began to whimper anew.

"You simply must hold on long enough to tell me what I need to know, Emory. Tell me, and I will ensure your safe passage, completely unharmed, into the Void and into a well-earned period of rest from your labors. But first—tell me what you know!"

T-t-terrible ... terrible power, was the reply that echoed, fainter than ever, from within the unseen realm of supernatural communication.

"Of what terrible power do you speak?" demanded Rowan, his own hair now bristling on his arms and on the back of his neck.

The ... the Cipher Disc, answered Emory, coughing up a small clot of blood even as the thought left his mind and entered Rowan's.

"The what? What is the Cipher Disc?"

Stone circle ... t-t-terrible power ... inscription.

"What has happened to Serenity?" pressed Rowan. "Was she attacked? What sort of power came against her?"

Accident ... The telepathic voice was now barely discernible and even Rowan had to strain his faculties to perceive what was being revealed. *Cipher Disc ... unleashed ... Serenity taken.* The familiar managed one more roll of its protruding eyes and made a pleading glance at Rowan. *You must beware. Terrible one ... so ... much ... power. Serenity is ... she is ...*

"Who? Which terrible power?" shouted Rowan, wanting to shake the pitiful body of the exasperating dog but not daring for the sake of whatever sliver of information might yet be extracted from it.

Doom to witches ...REVENGE ...

"Revenge?" gasped Rowan, his eyes growing wide in the radiance of his hovering light spell. He knew of only one "terrible power" that might seek revenge upon witches, and particularly upon those who happened to be in or around *his* circle of acquaintances.

"Please, Emory! I cannot work a spell to heal your form without destroying it completely! You must rally yourself a bit and tell me what you saw. Please try!"

Cipher Disc ... it's on ... the table. Forgotten. Poison and ... and ... fire.

Rowan looked frantically across the ripped and wildly tangled sheets of the bed toward Serenity's dressing table and saw in the warm light of his LuminoSphere, still rotating overhead, the flat amber form of the disc—the talisman Serenity had called her grandmother's "cipher stone." He used an edge of his cloak as a kind of glove, uttered a mammoth protective spell, and reached over to grab the thing. It was nondescript enough, this pale disc with a circle carved out of the middle, but he felt its undeniably inherent power through his cloak and even the Guarding Spell he had cast before touching the thing.

"Is this the Cipher Disc?" he asked, turning back to the smashed body of Emory.

Let me pass into the Void ... came the barest trace of a mental reply. *Beware ... beware of ...*

Those were the last words communicated by the familiar as its form finally expired and the inhabiting spirit was liberated, tumbling at once into the abysmal but inviting vortex of escape and safety, such as it was. Into the endless labyrinth of the Void he plunged, and not even the mighty Rowan Blaize, clutching the disc to his chest and hurling magical commands, as if from the distant opening of some long-abandoned well far, far above, could summon Emory back.

そんぐ

XII

BonSashay Rummy had been one of the most satisfying morsels that Dedwen the djin had savored in all of his two hundred-twenty thousand years of existence, and he had consumed his fair share of tender human children over that panoramic period of time. He had not only eaten human brats, but brats from all manner of species, mortal and immortal. Fairy-babies, imp-spawn, goblin-toddlers, witch-infants, and certainly a great many of the natal productions of fellow djinn who were of lesser stock in terms of power and the all-around ability to protest Dedwen's gastronomic selections.

Though he had long believed, as a connoisseur, that human offspring tasted best of all, Dedwen was prepared to admit that perhaps *this* little blonde shrieker had seemed an especially toothsome delicacy due to the simple fact that he had not eaten *anything* in nearly sixteen hundred years. Being trapped in the horrid grip of limbo had not presented him with any sense of the passage of time or any awareness of a grumbling stomach, but he had emerged ravenously hungry. The weasel-man's daughter proved to be a superb *amuse-bouche* in lieu of the long line of treats he had in mind for the coming days, weeks, months, years, and millennia.

The actual consumption of the girl had been routine. Dedwen possessed impeccable table manners (especially for a djin) and had not even needed to spit-out the foul tasting hoop skirt or any of the bleached blonde curls, the latter of which had not tasted exactly as intriguing as he had thought they would taste. Three, maybe four, sharp crunchings and his belly, as sturdy and as impenetrable as an iron furnace, was satiated. The father had only vomited a little bit at the sight of the swift snacking, but had recovered his composure rather impressively. Dedwen was beginning to feel a twinge of respect for him, despite his overarching contempt for all humans. This Crummy, whoever he was, was shaping-up to be a truly wretched credit to his all-too-irritating race.

Best of all, Crummy had been shocked (and possibly even exhilarated) to his core upon witnessing Dedwen peel the scalp back from his putrid skull and slough-off his behemoth outer-skin to reveal an exact replica of little BonSashay, right down to the last winsome ringlet, the gleam on the tap shoes, the pout on the lip-glossed rosebud of a mouth, the false-eyelashes beneath the six year-old brow, the faux fox-fur lining of the hoop skirt, and, last but not least, the Itty Bitty Kiddie of Panama City tiara.

"B-B-BonSashay, darling, is that you?" the fool had babbled upon seeing the unexpected reappearance of his recently masticated progeny. That "daughter" had bellowed back at him, but not in the trained poop-poop-bee-doop voice of a child-pageant veteran. Rather, she had slammed him with the roaring, guttural tones of a top tier djin.

"No, you idiot! I'm not your daughter. I only look like her. Eating that little snot-bag was not purely an act of hunger, you know. Meals can be useful to an *ifrit* in other ways, especially when it comes to assuming the appearance of another. Helps the magic. She was rather tasty, by the way. I must confess, however, that I was not expecting such a skinny child under all that finery. Didn't you feed your daughter properly?"

"Um … well … we, uh … I … er … her mama and me had to watch her like a hawk and, except for the occasional cheeseburger to shut her up, we had to keep her on a strict diet so she'd be able to compete onstage. You wouldn't believe how fast a little girl will stuff herself when you ain't watching and then she ends up looking like a little Jimmy Dean sausage in spandex before you can say 'Shoefly Pie.' We couldn't put up with that, not if she was to compete with the likes of Brenda Bob Parson, who is built just like a little praying mantis. Perfect pageant body. So we usually kept BonSashay on a routine of boiled chicken tenders and brown rice."

"Well, I could certainly taste the poultry," answered the new BonSashay, looking down at her finery in disdain. "At all events, I shall be inhabiting this form until further notice. There does not seem to be much subtlety to it, but if you say this is the customary appearance of mortal children who are going to compete for honors of beauty, and enter millions of homes through those fascinating TV boxes, then I'm afraid this is going to have to serve my purposes. I warn you, however," added Dedwen, holding up a gloved little girl finger and tossing a cascade of curls over a puffed sleeve shoulder with considerable pique. "Do not be deceived by this gaudy and pitiful form into thinking that I am in any way vulnerable. A High Ifrit still retains three-fourths of his power, even when occupying the shape of another—a little-known bit of djin trivia that I share with you merely in passing. You saw what I was before. Do you think that you want to challenge even a toe-talon's worth of *that,* much less three-fourths of it?"

"Oh, no, I surely don't, BonSash—er ... I mean, Mister Lord Dedwen ... or ... what should I call you now?"

"Ha! Under the circumstances, I suppose 'Djin Rummy' would do nicely for your purposes," snapped the pretty little monster that appeared ready to board the Good Ship Lollipop. "Is your skull filled with elephant dung? I told you already not to even address me unless asked. Mind your manners and you won't end up being slow-roasted over a spit in the middle of the Arabian desert. Obey my every whim and you won't be pulled into pieces, starting with your flabby earlobes, by my pack of pet Wraith-Jackals, who must be insane with hunger, seeing as they have been separated from their master for a millennia and a half. I do hope my wastrel of a sister, Deshasha, had the good sense to feed them in my absence. But there's no time to look into that now. There are important plans to set in motion.

"You say this strange competition was destined to be your ill-bred daughter's comeback? Ha! I can assure you that comebacks have been appreciated throughout the annals of history, even among my race. No one loves a flashy comeback more than the djinn, and I aim to launch such a comeback that elbow-spines and back-bristles will curl with envy throughout the *ifrit* aeries. It will be a memorable triumph due, especially, to its *unexpected* quality. Now, let us depart this stifling hole and journey to your dwelling so that I can meet the mother of that wheedling little whelp you called a daughter and we can finalize my plan to send shock waves across the mortal world through the medium of that noisy TV slab. On our way, I want to have a good look around this pathetic corner of the globe into which I have been released. I want to see what I'm dealing with."

Djin Rummy had then pulled the ruby ring from the folds of the satin hoop skirt and had gloated over it.

"Heh heh. I certainly have *this one* trapped for purposes of quick reference if you should prove fatally disappointing, Crummy. Come! Show me to your camel and let us be on our way."

Thus it was that, hours before Rowan Blaize made his discovery, the palpitating Chesterfield Rummy had been pushed—or, actually, thrown—from the front door of Serenity Turnbull's house that afternoon by a fiend that looked exactly like his little girl, but who possessed the strength of one hundred men, and Dedwen had only given the bumbling man a slight tap. Still, Chesterfield ended up sprawled at the far end of the lawn with a brutally sprained wrist and grass stains streaking down the sweat and vomit-soaked front of his pinstriped suit, not to mention the dashboard that was his forehead.

"Sorry," the little devil had sneered while tap shoe-ing out into the sun. "It will behoove me to remember that I must rein-in my inestimable might while inhabiting the meager and inconsequential shape of a minor harlot ... at least until the evening of this celebrated pageant. Then the whole world shall see a manifestation of strength and all shall cry out for the mountains to fall upon them in their misery!"

"Y-y-yes, they sure will, darlin,' I mean, Mister Lord Dedwen. Um ... I mean, Djin Rummy. Just give me a minute to pick myself up out of this spiky palmetto bush, here. I'll be right with you."

Matters had been complicated further by the confrontation of ancient djin with embarrassingly old (but hardly ancient) 1992 Cadillac Seville. Apparently expecting an actual camel, Djin Rummy was most skeptical about the "rather elaborate" mortal machine parked at the curb, but in the end decided that it could possibly pass for the complicated version of some imaginative emperor's chariot, and hopped with a scowl into the front passenger seat and away they drove. As they went along, a question regarding the whereabouts of the horses that ought to have been pulling the contraption segued into a small argument when Chesterfield attempted to explain the concept of horsepower to the supernatural murderer in child-flesh seated next to him.

"It cannot be that there are two hundred seventy-five horses hidden beneath the lid in front of this chariot! I would easily smell that many horses, even very small ones. You LIE!"

Disaster was averted by a quick utterance about developments in mortal technology and a comparison with the wondrous television invention, and the prehistoric beast seemed begrudgingly mollified as they cruised toward town. The nearly cross-eyed-with-terror Chesterfield could only wish that no airplane might be seen flying overhead during the trip.

There were to be, however, plenty of other attractions that would alternately fascinate, annoy, and/or befuddle the seething BonSashay-Monster on the relatively brief but rambling route from Vilano Beach to the Rummy residence on Avenida Menendez on the other side of St. Augustine's sleepy downtown district.

"What flimsy little boats, yet there are so many in formation!" noted the djin as they passed Comanche Cove yacht club and marina. "Are the mortal men of this place gathering for a naval assault of some kind? If so, they shall never win a battle with such unintimidating vessels. Desiccated old women would be able to repel an onslaught like that!"

That was hardly the last of the djin's various observations:

"Bridge-building seems to have improved markedly!"

"Behold! Lights that command the metal chariots to stop, and they *must* stop!"

"You tell me that this is the land that lies across the great Western Sea and that three hundred million mortals dwell here? You LIE!"

"What is a 'Dairy Queen'? Is that some shrine to Hathor? I thought you said these people followed the Nazarene."

"Oh. There is the sign of the Nazarene. It is quite ostentatious. They did not erect crosses that tall even after Constantine gave them the world on a golden tray!"

"Why are fleas being sold at market? Most mortals I recall always had more than enough in their armpits and never needed to *purchase* any."

"What is a 'Friday' and why must a god be thanked for it with a rectangular temple?"

"I see not one woman with a veil … no … wait—Behold! There are two who walk about with only small triangles of cloth strung around their dangling paps! You claim mortals have advanced? You LIE!"

"City roads in Trajan's day were much better maintained than these. Chariot wheels must sink frequently into the many holes I have seen thus far."

"Lo! That toothless mortal in the chariot with enormous wheels and two long-eared dogs at his side just cursed us when he sought to run us off the road! Ha! Do not worry. He shall reach his destination and discover that his testicles have shrunk to the size of barley grains. I have already performed the spell!"

"Do the natives make beer with such ineptitude that they require a selection of fifty-two different kinds in one establishment?"

"So, a bridge with lions upon it. That is much more familiar decoration."

"What is this? Mortals who cannot afford to put horses *inside* the lids of metal chariots and who must therefore ride in wooden wagons?"

"Why does that establishment invite mortals to enter for only *one* hour of happiness? Also, why is it that the bird who arrives early is more special than the bird who arrives at a later time? Would not a bird disturb the hour of happiness? In my day, mortals spent much time chasing birds *out* of their drinking halls and inns. They did not encourage birds to enter."

"Most assuredly, mortals are much more well-fed than I remember. In old Persia, only the kings and nobles were as fat as hippopotamuses, but look! Every mortal lumbering upon these walkways appears to have access to the table of a king. Can they *all* be kings?"

"Ah. At least there are still plenty of lepers that beg for coins. But why are they carrying signs and not ringing bells to warn other mortals of their approach? Since when have mortals allowed lepers to *work* for food? This is most peculiar."

"Signs! Signs everywhere! Words in every place and upon all surfaces! Surely this does not mean that everyday mortals can read like kings and wise men?"

"Why do cakes made in a pan merit the right to dwell in their own house? Moreover, what makes these cakes international? Why do these cakes receive so many visitors? I can see sixty humans through the glass. Foods apparently have their own residences in your strange era. Except for *that* thing, called a 'donut,' which is apparently not worthy of a home, but rather a mere 'hut'. The hut is, however, more impressive than any mortal hut I have seen heretofore, and it is likewise jammed with many bloated kings who are visiting the donut, and who have parked their metal chariots in great numbers around the hut. Explain these indecencies!"

Chesterfield's mind was about to gnaw itself with mangling mako-shark fangs into oblivion by the time they pulled into the palm-lined driveway of his two-story brick home on the corner of Avenida Menendez and South Street. He had wanted to let go of the wheel and throttle the chatterbox demon far more violently than he had ever wanted to throttle the real BonSashay, before the real BonsSashay had, to his dark and secret pleasure, been eaten. The promises of gold and inordinately long life had been enticing, without doubt, but how trustworthy were genies or "freets" or whatever the hell these sorts of devils claimed to be—Chesterfield had never read a single word about "genies" in the King James Edition—and how long would he have to put up with its presence before the benefits kicked in? Even in his own, dirty deal-devoted heart, Rummy began to wonder about his decision. He wondered if any aspect of this stunning supernatural opportunity was worth the already relentless torture of having a "daughter" one hundred times more irritating (and infinitely more volatile) than the daughter he had finally seen taken to a more punishing woodshed than any he had ever been able to imagine in several years of ghastly imaginings.

As he turned off the Seville's ignition, Chesterfield's wretched, tar-slathered soul wanted to believe that this would all end in a payoff more extravagant than any payoff his marginally gifted offspring would ever have been able to secure on her best day in her brightest ball-gown. He tried to reassure himself with the innate knowledge that hard bargains, even the most fiendish ones, were sacred in all worlds and planes of existence. Sometimes, however, despite a perfectly straightforward handshake between negotiating parties, one of the parties was the recipient of the old bait & switch, and Chesterfield was beginning to panic with the suspicion that he had exposed himself to that possibility. Worse, how was all of this going to play out in the presence of his wife, whom he could scarcely tolerate even on his most affable days, to say nothing of days when he happened to be saddled with the overriding concerns of Beelzebub-ish entities that emanated from hierarchies of a Hell too labyrinthine to comprehend?

He hoped the gold—at least a little bit of it—started to pile up very soon, or he might just have to haul off and let his brain turn into oatmeal, like it wanted to do.

"Heh heh ... well, here we are, uh ... Your High Lordship. Home."

Rummy's teeth gleamed in a burst of sunlight angling onto the rear view mirror. His forehead and flattop toupee, however, felt positively muddy, as if all his unclean thoughts had been oozing from his pores to blend with the constant stream of sweat. He also stunk like a cesspit, which was not surprising, given that his bowels had emptied several times into his trousers. Chesterfield was a man who could stand himself under a multitude of unsavory physical conditions, but even he was on the verge of a dry heave.

The djin did not seem to mind, and, as if sensing his thoughts, remarked, "Believe me. I know you are currently exuding odors that would frazzle the hair of any self-respecting mortal, but to a djin, your befouled state covers up, as it were, your unsullied fragrance, which is far more unspeakably offensive to my sensibilities. Let me enjoy it while I can, for I realize that you are going to have to clean yourself at some point, if we are to fulfill my plans without attracting inconvenient suspicions. Now show me how to get out of this claustrophobic chariot and take me inside to meet your concubine!"

Dedwen flounced at the velvet and satin fabric of the dress and shook mounds of golden ringlets in disgust. "I would very much like to get a look at the egg from whence *this* contemptible little vixen was hatched."

Begging his new sidekick's pardon, Chesterfield reached across and opened the unwieldy door of the Seville. He groaned and nearly flopped face first into the demon's hoop skirt. A frequently troublesome disc had popped anew in his lower back. How much could the human body endure in one day of interaction with pure devilry?

"What was that unseemly noise?" asked the djin.

"Oh … it's nothing at all," sputtered Chesterfield. "Just an old football injury that's done gone and ruptured again. I'll be fine in no time."

"Hmm. You humans are really nothing but sloshing skin bags of jelly and brittle bone. Let us move a bit more quickly. We've already wasted half the day and I have hardly seen enough of your repellent epoch to finalize my scheme for its ultimate downfall!"

White-hot pain zapped from Rummy's lower back to his over-heated brain and then back again as he sat up.

"If you gonna bring it all down, Djin Rummy—and I guess I won't be too sad about that if you do, I suppose the world's been asking for it—I just have to wonder if they's gonna be anything left for me to enjoy as your faithful assistant. Gold and glory and long life and such. You know? Our bargain?"

"Oh, shut up. There shall be enough, you greedy glutton," countered the djin, stepping gingerly out onto the driveway in the impeccable tap shoes. "There may be fewer humans around when the time comes to collect your spoils, but I promise to satisfy you with the resources of the ones that do remain. And you are my slave, not my assistant. Do not ever forget that fact or it shall go ill with you. But see here, what's this loitering? Get out and escort me into your abode." Dedwen crinkled his perfect little borrowed beauty princess nose and inspected the house.

"This dwelling is rather rudimentary. You told me you were an individual of some means and distinction in your world, but I can see from the decaying structure before me that you are not. The stupid witch had a far more impressive domicile, but then again she was a witch. Witches are crafty and capable of acquiring all manner of possessions for their pleasure, due to their sneaky ways."

Chesterfield Rummy's house was no shack, but it had seen better days. The profits of defunct ministries, bankrupt ostrich farms, rat-addled oyster bars, and tenuous City Council seats had not been bolstered by the rewards of regional beauty pageant forays resulting in the occasional tiara. As a result, the house displayed a vague lopsidedness and other telltale signs of poor upkeep.

A bright green gecko streaked across the front porch railing as they approached and Chesterfield was mortified when his "daughter" opened her dainty pink mouth and shot out a nine-foot scarlet tongue like a sticky, stinging whip and snapped the hapless lizard back into her hungry maw. She was chewing happily, with the gecko's tail just twitching across one of her dimples as he fumbled with his keys at the front door. His brain whirled. If the *real* BonSashay had been able to pull a stunt like that, they would have made a worldwide name for themselves, alright. The beauty pageant angle would have been jettisoned, but he would have thrown that child straight into a carnival freak show and lined-up little green lizards all the livelong day as crowds filed in and the dollars accumulated. If child protective services found it unsuitable, he would have packed his gecko-girl off to Asia to eke every last ruble from terminally stultified Siberian villages for hundreds of miles, if he had to.

Chesterfield Rummy turned the key in his front door and felt certain he was about to lose what little was left of the cheesecloth of his mind.

"Fancy, honey? We're home."

They entered the sparsely furnished mauve living room, which smelled of mothballs and regret. Chesterfield jangled his handful of keys, the salami-sized fingers bumbling over the lot until he found the shiniest and newest of the bunch. That one had been made for a brand new padlock a few weeks earlier, and its edges were sharp against his bratwurst thumb. Little Djin Rummy sauntered up, arms akimbo, to an aquarium mounted atop an outdated sofa table in the center of the dreary space. A dozen goldfish gulped and began to swim in frantic circles as she stared at them.

"Do these actually grow large enough to feed your family?" it asked.

"Uh, whuh? No. No ... them's pets. They was for little BonSashay to look at and feed," said Rummy as he opened the padlock hanging from a doorway beneath the large stairwell. "Just for decoration, really."

"Decoration?" snorted the djin as all twelve of the fish turned black and went belly-up, floating dead to coagulate at the top of the fishbowl. "It's clear that your bloodline did not stream from a reservoir of great artistic imagination. Tiny fish swimming stupidly in a bowl for decoration and amusement? Not much more evolved than you were in the days when my kind used to sit back and laugh as your kind picked lice from each other's heads for purposes of amusement."

"Ha Ha. Yeah ... imagine that," rasped Chesterfield, grinning maniacally at the deceased decorations. "Not really any artists in the Rummy woodpile. It was little BonSashay who inherited all the talent in the family, I guess."

"I find that difficult to believe, but it was quite easy to swallow," noted the guest, tapping a tap shoe with increasing impatience on the grimy surface of the hardwood floor. "Your offspring will certainly demonstrate an astounding array of new talents, now," added Dedwen. "So, where is this woman of yours? I'm hungry."

"Oh, she's in here," assured Rummy, unlocking the door under the stairs. "She'll be more than happy to fix you something to eat. I just have to rouse her is all. Won't take but five or ten minutes for the sedatives to wear off. A cold glass of water to her face usually does the trick."

"What is this locked room beneath the stairs? Is that where you sequester your *harim?* If there are several wives involved I am certain that one of them shall prove suitable for consumption."

"No, there's just the one wife," said Chesterfield, dragging from the musty crawlspace a woman who appeared to be the grown-up version of BonSashay—if BonSashay had managed to survive decades of chain-smoking, abject depression, the swilling of countless boxes of Two Buck Chuck, a steady diet of barbiturates and canned ravioli, and two years' off-and-on imprisonment beneath a staircase.

A masterwork of bleary-eyed befuddlement in neck-to-ankle lavender spandex, Fancy Rummy undulated and jiggled out of her prison, pausing to allow her husband to pry her, with a great scraping of the stretch-fabric, from the doorway where she had gotten stuck.

"*This* is your spouse?"

Fancy Rummy mumbled something incoherent and bounced, a bit, against the nearby wall until she gained her footing and something approaching a semblance of composure. The light of the living room, negligible as it was, seemed to blind and disorient her. She held up a plump hand to her haggard, pasty brow.

"A most distressing specimen," noted the djin. "I recall certain mortal tribes dwelling in the deep jungles of Nubia that were known to force feed their wives on pure goat's milk cream and lock them in cages that they might grow large and clumsy ... to the point of toppling over, if they tried to stand. This practice of the Fattening of Wives was thought to enhance the status of tribal leaders. Are you attempting to emulate those ancient tribesmen with your own female? If so, you are rather close to success."

"Awww ... izzat you there, li'l BonSashay, honey? Course it's you. Howza fundraisin' goin', baby girl? You bring mama home some nize money to make you a new drezzz ...?"

With that, Fancy Rummy careened forward, in as much as it was possible for one of such girth and clumsiness to accelerate to the point of an actual careen, into the living room and against the boat-sized sofa, where she executed a surprisingly graceful pirouette and collapsed, supine and snoring. In an instant she had become a behemoth Cleopatra in purple tights, asleep atop her barge. Fancy's great jowls quivered with every exposition of severe apnea. The interior had suddenly become stifling due to the tremendous body heat emanating from Fancy alone; she exuded a doughy humidity that gripped the room, along with Chesterfield's septic odors, and permeated it like a noxious fog.

"You told me this woman would be crucial toward confecting the necessary strange appearance required for my successful infiltration of the stage at this imminent child parade, or whatever it is," spat Djin Rummy. "How can I unleash a sudden and devastating surprise upon millions of mortals watching me through their magic window-boxes if I am not adequately prepared to blend in with a gaggle of *other* little whelps that shall be vying for the same attention? I must arouse no suspicion before the Great Moment arises."

"I swear to you, my Fancy can help you get ready for the pageant like nobody else can, once she comes-to in a few hours!" cried Chesterfield.

"Nonsense. This woman is of little use to herself, much less to my superior purposes. The framework of our little bargain, Crummy, appears to be suffering from the same structural peril as that unfortunate piece of furniture beneath your wife. If you do not maintain your part of the agreement, then I am not obliged to uphold my side of it. Needless to say, but that will not work out very well for you at all."

Chesterfield Rummy fell to his knees and tried to fan his wife back into a state of consciousness with a crumpled copy of the Lifestyles section of the Florida Times Union. It didn't work.

"Now, don't you go and worry, Your Deviousness. Fancy here is gonna come round any minute, I just know it."

The deviousness was unimpressed. "She could not 'come round' if a hundred camels attempted to drag her ruined faculties upright with an iron chain."

Rummy began to sweat as profusely as before and wondered madly how he could have so much liquid still left in his body at all, and how that liquid could be so annoyingly greasy.

"Look, Your Malevolence, you don't understand. My Fancy suffers from what us mortals call a 'bad case of the nerves.' She always has."

The djin rolled baby blue eyes and tossed the mane of Barbie Doll curls impetuously.

"No, I'm serious," asserted Chesterfield. "That's why I've had to keep her locked up under the stairs, yonder, and hopped up on horse tranquilizers the last few years. She used to be the driving force behind BonSashay's routines and competition schedule. She was just as wild to see our baby succeed as I was. And then ... well, then she started taking some of our daughter's pageant losses a little too seriously. It was all innocent enough, at first, what with snotty comments to the other pageant mothers and fathers, but things got real bad after Fancy brought that teeny slingshot to a pageant and shattered one little girl's kneecap with a ball-bearing while the poor thing was dancing the Mambo Number Five.

"See, my Fancy always had excellent aim. She was a real good shot. I managed to get her outta there quick—she was about two hundred pounds lighter on her feet, then—and I warned her about how that kinda thing could not only get us arrested, but it could put the brakes on poor BonSashay's dreams. Poor, poor Fancy. She was okay for about a month, and then she started slipping Ex-Lax into the other little girls' energy drinks. Why, one little pageant hopeful soiled herself so bad onstage, you'da thought a mud-bomb had gone off in her tutu. Only it weren't mud. You shoulda seen that little gal, standing up there, covered in her own feces, and she couldn't half-believe what had happened to her, and her mama's screaming, 'Get off! Get off! You can't mambo in a mess like that!' Then the heartbroken little thing tried to, you know, dance off the stage like a pro, with some dignity ... tried to save the number a little bit, but she slipped in a spray of her own poo and just sorta skidded off the platform right onto the judges' table. Oh, it was an awful scene, your Demonicness. It was—whaddaya call it?—*pandemonium*. Yeah, that's what it was, and in the middle of it all, laughing like there was no tomorrow, I saw my Fancy and knew she'd had something to do with it.

"I took her to a shrink. I swear I did, and they evaluated my darling and said their piece, but there was no way our insurance covered the electroshock treatments, so they put her on disability—the American way, you know?—and it got worse here at home. For a while I did think real hard about locking her up in the state booby hatch over by Maclenny, but then we wouldn't get her social security disability checks and I needed that money to keep pursuing our dreams. When you ate BonSashay, Djin Rummy, you ate *our* dreams, too. So, anyway, I just pumped my Fancy full of pills and all the high-carb food I could get in cans, and built that little parlor for her under the stairs. Put the padding on the walls in there myself. That's right. She started to calm down a bit, too. I could even let her out almost regular. You'd be amazed, Your Monstrousness, at the way my Fancy could still run-up a show-stoppin' ballgown. I was really hoping she could help with the cosmetics and the right gown this one last time, but, as you can see, I guess she's down, maybe for the week, so we'll have to go to Plan B."

"What, pray tell, is Plan B?"

"See, that's just the thing. We don't need Fancy, not with my know how and your magic devil hoodoo. I know the routines and dance numbers just as good as Fancy ever did, even though I couldn't sew a button onto my shirt to save my life. Couldn't I just show you the book with a picture of the Pint-Sized Princess champion's dress that Fancy was gonna try to bedazzle, and couldn't you, you know, just snap your claws or fingers or whatever you got and sorta pull that dress right outta thin air?"

"Of course I could do that, you braying ass. Do you mean to tell me that you have been chattering on with this grotesque and sickening tale about your mad wife and wasting precious time when all I need to see is an image or a drawing or a pattern?"

"Yeah," admitted Chesterfield. "I guess that's right."

Djin Rummy waved a white glove and Chesterfield was thrown up from the floor with gale force winds that sent him crashing against the living room wall. Another disc in his back was nearly crushed, singing an excruciating duet of pain along his spine. He landed in a heap near a toppled umbrella stand. Fancy, for her part, murmured and jiggled a bit around the abdominal region in her semi-comatose state. Both Chesterfield and the incensed djin looked curiously at her for a moment, as if she were about to spring to her tip toes and begin hemming ball-gowns with the nimbleness of a gazelle. This did not occur.

"Please, Your Possessiveness," croaked Chesterfield, struggling to even attain a kneeling position. "Hear me out. I think I'm talking too much because you get me all nervous, see? Think about it, will you? It ain't every day that a thousand year-old genie—"

"Two hundred-twenty thousand years!"

"Okay, okay … it ain't every day that a senior citizen genie just waltzes into my life and eats my daughter when we just so happen to ring the bell at a witch's house. That sorta thing just doesn't happen much nowadays. Things're a lot different from what they were in your salad days, as you have seen already while we was driving over here, and this whole thing has frankly got me on the edge. Now, surely, being as mighty and old and wise as you are, you can understand how a stupid fella like me could be a little flummoxed by all that, especially when all of it has taken place in only a matter of a few hours."

Djin Rummy began to pace thoughtfully around the grunting, eructatious heap of a woman on the couch, a little blonde moon circling a mammoth purple planet. The groveling, aching Chesterfield mortal *did* have a point, perhaps, and he had had the decency to refer to himself as the putrid human that he was. Dedwen the Great was not unmoved by self-abasement in others, no matter what the species.

"I suppose your claim to sympathy is tinged with a certain element of validity," it growled.

"Oh, see. I knew you was brilliant and amazing enough to see even a shred of reason, even coming from a worthless no good filthy rotten dog like me." Rummy was beginning to feel his fetid wheeler-dealer foundations again, his swindler sensibilities. They had brightened from dull embers to wisps of flame when he intuited that what the djin loved more than anything, or almost more than anything, was to see others willingly humiliate themselves. He groaned as his back sent electric fingers of agony throughout his body. Still, he was determined to get things back on track. Fancy had been a resounding failure.

"Most important of all, which we ain't even discussed yet, is the danger out there when you plan to show yourself—and I mean really *show* yourself—to the whole world."

"What could you possibly mean by 'danger,' little piggy-man?" scoffed the Goldilocks djin.

Chesterfield's bloodshot and yellowing eyes grew wide beneath the soaked twin caterpillars of his brows. "Well now, I ain't exactly an expert in ancient history, Your Awfulness, but I do know that there's been some pretty awesome developments in human achievement, and I ain't just talking about muscle relaxers and wine that comes in a cardboard box. No Siree. There's been some mighty scary advancements in weaponry, too, and if you been out of commission for a while, like you say, then I think you'd want to know as much as you can about this sorta thing, before you head out to, um, fulfill your diabolical plans and so on and so forth."

"What weapons are you talking about?" queried the djin, trying not to convey too much interest in the matter, even though it was most interested indeed.

In Dedwen's estimation, humans had been useful for precious little on the planet except as an occasional food source, as halfway decent builders before the onset of every Dark Age, and most of all for their ability to create weapons ideal for the wanton butchery of each other. The djin was loathe to admit it, but he had taken his share of hits when it came to the intricacies and innovations of mortal munitions over the ages. Pesky Roman legions had been the most distressing and inconvenient, and had made, by far, the most indelible impression upon him— especially when he had found himself particularly hungry and not quite as potent when it came to the command of his powers. This tended to occur in times of illness or when some other irksome affliction curtailed his magic. Wind-scorpions, for example, were common desert arachnids whose bites might produce pain and minor swelling in a mortal, but djinn were highly (and most secretly) allergic to the saliva of the fanged menaces. A fiend could be lamp-ridden and powerless for weeks following a bad encounter with one of the *solifugae*. Such a happenstance, along with a number of other hazards, could befall any spirit at one point or another, from the lowliest *nasnas* to the greatest of the *ifrit* and *marida,* although the most Powerful Ones were wise enough to lay low and hide themselves from rival spirits during such times.

Dedwen knew as well as any that there is nothing a djin enjoys more than getting the better of another djin down on its luck or in some sort of distress, usually in revenge for some slight, or a past mistreatment, petty though the incident may have been. Wild beasts were also trouble-some for a djin at a loss for power: wolves; jackals; lions; crocodiles; all could easily smell a djin on the skids. For that reason, as everyone in the magical realm knew, it behooved even the mightiest of their race to treat beasts with great respect and politeness at every possible opportunity. You never knew when you were going to run into such an animal when you were down at heel, and if you did, you hoped it might be a predator that remembered your former kindness and spared you in turn. Mortals, however, had never seemed to boast the decency and etiquette to respect anything less than aggression and brute strength. Dedwen himself had learned this the hard way on a few occasions.

In fact, there had been one exceptionally gruesome encounter during the reign of Antoninus Pius, when he had been in the Nile delta region in Egypt and had been trapped in the ruins of a temple of Isis in a town called Behbeit. He had been summoned there by one of the god-dess's First Prophets (Dedwen was, after all, a member in good standing of the Fearless-of-Faces) to perform some sort of task the sorcerer-priest had in mind. The summoning, however, had been recklessly managed and had caused an earthquake that brought the glorious rose granite sanctuary down in a heap of rubble, killing most of the townspeople and pinning Dedwen himself beneath one of the great columns in the hypo-style hall before he had a chance to flee.

Injured and weakened, he had been discovered by the local garri-son of occupying Roman forces when they came to loot what they could of the temple's fabled treasures. It had been a frightful scene. Oh, how their crossbow arrows pierced his great hide and spilled his black blood across slabs of the cracked courtyard! Alas, how their burning spears had

plagued his magnificent body with stinging fire! His magic was draining away, due to the injury, and it had only been through sheer malignance that he had managed to kill a few dozen of the relentless centurions
and then bound up and across the terrible ruins, arms flailing and great
yowls echoing across the creeping shadows of nightfall.

With their spiked whips they had pursued him as they fled through
barley-fields and splashed through swamps before reaching the stark edges of the desert, where even the vile Romans had not dared to pursue
him further. It was then that Dedwen had been forced to use all the
magic that remained at his disposal, shrinking himself into a size small
enough to fit into an abandoned fennec's lair, blocking the entrance with
stones and hoping not to be discovered in his vulnerability and agony,
licking his wounds in the silence until he regained a measure of his power
and could flee to more hospitable environs.

No, Dedwen did not care for mortal talent when it came to weaponry, not one bit.

It was in his best interests to learn more, even though his powers
were at a zenith, currently, and even though it would require listening
to the unbearable whines and whimperings of this slave he had deigned
to bargain with. What new terrors, indeed, had humans managed to
concoct in over fifteen hundred years? Their skills did tend to wax and
wane, and these present specimens did seem rather fat and slow and lazy
and misguided, what with their incomprehensible interests. Perhaps
weaponry, too, was on the wane and he had little cause for alarm as he
prepared to wreak gloriously mischievous havoc upon their communication boxes. If weaponry had been as interestingly developed as the boxes,
however, a few precautions might be in order ...

"Speak, you sniveling snipe, and enlighten me about these worrisome weapons, though I daresay that mortals can hardly have evolved the
kind of armories that might repel *my* power in its fullness. Ha!"

The djin realized that this did not sound terribly intimidating
coming from the dolled-up body of a girl-child, but Dedwen was not
in the mood for a premature display of visual potency. Chesterfield sat
down, unsteady and now turning various shades of gray on the surface

of his blotchy cheeks. His hands were breaking out in hives, as well. Funny, he thought, itching away, how it had taken him this long to get to hives, under the circumstances. Yet, he was not exactly laughing. In fact, his mind was still doing somersaults up, over, and around the notion that the blonde tap-dancing Tinkerbelle before him was not his daughter and, though their capacity for throwing tantrums appeared to be well-matched, this was indeed some impossibly ancient hellspawn whose temper would result in damages far more severe than a kick in the shins, or a splitting headache brought on by the jackhammer sound of incessant child-wheedling. The urge to strangle *this* militant moppet must not get the better of him. He had to stay on its good side, if such a side had a remote chance of existing at all.

"Your stupendousness, I have no doubt that you could open one amazing can of whup-ass on just about any army that was dumb enough to get in your way, back in olden days, but folks have got all kinds of unbelievable things they use nowadays. Stuff big and bad enough to take the place of hundreds, even thousands, of men. Why, there's bunker-buster bombs, rapid-fire artillery, grenade launchers, heat-seeking missiles, long-range missiles, stealth bombers, jet fighters, drones, and even nuc'ular warheads that could blow up an entire city and fry every one of its inhabitants to nothing but a bit of pork rind in seconds."

The djin listened impassively, knowing the words because of the spell it had first employed when confronting Serenity, but not grasping the particular nuances because not much spoke to its prior experience. The pouty BonSashay-face contorted into a grimace, but Dedwen did not wish to appear unduly taken by surprise in front of this mortal lackey, as insipid as the lackey was. Even so, the sheer list of weaponry sounded daunting, and the "warhead" that had the power to wipe out an entire city could certainly not be ignored, along with the warning that some of these things had the strength of thousands of men. It would probably be of little use to question the imbecile Rummy further. The little pig-man was now practically as immobile as his bloated wife on the divan, both breathing harshly and mumbling incoherent words.

A more thorough investigation into this particular problem, from a source that could be compelled to be *compelling,* was now required. Fishing around in the fluffy satin and velvet folds and pockets of the pageant gown, the ruby ring was produced and Djin Rummy stared at it with fiendish superiority. The witch would have to explain it all.

"Oh worthless witch within the jewel,
now hearken unto Dedwen, fool.
Emerge at once, my will to please,
that I your knowledge swift may seize!"

From the clunky ring now held by the tiny pink fingers of the disguised doll-baby, there emerged, not the rank and oily clouds that had marked Dedwen's first appearance from within the awful prison, but a gentle, sparkling vapor that betokened beams of sunlight dappled through a diaphanous mist. The substance billowed down to the floor of the Rummy living room and swiftly materialized into the stunned and panting form of Serenity Turnbull, sprawled on all fours and still in her nightgown and kimono. She caught her breath as if newly born and looked around wildly, first at the goggle-eyed and greasy, grass-stained face of Chesterfield Rummy, and then at the snoring mountain that was his unconscious wife on the sofa. Finally, she narrowed her eyes to behold the grinning, ring-bearing Pint-Sized Princess in frills and furbelows, tapping one tiny shoe on the floor with great impatience.

"Where in the name of Sibyl's Sixth Sense am I *now?"* Serenity managed to gasp, gazing with bewilderment at the weird, totally unfamiliar company. She struggled to her knees, but fell in a weakened heap. "Where is that hideous djin?" she barked.

"Right here, my agitated little lamb," said Dedwen, employing a tart BonSashay-style lisp.

"YOU?" Serenity hissed. "As a little girl dressed up like a streetwalker?"

"Hey, you're the lady what let us into that hell house in the first place!" blubbered Chesterfield Rummy from his place of shame against the wall. "And I resent you saying my gal is done up like a working gal."

"Who are *you?"* shrieked Serenity.

"Pay no attention to that moron," instructed the working gal. "Yes, it is I beneath all of this outrageous attire, but I am hardly a little girl, I assure you. The prototype for my current manifestation was consumed and proved to be a most palate-pleasing, if regrettably scrawny, tidbit."

"Despicable monster!" spat Serenity.

"Guilty!" trilled Djin Rummy, turning the ring over contemplatively in the meager light, admiring and loathing its power. "But there's no need for you to be redundant, my willowy witch. My, I *am* getting the hang of this cumbersome foreign tongue. Even its idiomatic nooks and crannies. That's what comes of plunging into the brain of a chatterbox-of-a-witch. But enough about my accomplishments, for the moment. Tell me, Serenity, how did it feel to be paralyzed inside the ruby stone, trapped like a pesky prehistoric mosquito in amber?"

"It was ineffably horrid and you know it!"

Serenity's mind raced to find the words of some spell—any spell she may have forgotten—that would give her even a sliver of hope to escape, rather than face a return to the ring. She knew, however, that it was as useless a hope as before; her imprisonment had made her weak. She still lacked the strength to even make it to her knees.

"I suppose you've brought me out to eat me in front of these mortals? Who are they, anyhow?"

"You have not been summoned to dinner, unfortunately for me," replied the djin. "But in answer to your query, I can tell you that these two buffoons are new associates of mine, though I suppose I ought to be embarrassed to say so. That embarrassment may not last long, believe me. In truth, they are the progenitors of what used to be the glamorous tot you now see before you."

Djin Rummy made a sinister and most sarcastic little curtsy.

"The deformed ape behind you, the father, has made a little bargain with me and his irritating offspring was part of the package. In fact, I think there's still a little bit of one of her tendons stuck in a back tooth. Ugh. I despise gristle!"

Serenity looked back at Chesterfield, who quailed a bit under her piercing, wild-witch glare. "You are a very evil, very damnable man, to strike any sort of deal with a creature like this one! Your own daughter. How could you?"

"Heh. Urghhhfghthphth," squawked Rummy in madness and metronomic pangs of terror.

"Oh, do stop preaching at the poor bit of camel-pie, witch. Mortals can't help themselves. You ought to know that by now. And I can be most persuasive, as you are certainly aware. Besides, he is going to serve a purpose, albeit an incidental one, as part of our little accord, our pithy arrangement."

"What sort of heinous thing are you planning in that ludicrous get-up?" shouted Serenity, narrowing her eyes in contempt. She hoped now to provoke the djin to destroy her, instead of facing the excruciating limbo of the ring for even another nanosecond. "You are without a doubt the most stupid djin anyone could ever encounter, and I can't imagine what sort of idiotic mischief a dung-brained piece of jackal fodder like you could possibly perpetrate in such a laughable disguise. Even the dimmest mortal will surely turn his nose up and sneer at your half-baked schemes."

Two jets of angry fire shot out of Djin Rummy's tiny pink nostrils and passed over the top of the ducking Serenity's head to scorch the remaining crew-cut toupee from the top of Chesterfield's persecuted pate. The man let out a strangled howl and the already repulsive air of the room welcomed the scents of sulfur, fried fake hair, and scorched scalp to the fragrant miasma. The djin fumed a bit more, taking a dainty but menacing step toward the witch.

"Half-baked?" it bellowed, causing Serenity to wince. "I have a good mind to half bake you and let the other half endure the agony without recourse."

"Do your best, you overrated desert goblin!" dared Serenity.

"Not yet," countered the djin, regaining control of its temper. "An eternity of torment in the ring is looking better and better for you by the moment, so just keep on provoking me with your pointless insults, weak as water witch-woman. As for my plans for mischief, they are superb beyond your wildest imagination, though what a shame that you shall not be privy to their climactic execution."

"This bad ass devil is gonna hijack the Pint-Sized Princess Beauty and Talent Pageant," blurted the filth-caked Chesterfield in an attempt to display pride for his new master and avoid more second-degree burns. He knew he was on thin ice. "Lord Master Dedwen BonSashay Djin Rummy aims to show the world his greatness through the wonder of TV!"

The master did not appreciate the earnestness of his swarthy puppet.

"Idiot!" trumpeted the girl-beast as the conscious beings in the room put their hands to their ears and gritted teeth, and spiders in their corner cobwebs shriveled into little drops of goo. "If I want a vote of confidence from the likes of you I'll ask for it. Until then, you are to keep your mouth—as red and as filthy as a baboon's anus—SHUT!"

Chesterfield curled and recoiled in pain, scrabbling as fast as he could to hide behind the sofa. Fancy Rummy wobbled and snorted, mumbling: "You can't put sequins on a skirt like that!" in her sleep.

"Is he talking about that creepy little-girl pageant that's been in the news?" said Serenity, aghast. "The one on Monday night? The one billed as a talent and beauty contest but which is, in fact, nothing more than an excuse to plaster children with cosmetics, put them in revealing outfits, and show them off for the twisted pleasure of unfulfilled and shameless parents, not to mention any number of sexually perverted adult strangers?"

"I think that is the one," replied Djin Rummy, future pageant contestant—one who intended to garner far more than a sash, a tiara, some flowers, and a Vegas wild card. "It is shaping up to be great fun."

"Ha! I might have known you would associate yourself with something utterly reprehensible right off the bat, after being cooped-up in that ring for so long. Still, it never ceases to amaze me how mortals manage to hitch their listing moral wagons to such wretched fallen stars with minimal prompting. You, Sir, hiding behind the sofa, are a very bad, bad man!" she called out to the cowering, burnt, soiled, stinking, hive-covered and indubitably pathetic Chesterfield Rummy. "You're even beginning to look like one of this festering djin's usual cohorts. I've been seeing grotesque demons and their minions for centuries, so I should know."

"Still, it is a significant improvement in the man's hitherto unacceptable mortal appearance, I assure you," interjected their host. "They always look best when they are mired in their own bowel movements. But this particular ambition of mine is no concern of yours, my worn out and world-weary witchling. I have summoned you out of this charming little trinket for one purpose only, and that is because I want information, and I want it now. Remember, you are in my power and subject to my every whim, so long as you—and no longer *I*—remain bound to the charm of Marutha's ring. It was your carelessness and stupidity, after all, which made my grand reemergence and your intractable doom possible!"

"Don't remind me," seethed Serenity.

"All the same, obey your new Lord and Master when he requires a boon. Let us waste no further time. This blithering mortal idiot hiding behind the slug he calls a 'wife' has proved to be most exasperating when it comes to communication that is direct and comprehensible. One realizes that it is perhaps far too much to expect sentience from beings that still ought to be dwelling in caves or swinging from one tree limb to another, but the nattering little monkey finds himself tongue-tied far more often than not. I could barely get anything helpful out of him as he drove me in his chariot through this most uncomfortably moist little city named, apparently, for one of those dreary Christian holy men I have always found so irritating."

"That's likely because no one can get a word in edgewise with a blabbermouth spirit like you," snapped Serenity. "And if I remember correctly, St. Augustine of Hippo, for whom this fine town is named, wasn't quite born yet when you were already locked away by Marutha, as you should have been forever! That is how long you have been out of the loop, O Dedwen, Most Asinine of the Djinn."

Dedwen put an immaculate white glove to his forehead bedecked with curls and sighed. "Spare us all the dreariness of witches," it breathed. "Please. You were not asked to provide unsolicited comments of a condescending nature. Be a good little ring slave and tell me what I wish to know. The pitiful progenitor of this garish little glitter girl tells me that mortals have developed a plethora of frightful weapons while I was so unjustly indisposed, and that these weapons are formidable. I cannot make head or tail of anything he babbles. He speaks of great arrows that can level entire cities down to their foundations and other, improbable projectiles that he says possess the strength of not merely a hundred men, but of thousands! Are there really flying things that can drop great thunderclouds of unquenchable fire upon a helpless little djin like me, right out of the air? Of course, it all sounds like rubbish, as I said, and he *does* appear to be overcome with delirium, but I thought it wise to consult someone marginally more coherent. Do mortals now possess such noteworthy tools of battle? Their chariots have certainly undergone some interesting innovations. I want full disclosure, witch, and will settle for nothing less."

Serenity tried once again to raise herself up at least to her knees, but the effort exhausted her and she merely toppled into a sprawled position onto the blubbery abdomen of Fancy Rummy.

"Oh, do stay prostrate on the floor, witch. That position is most becoming for the likes of you."

Serenity brushed wisps of hair from her eyes and ground her teeth together in mounting but ineffectual anger. She was compelled to answer and could feel the overwhelming will of her capturer, drawing a response from her unwilling mind like venom from a wound.

Then let it be venom, she thought, *for I am obliged to give this accursed creature the truth. Let the truth be as magnified as possible, and let it be crafty!*

"So you ask me about mortal weapons?" she said, panting as she stopped trying to fight the djin's coercive probing, and allowed herself to revel in a full and harrowing account of the truth. "Yes, mortals have at their disposal such weapons and forces that might vaporize cities a thousand times greater than this one, and cities of such size do exist, believe me. Much has changed since your hooves last walked the woe-begotten world. The sheer numbers of mortals being one of those changes. There are billions of them now, instead of mere millions, O Dedwen, and when stirred they can marshal armies and artillery that could lay waste to you and every djin upon this earth with as much ease as this worthless man over there might swat a fly away from his food plate. You would not even be as significant or worrisome as a housefly, were you to present yourself, in full power, in the face of even a miniscule fraction of the terrors mortals have crafted to eradicate each other and anything that might get in their way. Oh, they might shudder a bit at the rotten sight of such an ugly entity as you, but only for an instant, and then you would be blown to so many ... um ... so complete ... er ..."

"Smithereens?" croaked Rummy helpfully from his fetal position behind the sofa.

"Exactly. They would blow you to so many smithereens that even your spirit level would never be able to gather all the scattered parts and dust motes of your former self and put them back together again. Why, this one spoke to you of mortals' ability to blow up entire cities? Ha! Forget about cities! They could eliminate entire *continents,* if enough of them went berserk at the same time and gave the orders. The entire world would and could be reduced to noxious storms of fiery ash and acid torrents bucketing down from the dead, cloudless skies. The very air itself could be made laden with dread, invisible energies and poisons that burn flesh—yes, even djin flesh!—and which drift without direction and purpose to ruin and wreck all that exists. You, Dedwen, as strong and as ancient as you are, would be nothing against such power, if you should make yourself a target. That, Oh Master of the Ruby, is the truth!"

Djin Rummy raised an immaculately plucked brow and twirled a tiny Teaberry Sparkle-polished fingernail around a blonde ringlet, pondering this information with some solemnity. After a moment, during which Serenity waited in sad but satisfied triumph and even Chesterfield felt a pang of deviant pride for his race's power to Blow Up Everything on Earth, the Child-Monster spoke calmly.

"So what you are telling me—and it is, of course, the truth, for you do not have the power to resist my will in that regard, witch—is that nothing has really changed at all."

"What do you mean?" muttered Serenity, her brows knitting in frustration.

"What I mean is that mortals basically still teem like rats in certain vicinities, and that they still possess the power to destroy themselves and their surroundings on a massive scale relative to their numbers, to the point of extinction, even, if they got a little carried away."

"But ... but, the nuclear bombs that can make the air turn to fire and the skies go dark for centuries," murmured Serenity, Activist Sorceress.

"Oh, my dear. You have indeed been around for a few centuries, I expect, being a witch and semi-immortal yourself, but have you not learned by now that the air has been turning to ash and flame and that the sky has been raining acid down until the oceans boil for hundreds of thousands, even billions, of years? Oh, most certainly, I am not one of those Ruling Powers that was here at the Very Beginning of the stirring of the primordial soup. I am a latecomer to the scene, and the byproduct of other spiritual forces, Unhallowed Be Their Names, but I have been present quite long enough to realize that, whether this spinning ball of rock and water goes up in a conflagration of deadly vapors due to a few erupting volcanoes or due to the ignition of some collection of innovative mortal playthings, the modes are basically one and the same.

"It is the world, the very dust of the earth turning upon itself, when a great mountain sends liquid fire miles into the sky and blinds the sun. It is the same thing if mortals do it with their toys, at whatever stage, at whatever time, for mortals and everything they build, my dear, are the dust of the earth, too. Mortals and every last thing they build are *also* the earth turning upon itself. You therefore tell me nothing new, nothing I do not already understand. The astonishing thing is that you, who are a supernatural power—albeit rather dim—in your own right, do not grasp this. That is why we djinn have always had contempt for you sorcerer folk and your attraction for living life either within or dancing in-and-out of the mortal realm. You lose power and perspective when you do so.

"There is another thing you tell me by implication that is also not new, a thing I also fully comprehend. Namely, I and my kind are still just tricksters at the edges, as we have always been, no matter the ratio of our power to that of the mortals, be they in upward or downward spiral as a species. To accomplish the mischief that we wish to accomplish, and to do it with lasting impact, we have always managed—dare I say we have preferred to manage—by means of subterfuge and surprise, and that has not changed. Nor will it change. Not a century hence, not ten centuries hence. It will surely not change in a day or two when I shall treat the human world to a rather stunning spectacle of 'more of the same,' djin-style. I reiterate, witch … you do not frighten me, because you tell me nothing new."

Serenity felt her lower lip tremble in dismay. How could she have been so stupid? Truth or not, magnified or not, the narcissistic djin was right, and she had been a fool to feel even a sliver of triumph after her exposition. Even so, just as that particular sliver of triumph withered and slipped forever away, an entirely new sliver wiggled into her thoughts like a determined minnow, taking its place.

"Ah, but there is still magic, O Dedwen," she muttered in the gloom of the stifling space. "*That* is a power that comes not from this world, but from another—from several others—as you well know. There is still magic, and humans have nothing to do with that."

The djin laughed in the giggling BonSashay voice and threw the tiny shoulders back in their puffed sleeves.

"Yes, there is still magic and I am well aware of it. But behold, magic is hardly a concern of mine at this juncture. You are my prisoner and your magic could not even begin to stop me, once I was free from the ring."

"That's a fact," agreed Serenity, swallowing hard, even though she had never been a prideful witch. "But I am not the only magical force in this town that you may have to contend with. There are other supernatural beings in St. Augustine, other witches. Powerful ones, too."

A pink-shadowed eyelid twitched, almost imperceptibly, at this remark, but the djin maintained its grin. "Oh, yes, I do recall that bedraggled familiar of yours mentioning something about other hags in the region. Ones who did not find you worthy of fellowship, which is not exactly a surprise. My ardor remains undimmed, however. Judging from your talent, a dozen witches working in this town, all in concert against me, would be no more than a trifle, a nuisance. As you can attest, I handle witches in a rather authoritative fashion."

"You might not be able to handle the one I have in mind," said Serenity, allowing herself the slightest taunting curl of a smile.

"Oh, this seaside slumber-town is home to a genuinely potent enchantress, is it?"

"A warlock, actually," said Serenity. "One of considerable antiquity and skill, from what I understand. I wager that he could put an end to your deplorable adventures."

Now the devil frowned, for it knew that the witch was not lying. Even if it wasn't true, Dedwen knew Serenity believed fully in *what* she was saying, and such a certainty even on her part could not risk being unexplored.

"By all means, little worthless one, do tell me where to find this most reputable magus and I shall pay him a visit, trap him in this marvel of a ring in mere seconds, and the two of you can suffocate in limbo together until the End of All Things, if that end ever comes."

"His name is Rowan Blaize and I shall tell you exactly where you can find him. Tomorrow night, in fact, he will be at the Castillo, the old fortress in the center of town on the bay, hosting a midnight revel in honor of the solstice. You can go and pay him a visit there, unless you are afraid to do so, and I am thinking that you are."

No more shooting flames emerged from the pert BonSashay nostrils this time, but two puffs of black smoke shot out like a locomotive's exhaust as the djin grunted its displeasure.

"Do you honestly believe that I would be afraid to confront any wonderworker that a wormy witch like you happens to know? In fact, your Rowan Blaize does himself no favors of reputation by even hobnobbing with a lesser light such as yourself. This would indicate, to me, that he is not very impressive at all. By the by, if this is a ruse to distract me, it is as vain and as ineffectual as were your spells when the two of us first had occasion to meet."

Serenity set her jaw and shook her head. "I'm quite convinced that you are afraid to meet Rowan Blaize, to pay him a midnight visit tomorrow at the old fort," she said. "In fact, I dare you to do it."

Dedwen patted a heap of golden ringlets on his head and spit a wad of crimson saliva at the Rummy Family's prized Thomas Kinkade painting above the magazine rack stuffed with back issues of *Sugarbabies in the Spotlight* magazine. The shot burned a smoldering hole in the painting, just where Kinkade had imagined a luminescent creek-side cottage, and corroded a hole clean through the wall of the house. Palm leaves could be seen rustling in the approaching sunset beyond.

It is never wise to do two things with a djin, if one is to have anything to do with a djin at all. One mistake is to bargain with a djin in the first place, and the other is to dare a djin, to challenge one of them. But Serenity was in fact counting upon the veracity of this very ancient understanding. Djin Rummy took a few prancing tap shoe steps toward her on the floor. The witch looked up, unblinking. She refused to grovel. The enemy was fuming because he knew she was again telling the truth—after all, under his power she could not tell him an outright lie, or at least what she *believed* to be a lie—and he knew that, at least in part, he was beginning to feel a small, tickling feather of trepidation at the base of his vast and commanding memory.

Rowan Blaize.

Dedwen had heard that name, somewhere in the annals and desolate corridors of his extraordinary history, but it was as if trying to seize hold of a phantom every time the djin sought to fix his recollection upon the context in which he had heard the name! Where had he heard of Rowan Blaize, and why?

It was of no consequence, now. The dare, the challenge, had been set before him, and he subsequently reasoned that, if he could not remember the origin of the name in the first place, then that was yet another probable indication that this new magician was no one worth worrying about when it came to a direct encounter.

"I will be most delighted to make the acquaintance of your wonderful warlock tomorrow night at that pathetic fort we passed in the chariot on the way to this dilapidated hovel," cooed Djin Rummy, determined to betray not a hint of the irritation he was feeling as the petulant witch stared up at him, so smug and begging to be beheaded with a single swipe. "The meeting will give me a chance to flex my power a bit more in this outlandishly ridiculous little body, but too bad for your Rowan Blaize, and whoever is with him, that the practice session will last a mere moment, at best."

Serenity maintained her exasperating smile.

"Witches!" snarled the djin. "Oh, back in the ring with you, until you have proper company to keep for the day the sun burns out and this universe falls in upon itself and you float, tormented through Nothingness, for eternity, and an eternity beyond that!"

The ruby ring was held above Serenity's head and only then did she wince and throw up an arm to protect herself, but it was all useless. As swiftly as she had been summoned in a gay and shimmering cloud from the stone, she was dematerialized and sucked right back into it. Djin Rummy put the jewel into a satin pocket amid folds of velvet and began to pace, hands on hips about the living room, grumbling.

"Afraid of some half-wit warlock who's bound to be as mealy-mouthed as she is? I don't *think* so. In fact, it will provide a night of mild entertainment, surely. I have always enjoyed meting-out swift and merciless punishments upon unsuspecting fools on a solstice eve."

Chesterfield Rummy was, by now, a slobbering, jerking bundle of nervous tics and sweltering insanity propped against the sofa. What a terrible creature it was that had come to eat, and then inhabit, his terrible daughter! He wished he had never, ever met either of them, now that he thought of it. Why could he not have listened to his father and enlisted in the merchant marines, leaving land and women behind for a life of drudgery on the sea and a disconnected life of common debauchery upon every furlough? A man could not consider life very successful at all when an ancient demon was tramping around his living room, dressed as a pint-sized beauty pageant hopeful that had once been a family member, a family member now being digested in a belly of brimstone. Rummy was certain about few things, at the moment, but he was fairly certain about that.

"Wh-wh-what you gonna do when you meet this Roland Blade character that little strawberry blonde gal in the ring was talking about?" he jabbered, trying to make conversation.

Dedwen turned upon him with a look that would have turn less djin-experienced men's brains into porridge.

"Do?" said the creature with a prissy little stamp of a tap shoe. "What am I going to *do?* Why, you idiot, I can do just about anything I desire to do!"

Slovenly as ever on the sofa, Fancy Rummy gurgled and jiggled again. "Chester, honey, I'm hungry … fix me something to eat," she slurred in her stupor, eyes fluttering open like the weak wings of newly emerged butterflies. "Open me a big can of them raviolis."

The sneer of the djin's face was one of incomparable malevolence and mischief.

"I might even *do* something like this," it squealed, pointing a gloved hand at the gelatinous body of Fancy.

"BonSashay, baby? Izzat you? Why you lookin at Mama like that?" moaned the sedentary mother, unable to focus even as she was incapable of lifting her head from the cushion.

"Sh-prystk ashmmyrd tyshmaroul vijmal vijmal *vijmal!*" uttered the djinn in a series of awful, guttural syllables. Chesterfield watched as his wife, all three hundred twenty-five spandexed pounds of her, arched upward like an unlikely circus acrobat on the sofa, swelling and undulating until even the super-stretchy spandex split down the middle.

It was not a naked and obese human form that was exposed, but rather the writhing, twisting, slimy, and segmented body of an enormous white grub—a worm so large and disgusting in its movements that the sofa snapped in half beneath its oppressive activity. Fancy's burnt bottle-blonde hair was gone, replaced by the frantic, chomping, clicking, chattering mandibles of a grub's blind and blunt brown face.

Chesterfield screamed as the striking creature began to buck and flail like a bronco, knocking sofa, chairs, and a coffee table in a terrific clamor against all parts of the shuddering house. Then, as if hearing her husband's tortured screech, the grotesque grub-wife reared up like a swollen white snake's head and came down in a dive upon her mate's right foot, mandibles spewing the thick ooze of putrid saliva. It grabbed hold of his foot and gnawed in a frenzy, wrenching the entire limb completely off at the ankle, then gobbling it up as if nibbling away a bud on the stem of a plant.

"My foot! My foot!" wailed Chesterfield. "My foot is gone! She dang ate my foot!"

Rummy scrambled backward on his rear across the floor, waving a bloody stump that shot awful spurts of bright red blood onto the thudding, squirming, pasty-white behemoth before him. Then the grub reared upward again, but this time shot straight down and through the very floorboards, in a mammoth spray of splintering wood and ruin. Wriggling and working its horrendous bulk down, down, down through the rotting and rotted foundation beneath, the thing glutted itself and tunneled swiftly into the dirt below the house, writhing until its tail-end, translucent and bulbous, vanished in a final explosion of dirt and debris that clattered and covered the living room.

"That is what I might *do,*" whispered the djin, calmly surveying the frightful scene.

"Dear God! Dear God!" yowled Rummy. "It done chewed off my foot, shoe and all!"

Blood still poured from the now vacant hem of his pinstriped pants leg. The pretty little princess shrugged.

"Your wife said she was hungry, I believe. Also, I do hope you don't have many gardeners or farmers for neighbors. Because, if you do, you won't have many for long."

"But what about my FOOT?" hollered Chesterfield, his arms pounding like pistons on what was left of the filth-strewn floor.

"Oh, shut your baboon's hindquarters of a mouth. It's only—what?—five toes and a chunk of bone?"

Pointing toward Chesterfield's blood-soaked pants leg, a jet of searing light leapt from the child-finger to the gushing stump. Rummy screamed one last time and fell back, unconscious, the bleeding stemmed and the smell of burnt flesh replacing the foul odor of the carnivorous white grub-woman that had filled the living room.

"There. Cauterized. Are you happy now?" hissed Dedwen, who went over to the upturned magazine stand, picked up an old copy of *Sugarbabies in the Spotlight,* sat down in the only unmolested chair left in the room, and began to leaf daintily through the pages, smoothing the billows of the fluffy pageant dress on either side and kicking the white-stocking legs gently against the upholstery, a demure little angel pausing to enjoy her happy day. The photos in the magazine revealed much, and the articles were promising: *3 Knock-Their Socks-Off Routines That'll Get the Sash!, Vaseline Smiles and the Secrets of Blindingly White Stage-Teeth,* and *Dramatic Hand gestures Even Judy Would Envy!*

Chesterfield Rummy began to snore, just as his wife, who was by now worming and chewing her way through the tree roots of the neighbor's backyard next door, twenty feet down, had earlier snored on the sofa.

"You've got an hour to sleep it off, imbecile," murmured the djin toward Chesterfield's splayed form. Then she licked a velvet gloved finger to turn the next glossy page of the magazine. "I'm counting on you to teach me what all of this nonsense actually *means* tonight. Time is of the essence. After all, I have a warlock to destroy tomorrow, and a pageant to win the day after that."

ॐॐ

XIII

"The whole thing was probably just a spell gone awry, Rowan Blaize. Happens to our folk all the time, as if you didn't know. Wouldn't you agree that it sounds like a spell gone bad, Gert?"

"Sure I'd agree, Letty. I mean, look what happened with us. The perfect example. Our spell that went bad and resulted in utter destruction must've been the result of you getting a foreboding about Serenity Turnbull's spell that went bad and resulted in utter destruction. I wonder ... is that what they mean by irony?"

Letty Beauregard and Gertrude Gokey were polishing off cups of nightshade cider in great slurps as they offered their opinions of the apparent demise and/or disappearance of Serenity Turnbull. Everyone was in the main sitting room of Rowan's house. Miranda had her nose buried in a book, trying to ignore the houseguests as much as possible. Gert was using needles made of faery ulnae to knit herself a new scarf from the silk of a *nephila clavipes* spider, which was reluctantly offering its uplifted spinnerets on a lampstand beside her. She had found the needles while snooping most of the early evening through Rowan's rooms and crawlspaces, and she was having fun. A new scarf and the prospect of a big party on All Hallow's Eve had practically driven the day's discouraging events—the loss of everything she and Letty owned—from her thoughts. Letty was happily humming a discordant version of "Priapus Had a Pertinent Point When Asked for His Opinion," one of her most beloved chestnuts, much to the dismay of Bror, who slobbered and moaned and huffed and puffed in his accustomed spot near the fireplace, putting gigantic paws over his ears.

Rowan slouched in the midst of them on the minotaur-leather divan he had shipped over from his Aunt Ariadne's house in London, sipping a single-malt scotch. It just hadn't seemed like a wormwood martini night. The amber Cipher Disc glimmered softly in the light of the fire he had conjured; a slight cold front had moved in from the north across the bay, as usually happened in late October, but he felt another kind of chill even more keenly in the house. Both witches seemed deplorably noncha-lant about the mysterious circumstances surrounding Serenity.

"I am very much aware of the perils and risks involved whenever magicians attempt certain magicks above their abilities," he said, frown-ing. The flames in the grate danced in twisting columns of light reflected by his brilliant eyes. "But this situation did not at all look like some spell gone wrong."

"Hardly ever does, when that sort of thing happens," said Gert promptly. "Now take my poor cousin Dorcas, for instance. She thought she was the smartest thing since a good slap in the face, back when I was a girl. Her branch of the family was a lot like Letty's. Wasn't no spell too intricate or too ambitious for Dorcas to try, but of course she *would* think that way, seeing as she had a mother just as snooty as she was, a mother who sent her to train with some ole sorceress who'd supposedly been taught by an enchantress who had done *her* apprenticeship with someone who was allegedly a grand-niece of Erictho herself!"

"Oh, that was a whole lotta bunk," spouted Letty, a few tannis root shavings dotting her lips.

"Let me tell the story!" Gert retorted. "It was my cousin, after all. Anyhow, Dorcas fancied herself quite the talent and, to give her credit, she could pull off some nifty little tricks, as I recall. Shape-shifting, even though it'd never last more than an hour or two, and one time I even watched her cross a wide old raging river walking on nothing more than a strand of her own hair that she'd plucked and made long enough to throw across, like one of them circus tightrope acts the mortals used to fuss about, you know?"

"Your cousin Dorcas was an incorrigible show-off," snorted Letty.

"Yeah, I reckon she was," admitted Gert, putting down her knit-ting "needles" and giving the weary orb-weaver spider a rest from its labors. "But her showmanship caught up with her big time one day! See, the prefect of this grubby little city in what is now called 'Germany' once had the temerity to insult a whole group of us witches as we was passing through one summer on our way to some convocation or other. The man said we wasn't dressed like proper damsels and that if we wanted to avoid the stockade or the pokey or whatever they had in that town, well, we had better make tracks, and fast. Said we were a bunch of loose women, you see."

"Ha!" chortled Letty. Gert shot her a withering glance and gave a hint of a snarl from her curled up lower lip, but was not about to be waylaid from her tale.

"Now, I wanted to give that fat clod a fine and permanent set of donkey's ears right on the spot, and mind you I had more than enough zip in my zap to do it, even in them early days, but Dorcas holds me back and drags all of us out of the city like obedient lambs. Ever the show-off, as Letty noted correctly, she laid out her own plans once we were outside the city gates—plans to get back at the buffoon in a bigger, better way than any of us could have imagined. See, her idea was to go back at night, and I'm talking the dead of night, and use magic to teleport the prefect's house right up and out of town, while him and his wife and babies was still asleep inside. Dorcas aimed to take the house all the way out to some goat-addled hilltop far away and just set it down there, so we could watch their stunned reactions in the morning. 'That'll teach him to insult witches,' said Dorcas with that squeaky little voice of hers that I never could stand."

Gert jabbed a faery needle toward the ceiling and cringed in memory of the voice.

"Well, what happened?" asked Miranda, who had been intrigued enough to tear her eyes from the moldering pages of *Learning to Embrace your Inner-Changeling.*

Gert jolted out of her momentary trance and nodded pleasantly. "She took on way too much, is what happened, young Miranda. Confidence is a mighty useful thing in a witch, if she's got the skill to back it up. We all told Dorcas she was off her rocker to attempt such a stunt. We were afraid to even help, but she just charged head on back into town in the thick of night, mad as a bull chasing a red cape, so determined was she to make this happen. As Rowan knows ..." she paused and eyed him as if peering through centuries of delicate and predatory curiosity, "... what you might call 'heavy-lifting' ain't so easy to manage at all. The power needed to channel and maintain the pick-up and transport of an entire house is extraordinary, but there are some who can do that type of thing with ease, and my cousin Dorcas thought she was one of them."

Gert put her hand absently down upon the lampstand and allowed the Golden Orb Weaver to crawl languidly onto her brown, plump fingers.

"I can't remember what spell Dorcas used, but it wasn't anything any of us had ever heard before, and, much to our astonishment, up come that rotten prefect's big house right off its foundations without so much as the sound of a pebble falling, without even the creak of a rafter! There was Dorcas, grinning like the cat what ate the canary and up up up floated that house, and we was all beside ourselves, thinking she really *did* have the power to pull it off, when suddenly, POW!" Gert slammed one hammy fist down upon another, smashing her eight-legged silk factory to a pulpy mash and making everyone in the room (except Rowan and Bror) nearly jump out of their seats.

"Drat! Now look what I've gone and done," lamented Gert. "I just get too carried away with my own self. And that was probably the last banana spider of the year, too. Oh well, I can conjure up another one in a week or two if I find an egg sac."

"I presume that 'POW!' means your cousin lost control of the spell and dropped the prefect's house?" said Rowan drily, staring at Gert in the soft flicker of firelight shadows.

"She dropped it, alright," answered Gert, wiping up spider guts from her hand with a hankie she had plucked from her bosom. "Dropped it right on herself in the middle of town and that was the end of her! Dead as a doorknob, poor Cousin Dorcas. Nothing but her mashed feet, sticking out at us from under the baseboards. Most gruesome thing I ever saw."

"Oh. Give. Me. A. Break," muttered Miranda, who tossed her books aside and left the room in a huff, coaxing Bror from his rug into the kitchen for a late-night snack.

"It's true!" warbled Gert, calling after her. "You shoulda seen how rattled the prefect and his family was about the whole thing. The whole town was rattled, for that matter. Makes quite a shock wave, to have a whole house hit the ground from twenty feet in the air. Everybody woke up toot sweet. The rest of us had to skedaddle, let me tell you, with no time to do anything about Dorcas. There wasn't anything we *could* do. She was mashed. Just like this poor spider." Gert dabbed at a mangled leg still stuck to her fist. "And Dorcas had been wearing them turquoise pixie boots I had been coveting for years, too. If only I'd hung around long enough to make a grab for them! They weren't of any use to her anymore. But the town goons were up in arms by that time, so we had to run. Such a sad scene, and the whole point of my telling you about it is to illustrate what awful stuff can happen when witches try to do too much out of hubris, or spite, or whatever. That Serenity Turnbull may have seemed a bit on the ditzy side, but she also had a stuck-up streak in her, just like Dorcas."

"Heh heh heh!" cackled Letty, warming to the subject now that the cider had warmed her insides. "Serenity was probably trying to turn one of them sea turtles she's so fond of into a dashing beau to replace that nebbish Percival who took off to dig through the Middle East. The fallout when a spell like that goes afoul is unbelievable! I have heard it said," she was careful to enunciate, "that desperate love spells, when they backfire, backfire good and hard! Wouldn't surprise me in the least if such a thing happened to Turnbull. Great Cassiel! What're we gonna tell the folks tomorrow at the All Hallow's Eve party? It's not like Serenity ever attended, but a lot of the guests know her pretty well … or should I say *knew* her."

"We're not going to tell them anything," announced Rowan, "because we ourselves do not know exactly what transpired and, sadly, we no longer possess Gert's 'scrying pan' to ascertain the details, whatever they might be."

"Whull!" snorted Gert. "At least the brief vision in my wok seemed to confirm Letty's premonition migraine, and that vision pointed to trouble for Serenity."

Rowan shrugged. "I still do not believe it was a work of magic that blew up in Serenity's face. At least not *her* work of magic." His eyes searched the dark and shadow-shimmering corners of the expansive room, worried that the next shadow might congeal or take on some taunting form or other signal confirming his worst suspicions. He lifted the disc for another bewildered inspection. "And though I can sense that it is rather magical, we still don't know what this thing might be. Her familiar, Emory, was so intent upon mentioning it before he slipped away."

"Now, Rowan Blaize, you are going to have to stop worrying about all of this, at least for the time being," cautioned Letty. "You have a major metaphysical event to host tomorrow night, and we have all taken a look at that thing. It's magical, I'll grant you that, but not one of us can figure out its purpose to save our hides. Probably just another piece of that unfortunate witch's gaudy jewelry collection. You know how she was always traipsing around in them airy muumuus and wearing strange stones around her neck that didn't have a thing to do with spell-casting. And as for that familiar of hers, well, it got caught in whatever botched spell its mistress was trying out and became an unfortunate victim. But familiars know what they're in for when they get summoned, and they do tend to get a little incoherent when their assumed forms age or die and start to slip off into the Void. A fading familiar is bound to chatter all sorts of nonsense when on its last legs. Isn't that right, Gert?"

"Right you are, Letty."

"See? Now, Gert and I are gonna head up to those fine rooms you and Miranda were so kind as to prepare for our comfort because we want to have our sleep good and proper before tomorrow night's big gathering. It has been a most trying day but we're exhausted … and grateful more than you know. Miranda taking us clothes-shopping down by the outlet mall after all our insurance business was out of the way was especially sweet. Let us return the favor by getting out of your hair and catching a few winks, so we can be of assistance to you tomorrow night at the party."

"She's right again, Rowan," piped Gert, rising with some difficulty from her chair in the new pink housecoat she had purchased during their shopping foray. "We're more good to you with our wits restored, and only sleep'll do the trick on that count. We can all give Serenity's place a nice go-over the night after the party, to see if there's anything you missed. Heck, she's liable to turn up by then. Witches *have* been known to come back from the brink of trouble in the past, you know."

Rowan knew, but wished he did not know of certain *potential* cases.

The duo bid their host a prim goodnight and followed each other up the stairwell into the darkness, mumbling the entire way. Miranda came back from the kitchen just then, Bror in tow, yawning as wide as a chasm to reassume his spot on the hearth rug and begin to snore-off his snack.

"I gotta tell you, Rowan, I find it really difficult to wrap my head around those two bats," whispered Miranda fearfully, watching their bedroom slippers vanish up the stairs. "I mean, they're witches and they've got to be how many centuries old?"

"Don't know," said Rowan with a brief shrug of one shoulder. "Never was impertinent enough to ask."

"But what I mean is, they both have this huge history, possibly all over the world, if you believe half of their stories, and yet this prissy, folksy Southern dame 'act' just seems such a put on, when you think about it. Such an affectation. I can't figure that out."

"Then think a little bit more carefully about it," said Rowan, though not without a certain tenderness for his beloved foundling. "You've lived virtually your entire life around a wide array of magical beings, beginning with the inhabitants of Mad Ramble's Roam. You have seen firsthand how supernatural creatures are so often like quicksilver. They can be what they want when they must … and they can be what they must when they want. Witches and warlocks, especially, Miranda. We are very complex individuals, as you know. We have seen so much and we live, by choice or by circumstance, in so many worlds and eras, so many environments to which we, too, must adapt in one way or another. Magicians are adaptable because it is in our nature, and because we have to be adaptable.

"Gert and Letty may appear to be somewhat common, cranky old southern magnolias, very rough around the edges in some respects, very forward, dropping their Gs left and right, but this is only the current stage of their long journey. I guarantee that, if you had the chance to encounter them two hundred, three hundred or more years ago, you would have encountered two entirely different personalities, at least on the surface. Very different indeed. It is an 'act' ... yet it is most decidedly *not* an act. Am I making any sense to you?"

"You're right, obviously," said Miranda. "But even a mortal who has seen all I have seen will never be able to fully understand it. I suppose that's why magical beings live so comfortably along the edges, on the outskirts, yet long for a recognition and inclusion that they know they could never truly endure, or survive. I used to sense it was that way with King Narzell. That's where some of his immense bitterness came from. He knew he could never camouflage himself well enough to find a safe place in the mortal world, not like Letty and Gert have been able to do, and yet his world was swiftly falling apart because of humans and because of his own refusal to adapt. He's a different case, I guess. I don't want to confuse supernatural species, here, and I ought not to fall into that mistake, given my history."

Rowan lay supine on the divan and tilted his jet black mane over the edge, smiling at Miranda upside-down. "The day may also come when witches like Letty and Gert, together or separately, decide that they don't want to live in any sort of close proximity to mortals. I suspect one or both of them have already gone through several phases like that. I know that I have gone through it. Our needs and our perspectives change accordingly, when that happens. Our names change. Our appearances. Everything can change, to the observer, at least. When other worlds are involved, such changes can be even more pronounced.

"But you've seen more than enough of magical existence, Miranda. Besides, you are respected for what you know, for what you have learned. Many in your shoes have gone mad, or have not survived at all. That which is not within your power to grasp or understand will never be held against you. I can promise as much. Just be certain to live your life as you desire. For as long as you desire, that life can be lived safely with me, and with Bror. Now, apparently, it can even be lived with Letty and Gert … at least until they rebuild that shop of theirs! Let's hope it doesn't take them very long to get *that* ball rolling."

"Thank you, Rowan," said Miranda with a wistful smile. "You always manage to restore my confidence, but I wish I could restore yours. Oh, there's no use being evasive. I see you staring at the shadows again, with that disconcerted look in your eyes. Something's got you spooked, if you'll pardon my use of the term. Even the old biddies can sense it, though they haven't the temerity to say anything, yet. Do you really think Serenity Turnbull annihilated herself in a botched incantation, or do you think it's something—or someone—you've been fretting about for a while now?"

"No," protested Rowan. "Don't even think that. Not at this moment, if you please. I myself am not prepared to give it more than a mere flicker of thought, not yet. I don't know what has happened to Serenity, but I do know that we'll be likely to find out. Sooner, rather than later."

Miranda listened for a moment to the hearth flames as they crackled and snapped, and heard the palm leaves thrashing in the latest cool blast of wind outside. Bror grunted on his rug and dreamt contentedly of chasing elephants in India because, at one time in his life, he had engaged in just such an activity.

"Rowan, whatever has happened or is happening, the party is going to be outstanding tomorrow night. I don't know if that's any consolation," added Miranda, shifting uncomfortably in her chair. "But everyone is buzzing about it. Everyone—except for Serenity, of course—has RSVPed. You know, maybe we can even ask around about Serenity when we're there. The dryads are bound to have heard something. You know how they always get the best gossip there is to be had."

"I know," said Rowan, turning the smooth stone of what Emory had called the "Cipher Disc" over and over in his fingers and wondering about the steady army of storm clouds gathering, ominous and silent, in the corridors of his thought. "But let's just hope the truth, when we discover it, amounts to much less than the gossip we are bound to hear."

෨෧

XIV

Halloween night has, for decades, been far more the mischievous domain of adults eager to revel in an all-too-swiftly extinguished (or pathologically extended) childhood than a quaint trick or treat endeavor enjoyed by actual youngsters. In St. Augustine, as elsewhere, gone are the days when moppets merrily donned white bed sheets with swift scissor-cut eye holes, black and pointy buckle-hats, rubber masks, little devil suits, and other disguises painstakingly stitched together by amused mothers so their darlings could tote bags and jack-o-lantern pots through the blustery streets on October's last day.

The experience of kiddies skipping along in the darkness, accompanied by harried parents, prowling along the sidewalks and through the city's fabled alleyways like zigzagging specters and giggling columns of shadow, is largely extinct. Forgotten is the thrill of rapping upon neighborhood doors that would be reliably opened, almost to the last, with reactions of delighted surprise at being cornered by such mysterious and frightening imps—imps clamoring and squeaking and begging, asking the age-old question in a chorus of piping voices:

Trick or treat, trick or treat, trick or treat?

In the golden days of Halloween, viable trick or treating neighborhoods encompassed not only one's own block or lonely avenue of familiar houses, but the entire city—even the unfavorably regarded "other side of the tracks"—and outlying areas. Any spot where a human dwelling boasted a working porch light would attract the faux witches, goblins, ghosts, imps, demons, and assorted spooks seeking sweet reward for their brave nighttime forays, and these denizens were all the braver because they savored the mortifying pleasure of staying up way past bedtime. They gloated in the adventure of accosting the homes of

perfect strangers and requesting utterly unknown, untested, and uncertain quantities of items destined to be put in their mouths, chewed, and
ultimately swallowed with considerable glee.

Trick or treat, trick or treat, trick or treat?

In the era when Halloween belonged to children, the answer to
the relentless, take-no-prisoners philosophical chant was, except in very
rare cases involving urban legendary sociopaths fond of secreting shav-
ing-shards in shiny red apples ... *Treat.*

Treat after treat after treat after treat.

The greatest treat of all was the way in which children seemed to
become, if only for an evening, the very magical entities they were attempting to impersonate. Costumes were talismans, empowering them
to pierce the otherwise dreaded blackness like unbothered phantoms.
Children became fearless little night-conquerors, and the very partners
and cohorts of the Unseen Forces they only half-believed in on all *other*
eves. On All Hallow's Eve, however, these forces seemed more real than
anything else in the world, hurrying alongside children with every earnest breath, gathering spoil that would later be hoarded and lorded-over
in the dark forest of a bedroom, or by enchanted flashlight deep within
the cavernous halls found beneath Dwarf Mountains ... formed by the
perilous peaks of bed covers and blankets.

In those truly hallowed times, a child could sense the irresistible
allure and give in to the power of the Bright Spirit while trick or treating
on Halloween, dashing onward in his or her costume, arms flapping and
cape billowing in the wake of charmed whispers and other beckoning
powers. When that happened, there was nothing on earth, above earth,
or below earth that could convince such a child he or she was not genuinely soaring through the very air, as exhilarated with pride and purpose
as any mad or cackling creature able to cast a silhouette upon the moon
while crisscrossing the heavens. For that one night, Halloween had for
centuries made provision for children to enter the World Unspoken, the
Secret Sphere, because on that one night, children alone could sense that
the doors and windows to these realms were being opened ever so slight-

ly. Sensing this, they demanded the trick of entry and were rewarded with the treat of passage.

Only children understood that *they* were one and the same with magic—real magic!—on All Hallow's Eve, and only they understood that the sidewalk-shuffling, bell-ringing, door-knocking, bag-opening, candy-opening parts were all mere window dressing in comparison to what was actually going on.

Enchantment.

Then things changed. Over time, the night was flooded with streetlights and mistrust, porch lights were turned off, doors were locked and bolted, curtains were drawn, minds were otherwise occupied, candy jars were left unfilled, and children were hustled into brightly lit gymnasiums and dance halls to celebrate "Harvest" or "Autumn" dressed as whatever insipid Hollywood hero, grating Saturday morning cartoon character, or popular toy was deemed suitably trendy. The night was denied to children on All Hallow's Eve and, as a result, they no longer could hear its siren summons, and forgot its power altogether.

That, of course, was when adults stepped in to fill the void in the clumsy and often quite unseemly ways in which adults seem to specialize. The whispering, watchful spirits beyond the Veil were dismissed by adults, as well—adults, who tend to forget and ignore Everything Invisible, anyhow, and those once-beckoning powers and spirits were no longer offered the obeisance and flattery of imitation. Adults stole Halloween. Ghoulish attire was jettisoned by grown-ups in favor of "ironic" costuming. Witches were transformed into whip-bearing felines or saucy French maids. Werewolves were deemed unworthy of duplication—much too involved—and were replaced by middle-aged people carousing as boxes of laundry detergent, fast food containers, and other "harrowing" entities. Billowing shrouds were reconfigured into togas allowing for more uninhibited use of the limbs during consumption of enormous quantities of alcoholic beverages and the catching of leftover Mardi Gras beads. Over the hill revelers leaned and leered upon the balconies of nightclubs that hosted "Halloween Jazz Ensembles" and adults did not soar through the air in union with spirits on the great night. Instead, they staggered through the evening, or swerved menacingly across yellow-lined roadways. Once safe at home in their beds, passed out in the throes of intoxication, they did not dream of shattered glass doorways opening upon vast and splendid landscapes of magic, as did Halloween's authentic children.

The beings that inhabited the magical realm did not fail to notice the gradual hijacking and utter ruination of Halloween by adult mortals, and they responded in their own ways to the insult. With no more children to properly entrance and invigorate, they began to hold "parties" of their own, which was always considered a very distant "second best" to the way things had been before, no matter how hard they tried to make their own Halloween gatherings successful. Magical beings tried to convince themselves they were having a lot more fun than they used to have, but like adult mortals who told themselves the very same thing while dressed as cheerleaders in packed clubs drinking beer, they knew it was rather a lie.

Of course, it must be admitted that this state of affairs caused no small amount of resentment on the part of the magical community, all stemming from this pervasive Halloween snub, and it did inspire certain of the Ethereal Realm's more aggressive and cantankerous denizens to "act out" in various ways for purposes of retaliation, as it were. They did so in good old St. Augustine, even though the Ancient City was hardly alone in its status as a place that had turned its back on the true spirit of Halloween. Indeed, St. Augustine was just one of thousands of towns forced to deal with unsavory consequences on the very night that Rowan Blaize hosted his great All Hallow's Eve party, just as it had been experiencing these consequences for years. Normally sympathetic supernatural folk never did much to stop the mischief because they were too busy being forced to party on their own due to the unruly recalcitrance of mortal adults who, they believed, tended to deserve whatever they got.

On the night of Rowan's party, the "Thieves of All Souls Eve" got a great deal of "whatever."

For instance, a woman scantily dressed as a feline seductress of comic book fame, in an outfit she had fashioned herself from hand-sewn bits of black felt in a painfully obvious way, was one unwitting victim. Tottering on a pair of stiletto heels that seemed destined to become entangled with her drooping and dragging kitty-cat tail—made from black, spray-painted cotton balls strung along fishing line—the woman nearly reeled into the spines of a palmetto bush as she was leaving Belle Watling's. Belle Watling's was a St. Augustine hotspot that, on this night, looked as if it were going to be shaken from its very foundations at any moment and jitterbug across the street into the parking lot of Flagler College, so loud was the "Halloween Band" playing rock and roll songs, and so energetic were the people hanging out of every window and door, contorting their bodies in time with the music. A garbled call from an inebriated friend on the rickety front porch of Belle's spared the cat-lady a painful pirouette into the palmetto, distracting her long enough for the tacky tail to swing weakly away from the clicking staccato path of a stiletto.

"Yeah, Ashleigh, I'll—*burp!*—see you at the office tomorrow. So, yeah …bye. Happy Halloween. Woo hoo."

Off she minced up Hypolita Street toward old St. George, but in the dark she did not notice the figure that had been watching her as she passed beneath the balcony of the nearby Columbia Restaurant. She was surprised to the point of a blessedly immediate swoon upon her bed when, having clattered and stalked back into her apartment two blocks away, she reached up to remove her cat headdress and mask … only to discover that the mask was no longer composed of stitched felt, but of the slithery, slippery wings of a scargoyle that had dropped down and treated her to its usual trick of flesh-altering wraparound therapy. She would wake up in the morning with a skull-hammering hangover, the baneful breath occasioned by the ghosts of seven margaritas (rocks, no salt), and light blue facial skin pocked with over one hundred little scargoyle "sucker marks" where once her complexion had boasted the most fetching hue of peaches and cream.

That poor woman would spend the next two years in sunglasses and enormous floppy hats, flitting from one baffled dermatologist to the next, even ending up the subject of a scientific study in a peer-reviewed medical journal before the symptoms vanished altogether one day. The despair of her long ordeal would forever be in vain, however, because human adults had stolen Halloween from its rightful owners and *some* unscrupulous creatures wanted those human beings to pay for it.

Elsewhere in town, around eleven o'clock, as the moonlight streamed down over the usually placid bay and was dashed into thousands of glimmering liquid shards of white light, a trio of nattily attired partygoers dressed as commandos toted water-guns filled with vodka and approached the Bridge of Lions after getting rowdy enough to be tossed out of the Mill Top Tavern. Near the fabled bridge, an intracoastal naiad and her sisters—their hair drifting like tentacles across the surface of the moonstruck water, their nimble fingers encrusted with periwinkles— watched and waited for the loudmouths to get close enough to the edge of the promenade. Suddenly, combining their forces, the sisters smiled silently in the shallows and summoned a rogue wave that heaved up and over the seawall, dashing all three men in a wild series of somersaults as they rode the swell and spun out onto the street, coughing and choking and scrambling to regain their feet before oncoming traffic plowed them down for good. A few onlookers saw the extraordinary surge, of course, but no one accredited it to the magical intervention of saltwater naiads on Halloween night, which was *exactly* why the naiads, grinning and gliding in graceful circles beneath the chop like satisfied sharks, did the deed in the first place. Halloween had been stolen from its rightful owners, and they wanted those thought to be the thieves to pay for it.

Other incidents occurred all over St. Augustine, and these furious tricks befell even those who did not flaunt the decline of the holiday via loutish behavior and Bacchanalian festivities more appropriate to other sacred evenings and their associated entities.

For example, an old woman on Martin Luther King Jr. Avenue hobbled over to her microwave, leaning on a horsehead cane, reached over to innocently remove her second helping of pizza, and flailed her hands about her curlers, screaming as an entire colony of bats flew out of the contraption and circled the kitchen, shrieking for a few seconds before fading into mere memories of fluttering shadow. The old woman told herself she would be damned if she ever bought *that* brand of microwave pizza again.

"Must've been those no good pepperonis," she sniffed and tacked her cane as fast as she could into her bedroom to lay down because she figured she must already be asleep, anyhow, to have seen such a thing.

Several blocks away, on Riberia Street, a couple who had turned off all the lights to avoid even the remote *possibility* of being bothered by intrepid, retro-style trick or treaters, were watching *The Creature from the Black Lagoon* on television when they were interrupted by the ringing of the front doorbell.

"Don't answer it!" hissed Sheila, the young wife. "It might be some twisted person, like a trick or treating child!"

"But it might be my mother," countered Jim, the husband, whose mother lived next door and routinely forgot where she mislaid her reading glasses, or her dentures, or Mitzi, her Pomeranian.

"All the more reason not to answer the door, if it's her," counseled his spouse, and they settled back to watch the classic beast of the aforementioned lagoon. But the bell continued to ring.

"Look, Sheila, it's Mother. I'll just see what she wants and be done with it before the commercials are over," said the husband, rising from the love seat.

"I'll go with you," huffed Sheila. "I want to give her a piece of my mind about these constant interruptions, which I believe are deliberately calculated to undermine the quality time so necessary for our healthy marriage."

Of course, when they got to the door and opened it, they discovered that it was not Mother—not on this night, not on their lives.

It was, in fact, the Creature from the Black Lagoon, standing on their porch, dripping globs of pond scum, smelling like the muck that might be scooped from the bottom of the first bubbling cauldron of Primordial Soup, hissing great popping bubbles of stench-breath and flexing webbed claws and gills in the already unflattering radiance of Jim and Sheila's porch light.

There were screams—manly ones and womanly ones—for it really was a bit too much for the mind to accept, given what they had been watching. Afterward, when the police assured the couple it had been, unquestionably, a most inconsiderate seven foot-tall and expensively costumed prankster, Jim and Sheila were nearly able to get some sleep that night ... next door in the guest room of Mother's house.

They were all wrong, naturally (or supernaturally), for their visitor had *not* been the Creature from the Black Lagoon, who did not exist outside a re-mastered film reel from 1954. Instead, it had been poor WarrowWize, a creature that hailed, not from a lagoon, but from a massive, snot-colored swamp behind Old Moultrie Road. WarrowWize loved nothing more than to traipse once a year out of the little network of swamps he had been inhabiting for two centuries, particularly on Halloween. It was not his fault that he bore a striking resemblance to the rubber monster of cinematic infamy, and he certainly did have distant relations in various parts of the world who dwelled in small, fetid bodies of water that could rightfully be described as "black," but he had only stopped on his way to Rowan Blaize's party to ask for directions and maybe a glass of polliwogs, if anyone happened to have any around.

Humans!

WarrowWize and others were always forgetting how unreceptive they were to the magical world. WarrowWize had been forgetting it every year since he could remember, and had resolved to make a note of it before stalking off into the delicious camouflage of thick azalea bushes, palm groves, and magnolia trees, to say nothing of the night itself. Let the mortals work themselves into catatonia, for all he cared. Rudeness was the worst thing in the world, as far as WarrowWize was concerned. Besides, he had a party to attend, and he didn't get invited to parties by warlocks very often. So he dripped and wheezed his scaly way toward the fort along the bay-front, for judging from the moon's position in the sky, cobwebbed with wispy clouds, that party was just about to begin!

❧◈❧

The rest of old St. Augustine may have endured the revenge of Halloween magic or replaced it with revelry, ennui, and early bedtimes, but the Castillo de San Marcos, the great fort overlooking Matanzas Bay, was enshrouded with magic from the bottom of the hillside knoll to the very tops of the coquina walls against which seawater gently and unceasingly brushed. Rowan Blaize's All Hallow's Eve Party was already a tremendous success, and it was still half an hour before midnight and the time for various toasts and speeches.

Local mortals out and about passed by their city's signature monument and did indeed "see" a wild array of flashing lights, luminescent fallout from magical spells, and an endless parade of emanations, but upon seeing such things, their minds immediately turned toward the completion of their own activities and such bizarre sights were instantly forgotten. Even as guests of obvious non-human and decidedly immortal stock arrived to the fete by air, or by sea, or by enchanted vehicles as diverse as broomsticks and moonbeams mirrored upon the waves, mortal watchers took no substantial or lasting notice. Visions like that entered the consciousness and drifted away as intangible and inconsequential as gossamer on the sultry breeze of a Florida summer's day.

This was all due to Rowan's spell, of course, and it was a spell that he had not only utilized during the previous year's gala, but it was one he had employed on numerous occasions throughout his long and illustrious history whenever he and his kind decided to gather in spots frequented by mortals, or in areas where encounters with mortals would be possible. In such situations, the need to maintain privacy for the sake of order was paramount. Without a doubt, witches and wizards and sorcerers of all descriptions congregated with their varied and considerable coteries and entourages in out-of-the-way places for centuries on end without regard or caution for the potential interloping of mortals. They were indifferent to the issue of prying mortal eyes.

The general attitude in such circumstances had always been, "Too bad for the humans foolhardy enough to stumble upon *our* regalements or dare interrupt our proceedings," and such incidents had indeed occurred many times through the ages. Thus, the uninvited mortal had become a simultaneous object of contempt and amusement in many quarters, and few such hapless people ever returned to their own worlds following these encounters, intentional or not. Those that managed to return to their own environs rarely returned unscathed in some way. Once in a great while a savvy human being would prove charismatic, persuasive, or golden-tongued enough to form some kind of alliance or achieve some measure of impasse and walk away unmolested. Odysseus and his merry crew were the paragons of such good fortune, but everyone knew that *they* had extracurricular help, and this happenstance was a rarity of some magnitude.

Rowan Blaize, for his part, had never been a sorcerer particularly keen to toy with sneaky mortals or punish the genuinely inadvertent ones, and, privacy meaning as much to him as to any great magician, he had called forth the quartet of spirits inhabiting the very cornerstones of Existence, the lithe and shapeless entities responsible for the maintenance of invisible things, for the preservation of hidden realities. Since he was powerful enough to summon them, these Archons moved through time and through layers of otherwise impenetrable shadow to lend a measure of their own shapelessness to his magical weavework. Thus a great Cloaking Spell, a Spell of Ephemera, an Incantation of Transience, was nimbly and expertly created. It descended over the length and breadth of Rowan's chosen festival space, shielding it for the benefit of both guests and those very many who had not been, and could truly never be, invited.

Under the scrutiny of a watchful moon, the fifty thousand square foot 17th Century fortress, with its four diamond-shaped outer points, was alive with a rather satisfying chaos. It hummed with an exceedingly gratified miasma of guests who, for the most part, would not be caught dead, undead, or in-between at such a place on any other occasion during the year. Indeed, though some were friends, and others qualified as inherent enemies, and the majority simply had no typical interest in being one or the other, all differences were put aside in gallant fashion so that a most practical pandemonium and a capably incoherent coherence might be savored by everyone.

This was a magical convocation of some splendor, and all who were present sensed the enormity of sheer power in the atmosphere.

At the center of the gala, of course, was a roaring bonfire. No magician with any manners or the most miniscule grasp of ethereal etiquette would even ponder the notion of hosting such an event without a gigantic bonfire. The best part of all was that no wood or fuel had been required. Indeed, there had been no need for Rowan or for Miranda to personally prepare anything for the party—except for the cloaking spell and the invitations—themselves. The two (with Bror in tow) had arrived at the fort immediately after sunset and the Spell of Ephemera, with its attendant "tweaks" of local tourist councils, along with regional and statewide historical panels, was well in place by the time the moon was high and dominating the appropriately creepy sky.

Summoning the bonfire had been the first order of business.

Earlier in the day, at the house on lower St. George Street, Letty and Gert had fought with each other over which of the two of them would be the most honored to "help" Rowan by being the one to ignite the Great Fire, but both witches had ended up fussing so long over their attire for the evening (and ruing the ruin of their respective ceremonial wardrobes in the razing of the pepper shop) that both begged out of their previous offers of assistance.

"I can't possibly go without a turban to match this flying cape you loaned me, Rowan Blaize!"

And:

"It'll take at least another hour to get this braid tight enough around my head. You'll just have to go on without us!"

Rowan had sighed and donned his own, truly ancient apparel: the trollskin boots and dragonleather coat—the materials for which he had earned the *hard* way over two millennia before—as well as his own flying cape, a gift from his grandmother made partially from the plumes of one of Hera's own, beloved peacocks. Miranda was as excited as he was, not only because of how hard she had worked on the invitations and arrangements with special vendors, but because she was, above all else, a changeling. Even though it had been the most salvific day of her life when

Rowan had liberated her from her enchanted imprisonment, a change-ling she remained—one who had grown up among one of the rarest and most rag-tag assemblages of supernatural beings. Part of Miranda's imagination always thrilled to revisit that weird landscape, if only as a protected guest, for it would always be an element of her very identity.

Now, instead of regarding the collection of so many bizarre beings in one place as an oppressive experience, she enjoyed the opportunity to be included and respected. Due to her association with Rowan, and under the mantle of freedom he had secured for her, she had eagerly joined hands with her beloved employer and curled her fingers around Bror's ruhk-talon collar, and the three of them had stepped onto the widow's walk of the Victorian, into the milk-moon coolness of the night, and had flown to the fort under Rowan's power. Once there, the great warlock had raised his arms and coaxed a spectacular fire from the very earth in the center of the Castillo's interior plaza.

It was not long after when the "caterers" arrived.

They were four hobgoblin brothers from the town of Spuds, all of whom dwelled together in a crumbling old country mansion on a derelict but well-guarded farm estate. They were exceedingly secretive and had occupied the once-magnificent plantation house after the scourge of the Civil War. Each of the brothers was just humanoid enough to pass for particularly ugly (and possibly a bit inbred) men among the local mortals, who seldom ever laid eyes upon them, and thought them all to be descendants of the "original" owners, anyway. To be certain, the four were known and given a wide berth by the neighbors because of their family's frightening folkloric origins, their physically repulsive attributes, their alligator and rattlesnake infested acreage, and because they left mortal folk well alone in return. Most significantly for the party, however, these hobgoblin brothers were famous throughout the immortal community (or that portion of it that consumed actual food) for their talent in preparing spectacular low-country cuisine fused with a panorama of magical ingredients.

Tonight, the four great tables the brothers had trucked-in for the bash were laden with the fruits of their labors and the feast was lavish beyond compare: crab croquettes with chervil and *latrodectus* venom reduction sauce; cornbread with rosemary and spiced hummingbird tongues; salamander-eye caviar on roasted echidna scales; deviled albatross eggs which were served soft-boiled in the shell ("Those took some time to import, Master Blaize, believe us!"); poison honeycakes in platypus cream—the honey coming from mutant bees the brothers kept themselves and which fed exclusively upon the nectar of larkspur blossoms they cultivated.

The foursome had also wanted very much to serve their coveted grouper sushi-rolls wrapped in membranous batwing, but were mindful of offending the vampires that were bound to be in attendance at the party. Instead, they substituted pressed and marinated dragonfly wings, which they figured would sparkle more attractively in the firelight than the batwings, despite the concessions made in terms of sheer palette-thrilling flavor. Another highlight would be the okra stuffed with ground *chupacabra* meat and spiced with just a touch of nutmeg; the "chupa" tenderloins were another hard-to-get import that the brothers had been beside themselves with worry about obtaining in time. Gryffon's Nest Soup took up one entire table currently being swamped by a horde of ghouls that favored the gelatinous quality of the dish due to the sorry state of their decayed teeth. Nearby, a pair of dryads that guarded Tolomato Cemetery and its gnarly oaks raved about the quality of the starfish medallions, which were drenched in a key lime and black rose petal *coulis*. Even old WarrowWize, who had made it soggily and safely all the way from Old Moultrie Road, was trying to sop-up a bit of Coral Snake puree that had started streaming from his gill-slits after only a few spoonfuls.

Beverages of all sorts—ambrosia, muskmelon wine, huckleberry and wormwood cordials—were being ladled festively by the hobgoblin brothers' chittering offspring out of upside-down armadillo shells. Plenty of late-season flowers were strewn everywhere for the faeries to munch, and fey folk were milling throughout the expanse, mouths and cheeks stuffed with petals, faces like squirrels as they nibbled and gossiped.

The werewolves weren't eating because their preferred cuisine would have been downright unseemly for such an auspicious event. They were planning to feed right before dawn, anyhow, and they mainly came for the music and to ask nosy questions.

The vampires were strictly BYOB. That had been an unspoken understanding even before invitations were sent out.

Entertainment for Rowan's party was provided by a most beguiling trio. Dendara Cubbidge, a banshee from St. Ambrose Parish in Elkton, sang lead vocals while a Palatka incubus and a druid hag from Anastasia Island accompanied her multi-octave renditions of original material on sawgrass flute and ogre-ivory keyboard, respectively.

Within an hour, the success of the soiree had become evident to all. Rowan wondered why he hadn't thought to use the old fort for his previous gala; the venue was ideal. Miranda was leaning against Bror over by one of the Castillo's old jail cells, sipping muskmelon wine and debating the pros and cons of the vegan lifestyle with a bemused zombie named Garth. The evening's only changeling was animated and resplendent in her black strapless gown and lavender satin shawl. Rowan was so proud of her, and he made it a point to let everyone present know that she was as much to be thanked for the superb caliber of the event as was he.

Letty and Gert had not ceased to hold court since their typically spectacular (and separate) arrivals, which occurred not long after the music had begun. Letty, favoring the windy approach once more, had made her entrance first, emerging from the vortex of a gentle waterspout funnel she had conjured from a single cloud above the bay. The mini-tornado had hopped over the fort wall and deposited her regally upon the plaza to the oohing and aahing of the partygoers. It was a vast atmospheric improvement upon her disastrous sandstorm-on-the-beach entrance a year before. There was much enthusiastic applause. Not to be outdone, Gert came soon after. A great three-tiered, sugar-frosted cake had been placed with some ceremony on a table by the hobgoblin brothers, but it had turned out to be no cake at all, particularly when an imp in a cat-sized tuxedo attempted to grab a piece of the confection for himself, only to get its claw slapped by a suddenly emergent brown hand. Gert Gokey herself *was* the cake—an illusion the wily witch had managed in a rather form-fitting white gown studded with pearls and thousands of little fringed leather strips that looked like shredded coconut. The modes of entry were clever and, as usual, Letty and Gert felt the need to shoot each other mutual glances that seemed to snarl: "Nice try, but *my* spell was more creative."

Now the two ladies were shoulder to shoulder, giving and receiving gossip from a rapt circle of devotees, fully aware of their status as the city's patroness witches. Amid the cacophony of laughter, music, eating, drinking, hissing, shrieking, muttering, whistling, and all around supernatural buzz, however, Rowan could sense that the one-two punch news about Serenity Turnbull's disappearance and the destruction of the witches' pepper shop (and home) were the chief topics of conversation. Everyone was chattering about it, even the normally disconnected water nixies, who had managed to conjure themselves up from the bay to hover in an interweaving swirl of mist above one of the fort's dilapidated old wells.

Of course, Gert and Letty had seen personally to the pervasive spread of the news, thrilled to hear it crackling on tongues with the same ferocity as Rowan's magical bonfire. The witches were loving the drama and Gert, in particular, was commiserating with the four hobgoblin brothers as her captive audience. After all, they had brought the fabulous food, and wherever food of exceptional quality could be found, Gert Gokey was never far away, if she could help it. The brothers had, in fact, been the witches' exclusive suppliers of all the datil peppers used to make the products for their former atelier on St. George Street, so on this occasion they listened to the ladies' umpteenth mutually interruptive account of the terrible fire with obligatory interest. This was business, after all.

Rowan had been content to meet and greet for the first couple of hours, everyone praising him effusively and thanking him more than that for the rendered grace of an invitation. They also kept a slight and respectfully intimidated distance—even the werebeasts, which were, for better or worse, usually intimidated by nothing. Rowan remained, after well over a year in town, a mystery to the eerie community, and most of them could sense the enormity of his power acutely. Easy familiarity was not first and foremost on their minds in this regard. To be certain, Letty and Gert were highly respected witches, too, but they cultivated and encouraged a certain qualified intimacy with their supernatural peers, chiefly because such intimacy was crucial for navigating the ever-humming channels of metaphysical gossip down which they both craved to sail.

Rowan stood alone drinking brandy while watching a slightly tipsy succubus swat a gremlin away from her moth-wing skirts. His thoughts drifted again to the strange case of Serenity Turnbull when Letty Beauregard came up and tapped him firmly on the shoulder from behind.

"Still all bent out of shape about the unfortunate end of Serenity, I see. And you at your own All Hallow's Eve party, too," she added, fixing Rowan with her unusually penetrating gimlet stare and her trademark pursed, disapproving lips.

"Leticia. I was rather impressed by your entrance. Even more spectacular than last year, and with the added bonus of no drowned gremlins or goblins, too. You really have a knack with cyclonic spells, I must say. It isn't easy to conjure a towering cumulonimbus on a night of wispy cloud-cover in late October, but to whip up a waterspout to go with it ... I call that a job well done. How long, I wonder, have you been saving that ace up your sleeve?"

Letty grunted and took her place at his side, surveying the fantastic and energetic crowd, the kaleidoscope of merry movement and monstrous mannerisms.

"Gert believes she scored extra points for artistry, what with that surprise appearance in the form of a coconut cake, of all things. I suppose she has a claim to one-upmanship,"admitted Letty, rolling her eyes. "There's something to be said for subtlety. I've always believed that. Ha! Folks must've seen me coming a mile away in that little water twister, but you'll never catch *me* making an entrance dressed as somebody's dessert! That's for sure. Showy is best, in my opinion, if it's a show you intend to put on in the first place. But it's all in good fun and the spirit of

the evening, ain't it? All part of what has become the most talked-about
private event across the ectoplasmic continuum, at least in these parts."

"Thank you for saying so, Letty."

"You're quite welcome, I'm sure. And you don't have to avoid the
subject of Serenity Turnbull with me, my lad. I seen you moping about,
not really connecting with your guests, which is kind of your way, I admit. But you could at least look like you're here to have a good time.
Gert and me have been swept off our feet with chatter since we got here.
Couldn't brush the nosy pixies off if we tried!"

"Yes, I saw the two of you with your usual crowd of courtiers. I'm
glad you're enjoying yourselves and I don't blame anyone here for wanting to get all the news about the disaster at the pepper shop, much less
the conundrum regarding Serenity's disappearance."

"Our shop is the number one subject on everyone's lips, if they
have lips," confessed Letty, trying to look annoyed but failing; she was
proud of the buzz, even though it was a buzz based upon a grand miscalculation. Witches generally loved nothing more than a calamity to pro-
mote and promulgate through the very old-fashioned and decidedly non-
magical power of gossip … even if the calamity in question happened
to be of their own making. So long as they survived it, the incineration
of their beloved shop and apartment was now a legendary event worth
recounting at parties for another century, at least. In Letty and Gert's
eyes, one could never get enough mileage out of a gripping tale, particularly when they were the ones who owned bragging rights to the source
material. Rowan could imagine the scenario fifty years hence, when the
story would take on all sorts of jaw-dropping embellishments in both the
mortal and supernatural communities. Gert and Letty never went out
of their way to attract the spotlight, aside from grand entrances, but if
a spotlight happened to be trained upon them due to legitimate circumstances, and conveniently when a crowd of their magical peers happened
to be gathered in one spot, then they were more than happy to bask in
the glow.

As if sensing his thoughts, Letty cleared her throat like a school-teacher redirecting the attention of a pupil caught daydreaming. She nudged Rowan gently in the back with a bony elbow.

"We was not just talking exclusively about our own recent difficulties, you know. We done a fair bit of asking around about poor dear Serenity. Most folks was far more interested in what took place down at the pepper shop, naturally," she continued, "but I thought you'd like to know that we were careful to make inquiries about our unfortunate sister witch.

That part was a bit too much, even for Rowan.

"Letty Beauregard, I am not some sort of naïve tender-horn with the brain of a knobgoblin. The disdain and dare I say contempt that you and Gert held—I mean, *hold*—for Serenity Turnbull is hardly much of a secret, but I have never been one to meddle in the affections and disposi-tions of other magicians, no matter how much I may agree or disagree with their policies. Regardless of whatever awful thing befell Ms. Turn-bull. I find it rather rich that you now, and only in the aftermath of her apparent ruin, refer to her in even vaguely companionable terms as a 'sister' witch."

Letty was gobsmacked and Rowan was not disappointed in the least by the way a gnarled old hand clutched in umbrage at a cameo brooch of Queen Elizabeth I at her collar. An offended, almost heartbro-ken gasp escaped Letty's lips as she threw her shoulders back, astonished.

"Rowan Blaize, I am shocked and dismayed to hear you imply that Gert and I ever had anything less than the deepest respect and profes-sional admiration for our venerable associate in spell-casting, the late and grievously missed Serenity Turnbull."

"Oh, I wasn't *implying* anything," said Rowan in tones as unyield-ing as granite. Letty stared at him, aghast, for a few more seconds and then sniffed and shrugged her shoulders.

"Okay, so we didn't like her much at all," she muttered with a petulant little flounce of her long black skirt. "I guess there's no point in trying to hide that from the likes of you, but you're not entirely correct about the extent of our contempt, no matter what you think. Fact is, we tried reaching out to that girl when she first came to town, same as we did with you, only Serenity wasn't having any of it. Fact is, Gert and I probably should have done more to make the little thing feel welcome, instead of basically turning our noses up after the first try and always giving her the cold shoulder. Fact is ... well, fact is, we might just feel a little bit remorseful about that now. But there are a few more facts, too.

"One of them is that we did try to include her in certain things and another is that, deep down, we *did* sort of like her well enough in spite of our own stubborn skulls and sharp tongues. Last but not least, we did try to get to the bottom of my foreboding when I first foreboded." Letty pointed a finger of chagrin toward her host—it was a mild finger, but she meant it. "We tried to help to the point where we burnt down our own shop, our livelihood, and all we own in this cruel world. Fact is, we woulda done everything in our power to help that girl, or prevent whatever came to pass on her account, if we'd have been able to get a handle on it, instead of nearly turning the entire street, not to mention ourselves, to cinder. Please keep that in mind, Rowan Blaize. You're mighty respected by every charmed and enchanted denizen in these parts, and no one respects you more than Gert and I, but you do *not* know all of the facts!"

Rowan bowed his head once in dignified concession to that assertion, at least. "I am sorry if I impugned your hitherto clandestine reverence for dear Serenity," he murmured. "We'll just move on from the question of your devotion, for now. Were you able to find out anything about her potential fate from this network of immortals during your inquiries tonight?"

"No one knows a thing," said Letty, glowering with true disappointment. "And we asked everybody here because, of course, everyone made their way up to us to pay their respects and hear about our catastrophe and such. We didn't compel anyone to approach us, naturally. Why, I can run down a list of the big shots at the party tonight who are just as stymied about Serenity's disappearance as we are."

Letty pointed to a busy corner of the Castillo beyond the bonfire and Dendara Cubbige's Banshee Band. There, a dismal group sipped drinks and talked near one of the fort's several old munitions storehouses. "You see that bunch over there?" squawked Letty, raising her voice over a suddenly dramatic ogre-ivory keyboard arpeggio. "That's Mechthilde Frikk, the Swamp Beldam, having a little *tete a tete,* as they say, with Count Bulkagov and his irritating wife."

"I know who they are, Letty." Rowan narrowed his diamond eyes. Mechthilde was a true rarity in the occult demographic of St. Augustine, the love-child daughter of a great elemental spirit *and* one of the town's early immigrants. Her mother was, quite literally, the great Doomwater Swamp out beyond an especially lonesome stretch of A1A fifteen miles southeast of town. Her father had been a grizzled old gambler from Atlanta who had given up cards and carousing to become a hermit in the dank, steamy environs of Doomwater. Therein, he had built himself a cabin out of driftwood and clinging vines, catching his meals and living apart from civilized people, playing melancholy tunes on his harmonica when not wrestling alligators and trapping any small thing with fur that moved. Barefoot and bearded to his knees, Friedhelm Frikk became a wild man of the stubborn South, slowly bonding with his exotic, fetid environment, wooing the very essence of Life that inhabited the mucky expanse until, it was said, that elemental essence one day could no longer resist his grimy, tick-infested form, and rose up to embrace him in an appropriately swamp-scummy flurry of passion and inordinately humid desire.

The shock of the whole experience reputedly changed the hitherto eccentric hermit's worldview. He burned down his driftwood shack, cut off his beard, went into town, bought a three-piece suit and a Bible, and proceeded to hit the trail northward as a traveling preacher. He was never seen or heard from again in St. Augustine. Even so, the dalliance between old Frikk and Doomwater Swamp had not been without fruit of a different sort. Unions between elemental forces and other, far more tangible beings, especially humans, were quite uncommon, but they did occur. Friedhelm Frikk's night of unbridled carnal communion with the swamp-spirit spawned a love-child, as sometimes occurs in the world of magic. In this case, Mechthilde Frikk had been born of that connubial bliss, delivered among the water moccasins, lily pads, dangling mosses, inquisitive toads, and fertile layers composed of centuries of rotting life beneath the brackish pools and gaseous hollows of Doomwater.

No one knew for certain, but it had been whispered among egrets and possums that Mechthilde had emerged from the gaping heart of a decayed oak one oppressive and sticky afternoon, not long after Fried-helm's departure, fully grown and garbed in nothing but a slick of preter-natural slime. She had made her way out of the depths, it was rumored, beholding the new and hushed wetland world with her father's pale blue eyes, and as she waded through the swamp that had engendered her, al-ligators tumbled over each other trying to get out of the way. She was one of the more actualized productions of an elemental spirit's congress with another entity, or even an *actual* entity. The results of such unions could be disastrous, to say the least—many deformed and dangerous beings seething with hatred toward the physical realm had sprung into the world under similar circumstances throughout history. While the impulsive and inexorably feral Mechthilde was decidedly dangerous, she was not in any obvious manner deformed, at least in so far as mortal eyes would have assessed her.

She was, in fact, beautiful, with skin as flawless as the reflection of dawn's light across the clear mirror of her marshy domain, but she was now as brown as the acorns that fall with great plops into the murk from the creepy oaks of Doomwater. Her skin had been tanned by two centuries of life in the relentless Florida sunshine. Her hair was as black and shiny as the back of any raven that inhabited the lonesome cover of the surrounding forest, and her tresses wriggled and snaked downward and across her delicate shoulders like the endless tendrils of Spanish moss that dipped and dangled from gray limbs to slake their thirst in the un-moving mirror of water below.

Like other beings who were the offspring of bizarre and eminently incompatible parents, Mechthilde's constitution was a mixed bag. She had no overt magical powers to speak of, at least not in the way that witches or goblins or faeries do, and though she was humanoid, she was not exactly human and not at all mortal, as far as anyone knew. Over the years she had formed a secretive but satisfying relationship with the local populace, who accepted her as something of an alluring ghost. She became a legend much discussed and woven into the variegated strains of North Floridian folklore, but seldom glimpsed by those who entered her world. In truth, she had built a new version of her departed father's driftwood shack and within it she dwelled, the vigilant guardian of a gloom that was yet ever-vibrant and teeming with life. She learned to converse and even read books brought to her by Letty and Gert after *they* had settled in the Ancient City in the late 1800s. It was Gert who had given her the name 'Mechthilde' after discerning the story of her strange lineage. The Swamp Beldam was also besought by generations of intrepid mortal women who made pilgrimage to her domain, begging for just a bit of the musky black soil beneath the floorboards of her shack. Indeed, when that soil was mixed with a bit of spring water and swallowed, or worn in a poultice charm around the neck for several weeks, a wife who had never conceived eventually found herself swollen with child.

Such women had been welcome to make their risky forays to the Swamp Beldam's lair in past decades, but even the most persistent explorers who still believed the old lore could not find her anymore in Doomwater. Mechthilde had been withdrawing deeper and deeper into her shrinking kingdom as developers encroached over the years, and the toxins and wastes of the growing mortal world intruded upon her sanctum, exacting a toll upon its unkempt but pristine splendor. Mechthilde did possess the uncanny power of camouflage, which helped her significantly as she started to vanish into her shrinking realm. Birds, beasts, plants, and even the currents of that ecosystem were also at her command, to an extent, for she was bound to the life of the swamp by thought, blood, and being. More than once a careless speculator or inconsiderate group of poachers had found themselves stalked by the largest and most ill-tempered of Mechthilde's gators, or seized with terror as their motorboats were upended by sunken logs that had *not* been jutting straight out of the water just a few seconds earlier. Especially daunting was the sight of dozens of coral snakes and water moccasins slithering into a drunken intruder's fishing canoe all at one time—one of the Beldam's favorite tricks.

Even so, there was little that she could do to stem the tides of human progress and her kingdom had been reduced, comparatively speaking, to the size of a postage stamp, when one considered the scope of Doomwater in its heyday. All of the occult beings of St. Augustine that possessed anything resembling the power to sympathize felt pity for Mechthilde, and Rowan, upon hearing her sad tale from Letty and Gert, had made it a point to invite her to the All Hallow's Eve celebration. Like the witches, he had flown out to visit and confer with her on a few occasions and had always been well-received. She knew little of the cares and concerns of their world, but Rowan's own lineage consisted of preternatural spiritual powers, and he knew well how to communicate effectively with such elusive and sometimes volatile forces.

Standing in the midst of the humming party of friends and fiends with Letty, he sighed and wondered how long it would be before Mechthilde Frikk, born of a wild and lustful union between nature and humanity, would ironically be extinguished altogether because of an entirely different, but equally lustful, interaction between the same forces. He would not interfere, one way or the other, but found her an intriguing addition to the crowd. Tonight, the Beldam's arrival had been one of the most graceful of all in the vast and varied guest-list. She had come floating to the Castillo in a caress of moonlight upon a throne of driftwood, all the way from her swamp and across the unfamiliar expansiveness of the bay, helped along by two of the fattest and most fearsome alligators still in her command, a pair of fifteen-foot behemoths that carried her upon the ridges of their great rough-scaled backs. Even now they awaited their mistress, submerged and lurking in the shallows outside the barnacled walls of the fort, ready to take her home again when the festivities came to an end.

"Serenity had been working real hard to help old Mechthilde," noted Letty with an authoritative nod of her angular head. The iron gray braids were wound about her skull like an impenetrable warrior's helmet. "All that environmental stuff Serenity was constantly yapping to her students about over to Flagler College wasn't just a lot of talk. She had been going out to visit the Beldam a fair amount at Doomwater, as I understand. After they talked, she started writing cheeky letters to representatives and casting little spells here and there on land developers who looked like they was about to get too greedy with that strip of land along A1A. You know, gremlins in the bulldozers and concrete mixers. That sort of thing."

"I didn't realize that," said Rowan, emerging a bit from his trance-like thoughts about Mechthilde and her plight. "I don't approve of using magic to interfere, too much, in mortal designs. You yourself know the dangers inherent in that. They need to learn their own lessons, if at all possible. It's one thing if we, as witches and warlocks, find ourselves under direct assault, but quite another when we try to influence destinies. Serenity means well, but she does display the tendency to identify far too much with human concerns. The Swamp Daughter herself is the product of a kind of interfering human force. If she is destined to be undone by it, as magnificent as she is, then it is not wise for sorcery to seek to redraw the proverbial bigger picture. Those are the kinds of things that can get an earnest witch into trouble, and I wonder if Serenity has met that sort of trouble, indeed."

"I'm with you all the way on that one, Rowan Blaize. No one needs to tell me about the delicate balance we have to maintain living alongside mortals, but it's true that Serenity was assisting the creature all the same. I asked Mechthilde, but she didn't have any idea about any sort of unusual spells Serenity might've been working on lately, though she said that Serenity spent a lot of time in the last few months jabbering on about the frustrations of contending with human bureaucracy or some such twaddle. Mechthilde certainly didn't know what all that stuff meant. What can we expect? She's practically got muck for brains. But she was sure glad that someone cared, just the same, and is heartbroken about the news that Turnbull has been blowed up, or worse. She says she'll keep her eyes and ears open for any possible information that might be helpful, though I haven't the foggiest notion what she thinks she's going to hear, out there among the alligators and egrets."

"You might be surprised, Letty. The Swamp Beldam has got a lot of helpful eyes and ears at her disposal, even faraway out at Doomwater, or what's left of Doomwater."

"Nothing surprises me, Blaize. For instance, take a look at Mechthilde nattering away over there with Count Bulkagov, though Hecate knows why she's hanging around him. I realize it's a party, and people have to mingle and all, but she must be bored senseless. Still, I have to tell you—Bulkagov himself was nearly in tears when he heard the news about what happened to our shop and *whatever* happened to Serenity. He's one of them *sensitive* vampires, as you know."

"Indeed he is," said Rowan with a hint of condescension he could not quite conceal. There were only two beings of the *nosferatu* persuasion living in St. Augustine, and both of them were very low key. Count Bulkagov was generally known as "Dr. Bulkagov" around town, and he and his wife worked the graveyard shift in the oncology wing at Flagler Hospital for reasons that were both selfish and surprisingly humanitarian. Since the Bulkagovs dined regularly from bags "on the job" with the help of straws, the couple nipped and sipped upon actual humans for sentimental reasons only a few times a year, and never more than was necessary to get themselves and their victims mildly dizzy from drink and drainage, respectively. Rowan did not associate much at all with the Dr. and Mrs. Bulkagov, even though they sent him frequent invitations to lavish parties that lasted invariably from sundown until two hours before dawn. Rowan valued his slumber as much as any warlock and was not inclined to loiter around a punchbowl with vampires. In his long experience, vampires were not to be trusted, even the polite ones. Sometimes *especially* the polite ones.

In Rowan's estimation, the more genteel a vampire and its family tended to be, the more one had to keep one's eye upon them. Their species was not at all averse to having a good suck or two on a witch or a warlock who happened to be down on his or her luck, or coming up a trifle short in the magical power department. The most powerful vampires could be a bit of a nuisance, even to sorcerers as accomplished as Rowan, but Dr. and Mrs. Bulkagov were not quite of the Vlad Dracul "…

the children of the night! What beautiful music they make ..." varietal. They seemed to follow the contemporary westernized model of vampiric non-invasiveness and politically correct coexistence in most social circles. Thus, Rowan disapproved of the Bulkagovs only in token fashion and was careful not to let it show if he happened to encounter them, which had occurred only once or twice during late night flights across town for whatever reason. They likely knew he didn't care too highly for them, but the duo remained excessively deferential and were well-respected by other magical beings, or at least those who were never potential thirst-quenchers for vampires. Their absence on the guest list for tonight's party would have been seen as a telling snub and All Soul's Eve was a time for unity and at least a modicum of tolerance.

Doctor Bulkagov was in black tie and tails while Mrs. Bulkagov sported a trendy bob haircut and was dressed in a rather expensive frock by one of the more in-demand Italian designers. Both were smiling wide enough to display their fangs and raising their straw-punched bags of hemoglobin in a display of "Cheers!" to Rowan, who raised his goblet and smiled politely in turn. So long as he didn't have to get close enough to smell their rancid breath, he would be content with them as guests for the night. He wondered briefly why they were so intent upon chatting up the Swamp Beldam and hoped she knew what they were capable of. If they pulled anything funny on her, all she had to do was snap her fingers and two party-weary bats flapping their way home later on would be snapped up by big white swamp owls and the hospital would be searching for a new oncology department Team Captain and lab assistant.

"Dr. B and his wifey wouldn't seem to have much in common with stringy haired ole Mechthilde, but like I said, Serenity was the topic of conversation when I was over there earlier. Did you know that Serenity helped chair the local blood drive for the Red Cross last spring? I'll give you one guess as to who else sits at the head of *that* board in town! The Bulkagovs were nearly apoplectic when I mentioned what happened to Turnbull. Didn't bat an eye when I tried to talk about our poor pepper shop, but they gave such gasps when I mentioned Serenity that I had to step back and cover my nose. Their breath, you know. Pretty rank."

"I'm fully aware of the perils of vampire halitosis, Letty, but what I was apparently not so fully aware about is … or was … the extent of Serenity's involvement in the community at large. She had a much higher profile than even I had surmised, and I thought I had a fairly good handle on her."

"Just like you thought you had a handle on me and Gert being dead-set *against* Serenity Turnbull!"

"That's because you are … or you were."

"Well, no need to get your buckles in a bind, Blaize. That's neither here nor there, at this point, but if you look around, you'll see that just about everyone here is yapping away about the mystery of what happened to that sweet Serenity Turnbull. Why, she's the life of your party, and she ain't even here! I mean, look at them ne'er-do-wells over by the cornbread platter. Drunk on huckleberry brandy to the last, but barking a mile a minute about Serenity."

The group of "ne'er-do-wells" to which Letty referred was in fact a quintet of werewolves, each of whom Rowan recognized (when in non-lupine form) to be upstanding and likeable citizens of St. Augustine. In his opinion, they were far less-deserving of pejoratives than the vampire couple across the courtyard. But the shape-shifters—Lucas, Andrus, Dominic, Martina, and Bobby—lived a very "public" life of which Letty Beauregard apparently disapproved. They were a troupe of actors and comedians who staffed one of St. Augustine's oldest and most ramshackle dinner theaters sequestered down a slightly notorious but colorful side-alley near Cordova Street, where a smattering of do-it-yourself art galleries abutted a creaky little French bakery and teahouse, a New Age incense shop, and the crumbling, thatch-roofed El Casamanya Dinner House and Comedy Club.

They were a hardy lot, the quintet, if a bit swarthy and ill-groomed, but they owned and operated the place, which served only soup, salad, Cuban sandwiches, and the occasional roast stew "surprise" in steaming tureens as particularly adventurous diners sat at rickety tables clustered around an equally suspect stage. They called themselves *Los Cinco Incomprensibles* (The Five Incomprehensibles) and would perform entirely original and utterly ad-libbed comic and dramatic vignettes, created only the moment they all emerged from the pink, yellow, and purple rag curtains that obscured the "wings," which were basically two larger than usual broom closets. Their only thought to a business plan had been to adopt a Spanish name and cursory bits of Moorish décor to exploit St. Augustine's exotic heritage as a settlement. Some tourists fell for the gimmick, but the improv of *Los Cinco Incomprensibles* tended to stupefy whatever diners happened to wander in on any given evening. They fine-tuned their skills for the rats when there weren't any customers at all, which was generally quite often.

Rowan had to smile to see them drunk and literally letting their hair down now at his party. They realized their brand of entertainment was indeed incomprehensible to tourists and locals alike and therefore prided themselves upon being artistically misunderstood. It was a difficult existence, but they seemed not to care, or notice. All five of them lived cramped in a firetrap of a cottage out behind the restaurant, existing happily in abject squalor, as was the case with many wolf-specific werebeasts and shape-shifters, but The Five Incomprehensibles considered their quasi-poverty a privilege that signified their desire to suffer for art. A modest but regularly fortifying stipend from some embarrassed, rich *loup-garou* uncle in New England supposedly kept them on the survivable side of things when in humanoid form, and allowed them to keep El Casamanya Dinner Theater open and the bills paid ... barely.

Despite the fact that they were not very talented at comedy or drama or food preparation, this never seemed to them an insurmountable liability when it came to a career in entertainment or cuisine. Due to their relentlessly earnest attitudes and collective blindness to the pall of chronic failure, Rowan found it difficult not to root for them. Besides, he had always had a soft spot for werewolves. The quintet had invited him to one of their shows when he first arrived in the Ancient City and word had spread that a "big time warlock" had blown into town. Rowan accepted and found both the performance and the food to be as unfathomably awful as rumor suggested, and he had been the only customer on that particular night.

Their enthusiasm for their lack of ability being a strangely winsome quality, and Rowan being anything but a snob, an invitation back to their filth-hole of a cottage had also been accepted. There, everyone sat around smoking and talking about how successful the night had been, and about the new astonishments they would concoct for the dining crowds that would surely inundate their little *boite* on the following day. As werewolves, they were admittedly less discreet than the Bulkagov vampires, but in their favor they only raided cattle ranches in Ocala once a month, spurring a regular spate of *chupacabra* stories in the trashy supermarket presses and online. Oblivious to the problem that they were stealing ranchers' property as much as they were to stealing precious moments of an audience's life with their appalling performance art, the quintet loved the press clippings that invariably featured exasperated ranch foremen pointing to mangled cattle carcasses in black and white photos. The troupe referred to these kinds of notices as "critical raves" and, lacking real affirmation of any artistic accomplishment, promptly equated their ranch-raids with their awful stage forays in jolly fashion.

They had come to Rowan's party in full, mangy werewolf splendor, yellowed fangs glistening in the firelight. The smaller fey and imp constituencies were edgy, watchful and keeping a rather obvious distance. For his part, Rowan expected no trouble from *Los Cincos Incomprensibles,* and was honored by their acceptance of his invitation.

"Serenity was the best customer at that disgrace of a supper club them loopy werewolves operate," informed Letty. "About a year ago, she read some article in the Record about this struggling set of fools practically starving for their art—while owning their own restaurant, mind you—and she started going once a week to cheer them on as they do whatever abominable things they do on that little stage. They probably perform in the nude and do all sorts of twisted things, for all I know," added Letty with a grimace. "But you know how Serenity was. Once her heart started to bleed for some cause, she was a goner. And she didn't care one bit that they're a bunch of flea-bitten, matted-haired beasts that steal the cows right out from under poor farmers' noses. They were 'entitled' to it, as some form of community property, according to Serenity.

Oh yes, me and Gert have been aware of their nonsense for some time. What do you make of it, Blaize? Look at them carousing over there, surely getting vermin all over the cornbread. They come up and asked me what was going on with Serenity, but I just turned up my nose, as is proper. Gert, unfortunately, will talk to anybody, so she gave them the details, such as we know. Oh, Zeus in a Zebra Suit! Look at their runny eyeballs and the snot coming out their snouts. Is there any sight worse than a buncha werewolves that can't hold their liquor?"

Rowan ignored Letty this time and looked around at the myriad of other guests, all of whom did indeed appear to be actively enjoying the food, the music, the warmth of the fire, the moon, the setting, the camaraderie. Still, there was a discernible undercurrent of apprehension concerning Serenity. No magical creature likes to hear bad news about a beneficent witch. It wreaks havoc upon occult metabolisms across species. Perhaps at midnight, when he called everyone at the Castillo to attention to deliver his brief speech about how this night, more than any other night upon Earth, was the one that bound them together in a common magical heritage and allowed them a glimpse of their place in a packed mortal world that was either losing its touch with magic or utterly warping its perception of magic with mockery ... perhaps *then* would be a good time to poll the crowd for information, or say a few comforting words. But what would he say, given the aching reminder still lodged in his head like a stone? Rowan remained unsettled by the fact that he did not know what had really occurred, and even greater was his fear that whatever had taken place might have been the work of an enemy he dreaded to even imagine again, much less mention to his guests.

The *Ponce de Leon Fountain of Youth* nixies were whispering in the darkest corner of the Castillo's inner courtyard, as far away from the upward spiral of the bonfire as possible. Rowan could make out the name of "Serenity" on their watery, murmuring lips.

Rebecca, the spinster suicide who had thrown herself from the top of Lightner Museum a century earlier and who now haunted the enormous attic of the place, driving curators, cleaning people, and tour guides to the bottle for decades, was fading in and out of ectoplasmic visibility by one of the great cannons, and even she was discussing Serenity with Antonio Pacetti, another ghost-fisherman from one of St. Augustine's founding Minorcan families. Antonio had been dead for over a century himself—felled by the giant squid that washed up on St. Augustine Beach in 1896, after the thing had yanked him off the deck of his shrimp trawler. None of the remaining Pacettis knew of the connection between two of the city's greatest mysteries: the unexplained disappearance of a beloved fisherman and the startling behemoth that had drifted, dead on the tide, after a fateful struggle with powerful Antonio and his boning knife.

Not long after Rowan had come to St. Augustine, ghostly Antonio had come to him, asking if he would reveal to his descendants the true story of his demise, and how he had "went down with a fight, without being eat-up by the beastie, and inflicted upon it a most terrible wound before I drownt." Rowan had calmly explained that such a revelation to the current members of the clan was not only ill-advised, but unnecessary. After all, Antonio's legend waxed more radiant with mystery so long as no one ever knew for certain what had become of him, whereas closure was … well, a bit final and conducive to forgetfulness.

Antonio had taken Rowan's point about the tenuous nature of "proving" the squid battle-story, the likelihood that Rowan would be taken for a crackpot, and, since many in town had long been peddling the spicy tale that Antonio had discovered a sunken treasure off the coast and escaped across the sea to become a reclusive baron in a sprawling villa in his Minorcan homeland, the matter was dropped. Antonio vowed not to trouble any of St. Augustine's witches about the issue again, since he had already struck-out with Gert, Letty, and Serenity, too. Besides, a blossoming spectral romance with Rebecca had taken his phantom mind off the need to clarify his mythical legacy, lately. Even Becky and Antonio, however, were shaking their heads in dismay over the apparent loss of a local sorceress, moping as only ghosts can mope.

The rest of the crowd—a trio of horned shadnocks from the cellar of Zorayda Castle on King Street, a delegation from the Circle of Six-Winged Salt Run Faeries that haunted the Lighthouse on Anastasia

Island, an assortment of sewer goblins, scargoyles from the Presbyterian church belfry and razorback-goyles from that of the Cathedral Basilica, dryads, naiads, incubi, and imps of every description—drank, ate, and danced wildly, all happily allowing themselves to be caught up in a windfall of witches' drama. Rowan could sense the speculations and theories blending with typical All Hallow's Eve agitation and occult merriment to ensure that elaborate tales of Serenity's ruination were already being measured and cut to size from whole cloth. Several apocryphal stories would achieve canonical status by the time everyone departed around three or four in the morning.

Dendara Cubbige was just launching into a particularly window-smashing, barnacle-peeling demonstration of her banshee upper-register when Rowan felt a couple of gentle but determined tugs at his cloak from behind. He and Letty turned around at the same time and looked down to behold a party guest that neither recognized as a denizen of St. Augustine's magical metropolis.

It was a little human girl with glorious mounds of blonde hair, topped with a great polka-dot red velvet bow nestled in the middle of her confectionary coif of spectacular ringlets and curls. She was wearing a hoop-skirted sateen ball gown of exceeding craftsmanship, glittering with sequins even on the massive puffed sleeves. Each sequin gleamed in the reflection of the bonfire's light, like stars exploding in some distant galaxy. In her tiny, opera-gloved hands, the little girl held a kind of leash fashioned from barbed wire. At the end of this leash, wearing a spiked dog collar and crawling on his hands and knees upon the Castillo courtyard, was a bloodied, burnt-scalped man in a despicably filthy and torn pinstriped suit. His eyes crossed with agony and exhaustion and his teeth chattered from exposure. The little girl looked up at Rowan Blaize with eyes as blue as a robin's purest egg, and she was smiling in such a way that her dimples seemed to twinkle with the same star-like intensity of her bugle-beaded ensemble.

Rowan leaned forward slightly after taking in this most unexpected scene and his steely gaze morphed to dark, thundercloud gray as if to subdue the cheerful blue sky in the smirking eyes of this uninvited visitor. But those eyes could not be subdued. Letty and Rowan could plainly see that the hapless figure in the collar was a mortal man; they could smell as much. They could also smell a whiff of mortality upon the child, but it was mixed with another fragrance, one that combined with the brazen appearance of a colossal new energy and sent a palpable signal of alarm through their beings and then outward to grip the entire festive gathering. A sudden and bracing silence fell like a dense fog upon the party and all became attentive to the figures in the center of the court-yard, drawn by an irresistible power.

"Little girl," said Rowan, as low and as cold as a subterranean cav-ern flooded with icy waters. "I do not believe we know you, and I do not believe you were on the guest list for this particular event."

The fingers of his hands, clasped casually behind his back, began to clench and unclench, making also a series of intricate movements that built the infrastructure of a potent defensive spell. Letty noticed this and, sensing the depth of danger in the bizarre child-intruder, she fixed her jaw in grim resolve and backed slowly away to find Gertrude. Rowan maintained his burning gaze. The child before him began to giggle.

"I think it most advisable that you identify yourself without de-lay," instructed Rowan, calm and yet as intense as a glassy sea before an underwater eruption. "This form I behold is not your own, unless I am much mistaken. Party-crashers who arrive in deceptive skins are doubly unwelcome at *this* All Hallow's Eve celebration."

"Oh! Do look at the pathetic lot of you!" exclaimed Djin Rummy, her laugh tinkling like an outward explosion of glass-shards through the evening air. "I have seen some decrepit gatherings of magical minions in my day, but this one has to be the most depressing. Half of you are too insignificant-looking to even warrant a proper classification. What's left? A couple of wan-looking bloodsuckers, a smattering of louse-ridden werewolves, a horde of drab faeries, two desiccated old witch-bags, and a most arrogant young upstart-of-a-warlock at the very head of the bunch! Such a shame, but I suppose even rag-tag immortals are entitled to their own little parties, dreary though the company and the accommodations may be."

"Ohmigolly!" croaked Gert, her mouth crammed with salamander-eye caviar as Letty dragged her to Rowan's side. "It's that precious little Pint-Sized Princess gal from the television!" She beamed and leaned down with a simpering, grandmotherly admiration, spouting crumbs and sticky little black eyeballs all over the front of Djin Rummy's fabulous gown. "I didn't know you was gonna be at this party, you adorable little darling! What a big surprise for Rowan to keep from me. You know, I been a big fan of yours for weeks on end and I aim to be front and center to cheer you on at the pageant tomorrow night. Got my tickets at the will-call, don'tcha know. Say ..." Gert gazed behind the new arrival in sudden confusion. "Ain't that your daddy there in the collar and chains? He don't look too good. And what's with the barbed-wire leash? Rowan," she added, looking back over her shoulder, "I'm pleased as punch because you know I'm over the moon about this angel, but do you think it was a good idea to invite mortals to a jamboree like this? Besides, little BonSashay needs her beauty sleep for tomorrow's competition."

"BonSashay" recoiled in disgust at the cow-eyed adoration of Gertrude Gokey.

"Ugh! Get away from me, you loathsome old wrinkled-up crone! It is insulting enough to be present at a convocation hosted by a whelp and wastrel boy-sorcerer, but to be accosted by a common hag is the ultimate disgrace. And to think I had been expecting to encounter personages of at least somewhat formidable stock. Ha! Your face, old woman, looks about as dignified as a fig seed that has been freshly passed from the festering anus of a camel. Did you *know* about these disreputable peasants?" hissed the djin, turning to bore a wicked glare into Chesterfield Rummy's brain, as if he was in any condition to offer an answer, sprawled and bleeding as he was upon the flagstones.

Gert's face stiffened, then, to camel-constipating fig seed proportions. Her sentimental smile vanished and her appreciative eyes narrowed to slits. She stood straight and pondered this most unexpected assessment of her bearing from someone she considered to be practically a superstar.

"My, my," she breathed. "That's not a very gracious thing to say about anybody at all, young lady. I don't expect you'll be winning many of them beauty princess crowns, with a mouth like that. You'll certainly lay an egg in the poise part of the competition. For sure."

"You knucklehead!" snapped Letty, pinching her best friend's flabby arm.

"Ow!"

"Haven't you got eyes on your face, or have you emptied every last bottle of huckleberry brandy in this fort? That *ain't* no Pint Size beauty princess or whatever the heck you think she is!"

"No she is *not,*" added Rowan, seething as he took a small step forward. Nearby, the bonfire suddenly roared so high it spun and twisted up from the courtyard like a towering column of fire touching the scattered clouds. "Someone or something has seen fit to spoil this fine evening with a rather unworthy display of mischief and I intend to get to the bottom of the matter. Swiftly. Who *are* you, most unwelcome little miscreant in your moppet masquerade? I won't inconvenience myself further by asking you to reveal your identity and purpose again."

A great gasp of astonishment mixed with disdain exuded like a searing, bitter gust from the assembly of onlookers. Everyone could see and sense the magnitude of Rowan's anger and, beneath it, a chilling undercurrent of worry. They had all been insulted, and as a result, they all began to close in like a shimmering, gruesome wall of vengeance, closing in upon the offensive little wretch in child's skin, not yet perceiving the terrible scope of her power and menace ... only the outrageousness of the interruption.

It was at that moment that Miranda came tacking through the magical mob in her elegant heels, shawl drawn firmly around her shoulders. Bror, in all his great bearing and slobbering curiosity, was at her side. They had been chatting politely, if uncomfortably, with a circle of sewer ghouls when the ruckus began. Bror gave a few sniffs of his enormous Mastiff's nostrils and sensed something much more offensive than septic ghouls in the presence of the dazzling girl-child. He began to growl.

"Rowan!" exclaimed Miranda, her face a mixed mask of bewilderment and amused contempt. "I've never known you to play a joke this cruel upon any of us. How could you have invited disgraceful people like this to our party? I know they weren't on any of the invitations I sent out. I don't understand. What gives?"

"Miranda, get out of here quickly," said Rowan.

Bror's growl continued to rumble loud and low. Every muscle in his gargantuan dog's body seemed tight and flexing.

Djin Rummy threw down the chain and barbed-wire leash attached to Chesterfield and it clattered with a deafening bang and a shower of sparks on the cracked flagstones. Arms akimbo, she threw back her head and laughed, but there was no hint of levity in the frightful sound. The air around her began to tingle and snap as if electrified. The Bulkagov vampire couple and several of the imps began to back away with their faces contorted in distress.

"Of all the fools that would have the nerve to insult me at such a pitiful consortium of clowns, it would have to be a putrid mortal female who proves herself the most intolerably offensive," spat the djin. "Really, boy-warlock, the quality of your company is all the indication I need of your inferior status as a magician!"

With that, Djin Rummy swayed with a slight rustle of her fabulous babydoll skirts, petticoats, frills and furbelows. She wound-up and gave Miranda such a smack across the her torso with an opera glove that everyone heard the awful cracking of ribs and gasped in horror as Rowan's foundling friend was flung, air knocked from her lungs, forty feet across the courtyard where she slammed into a coquina wall and dropped, motionless, in a crumpled heap to the stones below.

"NO!" shouted Rowan, who surged through the air with scorching tongues of fire beneath his cloak and coattails to reach her ruined side.

Bror went insane with anger and power. Unleashing a bloodcurdling howl, he leapt with the snarling full force of his bulk upon the diminutive interloper. For the most fleeting moment, the "Pint-Sized Princess" appeared to be alarmed and caught rather off guard by the attack. The shock as she was knocked brutally to the ground, twinkling tiara flying off the gigantic velvet bow and rolling away across the court-yard, was only to last an instant. Even as Bror's mighty maw opened to clamp down and throttle the delicate ivory neck, a great flash of phos-phorescent green light erupted from the toppled djin-girl and Bror was hurled up and away with a heartrending yelp of agony and surprise, spin-ning like a terrible living boulder into a squeaking group of gravestone gimps too stunned and stupid to get out of the way. They were tossed and tumbled like so many red-fanged bowling pins, several of them crushed to their destruction as the Mastiff skidded with a colossal crunch into yet another of the Castillo's unyielding masonry walls. Bits of courtyard rocks and clumps of grass flew everywhere as the monstrous dog tried and failed to gain some purchase with his clumsy paws.

Djin Rummy had by now recovered from her momentary collapse and, eyes gleaming with the awful phosphorescent green aura, she rose up ten feet in the air, golden hair flying outward as if she were a child touching an electromagnetic ball in a museum display. Skirts billowed and flapped in an undercurrent of the djin's own magical malignance, delicate arms outstretched but incongruously threatening. When she spoke, the voice was that of the awful and ancient Dedwen, guttural and reverberating, it seemed, on the very blanket of midnight sky itself.

"Is anyone else foolish enough to meddle with the likes of me?"

Rocks atop the ramparts of the fort cracked at the shuddering power of the sound and denizens of all persuasions and potencies began taking to the air in escape or retreating to crouch in the various cham-bers of the Castillo, if they had not the power of flight. All trembled and backed away from the terrible little girl with the glowing green eyes. All began to flee like one receding wave escaping in a circle from an explo-sively volcanic island.

All, that is, except two …

Leticia Beauregard and Gertrude Gokey stood shoulder to shoul-der, as straight and as rigid as two immobile (albeit quite differently shaped) monuments of stone. The expressions upon their faces were grim—thickening storm clouds gathering swiftly against the horizon of a dark and brooding sea. The two witches stood as glowering sentinels of doom, ominous as a terrible abyss in their silent fury, even as every wraith, were-beast, and trickster in the Castillo courtyard scurried around and away in chattering pandemonium.

"Gertrude?" said Leticia, hoarse as a gust of wind over a dry creek bed.

"Leticia?" said Gertrude as both lifted their right arms in unison and pointed toward the ghastly floating girl-devil.

Then, with an eerie and discordant chant that pierced the maddened Halloween night and caused every being on-the-fly to stop in soundless astonishment, the twosome began to weave their spell:

> *"Hawks of Nephthys, keening high!*
> *O rays from Sekhmet's fearsome Eye!*
> *Buto's venom, Bastet's claws!*
> *Great Tefnut's foul and grasping claws!*
> *Horns of Hathor, wings of Isis!*
> *Heed ye all—attend this crisis!*
> *Lo, as we invoke such names,*
> *Engulf this foe in searing flames!*

A terrible wind, whipping with a razor whine and rotating with a magnificent roar, rose up around Gert and Letty as they continued to stand their ground, pointing, jabbing, stabbing with ruinous power upward at the djin-girl until the whistling cyclone surged and swirled about their skirts and plunged directly into the great bonfire nearby. The blaze was immediately transformed from a merry conflagration into a wailing, frightful orb that lifted up from the flagstones and separated into an explosive host of seven distinct and horrifying monsters of fiery vengeance.

Rending the very air with a ululating battle cry, these seven fire-spirits scorched the atmosphere and swooped down upon the grimacing, growling BonSashay at the command of the two witches, who called out:

"Attack it!"

"Destroy it!"

Present indeed, in the forms of screaming, crimson flame, were the avatars of the summoned entities. A hawk with white-hot talons ripped and shredded the djin's golden bouffant of hair, snatching at the radiant tufts and curls. What appeared to be a crackling fireball of an eye circled the girl like a blistering satellite that shot beams of laser-like fire out at the puffed sleeves and great folds of satin and lace. A writhing cobra reared-up and struck repeatedly with venomous jets of burning lava at the enemy's doll-face as claws and paws sought to pummel and smother. A great dazzling cow charged and gored again and again with sizzling horns, and a pair of tremendous wings that looked like violent bursts from the surface of the sun beat up and down, engulfing the stunned target and fanning the wrath of the entire ferocious entourage.

Gert and Letty smiled in solemn satisfaction at their handiwork. Djin Rummy was struggling and squirming and flailing at the relentless host of conjured attackers, overpowered and soon to be utterly consumed and reduced to a crisp in mid-air. The little shiny black tap shoes kicked in desperation as the fire-cobra coiled around stick-like legs in white stockings and squeezed. On the ground, Letty burst out with a triumphant cackle, for amid this infernal maelstrom the end was near.

Or so it seemed.

Behind them all, behind the mighty fort and without warning, there came from the tranquil Matanzas Bay a rumble and a roar as of the very foundations of the Earth being rent asunder and then up, up, up, towering and trembling arose a mammoth wave that blocked the midnight moon itself and, pausing to froth and boil at its crest, down, down, down it fell in a drowning dash upon everything and everyone inside or near the Castillo. In a single crash it extinguished the Fire-Assassins summoned by the witches as if they had never existed, and the slamming torrent tumbled and tossed Letty, Gert, tables, werewolves, goblins, imps, swamp beldams—*everything*—over and over in a salty, gurgling whirlpool. In seconds, the interior of the structure looked like a gigantic square pot sloshing mightily with the contents of a rather macabre soup. Only Djin Rummy, scorched in a couple of places on her gown and missing several clumps of golden hair that had been ripped from the scalp or singed away, hovered untouched above the fray, dry and laughing maniacally.

The magical inundation was beginning to drain away with great sucking sounds as creatures bobbed and gasped for air, some trying to cling to floating debris or being helped by the nixies and naiads who, of course, had been untroubled by the watery counterattack. Letty and Gert, however, coughed and sputtered and flopped about, completely reduced and unable to get a foothold in the bubbling flood that had caught them by such surprise. The djin saw them fumbling in the mess and laughed louder than ever, still levitating with mastery above the scene.

"Oh, ladies!" squealed the djin, now once again using the wheedling voice of BonSashay the beauty princess. "That was a most unexpected and impressive trick, I must admit, but perhaps not best utilized so very close to an entire ocean that will answer to my command. Look at you all, gawping like trout. I have a good mind to set this filthy stone kettle a-boil and turn you all into a flotsam and jetsam stew. Ha! Not even the Insatiable Ogres of Ingasha would deign to eat such dreck, though!"

Djin Rummy gestured, once again very princess-like, and one of the great spears displayed for tourists against a wall of the Castillo clanged from its place and whirred through the air to be caught by her petite, gloved hand. The dainty figure raised it high and aimed its rough and rusty point at the ample, plump, and still-bobbing target that was Gertrude Gokey.

"I can at least spear one purple whale for pure sport while I'm here," giggled the djin, and then she snarled with tiny peg teeth that gleamed in the reappearance of the indifferent moonlight. As she was about to cast the harpoon into the rolling, floating Gert, however, her gloved forearm was gripped in a crushing vise. Djin Rummy wailed in genuine agony and surprise, whipping her mad blonde face around to behold a white-knuckled hand squeezing tighter. That hand was attached to Rowan Blaize, who was himself now floating several feet above the rapidly draining pool.

"I don't think little children should play around with sharp objects," he murmured, and then squeezed until something began to crack in Djin Rummy's little arm and the spear was dropped with a splash into the murky drink.

"Let go of my arm, witch-boy!" hissed the freakish *ifrit*. Her eyes waxed phosphorescent again in the darkness. "I put those two old bags out like a couple of shoddy candles, so imagine what I could do to you, whelp."

"Gert was correct," said Rowan. "Little girls trying to win beauty pageants won't take many prizes if their mouths are so foul. Perhaps it's best if yours was kept shut until you have something more respectful to say."

Rowan reached up to his own mouth and, with his thumb and forefinger, pried from between his lips an enormous armored Siafu ant that thrashed and wriggled, its great mandible jaws clenching and un-clenching. He shoved it toward the flinching little djin-moppet's lips, where the ant pierced the pink skin hungrily and clamped down with a vengeance just beneath the precious upturned nose. With lightning speed, Rowan drew more Siafu ants from his mouth, one after the other, and hooked each biting creature into the djin's lips until its mouth was sealed shut by a row of dangling, living sutures, forty-two legs crawl-ing against her chin and each massive head pinching deeper and without mercy.

"Mmmmm! Mmmmm!" moaned the wild-eyed devil.

"Much more appropriate talk from an *enfant terrible,*" noted Row-an, not releasing his own crushing grip for an instant. "My little pin-pals are rather useful in a pinch, wouldn't you say? Oh, wait … I guess you *can't* say."

He gripped the djin's arm once again as if to break it in two pieces and scrutinized her now gruesomely infested face.

"When you've calmed down a bit, perhaps we'll unhook a few of those little beasties and let you tell us all who you really are, and what you're doing in a BonSashay Rummy suit. How would that be, tiny one?"

In response, Rowan received such a kick to his stomach that he was sent flying across the expanse of the soggy fort to lodge with a sick-ening thud between one of the Castillo turrets. Djin Rummy levitated down to the largely drained but debris-laden courtyard and reached up to rip each of the Siafu ants from her lips, one by one, their pinchers tearing right through the conjured child-skin in bloody tatters. For every ant she ripped away, she popped it into her mouth and crunched down happily until she had consumed them all, as if snacking on popcorn.

"Delicious," she remarked drily. "Haven't had any of these in centuries, but they are hardly worth what you've done to my dear little face." Indeed, the djin-girl's lips were hanging in gory flaps, exposing the teeth as white as the satin pageant gown. "Censorial insects!" she scoffed. "Is that really the best you can do?"

From his crumpled position in the turret, Rowan flung himself into the air and, as he did so, the clothing ripped from his body, exposing the chiseled musculature. His black mane of hair, glimmering in the moonshine, suddenly grew outward and spread like a dark plague of tendrils even as his body swelled, contorted, and changed color. He grew and grew and grew some more, swiftly covered in scales and callouses and bristles over lumpish, glistening muscles while his fair face morphed into hideous form. Curved tusks erupted and began to protrude from a festering, scabbed mouth beneath his nostrils, which were now as big and as forbidding as the openings of two dark and forgotten well-openings. Stinking and monolithic, grotesque and as tall as the Castillo walls, as hulking as a bull elephant, only Rowan's glorious gray-silver eyes remained intact, each now the size of a dinner plate. He landed on the Castillo courtyard with a thud that shook the entire edifice and sent the soaked, surviving denizens of the evening's party scurrying for what cover they could find.

Rowan Blaize had become a Goranthus Troll—one of his own most malignant and formidable enemies from centuries past, a being from out of the mists that deepened and clotted for all but himself and other magical beings who had trod through those very mists, age unto age, marked by the sure passage of their own designs. Indeed, Rowan had ever borne the scar from an outrageous encounter with a Goranthus, and it was the power of this scar, his possession of it, that enabled him to assume such a woeful and colossal form at this moment.

A great ringed and diamond-scaled Goranthus troll-tail unfurled behind him and then cracked like a whip in front of him toward the tiny child-figure that scuttled with the agility of a crab to avoid it. The bony barbs on the end of that tail—as heavy and hard as iron—slammed into the coquina wall near one of the fort's old jail cells and, instead of bouncing off the shell-addled stone like cannonballs of old, it shattered the portal in a devastating spray of debris. Rowan the Goranthus Troll lumbered forward, each footfall causing the flagstones to shudder. With a gnarled and pitted claw the size of a walrus, he gestured about and the party torches that had been doused by the djin's great wave sprang to snapping, undulating life, for he needed to see his enemy and everyone knows (well, a *few* "everyones" know) that one of the great weaknesses of a Goranthus is its poor night vision.

"Who are you and what are you?" Rowan roared from behind the mighty tusks, tail writhing and poised to strike once more. The matted and tangled hair drooped over his dashboard-sized troll's brow and down across his behemoth torso. "I see you now, you little impostor!" he growled, and the echo of the sound bounced out into the night and would have paralyzed the entire city with fear were it not already under a spell meant to keep the business of sorcerers a secret on this night, of all nights.

Djin Rummy was pressed against one great block of the Castillo wall, glaring balefully up at the looming adversary. This was definitely a miscalculation, thought the djin. The young warlock was perhaps not so young, after all, and he had power—enormous power—to concoct such a transformation. Dedwen the *ifrit,* fearful of nothing when fully potent, felt suddenly rather small in the ball gown and bouffant. Others in the gathering who remained soaked and stunned about the precinct, looked up in their own breathless astonishment. Nearby lay the "girl's" father, half drowned and broken, but gazing upward, too, with a new level of madness at this latest revelation. Two of the werewolves cowered and trembled with one of the hobgoblin brothers clutching them both in a dark corner. A dryad was trying desperately (and failing) to make her lily white feet take root amid some cracks in the masonry and disappear out of sheer terror. Even the two witches, drenched as river rats and just as beady eyed, were staring speechless upward at their friend Rowan.

"Letty, what we gonna do?" mumbled Gert, crawling back slowly in her bunching skirts across slimy stones. "You think we oughtta help him? You wanna try another spell together?"

Letty Beauregard gulped, which was a physical reaction that she, as a witch of some measure, had rarely been known to experience. "You reckon he looks like he needs any help right now, Gert?"

"I reckon not. Hoo wee! We couldn't pull off something like that even if we was four hundred years younger and five times as talented!"

"You got that right, girl. Let's just slide on slowly out of the way, now, off to the side there, and let him take care of business."

Djin Rummy watched with leering contempt as the old crones retreated. They could ogle in wonder all they liked, but Dedwen the Great, terror of every mountain pass from Morocco to Anatolia, had seen a few Goranthus Trolls in centuries past and was not about to simply skid away. The Evil Pint-Sized Princess pushed away from the wall and sneered at the monstrous contender overhead.

"If you think you frighten me, you are quite mistaken, warlock. Inside that manufactured troll carcass there's still just a young, uncertain prestidigitator, and I tend to eat *those* for breakfast, when it suits me."

Rowan the troll reached across the plaza with his left arm and pulled one of the fort's great iron cannons from its place among the ramparts. He brought it down and smashed the flagstone before him to splinters and then swung it menacingly before him like a pendulum. The massive cannon sliced the air in low, horrid whistles. Every Goranthus Troll needed a club. Now he had one.

"The only thing of which I am uncertain," breathed Rowan with lungs like the bellows of a gargantuan furnace, "is your true identity, and I intend to ascertain that identity ere the dawn breaks and this entire structure is leveled."

"I'll grant you no such courtesy," howled Djin Rummy, this time half in the shrieking voice of BonSashay and half in the bloodcurdling boom of Dedwen——a show of harmonic travesty that made the crouching werewolves yelp in agony and cover their ears.

"No mind, then!" blasted Rowan. "There are ways of discerning such things even after the victim is dead. I am a patient troll. Behold!"

He swung the black cannon with such speed and surprising suddenness that even the wary djin was not swift enough to fly off or counter with a defensive spell. The force of the monster-club's blow utterly smashed one of the white-stocking legs to a pitiful pulp, ripping off part of the gaudy ball gown along with it. Djin Rummy screeched in dismay and hopped away on one clicking tap shoe toward a corner, leaving a leg and tatters of gown behind. The new amputee wobbled in the sputtering torchlight and turned around. Tears ran down the seemingly innocent but cosmetic-ridden face. These were the bright, green-glowing tears of a djin, however, and not those of a little girl who no longer really existed.

"I have had about enough of you, warlock! Look what you did to my leg, not to mention the dress." Inwardly, Dedwen cursed himself for not anticipating such a swift blow. This was not at *all* going according to plan.

"For the last time, speak and reveal yourself!" brayed Rowan in the thunderclap voice. "Or have you another wave to hurl over the walls of the fort? It shall not avail you this time."

Djin Rummy made no reply, but crouched down on the one remaining leg and reached up with great cunning to pull a tremendous handful of golden hair from the bountiful supply atop the child-head. Rolling the hairball in opera gloves, muttering, chanting, turning it over and over, the djin spoke words so ancient and arcane that even Rowan Blaize would never have recognized them.

"Ishi lomal oro malarol rolamshala shasha vijnal prasht ormala masha lo tashin ballak tur raktashin ristal ristal kul ah shalank ta!"

The djin hurled the ball of now glittering golden hair up and outward across the expanse and, just as Rowan Blaize had earlier flung himself outward and grown into something terrible, so too did the devilish beauty-princess hairball. It spun and whipped and uncoiled and enlongated into what seemed like a thousand individual ropes of strangling gold that spread across Rowan's great troll shoulders and torso and clung to him, snaking up, down, and all around in devious tentacles that began to bind with inexorable force. They crisscrossed once, and then again, and then again and again and again, choking the breath even from a chest so unbreakable and from a throat like the trunk of an ancient but unyielding oak.

It was over in seconds ... the djin's spell was that powerful.

Rowan dropped the cannon club, which clanged mournfully upon a few of its companions along the fort's parameters. With the brutal troll's hands he began to clutch wildly at the strands, but it was impossible for such enormous and blunt fingers to gain purchase. He could not even roar as the coils pulled tighter all around, spreading and proliferating until it seemed as if he was enshrouded in some titanic spider's wicked cocoon. The djin had outsmarted him. Gagging and void of air, void even of the mind to craft some new protective spell, Rowan collapsed, convulsing and gurgling against the only wall of the Castillo that had been unmolested that evening. Rowan Blaize fell, slumped, and as he fell, the mammoth form of the Goranthus Troll deserted him and all that remained was a naked and fair hand, clutching, lifeless, at the scorched fortress wall, surrounded by sparkling golden strands now too loose and disinterested to strangle such a small form.

The torches sputtered and guttered. They snapped in the silence. Whoever was left at the All Hallow's Eve party had crept quietly into the deepest shadows possible, and they maintained stillness. The night made no sound, save for the familiar rhythm of the bay-front groundswell lapping against the base of the Castillo de San Marcos. Only the utterly disheveled, unkempt, and one-legged Djin Rummy muttered and kept a keen eye upon the conquered foe, hopping forward now like a wizened monkey, bent and suspicious. Chesterfield Rummy saw the thing move and cringed, but she reached over and dragged him, scraping across the wet stone in pain, with one wiggle of her telekinetic finger. Together they hunched over the motionless body of Rowan in the pile of golden webbing. The djin sniffed the air above and scrutinized. She leapt up on her single leg and kicked one of Rowan's naked knees that was sticking out from the strands with her tap shoe. There was no movement in re-sponse. No sound.

"Stick your filthy hand inside and see if he's dead," croaked the djin-girl to Chesterfield.

"W-why do *I* have to do it?" he whimpered.

His 'daughter' gave him a stinging box on the ear. His skull, al-ready fractured, rang inside like a decayed, corroded church bell.

"Because I tell you to do so."

"But how do I know if something like that is dead or alive?"

"You feel for a pulse. You feel for a heartbeat, fool, the same as you do with one of your own putrid race."

Chesterfield winced and stuck a shaking hand inside the mass of creepy golden hair. He felt around, eyes squeezed so tight that tears dripped from their corners. Then he pulled it out after a moment.

"He's dead."

"You are certain?"

"Yeah. No pulse. No heartbeat. No nothing. See for yourself, if you don't believe."

The djin kicked the lifeless knee once more.

"Heh! No need," it rasped. "The warlock is gone. I knew that spell would finish him off. Pull a Goranthus troll on *me*, of all the fiends!"

"I wasn't so sure you could beat him," croaked Chesterfield in his own tangle of chains and barbed wire. "I mean, he turned hisself into something so ... so ... awful and huge."

"Shut up," spat the djin. "Shut up or I'll give you 'awful' and 'huge' aplenty." Then it looked once more at Rowan. "Hmmph! He was good. Better than I expected. I'll give him that much. But he wasn't good enough. Now let us get out of here. This exploit was messier and more inconvenient than was necessary, but I did what I came to do. I still have a beauty pageant to win and an entire world to captivate through the mortal magic of television," she whispered greedily in Chesterfield's ear.

"B-but what about your leg?" said Chesterfield, staring in horror at the maimed Pint-Sized Princess hopeful.

"You idiot. Don't you know by now that this isn't my real body? Do I really have to slap you again? Or eat out your pithy brains, chew them up, and spit them back into your head with more sense than you had to begin with? I can fashion a new leg. The upstart warlock dealt me a smart blow, and it will take a few hours, but I can fix everything. Now let us fly. I want to get out of this filthy hole."

"We gonna just leave him? What about all them other witches and freaks?"

"Look at you with a bag full of impertinent questions all of the sudden," snapped the djin. "Forget about him. It's more humiliating to leave him as he is. We djinn specialize in humiliation. Believe me. Besides, I am weakened and have just enough power to fly out of here through whatever cloaking spell these fools put around this dreary dump. It was annoying enough that I had to breach it when I arrived at full power! And don't worry about those two hags. They haven't got the nerve or the strength to get in my way again. But I don't want to expend the energy required to destroy them right now."

Djin Rummy hopped a step closer, grabbed the shreds of Chesterfield's starched collar, and smiled. "There's still work to do, Daddy."

Looking into her eyes was, for Chesterfield, a nightmare reflected within the mirrored madhouse of a thousand nightmares.

"Off we go, shall we? Into the welcome of the lovely moonlight? *Happy Halloween,* everyone."

෨ඁ෯

XV

From jam-packed San Carlos Avenue to the columned balconies of Flagler College and the normally sedate interiors of the art galleries on King and Grenada, to water coolers where people nursed or suffered through unfathomable hangovers they had denied the need to anticipate, people were in shock. From the Cobalt Lounge at swank Casa Monica Hotel, where a smattering of the previous night's revelers simply transformed their hangovers into brand new levels of comforting inebriation, to the row houses on Riberia and the trailer parks flung hither and yon along Old Dixie Highway, the community of St. Augustine was shaken to its respectfully concealed petticoats by news of what was already being termed the region's greatest act of ransacking and vandalism since the attacks of General James Oglethorpe in the 18th Century.

News crews from Jacksonville, Birmingham, Atlanta, Orlando, and Miami were first on the scene, funneling coverage and live feeds to the national syndicates and network news programs, where the story was seen as both a novelty item—not many people across the United States really knew the historical significance of St. Augustine—and as yet another sad indication of the speedy decline of value for property and propriety. All of it was chalked up to the despicable fallout of moral turpitude and the pervasive sense that little was sacred anymore, that little had a chance of withstanding the tide of wanton debauchery favoring recklessness, instant gratification, and self-indulgence.

Though all the news outlets would soon drop the story and millions across the nation would forget it by noon in the thrall of some breaking celebrity pregnancy bulletin, regional editorial columns, internet message boards, and comments sections related to the Ancient City veritably hummed with indignation. The ever trustworthy pages of the *St. Augustine Record* were being rustled with more frantic interest and opprobrium than they had been rustled-with for years. Indeed, one news outlet's assessment of the disaster was particularly wrenching:

St. Augustine Police Department, St. Johns County Sheriff's officials, state investigators, federal officials, members of the Historical Preservation Society, and thousands of local residents and visitors remain mystified and shocked by the extent of the damage done to the renowned Castillo de San Marcos, symbol of the Ancient City, in what was, or what many are already describing as, a colossal and unthinkable act of unmitigated Halloween night vandalism.

"I could never have imagined how this caliber of damage could be done to our beloved fort in just one night without anyone knowing," said visibly distressed Castillo Director, Horace McLennan. "Much less why anyone would do it at all. Like everyone else, I've been walking around here in a state of shock all morning, while everybody from here to Washington D.C., it seems, is trying to get to the bottom of it. I mean, look over here—we've got three cannons ripped right off their platforms and thrown across the esplanade. There's twenty or thirty feet of soot and scorch-marks on the north wall. One of the old jail cells has been ripped apart. An entire flagstone is smashed like it was nothing but glass. Splintered rock everywhere. And over there is a massive chunk just knocked right out of the coquina masonry. And mud is everywhere. Along with hundreds of dead fish and shrimp. What's up with that? Oh, the stench!

"Sir Francis Drake himself couldn't have done this much damage if he'd ever seen the inside of our beloved monument! I haven't got the slightest clue how something this awful could have happened, and I don't think any of the big-shot investigators do, either. It's like the place was bombed or attacked or hit by a freaking meteor or something. I tell you, I just can't wrap my head around it. Not one person—not one credible

person, anyhow—appears to have heard or seen anything, even with all of the people out and about for Halloween festivities last night. Would you believe we even have a psychic out here? I don't know who brought the likes of her in, or if she came of her own volition, but she seems to think it all was the work of extraterrestrials. Gee, that's a lead for you. If you ask me, this is just one more example of how our young people in this country are going straight to the dogs. I wouldn't want to run into the likes of the kind of young people who could pull something like *this* off. Most disgraceful thing I've seen in all my forty-seven years, I can assure you of that."

༺ঌৎঌ༻

"Shall I read further?" said Letty Beauregard, her wide-eyed face a leathery landscape of frown lines and weary umbrage.

"Is there anything more potentially damning than what we've already seen for ourselves?" muttered Rowan Blaize, bruised and still slightly dizzy. He was propped against the pillows of his grand four-poster bed, its capitals carved like ponderous satyrs' heads. The wounded warlock was sipping irritably at a cup of tea infused with Gert Gokey's "not sold in stores" Datil Take the Ache Away elixir. Gert herself, marshmallow plump in a white terry cloth bathrobe, sat next to him on the bed, patting his knee reassuringly atop the merry gargoyles-doing-somersaults motif duvet. Letty pursed her lemon-curdled lips and scanned the newspaper again, squinting as her beaked nose moved up and down and side to side.

"No," she said at last. "Can't say as there's anything else out of the ordinary in print about our little evening. There's a bit down here about bats supposedly flying outta some old lady's microwave last night, but that could've been most anybody up to tricks on their way to the party. Or the old gal might be flat-out crazy. I'd say it's even odds in this town, on a night like we just had. The news folk don't seem to be too interested in peripheral hijinks, anyhow. This wreckage at the fort has got them pretty well riled for the duration."

"Oh, they'll be talking about this for the next two centuries, I figure," said Gert, not without a measure of pride that she was trying and failing to conceal. "Even with mortal attention deficits being what they are, they'll remember this snafu. And to think—none of them noticed a thing as it was happening, thanks to your ducky little cloaking spell, Rowan."

Then Gert took a bracing sip from her own teacup, though it was filled with potent elderberry brandy from a bottle she had been careful to pilfer from the ruins of the party scene. "All things being considered, you gotta say we know how to leave quite an aftermath!" she said.

"This is hardly the time to be bragging about our ability to leave a gigantic mess in our wake," said Rowan. "I'm appalled and embarrassed by what occurred last night. I should have never held the party at all, given the forebodings we all seemed to be experiencing and the strange circumstances surrounding Serenity's disappearance. Worse, we have drawn the attention of the mortal world to our 'aftermath,' as you call it, Gert. That sort of thing is never any good and both of you know it. Even ruins can be repaired. I've seen that often enough in four thousand years, but mortals—if they rise to the challenge of a mystery—can very swiftly complicate matters for the likes of us."

"This'll blow over in a couple of weeks, dear," said Letty. "Trust me. I know mortal folk and I know this town. They'll be wrangling over the politics of it all in short shrift. Whose responsibility is it to fix this? Who is obliged to spend the money to clean that? Ha! Our entire shop and home burning down was the talk of the town and a few days later it's barely the talk of the block, I'd expect. Mortal people can't be bothered to care or remember much of import for extended periods of time."

"She's likely right," said Gert. "There's always something bigger happening in this world, right down the pike, and then all the human heads turn thisaway and thataway, as if they was being mass hypnotized or whatever."

"That's precisely the point," retorted Rowan, setting his teacup and saucer on the table with a rattle that gave even the witches a start. They were still spooked, and there was no mistake about it. "We do not want 'something bigger' to occur at this juncture, particularly on the local horizon, and the fact remains that this scenario appears all too likely to happen. Ow!"

"Oh, poor boy," cooed Gert solicitously. "Is it your darling little neck again?"

"I'm fine," countered Rowan. "Just a little raw along my chest where those despicable hairs lassoed me. They burned almost as well as they strangled, I can assure you. Forget about my injuries for the moment. You ought to check and see how poor Miranda and Bror are faring. I covered them with healing spells back at the fort as soon as I could, while you two were attacking our unexpected little guest, and I know you have been working your own charms upon them all morning, ladies, as you have done for me. But their initial condition was so much worse than mine. Recoveries, even magically enhanced ones, can go away in the blink of an eye, in the sparkle of a star. Perhaps I shall get up and attend them myself. I'm feeling much, much better."

"No need to bother," said Miranda, smiling and leaning against the bedroom portal. "I'm as fit as a fiddle, thanks to all of you. Bror is fine, too, but he's currently snoring and drooling up a storm, so I didn't have the heart to wake him and bring him in to say hello."

"Well!" gasped Rowan with delight. "You *are* the picture of health, my precious foundling. Letty and Gert are even more adept at their arts than I thought."

"They are," agreed Miranda. She sauntered inside wearing one of her favorite sets of flannel pajamas and flopped into a chair next to Letty. "And so are you. I have a feeling I wouldn't have made it through at all if you hadn't rushed to my side at once. Bror either."

"I daresay you wouldn't have made it," said Gert, rising unsteadily to pour Miranda a teacup of her restorative brew. "Here, have some more of this for good measure, doll. You had several broken ribs and a concussion, among other things, but this is one instance where you can be quite thankful you live amongst witches and their little dramas. Now, you need to think about getting back to bed, just to stay on the safe side."

"None of us are going to be on the 'safe side' until this muddle is solved once and for all," said Rowan, ominously. "You all felt how powerful that … that *being* was, whatever it was. I threw my full strength against it, or at least one of my best enchantments, and still barely escaped with my hide."

"Oh, we saw that, alright," said Letty with a sparkle in her eye and a curt nod. "Mighty proud of you we was, too, or at least we would've had time to *enjoy* being proud if the entire ocean hadn't come crashing down on our heads. But we sensed the magnitude of magic in that miniature monstrosity, sure enough. We knew there was gonna be trouble from the get-go."

"I should say so," agreed Gert. "A most revolting disguise it had, too, dressed as that darling little Pint-Sized Princess child. I could tell it was a ruse the moment I got my wits about me and bent my thought upon the matter. What I *couldn't* tell was what sort of person, or thing, exactly, was lurking beneath them ringlets and all that puffy satin."

"Are you certain that this 'child' has not been some kind of sorceress all along?" said Rowan, exasperated.

Letty shook her head. "Not a chance. That gal and her daddy have been in the shop a few times over the years, looking for money to fund them deplorable girl-pageants."

"Why, you *never* told me that, Leticia Beauregard!" puffed Gert. "And you knew I was a big fan, too."

"Why do you think I never told you? You would've hawked your magic wok and turned over the store keys to those shysters if I hadn't given them the stink-eye on prior occasions. Anyhow, don't interrupt. As I was saying, I seen both of them up close and personal enough in the past to know that the child was, hitherto, just a typical mortal brat and the father a dime-a-dozen snake-oil salesman. But that sure as Sheba's Shingles *wasn't* the girl we saw last night. Not on the inside, anyhow. I'm fairly certain that poor horsewhipped fool in chains and barbed-wire was actually the little girl's father, but I couldn't get the slightest glimpse into what manner of thing was occupying her skin, though not for lack of trying. Perhaps if we'd had more time."

"Well, we didn't have that," said Rowan, brows knitting a dark blanket of anxious and disturbing thoughts. "Things fell apart rather swiftly."

"That wasn't your fault Rowan Blaize," said Gert. She wagged a pudgy brown finger at her patient against the pillows. "You displayed a great presence of mind and magic last night. Why, if you hadn't flown Miranda and Bror up into the ramparts of the fort as soon as they'd been attacked, they woulda drowned in that tidal wave! And you certainly saved *my* skin. I would have been speared like a bluefish if you hadn't taken that little minx in hand."

"Yep," added Letty. "And you were the only one of us who was able to wound the little varmint, to boot. Those Siafu ants! Well, that certainly had some flair, some pizzazz. But a Goranthus troll? My word."

"Oh, Simpering Cybele's Meteor!" cackled Gert, slapping her knee. "My hair nearly straightened of its own accord when I saw you transform into that beast. Great stars and satellites. They used to scare the likes of us with stories of Goranthus trolls back in the mountains when I was just a girl! Only ever *saw* one of them in my life, deep in some Romanian forest, I forget which one—it was at least six hundred years ago—but the brute was carrying what looked like a bag full of clobbered gypsies back to its cave. I happened to be flying low through the woods on an old willow branch when I ran into it, and it give me a look and knew I was a witch, and I gave it a look and knew what it was, and we both just decided it was best not to mess with each other, at the moment, so off we went on our merry ways. And the one I saw wasn't half the size of the one you turned yourself into."

"That's a lovely reminiscence, Gert, but I was still defeated," said Rowan. "And I have no more idea about what defeated me than anyone else here. I could not perceive its nature, only its threat, its potency. The rest was kept hidden from me. Did anyone in attendance at that luckless party say anything, mention anything they saw or may have intuited that might give us a clue?"

Letty and Gert glanced at each other furtively.

"Everyone who could manage to escape eventually escaped, Rowan," said Letty. "Several of them were lost. That was quite a showdown, as you know. Two of the werewolves from that dinner theater got themselves drownded. The Swamp Beldam got burnt up by accident."

"Yes, it was a total accident," gabbled Gert, looking quite ashamed. "She was caught in the crossfire when Letty and me cast our spell. A bunch of Greedle goblins or gravestone gimps—I forget which—got smushed underneath Bror and two of the hobgobby brothers from out Spuds way are pretty well injured, but they'll be okay in a week or two. The rest apparently got away or went into hiding."

"It was lucky *we* got away," said Letty. "I mean, a few of the wraiths were nice enough to stick around and help us clean things up, evidence-wise, as much as we could before dawn, and get you and Miranda and the dog back to the house, but you know wraiths. A wraith can't lift anything to save its lifelessness. That vampire couple, the Bulkagovs, ended-up helping the most. They carried you while we steered. You know, it was mighty smart of you to play possum like you did when she knocked you sideways and had the poor old Rummy man reach in to feel for your heartbeat."

"Ugh!"said Rowan, grimacing.

"And I know vampires turns your stomach and all, but ..."

"But they shall be properly thanked by me when the time is right," Rowan said, gathering himself as much as he could. "I appreciate *those* vampires, at least at this particular juncture. The fact remains that we are no closer to solving the mystery of our interloper's identity for the good of all our magical folk. Besides, taking into consideration all of our various odd forebodings, anxieties, and premonitions, and the fact that this disguised abomination crashed our festival specifically to confront *me*, I have no choice but to fear the very worst."

He ran his fingers through the shock of jet black hair and laid his head back against the pillow, sighing.

"Are you saying you might know who that was, after all?" mumbled Gert, teacup poised halfway between her bosom and her chin.

"In my worst case scenario … yes, I might."

"Oh, Rowan," said Miranda, clutching the collar of her pajamas in despair. "You really don't think it's … it's …"

"Frankly, I do," answered the beleaguered warlock, spring slightly forward in the sumptuous bed and spreading his arms wide. "I have only one sworn enemy, Miranda, at least in this world, who has the guile, the power, and the reason to seek vengeance upon me. Yes, Miranda my foundling, I think my worst fears may have at last come true. Who else could it be? In this town, especially? At this time? Oh, it would be just *like* her to pull a stunt as sickening as this, too!" added Rowan with a growl, crossing his arms and apparently speaking to the embroidered gargoyles frolicking on the duvet. "And to think she started her vicious campaign against me by probably killing that innocent little beauty pageant kid."

"But you were so very certain that you had finally ruined her!" said Miranda, a slight whine creeping into her normally soft and taciturn voice.

Rowan held up a gloriously long index finger. "One is never certain of anything in the world of magicians, dear Miranda. Never forget that, particularly when a specimen as despicably spectacular as *she* is involved."

"Who in the blazes is SHE?" squawked Letty and Gert in consternated unity.

"An old adversary," griped Rowan, making a miffed little kick at the bed sheets. "Damnation! Well, not an old adversary in terms of the establishment of our particular enmity, but she herself is incredibly old. Or is. Or was."

"Stop beating around the bush, Rowan Blaize, and spell it out for the rest of us," demanded Letty, sitting prim and expectant with the newspaper now folded neatly in her lap. "What is her NAME?"

"Circe," replied Rowan, calm and matter-of-fact, his eyes going from thundercloud gray to bright silver in a haze of sunlight that meandered through one of the bedroom windows.

The witches paused for a few seconds in consideration of this name, and then, as if both were telepathic twins from inordinately different wombs, brayed in perfect synchronicity:

"You don't mean *that* Circe!"

"I am afraid that I do," muttered Rowan, smoothing the covers over the hem of his phoenix-feathered bed jacket. "None other than her."

"Whull!" responded Letty with another great gulp. "I figured you may have rubbed elbows with some high-falluting personalities in your day—which apparently extends a lot farther back than any of us might've guessed—but Circe herself? Mightiest of all sorceresses, save for perhaps Hecate and Calypso?"

"Mightier than either of them, I regret to inform you," said Rowan. "As a matter of fact, Hecate and Calypso are no longer with us due specifically to Circe's machinations."

"You mean they've gone into some other world?" said Gert, breathless.

"I mean, they're both destroyed. By Circe."

The witches gasped in sheer horror, hands fluttering to their chins. Gert dropped her teacup of elderberry brandy to the floor. It shattered but no one noticed.

"Impossible!" Letty croaked.

Miranda squirmed in her chair. She knew well the whole story.

"Not only quite possible, but accomplished, I assure you," said Rowan. "I have seen the evidence with my own eyes and would have fallen victim to Circe's hideous schemes, too, had it not been for happy chance and some assistance from Hermes himself."

"Hermes?" screeched Gert.

"You do beat all, Blaize," added Letty. "But how on earth did you ever get tangled up with the likes of them Powers? They're of the Old, Ruling Race, and no mistake."

"It's a long story. I wrote a ballad, an extended poem, if you like, about the events after they happened twenty years ago. I wrote it in one of the truly ancient languages and Miranda, along with the help of another mortal friend of ours, Jonathan, helped to translate it as best they could into an accessible English form a while back. I was quite pleased with their results. You'll have to remind me to find the book for you some time. If I survive to find it at all. Suffice it to say, for now, that my family of magicians is a rather old and well-connected one, even as such families go, and at one time, thousands of years ago, both my Aunt Ariadne and my mother served as handmaidens and associates of great Circe on her catch-all of an island in the Aegean. They learned great sorceries from her in the course of their shared endeavors and, though my mother eventually struck out on a rather independent pathway, my Aunt—as it turned out—remained somewhat close to the Queen of Aeaea ... to her own doom, unfortunately."

"Are you telling us your Auntie was none other than Ariadne of Scythia? And that *she* was destroyed by Circe, too?" said Gert, eyes bulging as she clutched her extraordinary bosom.

"My Aunt was 'Ariadne of many places,' not just Scythia, though likely that is how you might have heard tales of her most famous exploits. And, yes, she was felled by Circe's power. You see, the great sorceress was collecting particularly gifted and powerful witches, wizards, warlocks, and magicians ... collecting them like a spider collects flies and draining the power and the life from them. She did this for the vile purpose of reanimating their spirits in the most gruesome way imaginable and using them to launch an outright plan for the eradication of the human race."

"Ttch!" clucked Letty, pounding a fist into her scrawny lap. "Comes as little surprise. Them really ancient enchantresses do end-up going a little haywire after so many centuries alive. As most anyone in-the-know recalls, Circe certainly harbored a well-known contempt for mortal kind. Always wanted to be treated like a goddess, like some of her superiors, but resented the fact that, while mighty, she wasn't quite suited for Olympian real estate. Mind you, the occasional mortal-to-pig transformation, simply as an experimental exercise, is nothing to be ashamed about."

"Absolutely not," Gert concurred with a somewhat defensive, jowl-quivering, nod.

"But wiping out the race of mortals entirely," added Letty ruefully. "Now that is a different can of worms altogether."

"So agreed the Ruling Powers, the Archons," said Rowan, picking up his cup of elixir once more. "That was one reason Hermes was dispatched to my aid. For, you see, Circe had put a most debilitating spell upon me and had drawn me into her web, and therein I was fatefully ensnared. She considered me to be one of that select cabal of wonderworkers worth collecting."

"Hmpf! Now I'm getting a bit of the picture, Blaize. Gert and me had never heard of you before you hit town, and you was a bit of a mystery, but we knew you was ... *special* ... despite your youthful trappings. And we have heard legends—rumors—of a mighty young warlock capable of amazing magicks. A figure from the shadows of the Old Days, and I mean the *really* old days. But as you know, Gert and me left the Old Country a long time ago ourselves to settle on this heap of continent, and we ain't been back or kept in touch too much. Off the radar, as mortals would say. We didn't put two and two together when you arrived, though we had our suspicions."

"Still, that Goranthus troll transmogrification was as clear a signal of your elite status as anyone could ever want or need to see," interjected Gert. "Yes indeed. No wonder Circe wanted you in her clutches for whatever it was she was planning to do. What I want to know is how in the Howling Corridors of Hades did you manage to get away?"

"I was not strong enough to withstand Circe's power on my own, prodigy though I may be. But I had a singular advantage in my plight because Hermes himself released me from Circe's jail and loaned me his caduceus."

"By the glittering girdle of the Gorgon!" exclaimed Letty. "A wand to beat all wands!"

"I suppose it was," said Rowan, wincing at the memory of power and pain mixed ineffably. "I used it to confront Circe in her dark and abysmal lair, her charnel house, and let us just say that a quarrel ensued. It was one from which I did not very easily emerge victorious, even with the aid of such a talisman."

"By all that's ghastly, how did you prevail?" said the hefty Gert on tenterhooks of considerable strength.

"Again, for the majority of the details, you'll have to read the ballad, the poem. Miranda, if any of us survives the next few days or weeks, be a dear and dig it out of the attic for them. But I tell you one thing, ladies: by speed and by savvy, I was able to … *misplace* the mighty demigoddess."

"Misplace her?" crowed the witches.

"Yes. I used the caduceus—and a particularly risky incantation—to relocate Circe, to put her some place where she could no longer do any harm, yet wherein I could also keep a very close and watchful eye upon her."

Letty gestured desperately for an answer.

"I 'misplaced' Circe in a constellation," said Rowan loftily. "One of her very own. A cluster of stars shaped like a weasel. In the Great Square of Pegasus."

There were more gasps from the witches. "But only the god-like ones, the Archons, have the power to exact a punishment, or bestow a *privilege,* like that!" said Letty.

Rowan shrugged. "Well, I had the scepter of a god in my possession, at the time. And, as I mentioned, my own family is of a certain interesting pedigree. I took a chance. It worked. As the awful smoke and fury of our battle dissipated, and I rushed upward from the earth into the night to behold the Firmament, there she was as I intended, splayed across the western border of the Great Square. Whether in agony or in limbo, I could not tell, and did not care, for she was defeated."

The witches were galvanized, even as Miranda lowered her head in dismay and tucked her cold fingers under the warm flannel armpits of her pajamas.

"Then you have nothing to worry about from Circe any longer!" trumpeted Gert. "You can just go out at night like you said and check up on her for yourself, anytime you want."

"Oh, I have checked, dearest Gertrude. I have. But her constellation is gone."

"Er ... now, that *is* what we would call a problem," murmured Letty, flopping back in her chair as if she, too, had been defeated by the ghosts of a terrible encounter.

"Most unsettling, isn't it?" said Rowan, sipping tea. "For over five years after I defeated Circe, five years after our fracas, I monitored her great float across the heavens, amid the trillions of other burning, spinning orbs and constellations known and unknown, and then, one evening fifteen years ago, she was gone. By what means, I do not know. But there you have that part of the story, and it is for this reason that Miranda and Bror and I have been moving about this world like vagabonds, lately. It is my belief—though not my certainty—that Circe has most truly escaped her imprisonment and is most assuredly plotting a fine measure of revenge, for vengeance is in her very ichor. I neither welcome nor do I fear another confrontation with her. I merely anticipate it, and this time I do not have the caduceus of Hermes to wield in my defense."

"Now hold on," said Letty, scratching at her grey, clutching braids, cogitating ferociously. "There could have been lots of reasons why that constellation disappeared, Rowan Blaize. I'm not entirely ignorant about such matters. I, too, am an immortal, though not of your stock, it would seem. For example, one of the other Archons could have—"

Rowan held up a hand and shook his head. His smile was a grim one.

"I know, Leticia, and have always been prepared to consider any or all of the more palatable possibilities, but after what happened last night, and after the immensity of the power and trickery we all encountered and somehow managed to endure, at least for the moment, I believe that Circe has made herself known once again. That is the most likely scenario, all things being considered."

"Well, that's a tale and a half and there ain't no doubt about it," said Gert, folding her doughy arms and blowing air out of her great round cheeks in an astonished, or exhausted, whoosh. "But, if that was Circe last night, why didn't she kill you outright, instead of taking a chance that you was just playing possum, which, in fact, you *was* doing? Why were you able to chop her leg off, if that was the mighty Circe? What was with the Pint-Sized Princess get-up? Did she just want to make fun of you? I don't get it."

"I don't know the answers to those questions," admitted Rowan, who had scarcely had time to ponder them in the first place, so recent had been his own recovery from the duel. "It's true, you all saw that she was wounded, though I question the severity of the injury, given that she is merely posing in a child's overdressed form. Perhaps that in itself is a sign. Perhaps you are correct and the outlandish appearance as the Rummy child was part of some plan to humiliate me. When it comes to Circe, I guarantee you: no plot, or postulation, for that matter, is contemptible enough."

"If that's the case," said Letty, swimming to the surface after time spent in the dark depths of thought, "then Circe may be a bit off her game, because she left something behind when she skedaddled away from that fort with her one crooked leg and the beat-up old pageant gal's daddy in tow. Here," she added, reaching into one of the deep pockets of the apron she had put on that morning to play magical nursemaid. "I been waiting for the right moment to show this to y'all, and seeing as everyone is now alert and accounted for, and we've got a bit of the story figured out, you might want to have a gander at this."

She had pulled from the apron a moist, slightly soiled shred of puffed white satin fabric and she dropped it on the coverlet near Rowan's feet. A gigantic ruby-stone ring in a warped gold setting slipped from the tattered piece of garment.

"There you are. Witches with a great deal on the ball don't normally leave bits of their clothes or godawful ugly jewelry behind when they leave a place under less than friendly circumstances. Witches with any sense know what kinds of spells can be finagled if someone with a mind to teach them a lesson gets hold of their paranormal possessions. I grabbed this after I saw it fall into a corner of the courtyard, after you ripped her gown and bashed one of her spindly little legs off with that old cannon."

"You NEVER!" said Gert, bustling over to ogle the thing.

"I certainly did."

Rowan was agog, too. Even Miranda had come out of her chair to peer at the thing from behind the protective shoulders of the witches crowding the bed.

"This is most unusual, to be certain," said Rowan. "You took a great risk, indeed, picking this up, Letty. It could well be a trap."

"Didn't look like one to me. Just looked like something that plopped off from that ridiculous outfit once you'd knocked her limb off and she was too stunned to remember it."

"Even so, a sheltering charm would have been in order before touching it."

"Already done," said Letty flatly. "Ain't nothing untoward happened to me, yet. Leastways, nothing that I know about. You might want to have a look at the band of that ring, there. It's got some kind of writing on it, but I'll be cornsnazzled if I can make head nor tail of it."

Rowan scrutinized her stern, gimlet stare for a moment and, muttering a defensive spell of his own, twitched the singed satin folds aside and picked up the ring for examination.

"It's a ruby," he noted. "Large and aesthetically unappealing, despite its potential value to the mortal market. Witches, of course, care far less for exquisitely cut stones to show off. Hmmm. This writing is unknown to me, as well. Most archaic and unusual, and I have seen a great many scripts in my ... wait a moment!"

Rowan's ice gray eyes went wide and he sat straight in the bed.

"What's the matter?" hissed Gert, wringing her chubby hands. "Did Circe's spell getcha?"

"No!" said Rowan, throwing off the covers and flying from the bed to the chest of drawers across the room. "By Persephone's Petticoats, this is not the first time I have heard of a strange inscription in the past few days. No indeed. How could I have been so slow-witted once you produced this for our viewing pleasure, Letty?"

He found the stone disc he had secreted in the top drawer of the bureau and held it up triumphantly next to the ring.

"Not that silly bit of hippie jewelry you found at Serenity's place?" complained Letty. "We're in serious trouble here, if all the signs are legitimate. What's that thing got to do with Circe and this ugly old ruby she dropped during the big snafu?"

"I intend to find out in very short order, my dear Leticia," said Rowan, his face now glowing with new determination. "If what that battered Shih-Tzu familiar tried to tell me back at Serenity's house makes any sense whatsoever, then I think I may know exactly what this piece of 'hippie jewelry' is, and I think I know exactly how to use it."

"What is it, then, Rowan?" said Miranda.

"I would bet my best cauldron and Letty's special-occasions-only broomstick that this, faithful foundling, is a *genuine* Babel Disc—wrought when the world was young and even more foolish and arrogant than ever it was. Stacks of these were built into the observation decks of the fabled Tower itself, before it met its doom. I heard that a few were found and preserved from the rubble ages ago, but never expected to see one. It can decode any written language known in the heavens or upon the earth!"

"Oh, for crying out loud," said Gert. "Them things only exist in legend!"

"According to mortals, so do we," blurted Letty, nudging her companion in the ribs. "Let the warlock talk."

"The only thing to do is put it to the test," declared Rowan, holding the golden band up to his face while peering at its faint inscription through the shiny, smooth stone.

"Aha! Just as I thought. Ladies, stand aside. Miranda, get behind them. In fact, I'd appreciate it if one of you would work up a spell over there on the area rug. Letty, don't fret about the value of the carpet. It's one of my best Tabriz acquisitions and it rides the thermals like an albatross when coaxed, but we need it for far more important purposes at the moment. Burn a Pentacle of Imprisonment into it."

"Why?"

"Just do it. And make it your best."

Shoulders that had been sagging swiftly firmed-up and the old witch trained an eye and a pitifully crooked index finger on the elaborate carpet across the far end of Rowan's bedroom. A thin beam of orange, laser-like fire emanated from the tip of her finger and with flawless precision burned the outline of a pentagram as she chanted her spell *sotto voce*.

"Ooo! Fabulous technique, Letty," snorted Gert, who loved nothing more than to see a witch being useful in a crisis, particularly if it didn't have to be her.

"And now for the translation," said Rowan, eyeing the terrible ring's band of gold. ""Whoever ... has the ... grave misfortune ... of speaking ... aloud ... the words ... of this secret ... inscription ... that I, Marutha ... inscribed ... hereupon ... will break ... the infernal ... seal ... and ... find ... themselves ... at the mercy ... of mighty ... Dedwen."

"Dedwen?" babbled the witches. "Who in Hades is Dedwen?"

No sooner had the words been spoken than a furious plume of yellow vapor and smoke swirled and steamed from the ruby-stone and began to coagulate in roiling clouds and swelling swoops.

"Look out, all of you," warned Rowan as he tossed the ring into the pentacle Letty had etched into the carpet. The witches and Miranda sidled over to gather at his side, their hands held out in a show of defense at whatever horror—and they had little doubt it was to prove a horror—might become manifest.

"Brace yourselves with spells of elves, ladies! We have absolutely no idea what manner of hideousness lurks in that noxious smoke coming from the gemstone. It is almost certain to be ghastly, so we must all be prepared to strike with full strength, if necessary! The pentacle ought to contain whatever foul entity may appear, but one cannot be too careful in such circumstances."

"Then why go and get us into such circumstances in the first place," said Gert, her voice quavering.

"Shut up!" snapped Letty.

When the otherwise benign, even pretty-looking smoke began to dissipate into the clearness of the surrounding air and they could all see the hacking, coughing, crouching "hideousness" on the carpet before them, they dropped their hands and their jaws as one, exclaiming in the same high-pitched chorus:

"SERENITY TURNBULL?"

"Ack! Phlack! ACK!" choked Serenity, discombobulated in her kimono and hair unkempt as a haystack in a windstorm. She was shivering. When she wobbled up and tried to stagger her way off the carpet, she was zapped by a sizzling bolt of orange lightning and fell back upon her rump, sobbing.

"Baaaaaahhhhh!" she wailed.

Letty flailed her arms and elbows about for an instant like a disoriented turkey—she really had been taken unawares by *this* turn of events—and gathered her wits together quickly enough to address the sorry scene.

> *Star of Shelter, points of five,*
> *obey the charm I now contrive.*
> *Throw down thy shield and quench thy fire,*
> *as I thy maker doth desire!*

As a unit, the four ran to the carpet and lifted the sniveling, pathetic Serenity from the floor and gently guided her lurching figure to the well-cushioned chair Letty had been occupying for most of the morning. All the while, they attempted to answer Serenity's frantic inquiries:

"W-w-where am I *now?*"

"Shush! It's alright gal. You're in Rowan Blaize's very own bedroom."

"WHAT?"

"You idiot, Gertrude! Haven't you got a lick of subtlety? How would *you* like to just pop out of a magic ring and find yourself in a daze in some man's boudoir?"

"To be quite honest, Letty, I don't think that'd be the worst—"

"Zip it, Gokey! There, there, Serenity, dear. You're safe in a nice powerful warlock's house."

"Serenity, it's Rowan Blaize. Are you injured in any way?"

"I ... I ... don't know. I don't think so. Not too badly. I just couldn't breathe. Am I really out of that horrible ruby? It was beyond tortuous!"

"Yes, I used the Babel Disc to speak the ring's inscription and it set you free. See? Here it is. Poor, poor girl. We are all just as surprised as you are."

"Babel Disc? That's my granny's old ciphering stone. You used it? Oh, my, I am a bit queasy. Is Emory here? My familiar? I want my familiar!"

"Oh, too bad, doll. Emory is all squashed up and dead. Gone into the Void, that's what Rowan said."

"BAAAAaaahhhh-ahahahah!"

"Gertrude Gokey!" the other helpers yelled.

"Sorry. Just trying to answer the gal's question."

"B-but where's that awful Dedwen?" Serenity rasped, her voice failing her and her fingers clutching the arms of her rescuers in white-tipped terror.

"Dedwen!" repeated Rowan as they finally lowered her into the chair. He looked down at her feet; the ears to her pink bunny slippers had been completely burnt off. She really had been having a bad couple of days. "Serenity, Dedwen was the name in the ring incantation and, instead of seeing this individual appear when I read the spell, we see you. How has this come to pass, dear girl?"

"Because Dedwen was the one who put me there!" shrieked Serenity, on the verge of some fit. "Would someone please bring me a glass of water or anything wet? There's nothing drier than limbo, let me tell you!"

"I can do you a sight better than water," assured Gert, pulling a golden flask from her unstoppable bosom and scuttling to Rowan's bedside table for a teacup. In very little time a dose of salvific ambrosia was poured, drunk, refilled, and then Serenity was coddled, soothed, smoothed, and petted to the point wherein she could tell them, in reasonably coherent fashion, the entire tale of her most accidental and ill-fated encounter with the ancient djin back at the beach house. Her associates were flabbergasted, but not quite certain they had a right to feel relieved.

"So, it wasn't old Circe, after all!" said Gert.

"Right, but it was still one of them *ifrits,*" countered Letty. "An upper-level one, to boot, it seems. I mighta known a darn genie was at the heart of such a tussle. Them rascals are big trouble, and no mistake. Well, except for the good ones. Never had any dealings with that accursed race myself, but I've known a few witches who've tangled with them in the past. The stories are *not* pretty. Rowan, you ever heard of this Dedwen character?"

"I have not, and to be quite frank, it doesn't surprise me, even given the tremendous power of this specimen, who must have a fearsome reputation. Djinn are the most secretive of all the demons. They tend to drop names almost exclusively amongst themselves to build, secure, or restore their status."

More worrisome to all was Serenity's tearful account of Dedwen's plan to hijack the Pint-Sized Princess pageant and unleash some sort of heinous surprise upon the watching, unwary world the very next evening. Gert, who retained the softest of spots in her heart for toddlers in tiaras, was particularly beside herself over this state of affairs.

"Imagine the wickedness!" she bellowed. "Eating up a sweet, precious little prodigy like BonSashay Rummy and then having the nerve to waltz around in her skin, attacking perfectly decent witches and other respectable weirdoes just trying to have themselves a good old-fashioned time at a Halloween party. Oh! By the Magpies of Mab, them other darling little contestants at the pageant are in for serious trouble if that djin is fixing to enter the competition. And to think I had tickets to the whole shebang, before the shop burnt to the ground!"

"You're pepper shop burned down?" sniffed Serenity, accepting a tissue from Letty and finally feeling a bit more like herself, whatever that was.

"Yep," said Gert. "It was all pretty much your fault, too, come to think of it."

"Whaaaat?"

Letty was forced to jab her pudgy pal once more in her well-padded ribs.

"Will you keep that trap shut for once and stop making things worse, Gertrude?"

"I was just talking about the forebodings and my scrying pan. All that stuff really happened, in case you forgot."

"We're not here to assign blame," informed Letty, turning with as much compassion as she could muster to Serenity. "Now, dear, don't you mind a thing about what this battleax says. It was that nasty genie's fault and you was only one quarter or maybe, at best, half responsible for the tragedy."

"Please, ladies," urged Rowan, standing behind the bewildered Serenity with his hands on her willowy shoulders. "More important for us is that we know exactly what we're dealing with, at last. Forget about the shop. Forget, certainly, about the party. We need to think of a strategy to stop this Dedwen the Great, as it apparently calls itself."

Letty glowered at their usually indomitable host. "Have you ever tangled with a High Genie, Rowan Blaize?"

"Gee, until last night, Letty? No. And you saw the results of *that* contretemps."

"But you still whacked her ... him ... it a real good one with that cannon when you was turned into the troll," offered Gert encouragingly.

"A minor wound, in the scheme of things," fretted Rowan, who began to pace back and forth before his bedroom fireplace. "It behooves us far more to ascertain more of the story behind this 'Marutha of Maipherkat' that our dear Serenity has told us about, the one so named on the ring's inscription, as well. Miss Turnbull, is there anything else you can remember the djin saying—they do love to brag, and have rather loose tongues when goaded. Did it reveal anything else about this Marutha? I myself know the city of Maipherkat and remember it fairly well from my younger days, but I am not at all familiar with Marutha."

Serenity shook her head sadly. "No. That disgusting monster only told me that Marutha was a Christian bishop who imprisoned him in that wretched ring over fifteen hundred years ago, or so."

"Yes, but how?" muttered Rowan to himself. "I've got to find out more about this Marutha before we make another move. I wish I had my complete library on hand!"

"Wait no longer," piped Miranda from the doorway. She had run out of the room to procure her smartphone. "Look!" Rowan and thoroughly modern Serenity were interested, but the other witches glanced at the thing as if it were a particularly uninteresting piece of roadside rock. "I found out more about Marutha, everyone! I googled it."

"You *what?*" muttered Letty, as if Miranda had been engaging in an act so unspeakable that the only fitting punishment was immediate ostracism from all decent civilization, magical or mortal.

"Oh, get with the times, Letty," said Gert, whose turn it was to nudge her partner in the bony arm. "Googlies is one of them internet thingamabobs the mortals is so crazy about. I've told you about the googlies before, haven't I?"

"You best not have mentioned mortal googlies to me," said Letty. "Besides, I don't trust those contraptions." She gave Miranda's phone a piercing glare. "It took me a century to get used to cash registers and I still ain't over the experience of them credit card machines we had to finally get in the store."

"What a lot of piffle," said Gert. "Don't pay her any mind, Miranda. Go ahead and tell us what you found out there in spyberspace, honey."

"Well, there are a number of articles online about Marutha of Maipherkat, but I found a relatively comprehensive one on Wikipedia."

"Wiki WHUH?" murmured Gert, her cutting edged-ness deflating before their eyes.

"Just listen," said Miranda, thumbs moving across her little phone with the speed and determination of a spider putting the finishing touches on a silken snare. "Okay. Saint Maruthas or Marutha of Martyropolis was a monk who became bishop of Maipherkat in Mesopotamia (Meiafarakin) for a period beginning before 399 and was still in office in 410. He's believed to have died before 420. He is venerated as a Saint by Catholics, Greek Orthodox believers and Copts, his feast being kept on 4

December. He brought into his episcopal city the relics of so many martyrs that it received the surname Martyropolis. He was a friend of Saint John Chrysostom. He acted as an ambassador between the East Roman Emperor and the Persian Emperor.

"In the interests of the Church of Persia, which had suffered much in the persecution of Shapur II, he came to Constantinople, but found Emperor Arcadius too busily engaged in the affairs about the exile of St. John Chrysostom. Later, Marutha was sent by Emperor Theodosius II to the court of Persia, where, notwithstanding the Magi, he won the esteem of King Yazdgard I of Persia by his affability, saintly life, and, as is claimed, by his knowledge of medicine. So Marutha managed to negotiate a peace between the two empires.

"He was present at the general First Council of Constantinople in 381 and at a Council of Antioch in 383 (or 390), at which the Messalians were condemned. For the benefit of the Persian Church he is said to have held two synods at Ctesiphon. A great organizer, he was one of the first to give a regular structure to the church, helped in his mission by the catholicos Isaac."

"That's it," cried Rowan when she had finished. "Brilliant, brilliant woman! Ha!" he added to the witches. "She may be a changeling who became a foundling, but thank our stars she has found the trappings of human progress so fascinating. While I do not know of Marutha, I have indeed heard much in the old days about King Yazdgard. He was well-known for possessing a cabal of very capable sorcerers at his disposal. Mother and Father mentioned that notorious clutch once or twice. I'm afraid their names have been lost in the crumbling away of time, but their mere existence provides us now with a profound clue. If this 'Wikipedia' is correct, and we can verify the information, which is probably a good idea, then Marutha the good bishop had some manner of interaction with Yazdgard's cadre of wizards, as Miranda related. I suspect that the key that opens the doorway to what we need to know can be found in one of those interactions. I smell it!"

"But how are you going to uncover any details about Marutha and these court magicians if you say their names have been lost?" asked Serenity. "How are you going to possibly find out what went on, and to what purpose would you seek that particular information?"

"I am going to have to take a little excursion, my friends," said Rowan, stalking over to his ornate and lavishly appointed closet of garments, magical and otherwise. "I need access to certain books, you see. Books that contain the kind of information even our lovely Miranda will never be able to discover with her very worthy Google and Wikipedia."

"Which books?" demanded Letty, suspicious.

"Exactly!" said Rowan, yanking a pitch black cloak from his closet. "*Witch* books. Now listen. I want all of you, Serenity included, once she's feeling better, to spend all of tonight gathering your strength and your powers and staying out of the line of fire, if you see any fire forthcoming. Weave protective spells around this house like you've never weaved spells before. This Dedwen thinks it has either killed me or has the rest of you on toast, so it'll be focused upon whatever twisted plans it has for that warped little girl beauty pageant. Tomorrow, I want Letty, Gert, and even you, Serenity, to move discreetly about the city and rally the help of the magical community. They'll still be in shock due to the enormity of last night's fiasco, but I know the three of you will use all your powers of persuasion. We may need their assistance when all is said and done, or we may not need it. I have to find out. Miranda, you stay here with Bror and wait for my return. Both of you need to recover a bit more than you've recovered and *no* arguing. If I have anything to say about it, I'll be back with a plan. It may not be a plan that works, but it will be a plan nonetheless. Right now, I need books. Special ones.

"And I know only one place in the world where I can find them."

XVI

The house had been closed up and locked—windows, doors, even the chimneys—for almost twenty years. The locks were magical, as well as conventional, and they were potent to the last. The place loomed, not far apart from the other majestic homes in that London neighborhood, silent and yet ever so swift to share stories and legends that were not ever of its own creation. Tales and whispers that had never in the least been uttered in the myriad hallways and hidden rooms of the stately mansion seemed poised to burst from the framework, but stillness ruled with a stern, unspoken dignity. If secrets abounded in this area, they were indeed the imaginings of others in Holland Park, for the house was widely considered to be haunted.

No vagabond, whether pitifully desperate in the cold or reckless with indifference, would come near the place. No mischievous packs of teens looking for something to despoil on the outside or a spot within which to hide came terribly close to the house. Many knew its reputation, of course, and even though such reputations can attract the genuinely intrepid and brazen out of the devious inner desire to cross and conquer all perceived boundaries, no adventurers or thrill-seekers bothered this dwelling, as much as their daredevil hearts may have compelled them to try. Oh, without question, a few vandals of the psychotic variety—those without the power of discernment—had made the mistake of trying to gain entry over the past two decades, for such criminals are not swayed by the aura of magic, even though they can be easily ensnared by wandering, blind, into the clutches of spell-craft in the foolhardy haze of madness. But those types who had jimmied-open a door here, or a window, there … well, those individuals had all been *absorbed* by the house, just as so many others in the marbled hallways and niches inhabited the space.

There they were and there they remained, in contorted, agonized, or sometimes graceful forms of dead and plentiful stone.

This had been the home of Rowan's aunt, Ariadne, and she had been famous in her world for many things, but stonework had been her specialty above all other talents. If one was of a nature so disposed, one could smell it in the very air—an enormous and fitting curse hung over the place, covering it like an avalanche poised to tumble down a mountainside. Rowan could smell the presence of the curse as he moved, black as a tar-pit wraith, through the halls, his hooded cloak billowing slightly out behind in the stale but magically charged air. The curse did not trouble Rowan, however, for he himself had leveled the enchantment upon the great abode years ago, when it had been his grim responsibility to close it up and move on, not long after Ariadne's demise.

It was Rowan's curse that now kept the house rife with dangerous and watchful spirits, with ever-vigilant and volatile forces that guarded the treasures within and breathed ominous warning constantly into the fogs and footsteps of London without:

> Keep away! Keep away! Lest this peril be your last.
> Keep away! Keep away! All gaze elsewhere as you pass.

Rowan ascended the winding staircase to the fourth floor of the cavernous dwelling, to his Auntie's old study, her most beloved chamber. Phantasms installed to guard and make secure the parameters bowed in deference and withdrew into the blackest of already obsidian corners as he passed, for Rowan was now master of Asphodel House, and he commanded them. The warlock nodded in solemn acknowledgement as he passed. The lonesome spirits, trapped in their duties for as long as he willed it, deserved that much, for even such as they could feel a sense of intransigence amid the surge of Time's passage elsewhere.

Rowan was exhausted. In broad daylight and as shaken as he had been after the battle with Dedwen the Great, he had left Letty, Gert, Miranda, the recovering Serenity, and even the slobbering Bror with their instructions and he had flown, faster and more furiously than he had remembered flying in centuries, to reach this place. Flinging open the door to his Aunt Ariadne's study, he gestured idly toward the gigantic Aswan granite hearth, stacked as it was with arid and magnificent logs (he had been careful to leave it so provisioned) and, speaking a spell of ignition, a fire was blazing bright, if not cheerful, in an instant.

He looked around the room and remembered that fateful evening twenty years prior, and the great conference with his powerful, dangerous aunt, when he had come to her from the very depths of danger and his own exceeding peril ... only to encounter a betrayal that would overwhelm them both and cost his mother's indomitable sister her very existence. He shook his head slowly in dismay at the memory of such affairs, at the waste of so much brilliance and spirit, and as he did so, shadows all about skittered away as if alive in their own right—some of them *were,* in fact, alive—to occupy the corners of the frescoed ceiling or flit among the vast collection of magnificent volumes lining the twenty-five foot tall, wall-length bookcases all around. He thought, too, of Bror, now his loyal servant (and Miranda's even more so, perhaps) and how the Mastiff had once been such a stalwart footman and butler to Ariadne. Bror had been granted the wish that had made him, for the first time in centuries, truly happy, but even he would not have wanted to return to this wraith-infested gloom.

Rowan himself preferred not to be here, but he had come back, at utmost need, and this room, of all the many mysterious and residually enchanted chambers in the sprawling house, still retained its incomparable usefulness. Books by the thousands made the room alive with a sparkle of its former mistress's magnificence. The magnificent pentagram his aunt had crafted with the full range of her considerable skill, was waiting for him, carved into the marble floor. Its black, sunken sigils were begging to be used. He threw back the hood of his cloak, let the burgeoning firelight play upon his face for a moment, and sighed. Then he obliged the summons of the terrifyingly potent shapes and carvings, speaking the words of a spell he would never, ever forget, drawing upon all of his own, exceedingly worthy ability.

He had not been considered the family prodigy for little reason.

His voice echoed in the great room as if through even more laby-rinthine spirals of time and space:

> *"Denizens of hidden spheres, O eyes behind the veil!*
> *Unfettered Sybil spirits who upon the swift wind sail!*
> *Ye foul and reckless demons of the festering abyss,*
> *now hearken to this mighty spell, and dare Ye not resist!*
> *From all forgotten corners of the worlds and worlds-within,*
> *from every secret landscape let relentless search begin.*
> *For I, great Rowan Blaize, now seek an imp to do my will,*
> *a seer among demon-kind—one willing to fulfill*
> *the task I have appointed, that the Truth be duly found.*
> *Arise, O GnostiKimp—within this pentagram be bound!"*

On cue, and with a great, slimy unfolding of shadow and shifting air, the desired denizen emerged from the Void and sat before Rowan in the unhallowed star. Similar by nature and species to the one his Aunt had summoned decades ago, this one seemed much younger, somehow, and more agitated. Rowan hoped that this mercurial slave would nevertheless prove useful and experienced. It spoke to him even before he managed to state his purpose.

"Argh! And woe to an imp like me," it sniveled and began to fidget, wary of the circle. "For I see that I have been conjured by none other than the mighty magician, Rowan Blaize. Again I decry my woe!"

Rowan raised a disappointed but curious brow.

"You seem to know me, spirit, yet I do not know you."

"Ha! And such would have been my continued good fortune, had you not wrenched me up from the Bleak Chasms on this occasion," prattled the thing. "Believe me when I say that I could have happily gone another ten thousand cycles of the Underworld moons without making your infamous acquaintance. But you know how it is with us, in the Within World." The imp made a dismissive swipe with one of its talons. "Your sort calls and our sort *comes,* and neither of us gets to choose quite exactly the sort we come face to face with! Oh, infamous! Infamous Rowan Blaize!"

"Why do you say that?"

"Please!" It held up a webbed and offended paw. "Word gets around, even in the Tunnels of Turpitude. My confreres have heard about what happened the last time Rowan Blaize summoned a GnostiKimp to his beck and call. It was in this same pentagram, too, I suspect. If I look around, will I see the splattered remains of Zvgghhttjjkdllkijxxn?"

"What is Zvgghhttjjkdllkijxxn?"

"You mean '*who*' is Zvgghhttjjkdllkijxxn!" squealed the imp. Zvgghhttjjkdllkijxxn was the poor sot you smashed beneath your wicked and warlocky feet, of course. A cousin of mine, if you must know. His mother has never gotten over it, though I doubt that makes any difference to the likes of you. He was her seven hundred-seventy seventh son. An incomprehensible loss! Oh, when it became apparent that I was being sucked up from the most pleasantly putrid of the Pools of Perdition to attend the needs of Rowan Blaize, I rued the day I had ever been hatched, you can believe me."

Rowan was already perturbed. His frown expressed but a fraction of it. Even so, his words were calm enough.

"Be that as it may, it was not I who obliterated your sad relation twenty years ago. It was a relation of *mine*. One who is not with us, at present. So, you see, your information about the matter is a trifle skewed, particularly for an imp of your milieu. Luckily, your sort provides obscure knowledge at direct command, rather than of your own volition. The Waning Wastelands would otherwise be even more rife with absurd gossip than they already are."

"Well!" snarled the petulant mini-devil.

"More to the point, you are here at my pleasure, and under my power ..."

"Yes, yes, yes, we all know that. Get on with it, O mighty warlock."

"You know, it is little wonder that so many of your kind get crushed underfoot, even after they have rendered their special services," said Rowan, and he was quite correct. GnostiKimps are among the most irritating and annoying of all the subterranean magical beings a magician is sometimes obliged to employ. His Aunt Ariadne had hardly been the first to lose her temper and scatter imp guts around a spell chamber.

"But my request is a relatively simple one, and then you will be exiled back to the Lairs of Lassitude with all expedience, unmolested, and with all your parts intact," continued Rowan. "I need, of course, information, and I need, I think, a book. I believe it to be one of the books in this room." He pointed to the towering collection that surrounded them. "As you can see, there are well over four thousand volumes on that wall alone and, time being of the essence, I haven't any to spare in sorting through the stacks."

"Of course you don't!" replied the imp. "Your kind never does, though many of you have the privilege of slipping in and out of time, just like Eldritch Eels slither so easily through the Estuaries of Angst back where *I* come from. What book do you seek and I will gladly use my gifts to become your very own living library card, not to mention librarian."

"I can count on you for that," snapped Rowan, catching a glimpse of his Auntie's old fireplace poker and wanting very much to use it as it had been used before in a similar circumstance.

"I am looking into the history of a great Christian bishop of the relatively ancient world, a certain Marutha of the city of Maipherkat, who had considerable dealings with the mighty King Yazdgard of Mesopotamia, and his bevy of wizards. My Auntie has—or *had*—the most complete collection of ancient lore, legend, and assorted grimmoires in the entire witchy world, and I want to know if one of those moldering volumes up there contains any information about Marutha's dealings with these wizards and the specific involvement of a djin, one of the High Ifrit. A djin named Dedwen."

At this, the GnostiKimp clutched its spiked and batty ears.

"Names! Names!" it shrieked. "You are after names that are better left unspoken! I know of this djin even without having to draw upon the inner gifts unique to my race. Curses! Do I *ever* know about *that* savage scourge! Why, he has been plundering the Pools of Perdition and the

Canyons of Calumny for ages untold, snacking upon my kind and our various collaterals whenever there's a particularly obnoxious rumble in his belly. Whatever do you want to know about *him* for?"

"That is none of your business," warned Rowan with a harsh tap of his trollskin boot upon the edge of the pentagram. "And I bind and abjure you not to breathe a word of gossip about our dealings when you return to whatever stench-pit you've been haunting back home. I have ways of punishing the recalcitrant, I assure you."

The imp sighed. "Yes, yes. You all do. And you never let us forget it, either. Let me think for a moment and summon my powers of Knowledge Hidden before I answer your question."

The imp buried its face in its hands as Rowan tapped his boot impatiently on the marble. Soon the creature popped up with a fetid-fanged grin and a snap of its rancid fingers.

"Why, yes, there *is* a book giving a rather lurid and detailed account of the very dealings you describe," it croaked.

"Is the book here, in my Aunt's collection?"

"May I show you?"

"By all means, but you are not allowed to step out of the pentagram."

"I couldn't even if I wanted to. Besides, there's no need." The imp reached with one of its talons, smudged with the rotting, gory flesh of who-knew-what manner of Within-World victim, and one of the massive leather-bound volumes on the shelves disengaged itself and floated down gently into Rowan's waiting hands. He read the Latin title, embossed in gold leaf before him.

"Myths and Legends of Provincial Mesopotamia and Fifteen Excellent Yet Little Known Hostels for Pilgrims on the Way to Jerusalem. I suppose this fits the category. I asked for obscure and that is what I got."

"Precisely," said the irritable demon, folding its spindly arms and sucking at a bit of Eldritch Eel gristle caught between its fangs. "It's a Latin translation from a Greek original, which itself was based upon a hodgepodge of fragments compiled in any number of dreary mortal languages."

"And you're certain the pertinent information I seek is within this volume?" said Rowan threateningly. "I don't want to have to track you down and summon you again."

"Believe me, that's the last thing I would want in any world," said the GnostiKimp. "You'll find the story you seek, or as much of it as has ever been written down, within that book. On page one hundred twenty-two, as a matter of fact. Now, may I be banished or what, O mighty Blaize?"

"With my thanks," responded Rowan. "And I appreciate your prompt and precise, if not very courteous, service. And you may feel quite free to brag to all of your friends in the Netherlands that you are *far* more effective than Google."

"Which devil is *that?*"

"Never-mind," said Rowan, and he waved a hand. "Just be gone."

❧❧

XVII

Belinda Bluebell Redondo, as she was known to friends, loved ones, a blind tabby cat called "Num Nums," and even to strangers who read her rhinestone-bedazzled nametag, had had about enough for the evening. She looked up from the Pint-Sized Princess pageant registration table with all the condescending moral superiority and simmering disapproval that little girl beauty pageant registration tables have been conferring upon obese, unfulfilled, and slightly xenophobic spinsters since the Dark Ages.

She adjusted her muumuu and lowered her false eyelashes, which looked like so many tarantula legs springing out of her face. Then she transformed her pancake-sized (and pancake-fuelled) jowls into great, flabby mechanisms, turning the bright pink banana-slug lips downward in disdain, creating a sort of "Doom Crevasse" on either side of her mouth—one fold of which was currently hiding the remnants of a substantial Krispy Kreme donut-crumb she had failed to snag in her usual manner. This technique involved an almost acrobatic probative maneuver of her great purple tongue, which itself possessed the size and debris-eliminating capabilities of a grade school chalkboard eraser.

Sometimes, when Belinda forgot to take her Xanax, for example, she was beset by the urge to send her impressive slab of tongue on all sorts of facial expeditions. She often felt compelled to do it in front of harried registrants, searching for an uneaten morsel of breakfast, a smidge of coffee-break residue, a tasty gob of smeared make-up, or all of the above. Her oral organ accomplished this with the precision of an exploratory device scouring and sifting the surface of some distant rust-colored planet. The sight of Belinda's impulsive tongue at work had been known to scare some of the more sensitive pageant moppets and induce dry-heaves in some of the more hung-over pageant parents during the registration process.

Belinda had thus been warned by the skinnier, bigger-haired women who occupied the FCP Oversight Committee—*Oh, how she envied those goddesses!*—to subdue her wayward tongue or face demotion to a concession stand, but her mood-altering substances were working at full-tilt today. She had taken two tablets, which was a good thing, since this was the Night of All Nights, and all contestants had now been registered and ushered into the dressing-cubicles behind the auditorium ... all except for the pair of winners who were straggling in the door as she prepared to shut down her table, alone in the little registration room. She looked at her Hello Kitty wristwatch. They were in time. Barely. *Drat.*

"Name, please," she drawled, scrutinizing this last-minute entrant and its Accompanying Adult. This one was with her father, presumably—a man who, despite a smile that could shame dust from the surface of a plate-glass window, looked as if he had been in one bruise-fest of a bar-fight the night before. He was leaning on a crutch.

Belinda Bluebell merely noted this; she was not surprised by it, for she had seen countless parents of both sexes appear in similar conditions throughout her career in the girl pageant racket. The parents of little girl beauty contestants were always being beaten-up for one reason or another, it seemed, or else beating each other up. Most of the time they merely reeked of alcohol saturation, but the *vibrissae* in Belinda's bloodhound-caliber olfactory cavity could detect no scent of the Demon Liquor.

This parent was simply beat up.

The child was immaculate. Even the most black-eyed, slurring, hepatitic, flopsweat-drenched pageant-parents usually managed to get *that* part right. It was the whole point, after all.

"Name, *please,*" repeated Belinda Bluebell, more forcefully. She was a woman who considered the need to repeat herself to anyone a catastrophic wrinkle in the very fabric of the time space continuum itself.

"Um, yes ... well, um ... Hello there, and mighty nice to see you, Ms. Bluebell Redondo."

"That's *Miss* Bluebell Redondo." The flapjack jowls flapped with menace.

"Right. Right. Miss Redondo. I don't suppose you remember us, what with all the little ones you see coming past your desk from here to Miami and back again, and sorry we were almost late, but I sure do remember you, and——"

"Tell this woman what she wants to know, you incorrigible piece of suffocating and pungent human fecal expulsion," said the pint-sized hopeful.

Belinda Bluebell Redondo raised an erratically penciled-in brow. She had to hand it to the child in the fabulous white wedding cake ball-gown. It was a good line, but it wasn't even close to the best she had heard earlier in the evening's registration process. Pageant day nerves always brought out the sass in teeny-tiny beauty queens.

"Heh heh! Yes, well, this here is my precious little daughter Bon-Sashay Rummy and I am her father, Chesterfield. Also Rummy. Heh heh? As I said, you may remember us from the Fabulous Li'l Filly Folly pageant down in Titusville, where BonSashay came in second and just about took the——"

"No time to hear about that. What song will you be performing in the musical portion of the competition?" said Belinda, who had never liked the stopover in Titusville, or in St. Augustine. She was moving her newly manicured and starburst-glittered hands like two bloated arachnids collaborating on a great multi-tasked web: preparing to write names on tags; fill out security passes to be stuffed into laminated badge casings; record entry information; and document the overall glory.

"I shall be performing an original selection of my own composition," sneered Djin Rummy, her arms crossed and both freshly tap-shoed feet tapping an ominous beat. The missing leg, of course, had been re-generated. The djin had been forced to eat a Jehovah's Witness—and child—that had fortunately knocked upon Chesterfield's door at 8AM that morning, in order to restore full power. It had not been a particularly satisfying meal ("How extraordinary. In thousands of years I have never consumed humans who tasted *that* stupid!"), but it had been enough to start the tedious day of practicing basic pageant etiquette, the kind of etiquette that would at least get the djin on the stage to unfurl its Great Scheme without arousing suspicion. Even Chesterfield had been magically gifted with a new suit to distract from his general busted-up "look." Now, everything had to go according to the sundial.

"What is the title of this original composition?" said Belinda, dispassionately blowing acrid breath from betwixt the banana slug lips.

"Title? Title? What need have I of a title for the inestimable greatness about to be unleashed upon the entire viewing planet by my unparalleled genius?"

"You need a title so that the emcee can announce your song to the audience in the auditorium and to the judges," gurgled Belinda. "You two are almost late as it is. I was getting ready to close the sign-in table down for the night. It's a great thing y'all filled out the pre-registration form months ago, or I would have to prevent you from taking the stage in this pageant altogether. Oh, Gosh, *why* did they opt to use the rear-entrance of this auditorium for the sign-ins?" lamented Belinda to the table and to her stack of papers. "I knew people would be dragging themselves in at the last minute on account of they'd get confused. I mean, the first part of the competition has already started."

Through the thick concrete walls filtered the faint sound of auditorium applause and then the first strains of some sequined little angel butchering the opening bars of "Somewhere Over the Rainbow" while accompanied by her destitute father on an out-of-tune ukulele.

Djin Rummy leaned forward across the registration desk, baby blue eyes suddenly afire.

"And just how do you think you would 'prevent' me from taking the stage in that festering foxhole of an amphitheater, my large and lethargic lady?"

"It is an auditorium, Miss Rummy, not an amphitheater," said Belinda Bluebell Redondo amid the quiver of several chins. She looked beyond the impeccably appointed Pint-Sized Pain staring her in the face to address the slowly retreating, profusely sweating Chesterfield Rummy. She pointed her registrar's pen at him threateningly.

"Sir, you need to get your contestant under control. I will not be disrespected, and I think it is very important to remind you that, although I was only recently promoted from name-tags to complete table-registration and sign-in, I was endowed with the full powers of disqualification, powers which can and will be used at my discretion. Now, if your daughter wants to gain last-minute access to the dressing rooms so she can go on as scheduled like the other girls, I need to know the name of the song she is planning to sing so that I may inform this evening's host and so her selection may be included in the pageant's digital set-list. That way the judges can follow along. I also need a lyric sheet and the name of her accompanist or the official licensing permission of a karaoke backing track, if applicable.

"This is all part of established pageant protocol, Mr. Rummy, and I don't think you want to be trying my patience right now. Your daughter's potential stardom could hang in the balance, and thirty-one other little divas have already come through that back door tonight to work my last nerve until I could just about yank the hair right out of my own head. Now, please let me know which song Miss Rummy is fixing to perform this evening so we can all enjoy the warm and dynamic old-fashioned American values that little girl beauty pageants represent to patriotic citizens across this blessed nation!"

"You want to know the song I am planning to perform?" shrieked Djin Rummy, splaying gloved fingers at the ceiling in a mounting paroxysm of fury. Miss Bluebell Redondo's registration table began to shake and clatter of its own accord. "You want to know the *song?*"

"Oh, no. It's gonna get bad right off the bat, ain't it?" moaned Chesterfield Rummy, skulking backwards toward the entrance of the registration room. Though he was still missing a foot, he was going to make a run for it. Forget about gold and world domination. Hell could not be much worse than what he had already experienced. Yes, he was going to make a run for it as soon as it was possible. He was prepared to jump in the gator-filled swamp near the parking lot and hide, if it came to it.

"SHE WANTS TO KNOW THE SONG!"

"Yes!" shouted Belinda Bluebell. "I've made that clear since you people practically came in the door!"

"Then I shall *perform* it for you!" hissed the wild-eyed BonSashay like some miniature, and in her case truly demonic, Norma Desmond.

Belinda shook her canned ham of a head. "I don't want to hear it performed here at my registration table. That is not part of my job description. I only want the ... what in hell's bells are *doing*, child?"

The "child" had levitated up to stand atop the hallowed registration table, two plumes of sulfurous green smoke billowing out of her ears and weaving through the copious mounds of piled, cotton-candy blonde hair.

"Is this a magic act or a song-and-dance?" Belinda peered around her to ask the crouching, quailing Chesterfield near the door. "Your pre-registration clearly stated song-and-dance, and it is way too late now to switch to a magic act the night of the competition. The judges will go out of their minds! The confusion will be unprecedented. Y'all can't just waltz in and flaunt years of established pageant procedure just to suit yourselves. I'm afraid I am going to have to disqualify you both," said Belinda with a dismissive shake of her chins.

This was it. She had seen enough tantrums over the years, along with everything from bleeding scalps due to hair-pulling fights, to nervous collapses and hysterics that degenerated into complete loss of Pint-Sized Princess bladder control. But levitating contestants? That was too much, especially if the levitator was a Grade A *weisenheimer*. She reached for her phone to call security ... and promptly dropped it clattering to the floor.

Djin Rummy had reached over and pried open Belinda's considerable mouth with one gloved hand on a porcine nose and the other grasping the second chin. Reaching inside, the djin took hold of the great, purple, lolling Belinda-tongue and slowly began to yank it as far as it would go from her mouth without ripping it off.

"You want to see a magic act? I'll *show* you a magic act."

The tongue grew longer and longer and longer.

"Unggghhh … ungghhh …" said Belinda Bluebell Redondo, her comparatively stumpy little arms and legs pumping helplessly, as if they were auxiliary vessels trying to escape the behemoth mother-ship of her extraordinary torso.

Beyond the registration room, other, nicer Pint-Sized Princesses primped and preened before mirrors or waited in the wings for their chance to take the stage and bask in the all-encompassing, id-affirming spotlight. Their precipitously large egos shivered for the chance to bask in rapturous applause emanating from an audience of the very same neurotics they would one day grow up to be, when beauty pageant days were over and were no more than a brain-warping memory they could share, or were an activity they could perhaps force upon children of their own.

"Unggghhh … ungghhh …" said Belinda Bluebell Redondo.

Throughout universe after universe, cycles of time spun this way and that, forward and backward, never and forever, but in the registration room of the Ancient City's Sandpiper Auditorium and Shuffleboard Coliseum, no one could hear Belinda scream—partly because she couldn't, and partly because the orchestra inside was currently staggering through "The Good Ship Lollipop" for a raven-haired, tin-eared contestant from Hialeah who would countenance no competition whatsoever from the outer world.

Belinda's tongue was now stretching, bloated, twelve feet out of her mouth. Djin "BonSashay" Rummy was dragging it across the floor and putting all of her magic and tap-shoe sliding power into the effort.

"Listen to me carefully, woman. Not in a million years could your pig-like brain comprehend the sheer scope of what I am about to achieve on that stage tonight. Therefore I will render you the final grace of proffering only a few, incidental details, not to mention a little background regarding my present endeavor. You see, I have been forced to endure the most appalling examples of mortal and immortal incompetence in the very short time that I have been restored to this ever-repulsive plane of existence, starting with that piece of freshly squeezed and steaming camel dung over there, near the door, preparing to make a run for it, which will be unsuccessful, and now I find myself faced with the most repellent example of gluttonous womanhood I have beheld since the days of the Cannibal Concubines of Collossae. That present example would be *you,* Belinda.

"Do not worry about the fact that you cannot begin to comprehend the bulk of the meaning behind the words I speak, and speaking of bulk, you yourself will not be alive long enough to regret the misfortune of your inculpably *human* stupidity and ignorance. Rejoice and be glad that you have led a life quite obviously free of even the remotest hint of a hunger pang. Others of your race are not so fortunate. Consider what I do for you as a favor, for you shall die more swiftly and with less pain when I destroy you than you will if I were to let your impertinence go unpunished and allow you to choke, partially, on that pickled pig's foot you would otherwise gnaw upon three years from now—looking into your alternative future, here, Belinda—only to be rendered as immobile as a common eggplant, but with part of your mind still quite intact enough to realize and rue your insatiable lifetime urge to snack.

"Yes, Belinda, consider this a favor, and, when I am through with you, I am going to make my way properly into that theater and reveal my true self to the world via the magical mortal picture boxes I have seen and heard so very much about. I shall do so through the most magnificent display of carnage the human world has ever been able to see, at least collectively speaking, and I shall do it with flair, Belinda. I shall accomplish it with an element of surprise. Do you know why? I'll tell you why. Because mortals love nothing better than *surprise,* and I aim to satisfy. Out I shall prance, just as 'Daddy' and I have rehearsed all day, perform an oration and a few minor tricks, bow to the adoring crowd, and then, dear Belinda, I shall rip off this tawdry little girly-skin and display all of my ancient glory as a djin of the Sixth Circle of Elite Ifrit. Thereafter I shall proceed to feast upon members of that terror-stricken audience as if they were nothing more than pieces in that triple-tiered box of crème-filled sweets currently languishing next to your pillow in that sty you call an 'apartment,' Belinda.

"I shall do all of this, my dear, because I have been trapped in a miserable ring for over one thousand five hundred-fifty years and I am

HUNGRY, Belinda. I am very, very, very, very hungry. I firmly believe that my unhappiness with humans and my famished state merits a public display the likes of which will never be seen again. It will soothe my troubled spirit and, as an added benefit, the whole world shall be entertained, for I have learned from the estimable Chesterfield Rummy that mortals have not changed in the least over the course of the centuries, as far as their greedy desire to be amused even by scenes of their own destruction. Now, pardon, me, Belinda, as I start with this twenty-foot portion of your well-seasoned tongue and then work my way quickly to those delectable chins layered below your face like grand globs of goblin pudding. This will be swift, as promised, for I can keep the glory of the prize in mind. I have a pageant to 'win' and an entire world—an entire *world,* Belinda—ready and waiting me to watch me do it."

"Well, I dunno. You might get yourself a fair slice of the viewership out of Orlando, but you sure ain't gonna have the whole *world* tuned-in, there, Dedwen. Heh! Funny old thing—turns out this little girl pageant ain't such a big deal, after all. This gig in St. Augustine is only being taped for a two-bit airtime on some lousy cable access channel next week!"

Djin Rummy dropped the mammoth slab of tongue with a gelatinous, wet sound upon the floor. The cross-eyed Belinda's head smacked the registration table and spun her brain toward blessed unconsciousness as the djin spun toward the cheerful voice that had spoken from the rear-entrance door. There, smiling and jolly in her finest turban (brand new ostrich feather in place) stood Gert Gokey, and, at her left, the perpetually disapproving flagpole figure of Letty Beauregard. On her right stood the willowy, trembling-with-sea-turtle-saving-passion Serenity Turnbull's frame.

"Not *you* old magpies?" laughed the djinn. "One hoped that my wave might have washed you out of sight for posterity, but I suppose that two witches as dull-witted and dried-up as you could absorb and conquer entire oceans of water! How foolish to come and face me here, as I stand on the brink of my greatest triumph since the Great Barbarian Barbecue of Blachernae in 232!"

"My, my, did you hear that, Gert?" Letty shook her grim, gray-braided head and narrowed her beady eyes at the seething impostor. "Us two are just a couple of dried out old has-beens who ain't worth the broomsticks we rode in on. Guess we shoulda stayed home and hid under the covers, eh?"

"Or tended to our knitting, like old biddies ought to do," added Gert, smiling wider than ever, but now there was a fury underlying her good-natured expression that few who had been on its receiving end had ever survived to pass remark.

"Oh, good God Almighty!" cried the cringing and ruined tangle of arms and legs that was Chesterfield Rummy, curled in a corner near a potted plastic plant. "Do you think you voodoo women can save me from this no-good babygirl-eating nightmare of a noonday devil?"

"Silence, you ungrateful dog!" spat Djin Rummy, sending a seething jet of fire toward Chesterfield, a jet that frazzled the second toupee he'd dug out of an old drawer right off his scalp with a bloodcurdling squeal. The djin turned back to the witches.

"And what sad adjunct have you worn out wonderworkers brought along as reinforcement, I presume?"

Serenity had borrowed a smart new blazer and some jeans from Miranda and had pulled her pretty blonde haystack hair back into a po-nytail. Djin Rummy's gleeful disregard for the interlopers segued into an overshadowing thundercloud of concern when Serenity was finally recognized.

"YOU? How is this thing possible? I left you imprisoned in that blasted ring!"

The djin felt frantically but in vain amid the folds and little pockets of the pageant ball gown, and then roared in remembrance of the confrontation at the Castillo and the original dress that had been shred-ded by the cannon's blow.

"Where is that accursed ring, you flimsy old—"

"Looking for *this,* Dedwen the Dreary?"

Rowan Blaize, still in his flying gear, walked out from behind the witches in the doorway as if he had appeared out of thin air ... which had, in fact, been the case. In his fingers he brandished the ruby ring of Marutha. Serenity, however, could contain herself no longer.

"You monster!" she spat, shaking from head to toe with conviction. "You are a very, very grave danger to decent society and must be taught a serious lesson. Putting innocent witches in suffocating places. Eating little girls, even if they *are* brats. Turning drugged housewives into giant grubs. Interrupting parties to which you are not invited and causing a ruckus. And look what you did to that woman's tongue!" Serenity shook a finger at the djin with all the reproach she could manage. "You are in for a very, very rude awakening."

Djin Rummy threw its head back and laughed. With a little kick of a tap-shoe beneath preciously upheld skirts, the fiend kicked Belinda's terrifyingly stretched tongue with such force that it swung back over the registration table and knocked the swooning woman head over heels onto the floor as well.

"You'll injure not another being in this world, Dedwen, mortal or magical," said Rowan, stepping forward. He playfully swung the great ruby ring on the end of his middle finger.

"You were supposed to be injured," hissed the djin, leering with rage at the warlock. "Injured and *dead!* It only goes to show that one cannot trust mortal morons as reliable servants." The softly weeping Chesterfield Rummy was the recipient of a marrow-melting glare. "I should have stuck my own hand in to test your pathetic heartbeat myself!"

"But you didn't," said Rowan, walking another few steps around and forward to stand directly in front of the three witches, who spread out threateningly to flank him on either side. "That was just one of your many foolish mistakes. But then again, the djinn are so prone to bumbling. I think it has always been part of their nature."

"How dare you besmirch the noble race of the Djinn?" hissed Djin Rummy, flexing little fingers in opera gloves. "You can't possibly think you can still stop me? Not after you saw what happened at that insufferable party! It strains credulity, to say the least. The first mouse-of-a-witch I brushed away like a mosquito. The two old ones I cooled with a dash of seawater, and you—whelp warlock!—were brought down by a little girl's hair!" A shining ringlet was twirled in mockery. "What makes you think I won't eradicate you all where you stand right now?"

Rowan paused in thought, half frowning, as if to ponder this very question. Then he shrugged.

"Greater powers than I have been brought down or held at bay by things even more mundane," he admitted. "When the magic is properly employed, or when one employs the proper magic, of course, amazing things can be achieved. Take … why, take a bit of compressed rock, for example." He held the ring aloft. "Really, it is just a colorful composite of pressurized bits dredged up out of the earth, dust from the first Great Cataclysm, in fact. Even less than hair, if you think about it. Less evolved. More static. And yet, it can be used to permanently imprison a being as awful and as terrible as you, Dedwen."

"Ha! I guessed already that it was the weakling witch who told you my name. I ought to incinerate her where she stands and don't know why I didn't do so when I first met her."

"Oh, she could only tell me so much about you from firsthand experience," replied Rowan, wary as a cat. "But she didn't need to provide a lot of information. As I mentioned, like most djinn you are sloppy and forgetful. Easily distracted by your own greed and arrogance."

"Kinda like mortal folks with them attention deficit disorders they all got nowadays," added Gert.

"Hush!" snapped Letty.

"No, she's correct, Leticia. Djinn can be very much like that, though far, far more ignoble than mortals could ever be."

"How dare you blaspheme, magician?" seethed Dedwen. "Comparing my splendid race, my elite order, with filth like the blob of nothing that languishes with her tongue around her neck on the floor, yonder?"

Belinda, for her part, appeared to be snoring happily. This only infuriated the djin.

"Mark my words—I will carve out your own tongue before this is through and then I will leave your skin flayed and tanned to use as leather for my codpiece!"

Now it was Rowan's turn to laugh. "You'll do no such thing, for you will be going back into the ring, Dedwen. Never to escape again."

"You do not have the power to command me at all, much less into that wretched prison!"

Then, in a blinding burst of radiance, the djin threw off the form and illusion of BonSashay Rummy and rose up before them, scaled and stinking, dripping with venom, the great chest heaving and tinkling with the hundreds of piercings. Dedwen's mighty forearms flexed and the triple claws clenched and unclenched in time with the opening and closing of the hideous mandibles. Gert and Letty, as strong-willed as they were, had to summon all of their wits to maintain facades of total composure. Serenity, who had seen this manifestation before, gritted her teeth and began, again, to think of spells she had never dared to ponder in all of her own, long years.

"Tremble before my magnificence, puny enchanters!" Dedwen roared as the orchestra in the auditorium beyond reached one of its own crescendos and a little painted girl caterwauled as if in agony to win the evening's coveted prize.

"That ring cannot trouble the likes of me anymore!" hollered the great demon. "You have all gravely miscalculated."

"It is you who have miscalculated, O djin," said Rowan, "for you were not only incompetent enough to leave the ring behind for our perusal, but you left behind far too many clues and failed, above all else, to retrieve the Babel Disc in Serenity's house after your encounter. You attention deficit is indeed your undoing."

The djin took a heaving step forward but the three witches put their arms up in unison and all of their power joined to create a force field that might hold him back for a moment longer, so that Rowan could speak.

"You worthless wenches!" barked Dedwen, struggling as if in air as thick as tar. "Those spells can't stop me for long. Do you not realize your doom?"

"They do not need to stop you for long, ifrit. And you should have paid more thought to your own doom."

"A Babel Disc?" spat the enemy, venom striking the walls and burning through. "So you saw the inscription through it. That means nothing. The words on the band of gold were only useful to free one who is imprisoned *already* within the stone."

"Quite correct," admitted Rowan. "But I have another incantation, one I very much doubt you ever expected to hear, even the first time you heard it, much less did you expect a 'whelp-of-a-warlock' to discover this incantation in the mere few days in which you have enjoyed a spree away from your rightful prison."

"What are you talking about, fool sorcerer?"

"Blaize, make it quick," whispered Letty. "We're doing our best, but we can't hold this one till they crown the next princess in that danged auditorium!"

"I am talking about research, you idiotic genie," said Rowan. "Mortals have gotten rather adept at it since you last bullied the world. Almost magically adept, in fact. And sorcerers have always been rather good in that regard. Due to some help both mortal and magical, I had an opportunity to peer, in a timely fashion, into your unique history with Marutha, Bishop of Maipherkat. I learned a number of valuable things."

"You lie!"

"For example, I learned that Marutha was quite entrenched and respected in the court of King Yazdgard and, though he clashed with the King's circle of royal sorcerers, there was one occasion in which the old bishop and a magician were to find themselves allies."

"NO!" roared the djin. The witches held him back as he fought. They were shuddering with effort. Rowan, however, kept his calm.

"The members of Marutha's flock in Maipherkat had captured a warlock in the nearby town of Kapur—a warlock who had lost his powers due to the treacherous spell of a rival. That warlock's name was Arabandal. The Christians of Maipherkat imprisoned him and were ready to boil him alive in oil when the old bishop, a kind and gentle soul, heard his plea for mercy and, refusing to judge a creature he did not know or entirely understand, Marutha took pity on Arabandal and commanded his flock to set him free on pain of excommunication. It was a dangerous and daring move for a churchman in his day, but Marutha stood his ground and his flock obeyed. The bishop, meanwhile, with great powers of diplomacy and compassion, waxed in favor in the court of King Yazdgard. Some years later, however, Marutha's flock was faced with an even greater problem than poor Arabandal."

"Hurry up, Rowan! Seriously!" squawked Letty. All three witches were sweating as if they had been drenched in another wave. Rowan paid no heed.

"One of Marutha's deacons had coveted a fabled treasure said to be hidden in the Zagros Mountains. He desired this treasure so fully and so overwhelmingly that the deacon was willing to attempt dark magic to conjure a simple crossroads djin and strike some sort of bargain. But the stupid mortal's attempt at magic backfired and he conjured far more than a mere crossroads djin. *You* were that djin he mistakenly conjured, Dedwen Great and Terrible. In exchange for revealing the location of the treasure, you demanded the deacon's firstborn daughter as future slave and wife—you who dare to disparage mortals and yet you have lusted after them! In his greed and vile passion, the deacon struck this bargain with a djin, for the djinn always love to bargain.

"The lost treasure of the Zagros Mountains brought the man no true satisfaction, as the 'gift' of undeserved wealth rarely does in the mortal realm. Yet, as you were coming one day to claim your prize, after the birth of his first daughter, the deacon repented of his bargain and feared for the fate of his child. In his despair, he turned to the kindly Marutha, his bishop, confessing his greed. Marutha, in turn, threw himself at the mercy of Yazdgard's wisdom, for he knew not how to thwart the freely struck bargain made between man and demon. The King could not help old Marutha, and the royal sorcerers, who had always despised the favored Christian bishop, turned their backs upon him in scorn. That is ... all but *one,* Dedwen. All but one.

"In the court of King Yazdgard there lived a warlock named Taltos, and it so happened that this warlock remembered well the inordinate and unusual mercy that Marutha had shown years before to the magician Arabandal, who had been captured by the Christians. He remembered, for Arabandal had indeed been the cousin of Taltos! Thus it was that Taltos took Marutha aside under cover of the night, when his fellow sorcerers did not perceive it, and he deigned to help Marutha and his beleaguered deacon's daughter. He gave unto the bishop a most powerful talisman, Dedwen, as payment for Marutha's act of compassion to Arabandal. That talisman was this ring, as you know!"

Rowan held high the glowing ruby.

"And as you know, Dedwen, this ring was fashioned by none other than Solomon himself, who alone of all beings in this heaven and on this earth, was given dominion over the race of the djinn—the good and the evil."

"How?" cried Dedwen. "How did you know this?" The witches' powers were fading, and the terrible djin was nearly able to break from their combined charm. Rowan held the ring up to the awful, slavering maw.

"How? Because the story was *written down,* Dedwen, as was Solomon's incantation itself, and many stories that are written down continue to live, even in secret, and most often in secret. This was one of those secret stories. Until now. You ask me how? I tell you it is because I once had an Aunt who loved to collect old books. Lots of them. That, great Dedwen, is *too bad for you.*"

Just as it was about to spring free, just as the witches had not a shred of strength left to hold back their foe, Rowan advanced upon the trembling, fighting *ifrit,* holding the enormous ruby ring high and speaking the ancient words of Solomon himself.

లు

XVIII

It was going to be a fairly lovely November day, just as it was, but magic made it splendid.

The previously hazy and cool Autumn morning, ten miles out on the Atlantic, due east of the Castillo de San Marcos, had been transformed ... partly by collective relief, but mostly by one of Letty Beauregard's more endearing, if seldom utilized, incantations:

> *"Solar disc, thou friend obscured*
> *by cloud that I have long endured,*
> *pass through these mists and come to me,*
> *to cast thy grace upon the sea ...*

"I only ever use that one in winter, when it's been a particularly rough week at the pepper shop, what with Gert and the looky-loos and all, and I want to sort of perk myself up a bit with a walk along the bay ... and the elements aren't able to cooperate of their *own* accord."

Letty was careful to add the last part, as if there should be any question whatsoever of her use of spells for frivolous personal purposes.

"You all probably think that's a bit selfish of me, to do that. Don't you?"

"Not at all, Letty," said Rowan. "Even our kind feels more alive when the day is pristine and particularly luminous."

"I think it's just a lovely little spell to use," Serenity Turnbull concurred. "I'm going to try it myself, sometime, if you don't mind, Letty. Why, have a look at how the sunlight is sparkling like little floating diamonds of all shapes and sizes and colors across the waves. I use a different sort of sunshine spell when I'm feeling a bit blue, but you should never apologize for employing it often. That's why we are who we are, after all."

Gert braced herself for a biting reply from Letty, who did indeed think for a moment about rendering a swift qualification of her intentions to the perpetually giddy Miss Turnbull, but no wisecrack, and no condescending correction was forthcoming. A tacit understanding had been reached. A bridge has been crossed without the need for fire. Friendships, however tentative and hesitant, had been forged.

"I'm glad to know you take the time to ... er ... enjoy a little sunbeam in your day, Serenity Turnbull."

It was clearly difficult to say, and it looked as if the words had to be pried from her brain, what with the rigid facial contortions, but Letty said it. She had said it and everyone breathed their own little sigh of contentment. The miraculously enhanced warmth of the gentle, approving sun bathed them all in a glow that approached something akin to unity, and that felt good simply because it was true.

Five of them were sitting on the deck of a deep-sea fishing boat, comfortable in chairs and gazing with no concerns in the world over the darkly brooding turquoise of the constant and self-satisfied sea. It was the sea that rarely, if ever, gave up any of its secrets in any part of the world, even in St. Augustine.

Rowan, Letty, Gert, Serenity, and Miranda were on deck chairs, sipping wormwood martinis prepared in the galley by Gert, while Bror, fully healed and drooling, as awkwardly loyal as ever, peered over the sides of the craft to catch glimpses of the manta rays that had been attracted to the overwhelming magical emanations of the boat, all gliding in an impromptu ballet around the spot where they had anchored. The boat itself, The Old Digby, had been courteously provided by the vampire, Dr. Bulkagov, and his wife, in thanks for all of their efforts to save St. Augustine, and ostensibly the world, from meddling djin-spirits.

The devastated magical community, from ghost to goblin, was still buzzing with a mood of good riddance about that matter and, despite regrets about the way the Halloween party had turned out, most vowed privately that they would be more than a little pleased to be invited back again next year, if Rowan was still going to host such a swanky affair. Rowan, for his part, was not at all certain. Would he still be in St. Augustine three months hence, to say nothing of a year from now?

He could perhaps ask Gert to find another scrying pan and give him a preview, but he had never been that sort of a warlock, not in any of the several worlds he had traipsed through to date. The unknown was still a deliciously intriguing thing, at least for him. Besides, watching Bror and watching Miranda laugh at Bror's maritime curiosity told him that those two, at least, may indeed have found a permanent home. Beyond that, he could not—or would not—deign to forecast. One thing was certain: he could get used to a life of idling about on a boat with a plentiful supply of wormwood martinis at hand. Despite his natural revulsion, he had felt obliged to accept the kindness of Dr. Bulkagov and his spouse, though Sisyphus only knew what those two *did* out on a fishing boat in deep sea in the dark of night. Rowan had never known a vampire to own a boat, but this was St. Augustine, after all. The lure of the waves could apparently work on just about anyone, in this town.

Now, Serenity was gently humming a little tune that he knew was boring a laser-like hole through Letty Beauregard's skull, but the old witch was sipping her own martini and enjoying the scenery with her feet propped on the prow. He was proud of everyone's cooperation and reserve, in this instance. It had been important for all of them to get together and "process" the series of events, as all sentient and contemporary beings ought to do ... even centuries-old enchanters and their foundlings.

"Quite crucial and fortuitous, really, that Gert knew exactly where to go when it came time to catch the Rummys at the Pint-Sized Princess registration table, down at the auditorium," said Rowan, watching a few pelicans sail across the soft pink of the afternoon horizon. "Of course, following them in secret didn't hurt much either."

"Oh, Gert doesn't miss much when it comes to knowing all the ins and outs of them disgusting little girl pageants," muttered Letty, watching, and perhaps envying, the same formation of birds. "But in this case we'll have to give her due credit for her vast reserves of tacky knowledge. A lot of lives was saved by catching them when we did. Including that poor soul at the registration desk. Belinda Ballbearing or whatever. Doesn't remember a thing, good for her."

"Right you are," said Gert, tipping her glass. "Even so, my eyes are a bit more open to the nonsense of it all. I tell you, this whole business may have just put me completely off Pint-Sized Princesses for good. I suppose I'll have to find a new distraction. A few more of those mortal reality shows, maybe. Them bickering Persian sisters out in Hollywood might be of some interest, do you think?"

"NO," said everyone else on the boat. Even Bror woofed his disapproval.

"Well, I already have my favorites and won't have time to fiddle with any entertainment luxuries," said Gert. "The shop is being rebuilt starting next week and Letty and I have to be overseeing that whole to-do."

"And I've got to explain to the board at Flagler College why I was missing for a few days without notice," sighed Serenity. "They're not best pleased. Mortals are all about the bottom line these days. Compassion is hard to come by. I might have to put a little see-things-my-way sort of spell on them if I want to keep my job."

This was something of which Letty approved wholeheartedly. "Now that is a classic witchcrafty approach to the matter," she said encouragingly. "It ain't your fault, entirely, that you was imprisoned in a ruby ring by a genie and I daresay 'the board' would never buy it if you tried to tell them, especially since you don't like to flat-out lie. Trust me—a little harmless manipulation never hurt mortals one bit, when used in moderation and for rational reasons. You just have to draw your boundaries, Serenity Turnbull, and keep right inside them. Mark my words, and, if you should ever need any advice, feel free to ask me. We are all here for you as guiding forces from now on."

"That's right, we are at your service," piped Gert. The ostrich feather in her turban was whipping wildly in a sudden tailwind as the boat spun lazily around. She reached down to fish about in the ice cooler for the shaker full of back-up wormwood martinis.

"Thanks ever so much, to both of you," said Serenity.

Rowan figured she half meant it, at least, and "half" was practically a job well-done when it comes to longstanding disagreements between sorceresses.

"What about Chesterfield Rummy?" he said, not wanting to darken their radiant excursion, but the question had to be asked.

"Straight to the Maclenny State Hospital in a padded room with prolly them shock treatments on the way," answered Gert promptly. She had, in fact, made all the arrangements herself. "And don't go feeling sorry for him on any count or thinking it's all impolitically correct, or whatever. This mess was just as much a result of his dirty disposition as it was that obnoxious djin. I mean, his own daughter, after all. Really provides a contrast to that whole ancient fracas with Marutha of Maipherkat and the deacon's daughter, don't it?"

Rowan shrugged. Everything was capable of providing a contrast, to him. Worlds rose and fell upon contrasts. He had seen it with his own eyes, time and again.

"And what about his poor wife, who last we knew was toppling palm trees at their roots while gnawing thirty feet below the earth?"

"That's been handled, too," said Letty. "I set the werewolves onto it. The remaining three, anyhow. You know how they like to dig incessantly. They found her last night, all the way over by South Street, about to gobble-up some poor old man's prize rose bushes, from the bottom up, of course. There wasn't much they could do ... the djin is still, well, *technically* alive, so the spell is still on her, and I got a look at her and I don't know that she dislikes her giant grub existence much more than she disliked her previous one, from what Serenity tells. Apparently she ain't a danger to anyone but herself and plants, and feet, I guess, so the boys have loaded her up and they're taking her down to the Everglades to drop her in the swamp. See how she fares against the gators and wild boar and all them boa constrictors they have there now, but I expect she'll more than hold her own. Survival of the fittest, after all."

"Just keep an eye on her, somehow," said Rowan with a sigh.

"The same way you've been always keeping an eye out for Circe?" ventured Gert, who was already onto her fourth wormwood martini and felt bold enough to inquire.

"Not really the same thing at all, Gert. In the case of Mrs. Rummy the twenty-foot grub, I'm more worried about the environmental damage she could wreak, but she can't breed—I hope—and the Everglades will be more than a sizeable containment facility. It's not like we can just drop her off at a zoo where they'll put her in a great big terrarium. As for Circe, perhaps this latest dilemma has opened my own eyes, just a bit. I suppose I've been too paranoid, too ready to jump to conclusions. Do I believe Circe is out there, in some condition, plotting some sort of retaliation against me? Yes. Am I going to spend the next nine or ten centuries constantly looking over my shoulder? Maybe ... and maybe not. It all depends. For now, for this moment, I choose to feel a bit freer than usual. Does that suit everyone?"

"It suits me and I think it's a great moment," said Miranda, who was enjoying a ginger ale in lieu of the deadly-to-mortals wormwood drinks and stroking Bror's sundrenched fur as he took his place faithfully near her chair, tired of the manta ray dances. "And I don't want you to worry anymore, because you are just as talented and just as capable as Circe will ever be. If she has any sense as a sorceress whatsoever—*wherever* she might be—she will be more worried about you coming after her. Whatever happens, or doesn't happen, you know Bror and I are on your side. We all have to drop some aspect of our past lives when it isn't contributing to our happiness in the present. Mortal, immortal, and everyone in between."

Rowan smiled at Miranda and an unseasonably balmy November breeze blew his black mane upward in rippling waves to match the water's expanse. She was correct, of course. Partly.

"Speaking of dropping dead weight, Serenity, how goes the situation with Percival and the engagement? Have you let him down gently?"

Serenity reddened and took what was, for her, a rather generous sip of her magical martini. "As the mortals are so fond of saying (hiccup!), Percival has been kicked to the curb, that troublesome boob. He's certainly (hiccup!) got some responsibility for what happened. No, I'm done with him and after the letter I sent, I can guarantee you he won't be bothering me in the future."

"Well done!" said Letty with another approving nod. Serenity was making great strides on this outing. "A witch can accomplish ten times more when she's on her own and independent."

"Hmpf!" was all Serenity would say as she sipped again.

"In that case," said Rowan, "I think you should be the one to do the honors, Miss Turnbull."

He pulled the dreaded ruby ring from the breast-pocket of his jacket. Percival the archaeologist wouldn't mind, particularly since his amorous ineptitude had started their terrific muddle in the first place.

"Will you favor us, Serenity? This is, after all, the main reason we're out here, floating our cares away in more ways than one. We're all here to see it done, to witness. No one has a greater right than you, I think."

Serenity crumpled up her face, threw back her shoulders with determination, and held out her lily white palm. Rowan dropped the ring into it.

Standing up and wobbling a bit toward the prow, she looked at the gem in which the awful djin was now forever trapped and she thought about marriage proposals. It was the only thing that came to mind after all that had happened.

Winding up her arm several times and sloshing the rest of her drink onto the deck, she hurled the ring off, off, off into the bright sunshine where it glistened and glittered once or twice, as if bidding farewell before it plopped some distance from the boat and sank into the secretive Atlantic, all the way to the centuries of mud and silt at the bottom, never to trouble the world again.

In that instant, all was good and right with the day, though unbeknownst to them, the following month would prove to be just a little bit *much*.

They moved forward into that future, as brave as magic and friendship would allow, just the same.

☜☞

Books by Jonathan Kieran

in

The Enchanted Heritage Chronicles

Rowan Blaize
Rowan Blaize and the Hand of Djin Rummy
Rowan Blaize and the Starbane Exile

For author news, interviews, extras, updates,
merchandise, and special offers,
visit
www.rowanblaize.com

All titles in the *Enchanted Heritage Chronicles series* will be available as e-books on Amazon Kindle following the official launch of the first three Rowan Blaize books in January 2013! Check the official website for up-to-the-minute information.

www.amazon.com